WARRIOR'S RANSOM

WARRIOR'S RANSOM

THE FIRST ARGENTINES

JEFF WHEELER

Text copyright © 2021 by Jeff Wheeler
All rights reserved.

Published by 47North, Seattle

www.apub.com

Amazon, the Amazon logo, and 47North are trademarks of Amazon.com, Inc., or its affiliates.

ISBN-13: 9781542027380
ISBN-10: 1542027381

Cover design by Shasti O'Leary Soudant

Printed in the United States of America

Quote from *Lord, I Would Follow Thee* by Susan Evans McCloud © by Intellectual Reserve, Inc.

To James

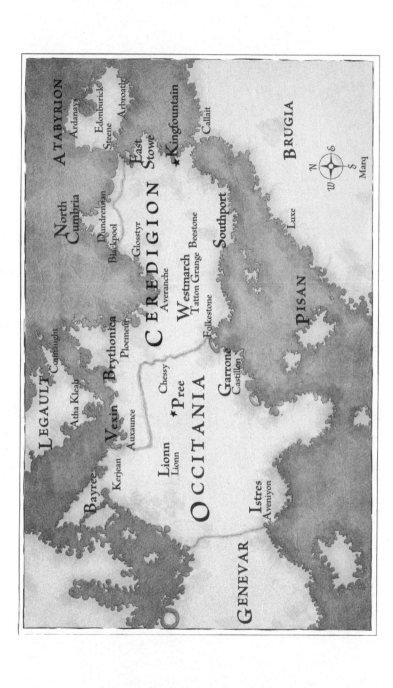

It seems that there will never be peace inside the fractious Argentine family. It didn't take long for Duke Benedict's visit to devolve into a full-throated shouting match between father and son. I'm surprised we didn't hear it up here in the tower. From what Sir Dalian told us, Benedict requested custody of his mother and asked that she be allowed to return to the Vexin with him. I don't know why Benedict believed his father might consent. He's not one to easily forgive an injury, let alone a betrayal. Of course, he was quick enough to allow his sons back into the fold, but his rancor toward his wife runs deep, like an underground river. It's said the son stormed off, against his father's orders. Is it all wind and bluster, or is this a portent of more rebellions to come? Because if I've learned anything about the royal family, it's that the festering has yet to heal.

A year has passed since the Younger King died during his second rebellion. The younger brother is nothing like him. He cares nothing for the bluster of knightly tournaments or the thrill of wearing the victor's crown. From what Emiloh has told me, I suspect he will pose a much graver threat to the king should he rebel again. I'm sure His Majesty realizes this. But I worry that he may be courting the very conflict he fears.

I'm grateful that Sir Dalian continues to bring us news. I enjoy talking to him. His father is Lord Kinghorn, constable of Westmarch, a very powerful man in the realm. I don't *know why the king doesn't make Lord Kinghorn the Duke of Westmarch. He should. But that's the thing about the Elder King. He grips power with a clenched fist that will not loosen. I fear it may be his downfall.*

—Claire de Murrow, Prisoner in the Tower
Kingfountain

PROLOGUE

The Chandleer Oasis

Heat, sun, and sand. Those were the three daily facts in Ransom's life as a caravan guard. But guarding the caravan was far better than being one of the camel handlers. He loathed the smell of the beasts, their noisy grunts, and their slow pace. There were twelve camels to defend, each laden with heavy burdens on their way to the outermost borders of the East Kingdoms. The head of the caravan—a merchant by the name of Kohler of Genevar—whistled an idle tune from the back of the lead camel.

Ransom rode a piebald destrier. It had a grayish coat that looked as if it had been splotched with ink. And while the incongruous coloring made the beast less elegant than others he'd ridden, he was grateful for the animal's relentless energy. Its previous owner had named it Dappled, which suited the coloring. It had borne him across the vast desert toward the Chandleer Oasis, their destination. His contract with Kohler would end at Chandleer unless what Ransom sought could not be found there and he had to go deeper into the East Kingdoms. It had been a year since he'd left Kingfountain following the funeral rites of Devon Argentine, the king he'd served, and they were almost to their first destination.

"Ransom!" barked Kohler.

He lifted his head at the merchant master and saw his arm pointing southward.

"What do you make of it? Bandits?"

His view was blocked by the train of camels, so Ransom urged Dappled forward, coming ahead of the lead camel. Kohler was wrapped in cloaks and headgear, layer after layer, to protect against the sun and wind. Ransom wore his armor beneath his own heavy robes for the same reason. He didn't like the smothering feeling of it, nor did it stop the sand from chafing his skin, but he'd learned from the ways of the desert people.

There were twenty or so riders approaching from the south. His stomach clenched with dread. Although there were twenty in their party as well, he was the only experienced fighter.

"How far is the oasis?" Ransom asked.

"I'd thought we'd get there by nightfall," Kohler said. "That's a lot of men for bandits."

"You have a lot of camels. They've no doubt been watching the caravan road."

"Close enough to Chandleer but still too far, even if we get the camels running." Kohler hawked and spat. "I'd hoped tales of our last run-in with thieves would be enough to frighten off any more vultures." Kohler lowered the scarf from around his mouth, revealing his bearded face. "Can you handle that many?"

"I guess we'll see," Ransom said. He heard the trickle of water, a sound that didn't exist in nature here in the desert. He'd sworn his loyalty to Kohler as part of the contract, and because he had, he felt a swell of Fountain magic whenever he was called upon to protect the caravan.

"*Hup!*" Kohler called out, signaling for the other camel drovers. "Like before. Tie the camels together so they cannot run. Grab your spears."

Some of the servants began to murmur with concern, but they had done this before. Ransom saw a few glance his way, offering looks of encouragement. He might be an outsider, but he'd proven himself as their guardian. The one everyone called when a scorpion wandered into camp or a thief attempted an attack. Serving a merchant felt different from serving a king, but this had taught him more about his power: it required him to serve someone else. When he had no master, the stores of strength faded and he felt darkness rise inside him. A darkness with which he was now familiar and that he feared.

Ransom rode south to face the riders, at the same time removing his cloak so his armor could be seen from a distance. He did this without really expecting it to affect them. The desert tribesmen were a hardy people, accustomed to living in difficult circumstances with oppressive heat and lack of water. Even if these men had heard stories about his prowess, the prospect of plundering a Genevese caravan was likely too tempting for them to ignore. Kohler was prosperous and would only become more so after this journey was done.

Ransom put on his helmet. His jousting helmet was in his saddle-bag. This one covered the top of his head with a nose guard in front, but it was otherwise open at the eyes and mouth so he could see and hear better. He cinched the strap beneath his chin and rolled his shoulders back, preparing his muscles for battle. His position gave him a powerful advantage. He was on the crest of a dune, which would require them to attack uphill. And their horses would be more wearied from the ride.

Dappled grunted, sensing the approaching danger. Ransom kept his eyes fixed on the incoming riders, the first of whom lifted hornwood bows. He waited, gazing at them. Black shafts lifted up into the sky and came pelting down around him, sticking into the sand. One came straight for his chest, but Ransom didn't flinch. He felt the ripple of magic and twisted at the last moment. Several more volleys of arrows came, and soon black fletching and shafts littered the ground nearby. He waited, unperturbed. So did his mount, which was an unusual beast and seemed to share its rider's confidence.

When the bandits began riding up the rise, Ransom finally reached down and drew his bastard sword, the one he had received from the armory in Tatton Grange in Westmarch. His lips felt chapped as he licked them. He observed the riders, looking for the leader, trying to sense which man he should target. As his gaze fixed on one specific person, a sense of understanding crept down Ransom's back. This was no well-organized or outfitted crew. They were a ragged band, with fur pelts sewn into their clothes, and those not holding the bows held curved scimitars. The leader rode straight at Ransom, his aim unfaltering.

Ransom felt the rushing of the falls inside his mind. He leaned forward in his saddle, listening to the thump of hooves on sand. Only twenty. He'd faced more than that when Lord DeVaux's men had ambushed him all those years ago. It was the voyage that had begun to twine his fate with that of the Argentine family, although his connection to them had been severed with the death of Devon Argentine, the Younger King. Still, even a year later, his mind lingered on what he'd left behind. On *whom* he'd left behind. He gripped the reins loosely in his left hand and glanced down at the braided, fraying bracelet he wore there. Many of the strips of leather had broken loose during this journey. The silver ends with the Gaultic design had tarnished. But Claire de Murrow, the woman he admired above all others, had given it to him, and so he'd kept it, doing his best to keep it intact.

He hadn't heard from her or about her in a year, but the thought of her soothed his soul like nothing else.

Shouts came from the attacking raiders, whooping cries meant to frighten him. He wasn't afraid. He simply lifted his sword, waiting patiently for them to get close enough.

As they swarmed him, Ransom began to fight. He killed the leader in the first pass and heard him topple from the saddle and bite into the sand. He deflected another scimitar and countered with a killing thrust. His ears heard every sound, every snort, every cry of rage, every moan of pain. Dappled flailed hooves, striking the horse of an advancing rider and biting another horse that came too close. Some of the raiders had rushed past him, heading to the caravan. Ransom blocked and parried, swinging Dappled around in a circle. He killed three more, leaving the remaining attackers rushing toward the caravan.

He whistled for Dappled to charge and went after them. The sleek stride of his powerful warhorse quickly overcame the band. He lopped off one man's arm as he passed and rode alongside another, who shrieked in panic when he noticed the knight bearing down on him. The man turned aside, forsaking the chance at plunder, and Ransom let him go.

Ahead, he saw the servants gripping spears and standing before the camels worriedly. The beasts brayed with concern, but they were tethered together in a circle and could not flee.

He killed three more men before they reached the caravan. The survivors fled down another hill, realizing they'd die if they didn't abandon their objective. He'd killed eight of the attackers, and his breathing had hardly picked up. It almost frightened him how efficient he was at killing people. The darkness inside him swelled with pride. He tamped it down.

Kohler grinned down at him and offered a salaam, a gesture of respect from the desert world. "I don't think we'll have any more trouble before we reach the oasis."

The Chandleer Oasis was an impressive sight in the middle of the desert. On the horizon, red- and orange-hued mountains jutted up from the dunes, forming a natural barrier to the east. The oasis was fortified, with a series of sandstone walls mixed with vibrant palm trees. The group reached it as the sun went down, and the guards opened the gates, allowing them to join other caravans that had braved the distance and were taking a much-needed rest.

There were many natural pools of water throughout the enclosure, enough to provide all the men and beasts with essential refreshment. Ransom refilled his flask and gulped it down, taking in the sights around him. There was a palace within the oasis itself, a grand structure with outer corridors, archways, and sculpted stone fashioned into dazzling parapets. Many travelers had set up their tents outside the palace, and Ransom helped his group do the same. Once the tents were up, Kohler broke off to speak to some of the other merchants in Genevese. Some of the other merchants had warriors with them too, and Ransom saw a few knights talking amongst themselves. One saw him and tapped his thumb against his chest in a familiar gesture. Ransom smiled and returned the salute.

Three knights walked up to him.

"Where do you hail from?" they asked in Occitanian.

He didn't want to announce himself, not sure how far his reputation might have spread. Although he'd been cleared of any wrongdoing after Devon's death, he knew it hadn't prevented people from whispering about him.

"A small castle in the country," he replied, matching their language. It wasn't a lie, as he'd won a small castle in Occitania at a tournament. "What about you three?"

"Much the same," said one of them. "How long have you been in the desert? It seems a good long time?"

"Over a year," Ransom answered.

"I took a ship from Brugia months ago," said another. "King Lewis is dead. It's said he died of apoplexy. The Black Prince is king now. Had you heard?"

Ransom almost physically flinched. The old king was the one who'd sent a cloaked woman to kill Devon. She was the same woman who had probably killed Claire's father. Ransom had seen her face, and she bore an uncanny resemblance to Queen Emiloh. He suspected the woman was the queen's daughter, born before her marriage to Devon the Elder. He had told no one.

"No," Ransom answered, shaking off the memories. "I'm surprised to hear it."

The knight shrugged. "We've been talking about going back to Occitania," said the knight. "The new king will need as many knights as he can take on. Might be another war with Ceredigion, eh?" He spoke the name of Ransom's country with a tone of open contempt. "You returning after this trip? Or continuing on to the East Kingdoms?"

"I don't know," Ransom said. "My contract ends here."

"Bah, who cares about a contract," said one of the other knights. "It pays the most to serve yourself."

The sentiment rankled Ransom. Their king, the one who'd died, had made a show of Virtus—the virtues of knighthood, which included honesty, valor, and integrity—but clearly it had failed to make an impact on his own knights. Or at least these three. "If that's how you see it. I must be on my way."

"You could come with us if you want," offered one of them.

He didn't but thanked them anyway and started walking toward the palace. The building was constructed of polished marble, and it struck him with wonder that such a place should exist in the middle of a vast desert. The gate stood open, and the armed warriors who guarded it stood by, allowing him to enter.

Torches in brackets lined the inner walls, holding back the coming dark. As he entered, servants approached with trays of apricots, figs, and cups of a pink drink. He took some of the fruit and waved away the drink. A few birds flitted around the indoor trellises, which were thick with fragrant star jasmine vines. He stopped and inspected them, inhaling the sweet fragrance, and noticed several of the merchants had preceded him inside. Kohler was among them. His robes and turban were gone; in their place, he wore his costly raiment, and his dark beard stretched into a massive grin. Laughter continued to emanate from the men as they shared experiences and stories. The celebratory atmosphere reminded Ransom of the end of a tournament, only this was a prize for merchants rather than knights—a reward for having endured the difficult journey.

A servant walked by with a tray of another kind of fruit. It had a mottled green rind and pink flesh. The bystanders took wedged slices and ate from them, spitting black seeds onto the marble floor. Other servants came and swept up the seeds.

Ransom continued to walk around, observing the guests and admiring the wealth on display. He wondered who ruled and defended such a place. It was a mystery to him, and it made him feel even more out of place than usual. Although he wasn't sure what he was looking for, he felt a mental nudge when he saw a set of doors at the far end of the luxurious hall. He walked to the doors and then outside into the gardens. There were others there, merchants roaming the space together. Beautiful dark-haired servants continued to offer delicacies to eat, skewered meat and green olives.

Ransom kept walking. Because of the fall of night, he couldn't see the mountains in the distance, but he imagined it was a splendid view during the day. Fountains shimmered throughout the garden, seemingly lit from within. His pulse quickened, and he felt a stirring in his heart. He'd come leagues through harsh terrain to reach this place. A pilgrimage to the East Kingdoms was, according to the deconeus of St. Penryn, a way for the Fountain-blessed to understand their calling. If he was lucky, the Fountain might also recognize him with a gift.

He walked past at least three different fountains, but the tugging sensation continued to draw him deeper into the gardens. Soon the glowing water sources were behind him. He wandered down a garden path, following it by instinct, and arrived at a small, nondescript well. A lip of stone surrounded it, and a wooden structure topped it, with a rope securing a jug to the wood. This was where servants came to draw water.

He glanced back, finding himself secluded from the other visitors and servants, and then rested his hand on the wooden structure. At first the only sound was that of distant laughter, but the sound faded, and in its wake came the rushing of waters, the noise of the falls outside the palace of Kingfountain. His skin prickled with awareness. It felt like he wasn't alone.

Ransom dropped to one knee by the edge of the rim. His chest began to heave as he felt emotions rush through him, unfamiliar, powerful.

Go down.

It was a thought, but it was not his own. Ransom didn't hesitate. He grabbed the sturdy rope and lowered the jug down into the well until he heard it splash into the water. After securing the rope, he gripped its fibrous length and began to lower himself down. The darkness engulfed him. He felt the strain from the weight of his armor, but he clenched his teeth and went down quickly. The water touched his legs, then his hips, and then he was hanging there, wondering how deep it went.

Let go.

Worry bloomed in his heart. He wore armor. He could drown. Looking up, he could only see the circle of stars in the sky above. Fear wriggled inside him. But he had not come this far only to turn back now.

Ransom let go of the rope, and his body sank into the well water.

He expected to meet stone at the bottom, but he didn't. The strange flooring was rough, uneven. Holding his breath, he went down, and his hands discovered wooden chests and iron coffers. Because of the blackness, he groped blindly, unsure of what to do, and then his fingers wrapped around a shape he recognized as a scabbard. He felt a strap, so he stuck his arm through it.

Go back up.

This was the gift from the Fountain. The blessing he had been seeking. He reached up, his lungs craving air, but there was no rope. He stood, straining for it, his chest aching with pain. He tried swimming, but the weight of his armor held him down. What was he to do? If he tried to remove the armor, he'd drown before he'd gotten even half of it off.

He stepped up on one of the chests, reaching as high as he could. Bubbles of escaping air came from his mouth. His heart thumping wildly, he tried jumping off the chest, but it toppled over. His knees smashed against something hard, shooting pain through his body. He gasped, and water rushed into his mouth. Ransom twisted, lights flashing in his eyes.

Then he heard the whisper again.

Nesh-ama.

And he knew what it meant.

Breathe.

The mad craving for air raged inside him, but every instinct battled the thought. Logic insisted it would kill him. And yet he'd promised himself he would listen if the call came, and so he obeyed the whisper and breathed in the water. Everything went dark.

$$\text{☓}$$

Ransom awoke lying next to the well in the darkness, stars sparkling overhead. He wasn't even wet. He quickly sat up, pressing his back against the stone wall, his heart hammering fearfully. The sensation of drowning hadn't left him, but he didn't cough. There was no water around him.

Something pressed against his side. He reached down and felt a scabbard there, the one he'd found at the bottom of the well. It was made of leather, wrapped around a wooden sheath, hand-stitched to a wide belt. The design around the hilt guard showed a raven's head, like the one he'd seen in Brythonica, and the bottom featured a metal chape with a filigree design. A few strands of leather had been tied into decorative knots. It seemed incredibly old.

The scabbard was empty, as if it had been waiting all this time for *his* sword. He was admiring it, grateful to be breathing again, when he noticed the braided bracelet was missing from his arm.

A gift for a gift, came the whispered thought.

꘡

Life has inexplicable moments. A small thing can remind us of events in the past. Sometimes it's a smell. Sometimes it's the way the breeze tickles your neck. I had one such moment this morning as the queen and I took our morning walk in the cistern courtyard. That is the only time each day when the Elder King allows his wife a small taste of freedom. The walls are too high to see over, although the ivy growing on them gets a decent view. It was during our walk this morning that I found something that triggered such a memory.

The cistern beneath the palace of Kingfountain is meant to hold rainwater because the castle is situated on a hill. The sluices and gutters within the palace feed it, but the courtyard is the place where the largest drain sits. There's a door, locked of course, that leads into the bowels of the watery place. At the edge of the cistern, I found a leather bracelet. It was very old, and many of the braided pieces had broken and been retied. The hook and clasp were made of silver that was so tarnished you almost couldn't see the Gaultic design. It looked so like the one I gave to Ransom, the one he wore for years before leaving Ceredigion. When I picked it up, little bits of sand came out of it. So strange. Ransom is still on his pilgrimage to the East Kingdoms. I've heard nothing from or about him, but finding this bracelet felt like a message of hope from the Aos Sí. Or maybe it was their intent to torment me.

So I've spent the rest of the day thinking about Ransom. I haven't seen or heard from him in over a year. Some people still titter about the gossip that he tried to seduce his master's wife, but they're the type who cling to anything sordid. I have good reason not to believe it, and my information comes from more reliable sources, not ignominious eejits. I wonder where Ransom is and if he will ever come back to the palace. I wonder if he still thinks of me as I do him.

The heart is a curious thing. Some days I just can't make sense of mine.

—Claire de Murrow
Cistern Garden, Kingfountain

CHAPTER ONE

The Elder King

Ransom stood at the dock, watching the handlers bring Dappled from the hold. The roar of the falls made him feel like he'd come home, and in a sense he had. He'd grown up in Kingfountain, under the wardship of King Gervase, the man who'd ruled before Devon Argentine, and the falls had become a part of him. His gaze shifted to the palace, which looked like a sleeping giant atop its hill.

Their ship had been assailed by an Atabyrion pirate vessel two days before, and Ransom had killed six of the pirates before they fled back to their own boat. The captain of the ship had offered him two thousand livres a year to stay on, but Ransom didn't enjoy being seasick, and he was only too grateful to return to land again. It took four handlers to get his destrier up the plank, blindfolded of course, but they finally managed it. Ransom came out and patted down the horse's withers. He wore a threadbare and torn tunic over his battered hauberk, and his armor was bundled up in a net and strapped to a palfrey, which had emerged from the hold with much fewer complaints.

He removed the blindfold from Dappled, and the mighty horse stomped derisively as it looked around.

"What?" Ransom asked the beast. "You don't care for the city? At least it's not as hot as the desert."

The horse snorted as if it understood his comment and disagreed. Ransom smiled, feeling a strange tension in his shoulders. His hand dropped to the hilt of his bastard sword, which hung in the scabbard he'd received in the oasis. The scabbard, when he'd drawn it out, had looked to be the length of a regular long sword. But he'd attempted to put his sword in it, and the scabbard had elongated until it fit the blade perfectly, revealing itself to have uncanny powers. However, while it did amplify his Fountain magic, especially during engagements with enemies, he had yet to figure out if it had some special purpose. Sometimes the raven sigil glowed blue, but the significance escaped him.

Grateful to be back ashore again, he climbed up on Dappled's back, took the guide rope of the palfrey, and continued his journey on land. He planned to stop at the palace, not to see the king, who was, based on what he'd heard, often at Tatton Grange, but because he hoped to learn the latest news from the kingdom and possibly find a noble in need of a knight. The second reason for his visit, the one closer to his heart, was that he wanted to see Claire again or at least get a message to her. His journey had been long and lonely, and he'd often wondered what Claire was doing. Whether she was looking up at the sky at the same moment he was, whether she was still up in her tower prison, and whether she thought of him too.

As he rode up the steep path leading to the city, he was met with the sights and smells of Ceredigion. Bakers were selling meat pies and ropes of juicy sausages. Ransom had plenty of silver in his money bag, so he treated himself to some food. His gaze drifted across the river to the palace, to the spire that rose above all others, and his stomach clenched with nervousness. On their stop in a Brugian port, he'd heard that Queen Emiloh was still a prisoner. What he didn't know was whether Claire still lived in the tower with her. The king had sent her there to serve as the queen's companion, although everyone knew it was a punishment for Claire's refusal to marry as he wished. As a Legaultan, she had that right. She was the heir to Legault and also to Glosstyr, which meant Ransom would never be allowed to marry her. Or if he did, it might cause a war. Unfortunately, that knowledge had little influence on his heart.

"You're a sunburnt chap, Sir Knight," said the merchant who'd sold him the sausage. "Where do you hail from?"

"I come and go," Ransom replied evasively. He thanked the man for the food and then walked Dappled through the crowded street. No one looked at him in recognition. A bridge straddled the river and the falls, and Ransom noticed some new construction had been done in his absence. The bridge had been widened, and some inns had been built along the sides. As he walked past the gate of the sanctuary of Our Lady, he was tempted to stop in and throw a coin into one of the many fountains, but he no longer felt the superstitious need to do so. His connection to the Fountain was stronger after his visit to the oasis. Instead, he mounted Dappled and rode to the palace gates, where he was met by a group of knights in tunics bearing Devon Argentine's standard of the Silver Rose. He recognized one of them, but the others were new.

"What brings you to Kingfountain, good sir?" asked the knight he knew, who looked up at him without paying him any notice. His name was Sir Bannon, and Ransom had trained with him years before.

"You don't recognize me, Bannon?" Ransom asked, wondering if his longer hair and full beard had disguised him.

Bannon's eyebrows furrowed. "You know my name."

"Is the king here?" Ransom asked.

The other man's brow knotted, but something lit in his eyes. "Are you Sir Ransom?"

He nodded in response to the question, giving the other knight a beleaguered smile. "I've come a long way."

"By the Fountain!" gasped Bannon, growing excited. "It *is* you. It's been years, man! Yes, the king is here. He's meeting with the lords of the realm. I'll come with you. What an ugly horse; where did you get it?"

Ransom dismounted. "I wouldn't trade Dappled for the finest black in the king's stables. He's a sturdy beast. And he won't bite off your ear."

"Good to know," chuckled Bannon. He ordered the knights to take care of Ransom's horses and belongings, and then escorted him to the main gate. Before they reached it, Ransom stared up at the queen's tower one last time, feeling a deep, familiar ache in his chest.

The interior of the palace had changed little since the funeral of the Younger King. He felt a stab of old pain from that memory. Even now, the corridors were so familiar to him. Two years of dirt, sand, and thirst seemed to melt away. He could have walked blindfolded to the great hall where the council usually met. They reached the doors, which were guarded, and the captain, who'd been speaking to the sentries, turned to look at him.

It was Sir Jude, one of Lord Kinghorn's knights. Ransom had defeated him at the siege of Arlect, part of the Younger King's attempted insurrection, and won a ransom from him.

"You!" Sir Jude said in astonishment.

"You recognized him before I did," said Bannon with a grin. "He came to see the king."

"Wait here," Jude said. There was no anger or resentment in his eyes. Just surprise. He opened the door, entered, and shut it behind him.

Bannon gave Ransom a knightly salute, which was reciprocated, and the older man left. The other knights at the door didn't look familiar.

Sir Jude returned and gave Ransom a measuring look but said nothing. Moments later, another knight Ransom recognized, Sir Iain, emerged from the throne room. He'd once served the queen, but his presence at the council meeting indicated he'd won the king's favor. When his gaze found Ransom, he shook his head in surprise.

"Look at you," said Sir Iain. "The king would see you. Now."

Ransom followed him in and found himself the immediate center of attention. The nobles had gathered around a table filled with trays of food and carafes of wine, but the Elder King was pacing in his usual restless way. When he saw Ransom approach, he offered a welcoming smile.

"You've aged five years in the time you've been gone," said the king with his typical caustic tone. "But there's no doubt as to who you are. Sir Ransom Barton, in the flesh. Well, you took long enough in your journey. You've just returned, or have you been idling elsewhere? Not at your castle in Gison, or I would have heard about it."

"I've just returned from my journey," Ransom said. "I was going to return to the Heath to see my kin, but there is no port in that direction."

The king chuckled at the humor. "Indeed not, I should say. It's been what . . . three years?"

"Two, my lord."

"Pfah, it could have been one for all I care. You're back. Well, are you ready to get to work? I have an assignment for you, which I think would be especially suitable."

Ransom stared at the king in surprise. "My lord?"

"Quit that courtly nonsense at once! I don't have time for it. Let me be clear. If you were serving one of the other kings, I would have heard about it. I pay well to remain informed of such things. Clearly you have no liege lord, and since I am in need of able men, you chose wisely in seeking me out first. I want you to serve me, Ransom. Beginning today. Is that clear? Do you need it in a writ?"

When Ransom had left, the Elder King had given him no indication that his service would be wanted. The man had simply told him, "Do what you must." He had intended to make the king aware of his return, but this welcome was entirely unexpected.

"Am I to understand that you want me in your mesnie?" Ransom asked, feeling the fires of hope. On his last day in Kingfountain, at the Younger King's funeral, he'd knocked James Wigant down with a staff and earned the king's ire. Or so he'd thought. Apparently, the incident had been forgiven or forgotten.

"Mesnie? Don't be a fool. I want you on my council. *That* is my true mesnie. You'll be starting your *own* mesnie now. You couldn't have returned at a more useful time. I'm about to invade the Vexin, but now it might not be necessary."

Ransom blinked in surprise. "The Vexin? Doesn't your son . . . ?"

"You've been gone a great while. Come, let's introduce you to the rest of the council." He grabbed Ransom by the arm and led him to a long table where the nobles had seated themselves with their food.

"Kinghorn . . . Constable . . . you already know him," he said, gesturing to the man who had overseen Ransom's training as a knight. Ransom barely had time to nod to him before the king moved on to the next man. "That is Duke Wigant. His son, a good friend of yours—am I correct?" He uttered a wicked laugh.

"I remember Sir Ransom," said the older duke with a glint in his eyes.

"Duke Ashel of Stowe," said the king, continuing around the table. "Duke Rainor of Southport. Also on the council are Sir Iain, you already know him, and Lady Deborah of Thorngate castle. Her husband was a great advisor to me, until he got the pox and died, and then I discovered that all of his best ideas came from her!"

Lady Deborah was a diminutive woman with gray-streaked hair the color of hazelnuts, but she seemed completely undaunted by the many large men around her, Ransom included. She gave him a gracious smile.

"And there, of course, is my chief steward, Simon of Holmberg, who you already know as well. See? We are all acquainted already."

Ransom's attention had been so firmly fixed on the king that he hadn't noticed Simon until he was named. Sir Simon was several years older than him, but they'd become friends and allies while serving the Younger King. Indeed, it was Simon who had brought him news of the Younger King's final illness. They exchanged smiles.

"And he will join the council of a sudden?" asked Duke Ashel with a hint of challenge in his voice.

"Didn't I just say that?" asked the king. "Stop eating and pay attention. He served my son, and now he will serve the sire. Simon, he already has some land in Occitania, but find him a castle here too. One of mine, of course. He'll need a wife. One of the royal wards will do, and another ward to stay at the castle."

Duke Wigant's hands closed into fists. The duke's reaction only buoyed the hopeful thoughts surging through Ransom, for he knew James had always had an interest in Claire. Would the king finally allow him to court her?

"I propose that we send Ransom to the Vexin to deliver a message to my truculent son. If anyone else, it would only rouse Benedict's scorn. I must be honest, none of you intimidates him as much as Ransom does. He'll need an escort of knights, of course. Bryon, how many do you recommend?"

"I should think fifty would be a significant show of force," said Lord Kinghorn. He had a wary look in his eyes. In fact, they all seemed uncomfortable with the king's suggestions.

"I agree. More than that and he'll treat it as an invading force. Make the arrangements."

"I will, Devon," said Lord Kinghorn.

"Good." The king clapped his hands, his face bright with eagerness. "I have work that must get done, but we will meet again for dinner." He draped his arm around Ransom's neck and thumped him hard on the back. "I've not felt this good in a while. Yes, this marks a change in the waters. I can feel it in these old bones!"

"My lord," Ransom said, trying not to stutter. He regretted that he had to voice his private feelings in front of the council, but there was no way around it. It seemed unlikely the king would provide him with a private meeting, and he dare not waste the opportunity. "Another reason I returned to Kingfountain was to see my friend, Claire de Murrow."

The king's brow narrowed. "You knew each other as children, did you not?"

"Yes, we both grew up in the castle."

"I see. That nonsense will not do. I've promised her to my son Jon-Landon. Let me douse any ardor you may still have with a bucket of cold reality. A match with her will never, ever happen. She's much too valuable to me."

Ransom's heart clenched. Disappointment was bitter in his mouth. "Does she not have a say? Is that not the way of her people?"

"A king always gets his way," he said flippantly. "I just need to make it worth her while. There are plenty of other lasses I can offer you instead. Sir Simon will help you understand. Off you go." He clapped Ransom on the back.

"May I at least send messages to her on occasion?" he persisted. "Not to court her, but because we have always been friends."

The king was about to turn away, but he gave Ransom a shrewd look. "I'm sure one of the other heiresses will be tempting to you, Ransom. Why not at least see who they are?"

"I thank you for your generosity, my lord. But my mind is made up."

The king shrugged. "You're young still. I give you permission to send her letters to rekindle your friendship, but nothing more. If you abuse this privilege, it will be taken away."

"We understand each other," Ransom said. "Thank you."

Ransom and Simon walked together down the corridor. "When did you start serving the king?" he asked, giving his friend a playful slap on his shoulder, which was instantly reciprocated.

"The previous steward suffered from gallstones. Do you remember Sir William Longsword?"

"I do." He was the one who had paid Ransom his wages as a knight in the Younger King's mesnie.

"He brought me on to help out and then became too incapacitated to serve." He glanced at Ransom. "How was your journey?"

"Long and hot," Ransom replied. He knew he was being vague, but at the moment the desert felt extremely far away, and he had no wish to discuss what had happened to him at the well. At least not while walking down a corridor in the castle. He smiled at his friend. "Rewarding too, but I'd prefer to discuss it at another time."

"That's fair," Simon said with a nod. "I correspond with Lady Sibyl, your mother, you know. I've helped her on occasion with some of the problems she's faced with your castle in Gison."

Ransom gave him a grateful smile. "Thank you, Simon."

Simon shrugged. "Being on the king's council is an incredible privilege. He trusts all of us to act in his name."

That earned another chuckle from Ransom. "I had no idea this would happen. I was planning to see Claire, if I could, and hoped to find a noble who'd give me a spot on his mesnie. I never dreamed of getting a spot on the king's council, especially not so soon."

"The king likes being unpredictable. No one else can think as fast as he can. Except Lady Deborah, perhaps. I think he listens to her the most."

"So the king said you're to give me a castle and a . . . wife?" Ransom asked with concern.

Simon grinned. "As I said, he likes keeping people off guard. You need a castle to pay for the additional expenses you will now have, although I should mention that your lady mother has managed your funds sensibly, and you have even more than when you left. Most knights are spendthrifts, always buying new clothes and entertaining people. The king has many lands he's inherited after the owners died without heirs, and he also has wardship over many who are too young still to inherit."

Ransom frowned.

Simon gave him another sidelong look. "I know you're stuck on Lady Claire, Ransom, but that's a concession you'll not get. I'm surprised he agreed that you could write to her. Everyone knows she's intended for Jon-Landon. Now, would you prefer a castle in the North, East, South, or West?"

"He has castles in all four quarters?"

"Of course! He's a rich man. But I should think the West would be the most suitable. It puts you in the place of greatest hostility. King Estian is always stirring up trouble. And you're the knight who dragged him off his horse in front of everyone at Chessy." He grinned. "You didn't think we'd forgotten, did you?"

Ransom tried not to smile, but he found himself doing so anyway. A flush came up his neck. "What is available in Westmarch, then? Can I have Averanche?"

"Sorry, that also belongs to Jon-Landon. The king has a castle on the border with Brythonica, however, that might suit you well, especially since you also own a manor in that duchy. It's called Josselin castle. Smaller than Averanche, but I expect you'll like it. They haven't had a master there since Lord Rakestraw died. What do you think?"

"I think the king is very generous," Ransom admitted.

"Oh, don't be so sure of that. You heard what he said in the hall. What he gives, he can take away. And he's done so, just to prove that he can. There's a cost in serving him. But I have to say this . . . I'm glad you're on the council now. He needs you more than you know." Then he smiled again. "So . . . you cannot have Claire, but she's not the only heiress who's available. Are you ready to learn about your future wife?"

A pit of dread formed in Ransom's stomach.

For the last two years, it has often felt like nothing would ever change. And then change comes so rapidly and quickly I cannot make sense of it. Sir Dalian brought news that Ransom returned today to Kingfountain and has been named part of the king's council. At first I thought either my ears weren't working or he was babbling like an eejit, but it's true. He has returned from his pilgrimage at last. King Devon snatched him up like a river trout before any of the other Fisher Kings could ply their lures at him.

He's the youngest member of the council, which is good for the king. He needs to hear different points of view, not just the opinions of his favorites. Sir Dalian said Ransom's been given the castle at Josselin, which is quite a gift. I've been there once. It's a solid piece, built during the older wars of conquest back when Ceredigion was first established.

I am so happy today to hear this news, especially since most of what we hear is grim these days. The conflict between the king and Benedict grows more fraught day by day. I've needed some good news.

I hope someday soon my path will cross with Ransom's again. I'd like that very much. Sometimes I take out that bracelet I found by the cistern. Touching it makes me feel closer to him. I've been keeping it in a safe place, but perhaps I'll start wearing it now and then.

—Claire de Murrow
(giddy with news at long last)

CHAPTER TWO

Broken Promises

Simon, who'd always had an observant eye, noticed the look on Ransom's face. He patted him on the shoulder, giving him a sympathetic smile.

"Let's go to the Hall of Records," he suggested. "Come on. You're not being dragged to a noose on the gallows, man. Not this time. Buck up."

The Hall of Records was beneath the main floor of the palace and smelled musty with books, scrolls, and dust. It was a cavern of shelves full of documents: writs signed, taxes due, and orders from the prolific king. It was buzzing with people coming in and out, some bringing documents that needed copying, others requesting information from previous decisions. The man at the desk had what looked like a perpetually pained look on his face as he gave orders to his underlings.

"That is Master Hawkes," Simon said, pointing at him. "The master of the rolls. He organizes all this mess. Pedigrees, histories, and anything the king needs in order to make a decision. Ah, he sees us."

The older man waved them forward, motioning for his underlings to back away from the desk.

"Who is with you, Sir Simon? I don't recognize him."

"Sir Ransom Barton," said Simon.

The man's furrowed brow relaxed somewhat. "I know that name. You're the lad King Gervase saved from execution all those years ago. I've read something about it. You are not a child any longer it appears."

"I should hope not," Ransom said, smiling at the man.

"He's been named to the king's council," said Simon.

"Has he indeed? Well, that is quite an honor. Or punishment, depending on how you view matters. Has the king granted him lands?"

"I think Josselin would suit him," said Simon. "And he's to start his own mesnie and take on one of the king's wards."

Master Hawkes rubbed his mouth thoughtfully. "Josselin . . . Josselin . . . the steward's name is Westin, I believe. The castellan is an aging knight who has been asking to retire for several years, but the king hasn't allowed it. He's done well enough, although I'm sure he'll be relieved to hear the news. What wards?"

"He asked me to choose them," said Simon. "I was thinking John Dearley."

"Ah, John Dearley, son of the late Malcolm Dearley of Coomb Manor. I believe the lad is sixteen and waiting impatiently to inherit his lands when he comes of age. A good choice. Shall I have him sent to Josselin castle? Along with a writ notifying the steward of the change?"

"That would be appreciated," answered Simon. "The king also wishes to give his new ally another ward, an heiress. Who is available?"

Ransom's stomach became queasy again.

"Lady Buttifer's daughter is six years old." Master Hawkes smiled and shook his head. "Probably too young."

"I think someone closer in age would be better," Simon said. He glanced at Ransom. "You don't have to marry the girl. It's just an . . . option. When I joined the king's council, I was given wardship of a young lady named Charlaine, Lord Nicholes's daughter. We became fond of each other and . . . well, now she's my wife."

"I didn't know you were married," Ransom said. "Congratulations."

Simon shrugged and beamed. "We are very different, but I've never been happier. If you take in someone who's too young, you become like a father to them. You know what it's like since that's how you came to Kingfountain. If the person you take in is a woman, and she's older . . . well, the expectation is that you'll marry her. If you want to."

The queasiness in Ransom's stomach only increased. He looked over at Master Hawkes, who had a shrewd look in his eye. "The king will expect you to take a wife, Sir Ransom," he said. "Posterity is power. I am a grandfather. The older I get, the more I understand that truth." His eyes narrowed a little. "I should think he'd be a decent match for Lady de Murrow."

Simon snorted. "So does he, unfortunately. The king still wants her for Jon-Landon."

Master Hawkes sighed. "That isn't a good match, but there's no convincing the king when his mind is made up. There are four other ladies under the king's wardship right now. I think perhaps . . . Lady Elodie."

"Of Namur? Isn't she twelve?"

Master Hawkes frowned as if he wanted to contest that, but rather than speak out of hand, he rose from the desk and walked to a shelf behind him. He withdrew a large leather-bound book and brought it back to the desk, then quickly opened it and riffled through pages.

"Lady Elodie of Namur, heiress of Lord Kenford of Namur, was born . . . ah, that would make her fifteen years old." He tapped the page and gave Ransom an assessing look. "A possible match. Namur brings in three thousand livres a year. Coupled with Josselin castle, you'd do very well for yourself."

"Her income would go to you while she's your ward," said Simon, looking more and more interested. "And you still have your castle at Gison and your manor in Brythonica."

"Impressive," said Master Hawkes. "Sir Ransom, you have a strong start in life. Not many knights your age have done half so well." He rubbed his mouth again. "You were the one Queen Emiloh ransomed, were you not? Ah yes, I remember that well. Five thousand livres she paid for you."

A heavy sum to pay for a single knight's ransom.

Thinking of it put him in mind of Emiloh's daughter, the poisoner who'd brought him a loaf of moldy bread filled with bandages when he was Lord DeVaux's prisoner. He'd only survived because of her, but she'd later reopened that very wound with a poisoned dagger and a crossbow.

He still had her dagger.

"And I am grateful that she did," Ransom said, realizing they'd both fallen silent during his reverie. "I owe her still."

Master Hawkes arched his brows. "Well, you'll be in a better position to repay her, although what good it would do her in that tower, I don't know. The income you get from these wardships is yours, but you must continue to pay the servants who maintain your properties and pay for any needed repairs—unless you decide to neglect what has been given to you. Many young lords squander their new income."

"I'm not worried about Ransom," said Simon. "He's prudent, like a true knight should be. So what do you think, my friend? Lady Elodie is one of the choices. What about the others, Master Hawkes?"

"The other two are also young children, eight and ten. Posterity is power. I'd advise you to take Lady Elodie. If you'd prefer an older rich heiress, there are some ladies who have already had husbands."

Ransom blanched, but he was only being asked to accept a ward at this point. He didn't have to marry her. Perhaps he could still convince the king to allow him to court Claire, or he could prove himself useful enough to earn that right. "No . . . no thank you."

"I thought not. Shall I send a writ and have Lady Elodie transferred to Josselin castle, then?"

Simon glanced at Ransom. "Of course. You know, Ransom, you look as greensick as most knights do on the eve of a battle. If I recall, you always slept like a man without worries before a big battle. You may know swords, destriers, and lances, but I think it's time you faced a different sort of test. Go to Auxaunce tomorrow on the king's orders. See your family on the way. Then you can stop by Josselin castle on the way back. I'll make sure they're expecting you."

"We will have a room prepared for you here at the palace as well," said Master Hawkes. "However, do not plan on staying in it for long. The king is always on the move, and you'll be either riding with him or acting for him for some time. I hope you have a sturdy horse."

Ransom nodded. Dappled might not be much to look at, but he was as sturdy as they came.

"May I get some paper and quills and ink? The king did give me permission to write to Claire."

"I'll arrange it," said Simon. "I'm sure she'd like to know you are back."

✕

Ransom had arrived in Kingfountain in a rotting tunic and a damaged hauberk, with no ties except to his family and the properties he'd won. He left Kingfountain with a trimmed beard and hair, a new royal tunic bearing the Silver Rose, the title to a castle, wardship of two young nobles, and the king's favor.

As Simon had suggested, he stopped by the Heath on his way, to visit with his family and share the news of his good fortune. He couldn't stay long, since he was on the king's errand, but it was a relief to see his family again. His sister had blossomed into a vibrant young woman, and his brother was working on an addition to the castle that added to its size and defenses. They were impressed to hear how the king had shown him such favor. Fortune was fickle, his mother had said, and indeed, his past ignominy seemed far behind him now.

After he left his family, Ransom and the fifty knights who'd been sent with him rode hard toward Auxaunce. He set the pace, and he was grateful that Dappled not only endured the journey but seemed tireless. They stopped at various royal castles along the way, where they were given shelter and food for the journey. They crossed Westmarch and then took the road leading past Brythonica to the duchy of Vexin. On that road, they crossed the very spot where the former constable of Westmarch, Lord Rakestraw, had perished in the battle with Lord DeVaux's men.

Ransom reined in and stared at the place, at the hedgerow where he'd been stabbed in the leg with a lance while defending himself. It felt strange to see the place again, especially since no signs of the skirmish remained. So many men had died that day. He had a strange feeling of the past and present colliding.

"Your horse never fatigues," said Sir Nigel, the captain of the force, riding up alongside Ransom's steed before stopping his own. He gazed at the road that lay ahead. "How far to Auxaunce do you think?"

"A league. We'll be there shortly." He turned around and saw the other knights approaching them.

"Shall we ride on, my lord?" asked Sir Nigel. He looked a little confused as to why they'd stopped.

Ransom shifted in his saddle, his eyes on that hedgerow again. He wondered if he'd encounter Lord DeVaux in Auxaunce. Part of him hoped that he did. The truce had ended, and Ransom was no longer a helpless prisoner.

"Aye," he said, "the courier will have arrived by now." The messenger would inform Duke Benedict of their arrival, ensuring he was there to receive them when they reached Auxaunce.

The fortress at Auxaunce was an impressive structure, one that rivaled the size of Kingfountain itself. Its walls were built around a thriving town, offering the populace protection from attack. The buildings inside were timber-and-plaster structures, and a main fountain bedecked the interior square, just before the ramparts leading up to the fortress. The stone castle had turrets and buttresses, but what stood out most were the statues arranged along the ramparts, looming stone guardians that stared down at the knights as they rode.

Ransom gazed up at the stone faces as they approached the city, imagining Emiloh riding swiftly up the rampart following the attack by DeVaux's men. Confined in the tower at Kingfountain, she had not visited her ancient homeland in years, and if her husband had his way, she never would. A steep price to pay.

The guards allowed them through the gates, and after all the men had gathered in the courtyard of the fortress, Ransom dismounted. His armor was still scuffed from his long journey, but his cloak was new. He rested his hand on the pommel of his bastard sword, which swung in the new scabbard strapped at his hips, and gazed up at the massive portcullis behind them. His thoughts were still fanciful after seeing that hedgerow, and it reminded him of the fangs of a mythical dragon. The courier had met them on the road and advised them that Benedict was indeed awaiting them.

Ransom gazed around at the men-at-arms gathered in the courtyard, wearing the badge of Duke Benedict, that of a rearing golden lion on a field of red. However, there were also several men wearing the Fleur-de-Lis, a symbol marking the ruling house of Occitania. He was surprised, and not pleasantly, to see it displayed so prominently.

As he approached the castle, he was met by a uniformed servant with an aged face, puffy hat, and tunic striped in gold and red. "Sir Ransom, this is an unexpected honor. My name is Jex. The duke is expecting your arrival. Come with me if you please."

Ransom had instructed Sir Nigel to be ready for action in case Duke Benedict became angered by the visit. Half the men he'd brought were to remain behind in the courtyard, eyes alert for any signal of treachery. The other half were to come with him.

As they walked inside, side by side, Jex said in a lower voice, "Have you any word of our lady, Sir Ransom? How fares the queen in her captivity?"

"I haven't seen her," Ransom answered.

"Very well," the man said, although his features drooped. "We often hear rumors that she's been poisoned. Not many have seen her."

"Idle rumors," Ransom said. But the words made him flinch, for they reminded him once again of the golden-haired poisoner, Emiloh's daughter. He wanted to ask Jex what he knew, but he didn't know whether the man could be trusted. So he remained silent until they reached the great hall.

Inside, Benedict was pacing. He'd only grown larger since their last meeting. He was almost as tall as Ransom now. Almost. And he had long golden hair and a red-flecked beard that he'd grown out, counter to the Occitanian preference for clean-shaven men. He looked like a warrior of Ceredigion as he paced like the restless lion on his emblem.

Upon seeing them, Benedict stopped his pacing.

"My lord duke," Jex said, "the embassy has arrived from Kingfountain." He bowed gracefully and doffed his puffy hat, revealing little stubs of hair on his bald head.

"I can see that," said Benedict, giving Ransom a wary look.

Ransom met his gaze. He felt his senses reach out, like water seeking lower ground, and envelope Benedict. The Fountain magic within him knew the younger man in just a moment. Yes, he was strong and hardened by years of conflict. He was gifted with weapons but preferred battle axes to swords, which allowed him to use his great strength to cut down his enemies. His health was in its prime, showing no signs of injury or impairment. Except for one—he was reckless and impatient. He always had been. In a long contest, his strength would flag, and he'd make costly mistakes. The knowledge that seeped into Ransom ensured he would win a fight with the duke.

That he should know such things seemed lopsided, unfair. But there was no denying he did know them, and if he had to use them to his advantage, he would.

"Have you come with a message for me?" Benedict asked with a cool aloofness.

"I have, my lord," Ransom said. He felt the reassuring weight of his hauberk. He felt the dignity of his office. And he felt the king's trust, which filled him with purpose. With power.

Benedict gave him a mocking look, a partial sneer on his lips. "Don't leave me waiting. What's the message from the old man?"

"It's a reminder and a warning, Bennett. Your father gave you the Vexin. He can take it away."

The duke was not amused, nor did he seem troubled by the threat. "I can see why he sent you to deliver such a boast, Ransom. Who else could he have sent that I wouldn't have laughed out of the Vexin? You serve the king now, like you did my brother. But I must ask you. *How* does he intend to take it away? Does he intend to wrest it from me, like a sweet from a child? Will he send a horde of mercenaries who are loyal to coin and not to him?" Benedict grunted. "You tell my father that if he moves against me, he will find that he has miscalculated my strength. And yours. I'm not afraid of you, Ransom. The last time we met, you bested me. I'm not so weak anymore."

Ransom stared at him, feeling the rage and hostility inside those blue eyes. "Fighting your father destroyed Devon. I watched it happen," Ransom said softly. He remembered the sunken face, the bloodied lips of the Younger King. The look of defeat in his eyes. "Don't make the same mistake. Make peace with him. Before it's too late."

The words affected Benedict. His bravado began to fade. "He makes enemies where there is no need, from his own sons to our neighboring kingdoms. But he was wise to send you. I want him to free my mother. If she must be in confinement, then let it be here, among her own people. His revenge is . . . blind. Whatever she may have done, it is not worth this punishment. I also wish to be named his heir. I want to see both orders in a writ before I meet with him again."

Ransom stared at him, knowing how implacable the Elder King was on this one issue. While he suspected the king wouldn't hesitate to name Benedict his heir—it was clearly his intention to pass the kingdom to him—he would never willingly free his wife. "I, too, wish he would free her, Bennett. But do not provoke him. Bend your knee to your father, your king, and he may be more willing to listen to wisdom."

The duke snorted in disgust. "What if I make him bend the knee to me?"

Pride. Ransom could see it seething inside Benedict like a hungry flame. He'd witnessed what it had done to the older brother. He dreaded it happening again. Ransom's talents flourished in battle, but he would prefer not to use them against his own countrymen.

Benedict looked away in the silence, his mood darkening then shifting again to reflection. "I am nearly the age my father was when he began conquering his lands. And I'm not like my brother. I could do this thing. I feel it in my heart. I would win."

"Why take by force what would be willingly given?" Ransom asked. "He sees you as his heir."

"Does he? That's more than he's confessed to me."

Ransom stepped closer. "His words are wounding. I won't deny it. And yet I find myself remembering the night he captured you and your brother. You heard your father's pain that night. We all did. Do not betray him again. Be loyal, and he will reward you."

"You seem so sure, Ransom. I almost pity you. But my father is good at making promises. He's not as good at keeping them."

The look of defiance in Benedict's eyes showed Ransom that the trouble between the sons and their father was far from over. And the prince's words were the sort that wouldn't leave him anytime soon—he had given his allegiance to King Devon, but all the king had given him could be easily taken away, like grains of sand slipping through a fist.

It was such a delight to get a letter from Ransom. He confided that he received permission from the king to send letters to me on occasion. His letter was much too short for my taste, but he told me a little about his journey—the sand and heat of it, the strange creatures he encountered in the desert. He told me also about the shock he felt to have so quickly found himself in the king's favor, which isn't surprising at all to anyone who knows him. Choosing Ransom is one of the only good decisions Devon's made.

Ransom actually asked if I would be open to writing back to him, the eejit, as if he didn't know this is the best news I've received in years. I don't know how faithful a correspondent he will prove, but the prospect alone makes the confinement of the tower more bearable. I already wrote one back, asking for more details about his journey to the East Kingdoms. I'm jealous to hear anything he can say about it. My world is so small now.

The queen grows more anxious every day. The palace is droning like a hive of bees. Knights flock to the castle bearing the standards of the various duchies. We may be in a tower, but we can still see. Sir Dalian says little, but it seems the Elder King is preparing for another war. Another war with one of his sons. Emi is worried and rightly so. The last war ended in the death of her eldest. Yet if Duke Benedict wins, it means our freedom.

It's like the game of Wizr the Occitanians enjoy so much. We can see pieces moving on the board, but confined to this tower as we are, we cannot understand the strategy of the hand that moves them. Benedict has spent the last several years fighting battles for his father. Does he know the kind of mind he faces? Can anyone understand the wild imaginings of this Argentine king?

—Claire de Murrow
Queen's Tower
(For how long?)

CHAPTER THREE

The Threat of War

Josselin castle was protected on the west by the Orme River. Thick woods gathered around it, except on the north side, where a hamlet of about thirty buildings had been built outside the castle walls. It was larger than the Heath, with tall round spires bedecked with conical roofs in a row. As Ransom and his knights came down the road, it seemed as if the towers were bunched close together, but when they drew near, their perspective changed, and he saw they were spaced evenly on a narrow wall. The hamlet smelled of sheep, and there were many chandler shops making candles from the tallow.

The walls of Josselin were uniformly gray, although moss grew on the lower third of the walls, and the slate shingles on the turrets had a blue tint. The river was placid, lined with pink-flowered plants, and there were many fishing boats in it. The windows were all high up on the higher floors, showing the castle had been designed to be a fortress of defense.

The peasants of the hamlet watched with curiosity as his troop of knights arrived, but no one approached or welcomed them. The main door of the castle was constructed of thick oak bound in iron, and it lay open to their approach. A servant wearing a comely tunic and a thick velvet hat stood fidgeting at the doorway.

He bowed as Ransom drew near. "Greetings, my lord," said the servant. "I am the steward of Josselin castle. My name is Westin." He doffed the velvet cap, revealing a shock of hair the color of carrots. "Greetings to you. Are you Sir Ransom? I was told you were coming. A letter from the palace arrived for you."

"I am. Good day to you." Ransom gave him a nod and a kindly smile. He took the proffered letter, his heart soaring at the sight of the fine handwriting. A woman's hand had written it. Although he'd hoped, he hadn't dared to expect a reply so soon.

The steward bunched the cap in his hands and nodded vigorously. "If you'd come this way, my lord." He walked ahead, and Ransom entered, the noise of clopping hooves drowning out other sounds. The fortress walls enclosed a private garden, which was being groomed by a half-dozen servants who glanced up from their work to study their new master.

Ransom dismounted and gazed at the castle. It was a fine building, well maintained and with a pretty view of the gardens. The roofline of the manor portion had steeply sloped gabled windows. He caught a glimpse of someone standing at the window, looking down at the courtyard, but the curtain closed as soon as he noticed. He wondered if that was one of his wards.

"Make sure our horses are taken care of and fed. We'll be riding back to Kingfountain on the morrow."

"As you command, my lord," said Westin nervously. He gave instructions to the groomsmen and then signaled for Ransom to follow him into the main portion of the castle. It was Occitanian in design, reminding him of the structures in Pree.

"Where are you from?" Ransom asked the steward as they walked together.

"Legault, originally. But I was raised in Brythonica and then came to oversee this castle several years ago. It's my first time as a steward."

He still had a nervous look about him, and it occurred to Ransom that the man feared he would be replaced. Clapping him on the back, Ransom said, "I'm sure you have done a capable job. I'm new to this property. I was only just given it. I don't plan on making changes unless they are needed. If you serve me well, you will retain your post."

A smile brightened Westin's mouth. "I intend to serve you well, my lord. Your two wards are here. Would you like to meet them?"

"I would. But I'd like to get out of this armor first and read this letter."

"I'd be honored to help you, my lord."

It was a strange and unique experience being the lord of such a fine castle. The fortress of Gison was much smaller and had no hamlet, and in truth, Ransom had spent little time there before leaving for the East Kingdoms. The master chambers were lavish, and the huge bed made him momentarily stare in surprise. The windows overlooked the gardens on one side and the river on the other. With Westin's help, he removed the suit of armor, and the steward hung the pieces on the waiting armor rack. He studied the tables, dressers, and the single chair, and thought the space too enormous for himself alone.

Of course, it is not meant for you alone. The king expects you to take a wife. He eyed the letter he'd put on the table.

"Are you hungry, my lord? I could have the cook bring something for you."

Ransom shook his head no. "Feed my men first. If there is anything left, I'll pick at that. I'd like to see John and Elodie soon. Give me a few minutes to read this."

"They are awaiting you in the sitting room. I'll bring you to them after I've seen that your men are fed."

"Thank you, Westin. You're doing very well."

After his steward was gone, he broke the seal on Claire's letter and quickly devoured it.

My dear friend,

Thank you for telling me of your arrangement with the king. I'm eager to hear about your journey to the East Kingdoms. Don't be stingy with details, now! I've nothing but time to read. Maybe your words will help me visit the vast deserts and strange customs in that foreign place. In return, perhaps I can tell you more about my homeland. Of the barrow mounds and hunting lodges in Legault and the tales of the Aos Sí. I'm grateful that you still consider me your friend, and you may rest assured that I shall always consider you my friend. So much has changed. Some memories should best be forgotten. But I will always remember the little boy at the palace, Gervase's favorite. Remember the tree we got stuck in? The one in the garden? It always makes me laugh to think of it. Now you serve another king. He has good qualities that are constantly disguised by his many terrible ones. Emiloh wishes to add her regards. She and I have become very close. But it is good to have someone to write to. It is good to be able to write to you. Hopefully, the king will allow us to speak in person one day and not just through words scrawled on a page. I should like that very much.

She'd signed her name with a flourish that made him smile. Hadn't he seen her sign letters to her family like that when they were younger?

Westin returned shortly afterward, and Ransom followed him down a long corridor to the sitting room, his mind still on Claire, his heart aching to read her words again. He knew he would read them over and over.

When they reached the room, Westin rapped softly on the open door, and they entered the space. Two young people stood waiting for them, their nerves showing as surely as Westin's had.

Ransom appraised them both, wondering what was going through their minds. What did they know about him? What rumors or stories had they heard?

The young man, John Dearley, was tall and rather spare in his frame. He had unruly brown tresses, serious eyes, and he looked pale with concern as he gazed at Ransom. Although the sword belted to his waist indicated he was not without battle training, he had all the insecurity and bravado of a youth trying to appear a man.

The girl, Elodie, was slightly younger. She was lovely, with golden hair that hung in ringlets, but the fidgeting of her hands suggested she was ill at ease. She couldn't even meet Ransom's gaze.

The two of them looked like birds trapped together in a cage. Ransom wondered if he'd appeared the same way to Lord Kinghorn when he'd first arrived at Averanche to begin his training as a knight. They both seemed to be waiting for him to speak first.

Ransom approached them, the sense of being an imposter shuffling in his chest. His first concern was putting them at ease.

"Welcome to Josselin castle," Ransom said. "I'm sure this change of events has been a surprise to you both. But I look forward to getting to know you."

The young man, John Dearley, nodded quickly in agreement. "I've been here two days. Lady Elodie came yesterday."

"And I've only just arrived myself," Ransom said in a pleasant tone. He directed his comments to Elodie. "I'm certain once I leave this room, I'll become lost immediately. Have you walked the grounds yet?"

"Yes, my lord," said the girl, giving him a guarded look. She glanced back down again quickly.

"We both have," said Dearley. "It's a beautiful castle. I'm rather envious. My given name is John, but I actually go by my family name,

43

Dearley. There was another boy, another child, who lived nearby, and he had the same name. We were both called by our last names instead, and I've come to prefer it." His explanation came out in a great gush of words, after which he flushed with embarrassment and looked away.

Ransom wasn't sure what to say. He saw the discomfort in both of them. They seemed so innocent, so young. He thought it best to end this first conversation quickly.

"Well, I'll call you Dearley, then. As for the castle, I should like to see it myself." He looked at Dearley. "We'll be leaving tomorrow morning to rendezvous with the king and report back on my mission to the Vexin. Be ready to ride by sunrise."

Dearley lifted his head, his eyes widening with surprise. "You mean . . . you wish me to come as well?"

"Yes. You're part of my mesnie now. You go where I go. It's just the two of us for the time being. I want to see how well you can handle a blade. There may be trouble in the near future. You must be ready for it."

The look of surprise turned to one of excitement. "I will . . . of course! Yes! Tomorrow at dawn. I should bring my armor?"

"That would be a wise thing. Now, Lady Elodie. I will leave instructions with Westin . . . he's the steward . . . ?"

She looked at him and nodded, her brows knitting in confusion.

"Good. While I am gone, you are the lady of the castle. You are in charge." He gestured to the room. "My younger sister, Maeg, is someone you can rely on for advice. You can write to her at the Heath and even invite her for a visit if you wish for company. I don't know how often I will be here, but I'll always try to let you know in advance before I come. Does that suit you?"

She swallowed, but her look of nervousness didn't fade. Was she wondering whether he would force her to marry him? According to Simon, that was the usual way of things. He had no intention to follow through, but he suspected it would be a mistake to address the matter so soon. It would embarrass her, no doubt, and she already looked desperately uncomfortable.

"That is all. I bid you both good day."

As he left, he found himself remembering the young man he'd been. Feeling the wheel of time turning.

Ransom and his troop of knights left at dawn as planned, and John Dearley was the first one in the courtyard ready to go. They rode into the morning together, keeping a slow-enough pace that they could speak comfortably, and Ransom discovered the young man was quite adept at diplomacy, languages, and the history of treaties. As the day progressed, Dearley became more comfortable with him, more affable and friendly. Still, it was not until they arrived at Beestone castle to rest for the night that Dearley broached a delicate topic. The castle stood on a bluff, easily seen above the tree line.

"I'm grateful for the chance to serve you, Sir Ransom. I was surprised to hear you were chosen for the king's council so quickly, but now I understand. I just . . . I'm curious . . . if you plan on taking Lady Elodie as your . . . well, you know . . . as your wife?"

Ransom was listening to him, but his gaze was on the castle they approached. Seeing it brought many dark memories to Ransom's mind. Beestone was the castle where the cloaked lady had attacked him. It was where she'd killed Devon.

The brooding on his face must have made Dearley assume he was offended by the question, because the boy quickly retreated from it. "I'm sorry. It was impertinent of me to ask."

Ransom looked at the young man. "It is fine that you asked, Dearley. And I'll answer you. No, I don't want to marry her. The king wants me to, but I've given my heart to someone else. Someone I cannot have."

Dearley listened to that and nodded, his eyes lost in thought. "I see. She'll be relieved, I think." He paused, as if weighing his words, then said, "She told me . . . before you came. She said that she was to be given to you, without any choice in the matter."

Ransom chuckled. "Oh, I can believe it. You may tell her, on my behalf, that she's safe from me."

Dearley grinned. "With your permission, I shall send her a message."

"You don't need my permission, but yes, tell her, by all means."

Dearley nodded, his smile fading. "Your lady love. I'm sorry it did not work out between you."

Ransom shrugged. "Maybe it will someday. I don't know."

The young man's eyes widened. "I find that difficult to believe. She's in the East Kingdoms."

Ransom looked at him in bafflement. "Who are you talking about?"

"Princess Noemie, of course. King Lewis had her marry again. You went there yourself . . . to the East Kingdoms, did you not?"

He felt the burn of resentment in his heart, not against his ward but against those whose wagging tongues had perpetuated the myth that Ransom had tried to seduce Devon the Younger's wife. His name had been cleared in the end, but many people preferred the salacious lies.

Ransom looked into Dearley's eyes. "I tell you on my honor as a knight, that what you heard is untrue. I value loyalty above all. And I was loyal to my king, to the Younger King. The stories are just that. Stories. I did not go after her. I left *before* her." Ransom shook his head, feeling the anger crackling inside him, his dark side straining to emerge. "I traveled with a caravan into the desert, providing protection for a Genevese merchant and his men. We did not venture far into the East Kingdoms. That is the truth. And I swear it on the Fountain."

Dearley gazed at him, nodding with great seriousness. "I believe you, Sir Ransom. I . . . I admit I've heard many stories about you. The queen once ransomed you for twenty thousand livres, did she not?"

Ransom sighed. And then, because he wished for there to be no misunderstandings, he proceeded to tell Dearley his story from the beginning.

When he arrived back in Kingfountain with the cohort of knights, Ransom saw that the palace was thronged with soldiers, most of whom were mercenaries. The stables were all full, and horses were being tended in the courtyard. He left Dearley to find provisions and a place to stable their mounts while he went into the castle to report back to the king.

He was brought to the king's chamber, where he found Lord Kinghorn and Lady Deborah with the Elder King.

King Devon smirked when he saw Ransom. "Do you like my little army?"

"I'm not sure 'little' is an appropriate description," Ransom said. "Has something happened while I was gone? It's been a fortnight since I left you."

The Elder King rubbed his hands together. "And why waste a fortnight? You went to the Vexin. What happened?"

Ransom looked at each of them in turn. "Benedict was defiant, as you might expect him to be. He wants to be named your heir—"

"Of course he does!" interrupted the king.

"And he suspects you will dangle promises over him. Promises he doesn't trust."

"Is he afraid of me, do you think? Is he fearful that I'll wrest the Vexin from him?"

Ransom saw a look that bordered on giddiness in the king's eyes. "He'll fight you for it, my lord. He won't give it up."

"Of course he won't," said the king. "What do you think, Sir Ransom? What if I offered him Kingfountain instead? Let Jon-Landon have the Vexin now that Benedict's tamed it. Do you think he would agree to forsake his duchy for a better prize? A greater kingdom?"

Ransom shook his head. "No. It's clear to me he doesn't trust you. And he's worked hard to prove himself to you. My lord, I counsel you . . ." He glanced at Lord Bryon and Lady Deborah. "Do not invade the duchy of Vexin. It would make him desperate. He might seek out dangerous alliances."

The king pursed his lips. He glanced at his companions much like Ransom had done. "But does he fear that I will come for him? Is he ready to fight me?"

"Yes," Ransom said firmly. "And he is."

"Good," said the king. Then he laughed.

Ransom's heart sank. The king's mind was already made up. He'd made it up before Ransom's trip to the Vexin.

"Don't look so forlorn, Ransom," said the king. "You were most useful to me. Your visit increased Benedict's dread and fear. But let me be clear. I have not won this kingdom by doing what everyone *thinks* I will do." He bowed to Lady Deborah. "You see my wisest counselor before you. This plan was Lady Deborah's idea. I reward cleverness. I reward cunning. I reward candor. Word will reach my son that the army is gathering. But I tell you this truth since you are now part of my council and are entitled to hear my plans but not to share them with others." He grinned like a wolf. "I'm not going to attack my son. I'm going to attack Occitania. They led my son astray and murdered him, and I've not forgotten it. Nor will I ever forgive it. They will pay until their treasury is empty and their hearts quail with fear."

‌

What a vexsome king we have. Is that even a proper word? It should be, for vexsome he is. The palace is quiet now that the king has taken his army away. They ride to tame a young lion, yet one with claws and teeth. The Vexin lands have always been troublesome, but this problem was sown by the king and will now be reaped by him. Jon-Landon has been left behind in case the worst happens.

When the king is gone, we have a little more freedom than normal. That should be a blessing, but I chafe with the uncertainty of everything. I heard from a maid that the king is encouraging Ransom to marry an heiress. He may have a longer leash than I do, but both of us must depend on the king's mercy. Will he stand up to King Devon, or will he take what he's been offered and demand no more? He did send me an answer from his castle in Josselin, though he was maddeningly vague about the heiress. He was more verbose about his journey to the East Kingdoms, thankfully, and loves to talk about his new horse, Dappled. I wrote him again but haven't heard back, although I expect he's traveling.

I loathe myself for feeling these things. It is jealousy, that is all. I had hoped things might be different between us. A spark still remains, but hope won't light a candle. I fear I'm doomed to remain in the dark.

—Claire de Murrow
Kingfountain Palace
The eve of war

CHAPTER FOUR

Fair Winds or Foul

Riding to war with the Elder King, Ransom couldn't help but compare the experience to that of fighting for Devon the Younger. He and his master had thought the odds were on their side, that victory would be easy, but now he understood they'd been deluding themselves. The king had a cunning mind, and he'd known of their betrayal before it happened. What lessons had Benedict learned from that?

Was the king underestimating his son?

After stopping for supplies and men at Beestone castle, they rode directly through Westmarch. They next made camp on the road to the Vexin. Most of the soldiers slept on the ground and ate rations they'd brought from Beestone. The object was to travel light and fast so the enemy wouldn't discover what they were about.

Ransom walked through the camp toward the royal pavilion, listening to the chatter amongst the men as they talked about whipping Benedict's force. He smiled inwardly, for none of the common soldiers knew their master's true purpose. It was possible the plan could backfire and the king's son would preemptively strike them on the journey, but Ransom doubted it. No, Benedict would hunker down and prepare for a storm.

When he reached the pavilion, he entered it and found the king pacing. He had the confident grin of a man who was enjoying playing the aggressor for a change. A map was stretched out in front of him, the corners held down by cups, and several knights stood before him. Most of the soldiers in camp, Ransom included, were clad in armor, but these men had been off gathering information. They were wearing merchant tunics to conceal their hauberks and cloaks to hide their swords. It was the evening report from the outriders.

Sir Harrold was speaking as Ransom entered.

"Some men saw us along the Westmarch border," he said to the king. "I think they were Occitanian, for they fled quickly."

"Did you give chase?" asked the king with interest.

"Aye, my lord. Just for a bit, to rouse their blood a little. They rode hard, and there was no chance of catching them before they could get to the safety of one of King Estian's castles. They know we're on the move."

"Of course they do!" snapped the king. "Well done, Harrold. Sir Axien, what news from the Vexin road?"

"I spoke to some farmers about three leagues west of here. They've not seen any soldiers, except the knights who passed this way with Sir Ransom recently. They've no idea we're coming."

The king smirked and nodded. "Good. Sir Rawlin, what news from Brythonica?"

"I delivered your writ to the border guards," answered Sir Rawlin in a slow, plodding tone. He was a bearlike man, even larger than Ransom, but slack of speech. "Received no answer, so I came back."

The king glanced at Lord Kinghorn. "What do you make of it, Bryon?"

"Goff is wary. He's probably deciding what to do. He might wait and see what happens first."

"I agree," said the king. "Churlish boy. Now that he has an heir, he's more careful, more likely to stay within his own borders. An obedient son would have sent his guards straightaway, to answer the summons at least."

"Maybe his men are defending the border with the Vexin?" Bryon suggested.

Ransom agreed. The two brothers had a history of rivalry. Being the third son, Goff had never presumed to rule the kingdom. Now that he was in line after Benedict, his fortunes had altered, especially since he had an heir, and his brother did not. He'd be very cautious.

The king shook his head. "Even so, he could have spared someone. Maybe he's sent a messenger to warn his brother? These faithless sons of mine. Perhaps I'll just give the throne to Jon-Landon and be done with their schemes." His good humor had soured. "What news from the east, Sir Thatcher?"

The final report was given by a knight with golden hair and a handsome face. "Nothing of note, my lord. Duke Wigant's forces are coming, as requested. The duke is having a bit of a problem with his joints of late, but he's coming anyway. He's making progress."

The mention of Sir James put a bitter taste in Ransom's mouth. As far as he was concerned, his school companion had hastened Devon the Younger's downfall, something he would never be punished for. He felt someone's gaze on him, and looked up to see Lord Kinghorn watching him carefully. His kinsman knew about his past with James, how the two had clashed since they were knights training in his household.

Careful not to allow his feelings to show, Ransom nodded to Lord Kinghorn.

"How much progress? Where is he?" asked the king.

"We met his outrider at Shackletown," said Sir Thatcher.

The king considered that for a moment. "He's farther ahead than I suspected. Good. That means he'll arrive in time. Excellent work, men. Get some food and rest. Start your journeys before dawn."

The knights grunted in agreement and dispersed from the tent, leaving Ransom, Lord Bryon, and Dukes Ashel and Rainor behind. The force of three duchies would soon be joined by a fourth.

After the others had left, Ashel grabbed one of the cups holding the map down and drank from it. He had a long beard streaked with gray and the cold eyes of a man used to battle and carnage. "When will you tell the men where we're really going?" he asked with a glint in his eye.

Devon shook his head. "Not yet."

"Have you chosen a target yet?" asked Duke Rainor. He had copper-colored hair and a matching beard. Although he was only in his midthirties, he'd grown fat during the years of mercenaries fighting the battles. Ransom didn't need his Fountain magic to see his weaknesses.

The king moved to the map and pointed to a place in Occitania. He looked at each one of them in turn. "Say nothing," he whispered.

The spot he pointed to on the map was the duke of Bayree's lands, which was on the northwest border of the Vexin and was nearly surrounded by water. If they took Bayree, Ceredigion would control the entire northern coastline of Occitania. It would be a grievous loss to King Estian. Even if he managed to cut off their supply route to the duchies by land, they could all be supported by sea.

Duke Ashel frowned. "He'll not give it up easily," he said in a serious voice. They were all being careful not to mention names.

"No, I don't imagine he will," said the king. Then he tapped the spot again. "That's why I'm bringing all my might. A blacksmith doesn't ask the iron to submit. He bends it to his will. The furnace is war, not diplomacy."

※

When Ransom retired to his tent, Dearley was still awake, sitting on his bedroll, arms wrapped around his knees.

"I thought you'd be asleep by now," Ransom said wearily.

"Is there going to be a battle tomorrow, do you think?"

"No, not tomorrow. But soon."

Dearley rocked back and forth, staring into the darkness. There was enough moonlight for Ransom to see his ward's worried look, but when Ransom went to unbuckle his armor, the younger man sprang up to help.

"I think I'm going to be sick," Dearley said in a half-hearted voice after they'd removed all but Ransom's hauberk. He'd sleep in it with his sword by his side.

"We've all felt that way," Ransom said. "What we're doing is dangerous work. It's natural to be nervous. But trust me when I say the king is prepared. He's not lost a battle these many years. They're more afraid of us. And they should be."

Dearley smiled at that and nodded. "I hope so. I'm terrified. When I was twelve, my father sent me to train under Lord Eros in North Cumbria. I never did well when we fought in teams. We always lost. We were the ones others went after first." He shook his head. "I did the best I could, but I'm not the most skilled swordsman in the kingdom."

"Were you good at languages? Managing a castle?"

"Those came more naturally, yes. But a knight needs to be able to defend a castle too." He looked up at Ransom, his gaze intent and worried. "All those times we failed . . . it wasn't real. We weren't trying to kill each other. If someone defeats me this time, I could die."

"It's your first time at war. You'll learn from it. My first time was when the Brugians invaded, as I told you. We were outnumbered, and help was far away. You do what you must. I'd rather be in this circumstance than that previous one. We never know what will happen. The moment you think you know, circumstances will surprise you. Just be prepared, don't give in to fear, and remember your training. Stay near me, and pay attention. I'll do what I can to watch over you."

Dearley sighed. "Thank you. I don't mean to be a burden on you."

"You're not. You're the first in my mesnie. There will be others. I promise we'll go back to Josselin castle. We'll make it through this."

And yet, even as he said the words, he wondered if he'd be able to keep his promise.

X

Two days later, everything had changed.

Ransom stared down at the same map with a look of incredulity. The members of the king's council stood around him, and the tent smelled of sweat and dust. The Occitanian army had gathered at the town of Bloissy, just south of their position, and reports showed that Benedict's men were not defending Auxaunce anymore but were riding hard to intercept them. If they continued west toward the duchy of Bayree, then King Estian and Benedict could join forces and strike them from the rear.

"How did he know what we were going to do?" asked Duke Rainor in confusion.

The king looked furious. His arms were folded, and he paced back and forth by the table. "Estian's army didn't appear until *after* we spurned the road to Auxaunce. Either he *guessed* my intention correctly, or one of you has betrayed me."

His words caused a chill inside the tent.

"My lord," said Duke Ashel angrily, "how can you accuse us?"

"We've been loyal to you all along!" Rainor said defensively. "Why would we—?"

"Enough!" barked the king. He turned and gazed at them, his eyes searing. "The only one *likely* to have betrayed us is Sir Ransom, the newest member of my council."

Ransom stared at the king in dread, his stomach clenching, his heart pounding wildly. Not again. One false accusation of treachery had been enough.

Before he could speak, the king shook his head. "I've had him watched since he came back. My spy in Auxaunce reported the confrontation with Benedict exactly as Ransom described it. And yes," he said, his gaze shifting to Ransom, "I have people at Josselin as well. I've been testing him all along. So no, it is not him! And I do not believe it was any of you either."

The words sent a spasm of relief through Ransom's heart. Cold sweat had formed on his brow, but he felt the tension ebb. Never had he been so glad to be spied on.

The Elder King shook his head, muttering something under his breath. "Nor do I think that Lady Deborah, who inspired this plan, used it to sell me out to the Occitanians. No, I've long believed the Occitanians have a way of spying on us from within. That they have some uncanny means of tracking the movement of my armies. I do not know how. Regardless, this turn of events leaves us with but one choice. We attack Estian. Now."

Duke Ashel gave a vicious grin, but Duke Rainor seemed full of misgivings. "We don't know how big his army is yet," he objected.

"It doesn't matter. We defeat it. It's as simple as that. He's trying to frighten us. To make us turn tail and run back to safety. I will not. This situation gives Benedict a choice to make. He either fights with us or against us. If he fights against us, I hereby decree that Goff is my heir and command you to show loyalty to him in my stead. I say this because I will not quit this battle until they yield, or I meet my end. Through fair winds or foul, I will not relent in my purpose. I will not yield the field unless I give it my corpse. Rouse the men. Have them prepare. We fight tonight. Any who stand in our way will be hewn down like grass. That is my command."

"But if we wait another day, Wigant's son will get here with his army," said Lord Kinghorn. "That could turn the tide of the battle."

"No. It means his men will be fresh and can help the rest retreat if need be." The king clenched his fist and pounded it on the table. "We fight. Tonight. Now! Bryon, you take the vanguard. I want Ashel on the right and Rainor on the left. Don't let them flank us. Ransom, you will command the reserve and await my orders. If Benedict tries to strike us from behind, you will be my wall to hold him off. I've cast the dice, let the pips land where they may. Rouse your men."

Ransom felt a surge of gratitude to have been given such an important role in the battle, and despite the challenge before them, he felt buoyed by the force of the king's determination. By the vow he had made to serve him. By the knowledge that they would be fighting Ceredigion's true enemies. He marched out of the tent and went to his pavilion. Dearley was fast asleep, breathing softly. Ransom crouched and shook him by the shoulder, startling him awake.

"Is it morning?" Dearley asked, wincing, trying to see in the dark. His eyes were confused.

"The king has given the order," he said. "We're going to fight the Occitanians. Tonight."

Dearley's jaw fell. "The Occitanians? W-whu? Where are they?"

"In the town of Bloissy, just south of here. Remember what I told you about expectations? We're not here to fight Benedict. We came to defeat Occitania, to carve another duchy from her. Get your armor back on. I'm going to make you a knight this evening. I'll go ask Lord Kinghorn to stand witness."

Dearley's look of shock made Ransom smile. He remembered being knighted before his first battle, and he felt it only appropriate to do the same for his ward. "I'm—tonight? Are you serious?"

Ransom nodded, rose, and put his hand on his sword. "Be ready when I get back."

X

A visitor came to the cistern garden today. Prince Jon-Landon Argentine. I know I have written previously about my disdain for him. He's dark-haired, unlike his older brothers, with a sallow face and a look that shows he holds much of the world in contempt. He is seventeen now, or almost—I cannot remember his true age. He has rancor in his heart for his mother. That is obvious in the overly courteous way he speaks to her, his eyes always shifting to distrust. He's his father's son and has been rewarded for despising his mother. Yet still he came to see her, or did he just come to see me?

I do not like Jon-Landon. I cannot help but think he is watching all of us, sizing us up, trying to seek a weakness he can tuck away for later use. The conversation was stilted and awkward. The only time he seemed genuine was when he expressed his concern for his father, the king, and what is happening during this present unrest with his brother. It is a concern I share.

There is no news yet from Westmarch. Everyone is looking for riders to come.

—Claire de Murrow
Cistern Garden
(the dreadful silence)

X

CHAPTER FIVE

The Desolation of War

It went against all of Ransom's instincts to watch the battle rage in front of him without charging into the fray. He sat astride Dappled, two lances couched in holders fixed to the saddle, his bastard sword in the Raven scabbard at his side. The rear guard of the army surrounded him, the men's eyes fixed on the scene in front of them as the armies of Ceredigion and Occitania battered each other.

Ransom's blood sang with the thrill of battle as he watched the clash, as he listened to the sounds. Horses screaming. Swords clanging. Lances shattering against shields. Men groaning or screaming in hate. It all swept over him like waters from a flood, igniting the trickling sound of the falls in his ears. He could sense the battle as if it were a living thing, a creature of enormous size, a monster made of armor, axes, swords, and helmets. And like a monster, it seemed on the verge of engulfing them all in blood.

In his mind, he heard echoes of the rallying speech that Devon had given before the attack. It had charged up all the knights and soldiers, Ransom included, and compelled a throaty yell from them as they rode onto the field.

"Fear them not, my brothers!" the king had shouted from his horse, brandishing his sword. "They're used to tournaments and flowers, not the sour harshness of war that you lads have drunk since your mother's milk! A debt of blood is owed this day. Blood like that which dripped from my son's mouth and eyes as he lay dying at Beestone, a victim of Occitanian treachery. They mock us and claim we are weak. We will prove our strength is mightier than theirs. Onward, lads! Onward until they cry for peace! Spare none until it is over! We shall be avenged this day!"

Even now, Ransom's blood surged with the will to fight, to follow his king into battle. Instead, he stood watch vigilantly, waiting for a time when he was needed. His senses searched too for any signs of the Occitanian poisoner. Estian's father had not hesitated to use her against them, and Ransom suspected the same of the son.

Time was no longer a concept that made any sense, so he wasn't aware of how much of it had passed when a prickle of awareness shot down his spine. He sensed riders coming, could feel the thrum of hooves as they approached from behind.

"Sir Ransom!" one of the knights called out in concern. "The Lion banner! It's Benedict!"

Ransom turned at his waist and gazed at the approaching men. A host of knights rode toward them from across the field, a small group leading them, one rider carrying the red banner with the golden lion.

"What do we do?" asked Dearley in concern. He'd looked pale all night, but somehow he'd lost more color. "Will they attack us?"

"I don't know," Ransom replied. "Stand ready. Front ranks, stay where you are. Back ranks, turn about. Prepare your lances!" He grabbed one of his own and pressed the wide shaft against his side. He circled Dappled around and came through the line to put himself at the forefront. The riders from the Vexin were coming fast, most on horseback, but he also saw foot soldiers running, holding pikes and halberds. He grimaced at the numbers he saw. If Benedict decided to attack, they would be in trouble.

"Sir Dearley," Ransom said, turning to the young knight who had just received his rank. "Get word to the king that his son approaches. Quickly now."

Dearley nodded and began riding toward the battle lines they'd been observing during the conflict. Ransom saw that Benedict was one of the vanguard, along with four knights. The group was riding hard and fast toward them.

Ransom kept his lance raised and rode to meet the five of them by himself. If they all lowered lances against him, he was a dead man. But he judged that Benedict was ahead of his army for a reason. It meant he sought more information before he acted.

As Ransom came closer to the group, he felt more confident of his appraisal. Benedict and his men had lances too, but the tips were pointed skyward. No one signaled they wanted to challenge him. Benedict made a signal, and his four companions slowed while he rode on until his lathered horse was right in front of Ransom's.

"Have I come too late?" he gasped, his cheeks flushed. He pulled off his helmet, spilling out his tangled hair. His beard and his bulky armor gave him a menacing look.

"Too late for what?" Ransom asked. "Are you friend or foe?"

"I am the Duke of Vexin!" Benedict said hotly. He looked at Ransom in disbelief. "I thought Father was coming to fight me— unjustly, I should say. His target was Estian all along?"

"Yes," Ransom said. "Though Estian was waiting for us here. Somehow he knew."

"*I* didn't know," Benedict said. "I swear it on the Lady. We came to answer the call to arms. If my father is fighting Occitania, then I will join the assault. Where can we aid you?"

Ransom felt a huge swell of relief. "This is good news indeed."

"Enough talk!" Benedict said. "Direct us. Where are we needed?"

"Duke Rainor has the left flank. He's been hard pressed and is giving ground. Add your force to his, and see if you can block the road back to Pree to prevent Estian from escaping."

"I will do so, Sir Ransom. Are you commanding the rear guard?"

"Yes, my lord duke."

He shook his head ruefully. "You belong in the thick of the fighting. I should have liked to fight alongside you."

"Perhaps another day," said Ransom. "See to it. The battle isn't yet won, but with your help, the day will be ours."

Benedict nodded, his eyes burning with determination. "I'm grateful we're not too late." He turned and lifted his lance. "To arms!" he shouted.

Ransom watched as Benedict went back to his men and changed their course, leading them directly to the left flank, as ordered. He would have to keep watch to ensure his trust in the duke was not misplaced. If Benedict attacked Rainor's men, Ransom would have to strike his forces from behind.

But those seedling doubts were only that. The knights of Vexin charged into the fray, clashing violently with the Occitanians. The additional men upended the balance, and the knights of Pree began to give way.

Ransom saw the king with his guard returning with Dearley. The king was breathing hard and had blood-spattered armor, but he looked fresh, enlivened by the energy of the battle.

"Is it true?" the king said, panting. "Did Bennett come?"

"I sent him to the left flank," Ransom answered. "Look, he's already breaking through."

The king grinned with triumph. "I'd almost feared to hope. Look at him! That's my son!" His grin was tremendous. It was *proud*. "Good lad. If he'd turned on us, we'd have failed. It's still . . . it's still not certain. But this has shifted the tide."

"Send us to the fight, my lord," said Ransom earnestly.

"It's a mess down there," said the king. "Hard to tell who is who." For a moment, Ransom thought his request would be denied, but the king shook his head. "Get in there. Help Duke Ashel. He's taking a beating, but thank the Fountain, he isn't giving in. Go!"

Ransom nodded and shouted the order to his men. Dearley swallowed and grabbed his lance.

"Stay by me," Ransom told the young knight.

The younger man nodded in agreement, but he looked greensick. Ransom took off on Dappled, and the knights of the rear guard came after him, their horses' hoofbeats adding to the cacophony of the battle.

Rather than risk wounding their countrymen—the chaos of battle made it difficult to discern between friend and foe—Ransom led his host to outflank the Occitanians and strike from the side. Shouts of warning came, and the soldiers swung around as the horde of knights from Ceredigion came upon them. Several knights wearing black tunics rushed forward to keep them from crashing into the melee.

Ransom lowered his lance and charged straight at the black-garbed knights. These were Estian's personal men, the ones who'd fought in the tournament circuit.

Ransom's blood screamed as the magic tingled through him. He knocked the first man off his horse without losing his lance. Another knight tried to skewer him, but Ransom leaned to the side and then couched his lance again and struck a different knight. The timber shattered, raining broken fragments onto the field. Distantly, he registered that his men had joined the attack. He acted on instinct, grabbing his second lance and using it to knock down another man, but it shattered on impact. Dappled screamed with rage and took a bite out of another horse's withers.

When he had no more lances, Ransom drew his bastard sword. One of the black-clad knights charged him with a lance, and Ransom was able to deflect it with his blade and then strike a blow as the knight rode past. A throb of warning struck him, and he turned to the left. There was Dearley, the stump of a lance under his arm, as two knights bore down on him with fresh lances. The young knight looked stunned as he watched the two men charging at him.

Ransom felt a throb of protectiveness. Two against one was unfair in any contest, but against such a stripling? He swatted Dappled with the flat of his blade and charged forward to intercept.

The clatter of arms swelled around him as he urged his horse to greater speed. Ashel's men were pressing the Occitanians back, sending them toward Ransom and his men. Despite the confusion of the battle, he sensed what was happening, like the tune of a song that was familiar to his ears.

Dearley leaned forward, gripping his shattered lance in preparation to receive the attack. His face looked calm, as if he were expecting to die.

Ransom arrived, putting himself and his horse in front of Dearley's. A lance pierced his armor and the force of the blow nearly toppled him off the saddle. Cracking wood. Agony. He gripped the saddle horn, feeling his body sliding off the seat, but he clenched and grimaced and managed to remain on his horse. His interference had broken both of the attacks.

Suddenly he was surrounded by Occitanian foot soldiers, pushed back by Ashel's front, trying to retreat. They surged around his horse, fleeing, but some took aim at him. Spears began to dent his armor, and one such blow actually helped him regain his balance.

Black knights astride their horses struggled to reach him, caught in a swift current of fleeing bodies. Another blow hit Ransom from behind, and he felt the second sting of pain. He swung his sword arm around, deflecting a halberd tip and then slaying the man who held it. Clinging to the saddle horn, having lost hold of the reins, he fought against the surge of foot soldiers. One of the mounted knights in black managed to get past the flood of fleeing men, and he attacked Ransom with a bastard sword.

Ransom's arm felt strange and weak, but he blocked the blows and tried to change position so he could use his other arm. Another blade struck his armor from behind. The chaos was overwhelming, but he narrowed his focus on the knight he could see and parried two more blows, looking for a weakness. The knight was highly skilled and a relentless attacker. But he'd been fighting for hours, and Ransom had not.

They traded blows, their horses alongside each other, and Ransom fought until his arm went numb from the effort. He felt more attacks against his back, but his armor protected him, somewhat, and he was past feeling pain. His blood raged with the passion of war, and he felt himself carried on a current of determination.

The knight couldn't defeat Ransom, and so he turned his horse aside and fled. And as the man left, Ransom realized it was Estian himself, disguised as one of his men.

Ransom went after him, knowing their victory would be complete if they could capture the Occitanian king, but another warrior immediately rode forward to bar his way. The man wore ceremonial armor, with fluted designs and elaborate frills. It was the armor of a royal knight, one who could afford such a costly expense. A count or a duke.

That a duke was interceding told Ransom he had guessed correctly about Estian's identity.

The royal knight lowered a lance and came straight at him. Ransom tried to block it, but his own limbs weren't responding as quickly or efficiently as they usually did. The lance caught him in the middle and would have knocked him off his saddle if they'd been riding faster. It knocked him sideways instead. Ransom delivered a counterstrike as they passed each other, his sword biting into the man's neck, and the royal slumped from his saddle.

Ransom searched for Estian, but there were so many riders now, many of them in black, and it was impossible to identify him in the crowd. The Occitanians had completely broken ranks, and the remaining soldiers were fleeing. Cheers of victory came from the throats of the warriors of Ceredigion. Men with faces contorted in fear rushed past him, dropping weapons, trying to escape the carnage with their lives.

Ransom slowed, his right arm feeling strangely weak. It was hard to keep his grip on the handle of his bastard sword. Dappled let out a shriek and snapped at a soldier who had come too close. Everything felt sluggish and slow. A buzzing noise sounded in Ransom's ears. He wanted to lie down and sleep on the trampled grass. Where was Estian? His mind fogged over, the buzzing growing louder. Was it in his head?

No, he realized, it was coming from his left side. He looked down and saw the raven's head symbol on the scabbard was glowing.

"You're hurt," said Dearley, riding up alongside Ransom. He'd dispensed with the shattered lance at some point and now held a bloody longsword.

Ransom turned to look at the young knight and felt a spear of pain in his shoulder. Dearley was staring at Ransom's back in horror.

He lifted his visor so he could see better, which was when he saw the broken end of a lance protruding from his flesh.

Good news, at long last! A fierce battle was fought between the Elder King and Estian, not with Benedict as we feared. The cause is one anyone can support—the Occitanians were horrible to Devon the Younger, and I suspect they also killed my father—and it was a major victory for our people. Many people are undoubtedly dropping coins into the fountains to celebrate our good fortune against our enemies. Emi's son Benedict turned the tide of the battle when he arrived with the men of Vexin. Their stout hearts and sharp blades and shattered lances brought the victory. I was told that Benedict himself rode after Estian, hoping to capture him, but he gave up on the chase when it led too near the Occitanian border. We are all relieved. Well, those of us with sense. When Jon-Landon was told the news, I heard he threw a chalice against the wall and stormed off. What an ill-bred eejit.

My joy has turned into sour dregs. Since writing the news of the victory, I have learned that my Ransom was grievously wounded in the battle and may not survive. Witnesses claim he nearly defeated King Estian after being pierced by a lance. He also slew the Duke of Bayree, and they said the duke's head was nearly taken from his shoulders in a single blow. Ransom was brought off the battlefield by his young ward. That is why I've had no news from him myself.

I'm sick inside. I can't bear to lose him, even though he isn't mine. Everyone else is praying to the Fountain for those they love. But I have made a petition to the Aos Sí to spare his life.

—*Claire de Murrow*
Accursed Tower of Waiting, Kingfountain

CHAPTER SIX

The Raven Scabbard

he pain had set in as soon as the Fountain magic deserted him. Dizziness and nausea roiled in Ransom's stomach, and he turned his head and vomited noisily. Each spasm made the anguish from the broken lance dig deeper into his wound. Each breath of air was a lungful of fire. His back ached, his left elbow throbbed, but it was the agony embedded in his shoulder that made him groan.

Lord Bryon knelt by the side of his cot—How had they gotten him back to his tent?—his expression grave, his cheek spattered with dried blood. "I've sent for a barber, Marshall. But there are none to be found here, someone's gone to the nearest town to fetch one."

Ransom squeezed his eyes shut. "I'll wait," he grunted.

Dearley choked on his tears. The sound of his anguish made Ransom feel even worse.

"I've never seen a man survive such a wound," Lord Bryon said. "That piece of lance has to come out. But your arm . . . you won't be able to use it again."

Ransom heard the words and silently dreaded they might be true. His sword arm. "I plan on keeping it, my lord."

"I'm going to pull the piece out. It'll hurt. Do you want something to bite on?"

Ransom remembered the injury he'd sustained in that long-ago battle with Lord DeVaux. The pain of a lance wound . . . that was a memory he wouldn't forget. He opened his eyes and looked at Lord Bryon.

"I've had worse. Pull it out."

Lord Bryon nodded and looked over at Dearley. "Hold him down."

The young man wiped his nose on his arm and came to the edge of the cot. His eyes were watery and swollen from tears.

"He's not going to live?" the young man choked.

"I intend to," Ransom answered, glaring at his ward. "I'm wounded, not deaf!"

Lord Bryon chuckled. Someone shoved open the curtain of the tent, letting in a blinding shard of light that made Ransom's skull throb and his teeth ache. He grunted and turned his face away.

"What is it?" Lord Bryon demanded, his patience faltering.

"The Duke of Bayree is dead!" the newcomer announced. Ransom recognized the voice as that of Sir Jude. "Ransom killed him!"

The Duke of Bayree was one of Estian's most powerful supporters. Another wasted opportunity to ransom a nobleman. Gritting his teeth, Ransom exhaled sharply.

"Has Benedict returned yet?" Lord Bryon asked.

"Not yet. He's riding after King Estian, who fled the field. Everything is still in chaos. We've routed them, and the king is rallying the men to give chase."

"If we catch Estian, everything changes. Praise the Fountain. Bring me word when Benedict returns. Tell the king I'm trying to keep this young man alive."

"I will, my lord. Thank you." The tent flap closed, and shadows smothered the space again, causing a pang of relief.

"Prepare yourself," Lord Bryon said. "I don't have tongs. I'll have to pull it out by hand."

"Just do it," Ransom said, feeling himself grow weaker with each breath. When he opened his eyes, he saw darkness closing in around his vision. His inner stores of Fountain magic were all spent. They'd kept him alive during the fight, but they'd run out at the end. He felt like a coil of rope dropped to the floor—lifeless, inert.

And then he felt it when Lord Bryon gripped the piece of the lance sticking from his armor. Dearley shoved down against Ransom's body to hold him as he started screaming in pain.

Everything went dark.

It was a humming that awoke him. At first he thought it was the drone of bees, but this was a deeper, more resonant sound, almost like the throb of a deep horn coming from the bottom of the sea. Something about it was achingly familiar, although he couldn't place it.

Ransom opened his eyes, realizing he'd passed out. He vaguely remembered the shard of wood coming out. The tent was brighter now, the sun falling heavily from its midday position.

A little grunt came from his lips when he tried to move.

"Sir Ransom?" croaked Dearley, suddenly rising from a stooped position on a camp stool. He turned and dropped to his knees by the rim of the cot. "Are you awake?"

"Yes," Ransom said, his throat dry, the sound gravelly.

"Bless our Lady!" whispered Dearley. He looked down on Ransom's face, his mouth slowly turning to a wide smile. Tears of relief came to his eyes, and he brushed them away.

Ransom lifted his head to glance at his back, relieved to see the wooden spur was indeed gone. A crumpled cloth lay on his flesh, but it wasn't red with blood. That fact astonished him.

"Where's Lord Bryon?" Ransom asked.

"He went to the king. He asked me to stay and watch over you."

Ransom's stomach gurgled. "Fetch me a drink."

"Do you want some wine?"

"No. Just water."

He could still hear the hum, the source of it quite near. Dearley went and fetched a water flask. After unstoppering it, he gently put his hand behind Ransom's neck and lifted his head higher so he could drink. Ransom expected a jolt of pain from his wound, but he only felt a deep soreness. Strange blue light shone on half of Dearley's face. Ransom shifted his left elbow to support his weight, a maneuver that caused him a little pain, although nowhere near as much as he would have expected. The water was cool and refreshing. He took a few swallows and then noticed the raven's head on his scabbard was glowing. Although he'd seen it shed light before, it had never glowed this brightly.

He stared at it, remembering vaguely that it had started glowing during the battle. Through the fog of war, and that of his injury, he had forgotten that.

"Do you see that, Dearley?" Ransom whispered after his drink.

"See what?" His ward looked at him inquisitively.

"Do you see my scabbard?"

Dearley glanced down and looked at the empty scabbard wrapped around Ransom's waist. The raven's head was glowing blue as clearly as the moon on a frosty night. "Yes," the young man said. "Are you worried about your sword? It was brought in from the battlefield. I've already cleaned it."

"Does the scabbard look . . . strange to you?" Ransom asked, still staring at it.

He cannot see the light.

The whisper from the Fountain alarmed him, and he stiffened. He'd not heard the voice since he'd retrieved the scabbard from the well at the oasis. *A gift for a gift.*

Dearley frowned. "It looks . . . old. Where did you get it?"

"It was . . . never mind." Ransom tried to sit up, but he felt that same aching soreness.

Dearley gripped his arm and helped him up. The rag fell away from the wound, dropping onto his lap. He glanced back and could see flesh through the hole in his tunic. His breastplate had been removed. The skin was livid, inflamed, but there was no scab, no dried blood.

He looked at Dearley, who stared at him in shock, his lips quivering.

"What happened?" he asked the young man.

Dearley's voice was but a whisper. "When Lord Kinghorn removed the broken lance, he told me to press the wound hard. He told me to be prepared that you might bleed to death. I did as he said. After you fell unconscious, we removed the armor so we could tend to the wound better. There was . . . there *wasn't* any blood leaking out. I kept lifting the rag, unable to believe it. The skin was torn, and I could see blood inside the wound, but none came out. Lord Kinghorn looked at me and told me to tell no one what we had seen. He said that you were Fountain-blessed."

A tingle of apprehension shot down to Ransom's hungry stomach. The wound had sealed itself. He swiveled his shoulder in a circle, feeling the muscles groan, but it didn't hurt. It was only sore. His left elbow, which he suspected he'd broken, felt the same way. The scabbard had healed him, not his Fountain magic.

Ransom swung his legs off the edge of the cot, amazed that he wasn't light-headed. Gratitude thrummed in his heart for the gift he'd been given at the oasis. Part of him wanted to reveal its power to Dearley, if only to explain what had happened, but he remembered something Lord Kinghorn had told him long ago. He'd said the Fountain-blessed of old had sometimes been killed for their relics, and a scabbard that could heal mortal wounds was indeed the kind of prize someone would kill for. While Dearley would never do such a thing, of course, he might mention it to someone else—either unwittingly or under duress. It was too great a chance for him to take.

Dearley was still on his knees, staring into Ransom's face. He looked haunted by what he'd seen.

"It's all right, lad," Ransom said. He reached with his right arm, which obeyed, and put his hand on his ward's shoulder.

Dearley bit his lip and sniffed. "It's not. It's my fault."

Ransom wrinkled his brow.

"It's my fault that you were injured," he blurted. He looked down in shame. "I froze. I was so terrified. They were coming at me . . . I saw them . . . two knights with their lances drawn. I just sat there, watching it. I'm so . . . I feel so terrible." He lifted his head and looked into Ransom's eyes. "You took a lance for me, Sir Ransom. One that nearly killed you. It's a miracle of the Fountain that you were healed."

Ransom saw the shame in the young man's eyes. But he also saw the respect, the commitment, and the sense of purpose. How young he looked. He reminded Ransom so much of how he'd felt as a new knight.

He squeezed Dearley's shoulder. "Of course I did, lad. You are in my mesnie now. It is my duty to protect you. I couldn't let those Occitanian miscreants kill my first knight during his first battle, could I?" He smiled at his ward. "Battles are chaos. Everyone flinches. You'll be better prepared next time."

Dearley breathed deeply, then he clenched a fist and pressed it to his mouth. His shoulders quivered. "You s-saved my life," he croaked. "I cannot thank you enough. But I will try." He looked at Ransom again. "I swear on the Blessed Lady I will make you proud of me someday. You won't regret what you did." He lowered his fist and swallowed. "I swear it. I will be faithful to you in all things."

Ransom felt tears prick his own eyes. He clapped Dearley on the back, unable to speak for the moment. When he did find his voice again, it was thick with emotion. "Thank you. You helped get me out of there alive. That means something to me as well."

Dearley flushed with pride. "Well, I wasn't totally useless. After what you did, I drew my sword. Someone kept striking at you from behind while you were fighting the Black Prince's knights. I . . . I killed him. And then the one who attacked you with a poleaxe."

"Did you now?" Ransom said, pleased.

Dearley nodded vigorously. "After what you did to protect me . . . I could do no less."

They both heard the sound of steps coming toward the tent. Dearley rose, and Ransom heard his stomach growl again. The tent opened, and a stranger carrying a leather bag entered. Lord Bryon came in behind him.

"I brought the barber . . ." Lord Bryon said, then fell silent. The barber saw Ransom sitting up on the cot, and his brows knitted in confusion.

"I thought he was mortally wounded?"

Lord Bryon studied Ransom for a moment, and a small smile came on his face. "No, that was someone else, and he died already. This is Sir Ransom, a member of the king's council. Just have a quick look at him before he reports to the king."

The barber frowned in confusion, but he came forward and examined Ransom's wounds. He prodded his chest with a forefinger and then examined his neck. "He's about as hale as you'd expect," he said with a shrug before standing again. "I'm sorry the other man died. I came as fast as I could."

"Thank you," Lord Bryon said, reaching into his coin purse and handing some livres to the man. "You'll earn more by tending to the wounded."

"Of course! That's why I came."

The barber left, and Ransom slowly stood. He felt a certain emptiness inside—one that came from his depleted stores of magic—but his body was growing stronger by the moment.

Lord Bryon looked at him, that secret smile growing. "Can you come to the king's tent?"

"I think so," Ransom said, flexing his arm muscles, feeling the health in them.

"A new tunic, perhaps?" Lord Kinghorn said. "Everyone in the camp thinks you won't survive the night. Many saw your condition when Sir Dearley brought you here." His smile broadened. "I never thought I'd live to see the day. Well . . . this makes our victory more noteworthy. The legends say King Andrew had a knight that no one could defeat. It would seem your pilgrimage to the oasis has served you well." He nodded encouragingly. "I'd enjoy discussing it with you someday. Come when you're ready. There's much to share."

"I'll be there shortly, my lord," Ransom said.

"I know you will be," Lord Bryon said, and from the way he said it, Ransom knew he'd finally won the man's respect. He watched as his kinsman left the tent, and then he turned to Dearley, who had been a silent witness to their exchange.

"I'll fetch you some food," Dearley promised, and he left the tent as well.

Ransom stood there in the midday heat. He saw his sword leaning against the armor stand and walked over to it. He gripped it in his hand and felt strength radiate through his arm. Overcome with wonder, he lifted it and slid it into the scabbard.

As the blade screeched against the material of the scabbard, he heard the Fountain's voice whisper to him again.

The scion of King Andrew will be reborn through an heir of the Argentines. They will try to kill the heir. You are all that stands in the way.

Jon-Landon came to see his mother again. But this time I knew for certain I was the one he wanted to see. He had a fevered quality to his eyes, like a dog following a cook with a juicy bone. Jon-Landon wants power. He wants it at all costs. His hope of becoming his father's heir has, it seems, been dashed, but the duchy of Glosstyr is still a crown title to be given away. Jon-Landon wants it. But I don't want him. Oh how it galls him that his father cannot order me to accept him. Well, he has tried to do just that, but I have a voice and I have a will and I will not be bound to such a tick-bitten dog. Jon-Landon wants to threaten me. I can see it in his eyes, yet he's not that foolish.

The only news he had of the battle was that the Elder King had been pressing the flesh of Estian, jabbing a bruise that was already painful. Both sides lost a lot of good men. Still no word about or from Ransom. So I don't know whether I should weep for joy, relief, or misery.

—Claire de Murrow, Queen in Her Own Right
(from forsaken Legault)

CHAPTER SEVEN

Temptation

With some food in his belly and a fresh tunic, Ransom walked to the king's tent, only to find that he had already gone south with Benedict. Ransom fetched Dappled and rode hard after them. Peasants were gathering the remains of the dead, and the cheery banter of the folk contrasted strangely with the solemnity of the moment.

Ransom knew the road, for he had ridden it before. It led to Pree. He passed soldiers marching with spears and halberds, heading to catch up with their king before dark. The faces he saw were grim and determined. There was no fear in their eyes, only a strong drive for vengeance. The king's rhetoric before the battle had worked well—the hackles of Ceredigion had been raised. A mood to conquer pervaded the air. He passed the front ranks and rode ahead alone, wondering how far the king had ridden.

His answer came as some knights barred the road ahead. He sensed them before he saw them in the shadows, and he reined in, hand going to his sword.

"Who are you?" one of them asked.

The king's voice erupted from the shadows clinging beneath some yew trees. "It's Sir Ransom, you dolt. Let him through."

The knights parted, and Ransom passed between them, earning nods from both men. Their armor was battered and blood-spattered. Both had seen hard fighting that day.

The king was in his full armor as well, a chain hood on his head with the hollow crown resting atop it. Benedict rode next to his father on one side and Lord Kinghorn on the other. A few other knights lingered in the shadows. Ransom sensed them all, and now that he was back in the presence of the king, of the man to whom he'd sworn an oath, he felt the trickle of energy flowing back into him.

"Look at you," said the king. "All that fuss and nonsense over a few scrapes. They almost had me believing you were ready for a boat and a trip down the falls to greet the Deep Fathoms."

"I feel much better," Ransom said, trying not to smile.

Benedict eyed Ransom with a look teetering between jealousy and awe.

"Indeed you should," the king said. "We defeated Estian's army, but he wriggled out of the net like a slippery fish. Now he's nearly back in Pree."

"Where are Duke Ashel and Duke Rainor?" Ransom asked, noticing that neither of them were present.

"I sent Ashel westward with his army. No one is opposing us. He's to wait at the border of Bayree for orders. And Rainor took a nasty blow during the fighting. He's in his tent back at the camp. But we have all the leaders we need right now." He glanced at his son and gave him a proud smile.

Benedict nodded solemnly.

"It will take time to bury the dead," Lord Bryon said.

"Let the dead bury the dead," the king snapped. "No, we're going to Pree."

Lord Bryon frowned in concern. "We don't have siege engines. There is no way we can conquer that city without them."

"I know that, Bryon. Estian knows it too. He's no fool. But if our army is camped outside his walls, it limits his options. I'm not leaving Occitania without getting what I want. And I want the duchy of Bayree. Its duke is dead—he no longer needs it. I want it and payment for the widows and fatherless we've gained in this skirmish."

Benedict gasped. "You're going to ask him to *pay* you to leave? If he summons the rest of his forces, we'll have no choice but to flee!"

"I am not leaving without taking something that will hurt him," said the king with an intensity bordering on madness. "I'm weary of this foolishness. The hypocrisy of his people. They parade their banners on the tournament grounds. They grant laurels of victory and reward knights who show Virtus. But it's all an act. A game. And when it came to a contest of wills, we won. I mean to show him that I will take what I wish as retribution for my son's death, and he cannot stop me."

Ransom stared at the king, sensing the implacability of his will. King Devon had an unconquerable spirit. But Estian was proud. He would know that giving in to the king now would hurt him down the road.

"How long must you bear grievance against Occitania?" said Benedict boldly. "We are not entirely innocent of wrong in the feud between our peoples." He lifted a hand, sensing his father's objection before it was spoken. "Don't mistake my words. They overstepped when they attacked Devon, and I'm not at all opposed to making Estian sue for peace between our people. There is no loss of honor, on their part, in yielding to a more determined foe."

"But if we drive them to desperation, we risk creating even more widows on both sides," said Lord Bryon, shaking his head in frustration. "We risk bleeding our own strength, making ourselves vulnerable to Brugia. Word of this battle will spread like doves. Kingfountain is exposed now."

The Elder King turned in his saddle. "I will not leave until I get what I want. But let us hasten the outcome." He twisted back and looked at Ransom. "My boy, at dawn you will ride to Pree with five hundred knights. Demand to speak with the king."

Benedict looked startled. "Send *me*, Father!"

"Confound it, boy! I know you want to go, but it is my will that Sir Ransom goes. Estian fears him. He does not fear you."

"Only because he's never faced me in battle. I'd kill him."

"Well, if he kills Ransom, then you can have him." The king chuckled with dark humor. He pointed at Ransom. "Ride up to the gates, but do not enter without a writ of safe conduct with the royal seal. You tell that pox-marked Estian that I'm at your heels. Ask him to surrender. He won't. Negotiate. I'll take the duchy of Bayree and fifty thousand livres. Hmmm. See if you can get more, but I want not a livre less than fifty thousand. You speak on my behalf. None of this running back and forth. If I don't get what I want, then I will squeeze Pree and every village and town surrounding her, starting with Chessy. You are my man, and you will come to terms with that boy king. If he sends you away, we will burn his fields and make all the fair demoiselles in Occitania shriek when they hear his name. Bring me back a duchy, Sir Ransom. I'll accept nothing less for my son's death."

Ransom had never seen the gates of Pree shut before, let alone with so many soldiers defending the ramparts. He rode with Dearley at his side. Ransom's broken armor had been mended sufficiently to defend him, and he wore it now as they approached the walls. His insides squirmed with dread at the coming meeting. If there *was* a meeting. He feared the cloaked lady might make an appearance, although he did not sense her presence. The sounds of the knights behind him offered some assurance they were not without help.

Ransom gripped the standard of the Argentine king, a banner with the Silver Rose, its pole fixed in the saddle where the lances usually were kept. It was the king's personal banner, the one usually held by his herald.

When they were close enough to see the faces of the men atop the walls, Ransom reined in and halted.

A tall man came to the edge of the rampart. "What news comes from our brethren of Ceredigion?"

An interesting choice of words.

"I am Sir Ransom Barton of the king's council. He sent me to speak to King Estian and negotiate terms."

A murmur went up among the armed soldiers atop the wall.

The man waited for silence and then said, "Should not a king treat with a king?"

Ransom knew his presence was an offense, and a carefully calculated one at that. There were many in Pree who remembered him. How many of them believed that he had disgraced the king's sister, Noemie? Certainly no one had forgotten his tournament victory against their king.

He waited in silence a moment as he stared up at the men.

"It is not improper for a knight to speak with another knight," he answered. "If my king comes to Pree, it will be to ruin her walls."

More gasps, and he saw frowns of outrage. He waited, staring up at the battlements. He felt vulnerable to sudden attack.

The murmuring continued for a while, increasing his suspense.

"He will meet you," came the answer. "Approach the gate, Sir Ransom. Bring two dozen knights. No more."

"I demand a writ of safe conduct. No one doubts the king's seal."

And the herald brought one from the gate himself, holding the scroll out to Ransom from atop his milk-white stallion. He was clean-shaven, like most Occitanians, and wore a purple tunic. Ransom unraveled the scroll and inspected it, taking note of the seal of the Black Prince—a white sword against a black field, the blade shining like a torch.

Ransom handed the writ to Dearley. "Take this to the king and then return."

"Aye, Sir Ransom," said Dearley, his look suspicious. But he did as he was bid.

They followed the messenger into the city of Pree. It was completely dead, with only soldiers walking around, a stark contrast to the lively streets Ransom was accustomed to. People were hunkering down in their homes and shops, worried about the enemy at the gates.

With the streets being clear, they soon made it to one of the bridges leading to the island where the palace sat on a spit of land astride the massive river. Seeing it brought back more cascading memories. It was here he'd discovered, for the first time, that Devon intended to challenge his father. It was here it had all begun.

They crossed the bridge, but instead of going to the palace, they rode to the gardens on the north side of the island. King Estian was waiting at the gate. He had a bruise on his left cheekbone and a gleaming coronet band atop his head. His tunic was black, stitched with silver and blue threads, along with seed pearls forming a diamond-shaped pattern.

"Walk with me," Estian said, gesturing to the gate and the gardens beyond.

Ransom looked at the knights who'd come with him and motioned for them to remain behind. He followed Estian through the gate and down one of the sculpted gravel paths, flanked with neatly trimmed hedgerows covered in budding pale flowers. There was an intoxicating smell that he suddenly recognized. It was star jasmine. The last time he'd smelled that was at the Chandleer Oasis.

"I'm surprised to see you still on your feet," said Estian with a calm smile. He cocked his head slightly. "When we last met, you had a piece of wood stuck in you."

"I suppose I did," Ransom said.

Estian snorted. "I tried to kill you, but I couldn't. Just like I couldn't defeat you in the tournament circuit. That's why Devon sent you to face me. He thought it would intimidate me." He smiled as if at a private joke. "I've requested aid from the southern dukes. They'll be here shortly, so I don't fear a siege. I also have mercenaries coming from Genevar. It won't take them long to arrive by ship. So. I will ask the question I've long wished to ask."

Ransom looked at him with curiosity.

"Name your price, Sir Ransom."

"The king wishes—"

Estian held up his hand, his eyes flashing with anger. "No. I don't care what *he* wants. I care about what *you* want. And I think I know it, so I will make the first offer. You want Lady Claire de Murrow. Ransom, I can get her for you. You won't have Glosstyr, but you could be ruling Legault alongside her."

With those words came a throb of temptation. Estian was good. He knew from Noemie, undoubtedly, where Ransom's heart was bound.

"Oh?" Ransom asked curiously. "Your reach extends all the way to the tower in Kingfountain?"

"You think I make an empty boast?" Estian said, his eyes flashing. "I could have Lady Claire here in Pree tonight. I know you are Fountain-blessed, and not because of the deconeus of St. Penryn. A Genevese merchant named Kohler told me so. You are a valuable man, Ransom Barton. So tell me. What will it take to secure your loyalty? What do *you* want?"

The words of King Estian twisted into Ransom's heart. He had to admit he felt tempted. Here was the King of Occitania offering him the one thing his heart desired—something he feared his own king would never give him. Doubt was a subtle poison. He breathed out slowly.

"Why do you hesitate?" Estian asked.

"Because I do not trust you, my lord," Ransom answered honestly.

"You've given your loyalty to the wrong man," Estian said. "He will not be king for long."

A bur of anger pierced Ransom's heart. "Yet I will stand by him." As he said the words, he felt the Fountain magic pulse through him.

"Even if you stand alone?" the king asked. "I knew you were coming. I didn't think Devon would be foolish enough to invade Occitania, so I didn't muster all of my strength. But I am doing so now, and I will use all of it against him. He's too proud to see it. And too blind to prevent it. Help yourself, Ransom. If he falls, you will not get the woman you adore. I do not reward my enemies. And if you fear for your countrymen, know this. I'll give Devon anything he asks for as long as I get you."

"How would you get Claire out of Kingfountain by tonight?" Ransom demanded.

"I won't tell you that unless we are agreed. But I do not make boasts I cannot fulfill. You know I have ways of getting what I want. Of seeing things I should not be able to see. I will share those secrets with you if you serve me."

Ransom stopped walking, his head buzzing with anger and with the allure of the offer. But there could only be one answer—his integrity demanded it. So did the Fountain. He could not forget its last whisper to him. Even if he did not always agree with the King of Ceredigion, he needed to protect the Argentine line.

"I cannot serve you, my lord. I already serve a king. I came here on his behalf."

Estian's face darkened with the rejection. "And what does Devon want now?"

"The duchy of Bayree. And fifty thousand livres."

Estian's eyes widened with surprise. And then he started to laugh.

Good news at last! I can't trust my hand, or my heart, to write any more than this. But I am so grateful he finally wrote to me. He assured me that he is completely hale, although I assume he's just being brave. Most of the letter was about the young knight in his mesnie, Dearley, who sounds like a charming fellow. Ransom told me that Dearley and his other ward, Elodie, remind him of the two of us when we were young, which is a bit peculiar considering we were so much younger when we lived at the castle together. I'd like to think he means they share an affection for each other, for it might mean that Ransom still thinks of me in ways he dare not say.

—Claire de Murrow
Queen's Tower
(gratefully)

CHAPTER EIGHT

Writ of Peace, Frown of War

When Ransom reached the king's pavilion, he quickly dismounted. Dearley took Dappled's reins with the promise to tend to the horse. Ransom fished the signed scroll from his saddlebag, smelling smoke and cooked bacon in the air, and then strode into the pavilion, through the tent door tied open to let in air and light.

Within he found the Elder King with his two sons, Goff and Benedict, along with Duke Wigant of North Cumbria and Lord Kinghorn of Westmarch. When Ransom and Benedict exchanged a look, the young duke's lips became a tight line.

"So he is back already," Benedict said bluntly.

Goff turned quickly, and his eyes flickered with resentment. Was it because of Ransom's last tournament in Brythonica, he wondered? He'd cut off the arm of his wife's champion in the midst of a duel.

"Ah!" said the king eagerly. He rubbed his hands together and came to meet him in the center of the tent. "What is that scroll? Have you done it?"

"Estian wants peace, not war," said Ransom, handing the scroll to the king. "Although he's prepared to fight you still, he's agreed to these terms, along with the condition of a truce of two years."

The king accepted the scroll and broke off the sealed ends. "Does he now? How like a dog to want to start licking his wounds. Let me see what I find here. Hmmm . . . some courteous nonsense, superfluous titles, ahhh! The meat!"

Benedict and Goff both came to stand by the king and peered over his shoulder. Before Benedict glanced down at the writ, he flashed another glance at Ransom. He held some resemblance to Devon the Younger, although his eyes were bluer, his face rounder, and he bore the signs of battle, the white scar on his cheek and cheekbone, his temple. The younger Goff had no battle scars at all.

"Interesting," said the king. "He does give us the duchy of Bayree, or the rights to control it through the duke's niece and heir, Alix, through a marriage alliance." He lowered the scroll a bit, his brow furrowing. "Where have I heard that name? No matter. She is the heiress, her uncle is dead, and thus we gain control of the duchy through her, along with the rights of wardship—a yearly increase of twelve thousand livres—" The king stopped abruptly. "You didn't count that living as part of the treaty, did you? I said I wanted fifty thousand."

"Read on, my lord," said Ransom, having anticipated that very reaction.

"It's there, Father," Goff said, pointing to the scroll.

"I can read for myself, cub. My eyes are not failing. Ah, there it is. You negotiated seventy-five thousand? To be paid . . . let me see . . . annually over the span of two years beginning now and ending at the culmination of the truce. But I want it now."

Ransom inhaled slowly. "You got more than what you asked for, my lord. I could have gotten close to fifty now, but by extending the term, I was able to press him for more."

He had hoped that the king would be pleased by the terms. But it felt like the Elder King was never satisfied by anything. He had the notion that the king's two sons, standing there with him, would agree with his assessment.

"I would have done better," said the king with a smug look. "But you did well enough for your first negotiation. I think I'll send you to Brugia soon so you can get them to heel next. I'd like to make it a practice to have all of my neighbors pay me to keep the peace. This is good work, Sir Ransom. How did King Estian the Black receive you? Did he try to bribe you?"

"He did."

"Of course! And you showed him your measure, no doubt. Some men are not so easily bought." He looked over at his two sons, his eyes narrowing. The message was clear—he may have allowed them back into the fold, but he had not forgotten their betrayal.

Benedict's cheeks flushed with simmering rage.

"What did he offer you?" asked the king.

Ransom found himself at the center of too many eyes, and he felt his own cheeks begin to burn. "A duchy," he said simply.

The king snorted. "Well, you can have one! I'll give you Bayree myself." He rolled up the scroll and handed it back to Ransom. "Be my vassal at the farthest reach of my domain. That will force Estian to keep his promise."

"You're giving him Bayree?" said Benedict incredulously.

The news came as no greater shock to Ransom himself. He stiffened.

"What about Jon-Landon?" spluttered Goff.

"He's too young to manage it," said the king, shaking his head. "You remember taming the Vexin, lad," he said, looking at Benedict.

"I was his age when I did it," he replied.

"But you've always been a lion, lad. That is not Jon-Landon's way. If I give it to Ransom, then I know it will be tamed, just as I know it would be if you were to rule it."

"Then why not give it to me?" Benedict demanded.

"Or to me!" Goff pressed in resentment. He glanced quickly between his brother and father.

"You have a wife and a duchy already," said the king to Goff. "And a son. Benedict, there are many daughters of lords in your realm, yet you've ultimately balked at their youth. If they are all too young for you to be agreeable, would you give up the Vexin to your youngest brother? Hmmm? But you won't give up what you've won. Even if I commanded it."

Benedict glowered at his father. "I haven't married because you've kept me running to and fro across the lands, leading your mercenaries and putting out campfires that could become wildfires if I didn't smother them. Are you saying you've been expecting me to pick a wife all this time since I was loathe to marry one too young? You could have said as much."

Here it was, the discord that was so rife among the Argentines. Queen Emiloh had been a restraining influence. But no longer.

"I'm trying to explain, Bennett, why I'm giving the duchy of Bayree to Ransom. To help you understand my thinking so that you may learn to—"

"Toy with other men, as you do?" interrupted the son hotly.

The Elder King's eyes blazed. "What I have gained is mine to give," he said, his voice trembling with rage.

"And to take away. Yes, you've said this before. I've done everything you've asked of me, Father. And still it is not enough."

"At least you have Father's respect," said Goff with a look of jealousy. "I've increased Brythonica's wealth fourfold, but spilled ink does not matter so much as spilled blood."

Ransom wished he were anywhere else. The tension in the tent increased with each stifled breath. He glanced at Lord Kinghorn, saw the look of disappointment on his face. Duke Wigant looked impassive, but his nostrils flared with disgust.

"Listen to you both, mewling like cats for a pail of milk," said the king with scorn. "You have no idea—still—how fortunate you both are. Bryon could tell you, if you'd but listen, what it was like under the reign of Gervase. Your whining is pitiful, truly." He glared at Benedict, shaking his head. "Have you learned nothing from me, boy?"

"I've learned what it means to be tight-fisted and greedy," said Benedict with accusation. "I've learned revenge and the cost of betrayal. But what I've learned most is that fear brings failure. I'm not afraid of you."

The king glared at his son. "Maybe you should be."

"We shall see. Is there any duty I may perform for you before I depart?" It was asked with a tone that held an edge of mockery. Benedict's blue eyes stared daggers at his father.

"Escort the Duke of Bayree's body to Lord Ashel. Inform him of my will and my decision. Have him remain at the border until Ransom comes with an army to replace him."

Benedict nodded and then left the tent.

Goff looked at his father, some of the fight having leaked out of him. "Is there something that I—"

"Just go," said the king, waving his hand as if a fly were annoying him.

Goff's mouth tightened with offense, and he stormed out of the tent.

Bryon placed a hand on the Elder King's shoulder, a gesture of simple sympathy, before he, too, departed. Duke Wigant coughed into his hand and then departed as well. Ransom stayed put, looking at the king, trying to understand his own roiling emotions. The king was going to give him the duchy of Bayree? Another heiress?

The king faced away from him, his head slightly bowed. Long moments came and went in silence. He stood somberly, then shook his head and turned around, startling when he saw Ransom standing there.

"I thought you'd gone with the others," he said.

"Would you like to be alone?" Ransom asked.

"It seems that is my destiny," said the king with a sad smile. "Jon-Landon will be disappointed I'm giving Bayree to you as well. He'll rail against me for his many disappointments."

"I don't want the duchy of Bayree," Ransom said. "Why not give it to your son?"

The king snorted. "Why is it that no one I reward is satisfied with what they are given? I've told you that you cannot have Archer's daughter, but I have given you a duchy instead. And yet, it's still not enough. Why are you still on that stubborn girl? I'm not in the habit of saying what I don't mean. I will never allow it to happen. Never."

Ransom felt the urge to defend himself, but arguing with the king had never gotten anyone anywhere, and it only added to the man's personal pain. So he said nothing.

The king put his hands on his hips. "My boy, let me be frank with you. You need a wife. I need a faithful vassal. I chose my wife because she ruled the Vexin, but we did fall in love. And that is what made the pain of her betrayal even more unbearable. Love is poison. You think you know what you want." He paused, chuckling. "Your youth blinds you. I won't force you to marry Lady Alix of Bayree, but at least do me the courtesy of meeting the lass before you reject her. Hmmm?"

Ransom sighed, feeling the conflict wrestling inside him. "I will, my lord." He had already written to Claire to assure her that he'd survived his wound. Part of him felt he should warn her about the king's request, but he decided it wasn't necessary to send a second letter. Why worry her unnecessarily? His heart hadn't changed.

The king looked surprised. "How strange that I should find more joy in your honest declaration than I do in my own sons. You were a comfort to King Gervase, as I recall. I never should have sent you away." He sighed. "But I must again. Take the men to Josselin and see that they get some rest, food, and a little wine. But not too much. Then go west and relieve Ashel."

Ransom wondered if now was the right time to bring it up. "My lord . . ."

"Yes?" asked the king, his eyebrows rising.

"There's another reason I'm reluctant to go to Bayree. When I made the demand of Estian, he . . ." Ransom wasn't sure how to say it.

"Go on," urged the king.

"He . . . laughed at me."

"Why were you surprised? Laughter is often a reaction to shocking things."

"I know that kind of laughter, my lord. This was different. He haggled more over the price of the peace than he did giving up one of his own duchies."

The king looked at him with curiosity. "Perhaps Bayree was giving Estian more trouble than it was worth to him." He chuckled. "Well, lad, it would seem you have a challenge to face. Get to it, then bring me word at Kingfountain what you have learned about your new domain."

Ransom bowed his head and left the tent.

The view of Josselin castle filled Ransom's chest with relief. The smell of tallow again became unmistakable, and as they rode through the town, several of the townsfolk waved and called out cheerful greetings. That had never happened to him before, and it brought a smile to his face. He nodded politely in return.

After crossing the threshold into the castle courtyard, he dismounted, and his steward, Westin, approached.

"Welcome home, my lord," he said with a bow. "Your sister is here."

Ransom barely had time to process the words before Maeg appeared in the entryway, grinning, and rushed down the steps to embrace him.

"What brings you here?" Ransom asked her, grateful to see her. It made it feel like more of a homecoming.

"Lady Elodie asked me to come. She wanted to know how to make this castle more suitable to you." She pulled back. "You look well, Brother. I'd heard you were injured during the fighting."

"It wasn't much," Ransom said.

"He's not being truthful," said Dearley, who came up to them. "Or he's simply being modest. I am Sir John Dearley, the first knight in your brother's mesnie. How do you do?"

"I am well. It's a pleasure to meet you, Sir John. My name is Maeg Barton."

"Everyone calls me Dearley," he said, bowing slightly. This time he didn't tell the story. His gaze lifted over Maeg's shoulder, and his eyes brightened.

Ransom followed his look and saw Lady Elodie had appeared in the doorway. Suppressing a smile, he clapped Dearley on the back. "Would you have Elodie prepare food for the knights who came with us? Westin, can you make space for them to bed down for the evening?"

"Of course," said Westin and Dearley simultaneously.

As they branched off to fulfill his commands, Ransom felt Maeg grip his arm and guide him toward the little park on the far side of the courtyard.

"It's a pretty castle," she said. "Larger than the Heath, for certain. You've done well for yourself, Brother."

"My fortunes continue to change," he said as they walked. "I've not been to Gison since my return or the manor in Brythonica either. Did Sir Kace escort you?"

"No. Marcus wouldn't have condoned it. I came with Sir Veren instead. But enough of my woes. Surely you will have more time now to enjoy your new home?"

"No. The king is sending me to Bayree in Occitania."

"I heard that the duke had fallen." She turned her head to study him. "No . . . what I heard was that *you* killed him. Why not capture him instead?"

He had it on the edge of his tongue to tell her it wasn't always possible to control the outcome of battles, that sometimes you needed to do what you could to survive, but he didn't wish to frighten her. He didn't want her to know how close he had come to dying.

"I'll remember that next time a duke tries to kill me," he answered.

Maeg shook her head, her dark hair fanning over her shoulders. "And why are you going to Bayree?"

"The Occitanians will only relinquish Bayree to us as part of a marriage alliance. The duke's niece is his heir, and King Devon wishes for me to marry her." The thought made him wince, and although he tried to hide his reaction, it didn't escape his sister's notice.

"That doesn't please you, does it?"

Ransom sighed, looking at the sculpted hedgerow on each side of the gravel path. The hedges had been shaped into large spheres as well as a low wall bordering the path. A few gardeners were milling about, cutting away the excess growth.

"I'm still devoted to Claire," he said. "Besides, I don't trust any of this. I've not been home that long, Maeg. Every time I think I've found my place . . . it gets ripped away from me. Bayree is so very far away, a spike of land in the sea. I saw the map in the king's tent. It's next to Benedict's land, and he'll make for a surly neighbor."

"How does Claire feel about you?" she asked.

"We are friends," Ransom said with a shrug. "I have permission to write her but not to court her. I wish I knew her feelings, but I cannot ask. It would violate my agreement with the king, and it would be unfair to her. I can't marry her unless he changes his mind."

"It would not be wise to upset the king," Maeg agreed. "What of Benedict? Is he still at odds with the king?"

"Yes. And he's angry with the king's decision to give me the duchy. He feels it should go to Jon-Landon."

"Shouldn't it? Wouldn't you rather have another duchy instead?"

"I would. But the only prize left for the taking is Glosstyr, and he means for Jon-Landon to marry Claire and take ownership of it. I cannot bear that thought. I . . . I don't know what to do."

"I'm glad I came. You need advice from someone who loves you. I think Mama would say the same thing. You need to be clear on how you feel. I take it you don't intend to marry Lady Elodie?"

"No!" Ransom said, surprised. "I told Dearley as much and asked him to tell her."

"I know," said Maeg, giving him a gentle but scolding look. "You need to tell her yourself. She's confused. I think she cares about your first knight. But she also feels obligated to you as her guardian."

Ransom's brow furrowed. "I'm not—"

"Just talk to her," said Maeg. "It's frightening, being in her position. Knowing that she might be given to a man to further his fame or wealth." Her voice hinted that the struggle she described was one she knew well. "If you will make no claim on her yourself, then tell her. Don't make her wait."

He stopped, and she stopped too, looking up at him. "Is that what is happening to you?" he asked softly.

She tried to smile, but then the tears came instead.

"Sir Kace?" he asked. "Was he bold enough to ask?"

"Yes," she said, the sound of her voice heartbreaking. "But Marcus . . . our brother . . . said no."

He put his arm around his sister, pulling her close to him, understanding the pain she was feeling. The ache in his heart was still there. It would always be there.

He had offered to help Marcus with their sister's dowry, and if he could do it without causing offense, he'd make a case for letting her marry for love. But he didn't want to say anything that might raise her hopes. As much as he wished he could solve her problem, he couldn't. Nor did he know how to approach his own dilemma. He looked down at the wrist where he'd worn Claire's braided charm for so long. The bracelet was gone, but it had only been a symbol. His love for Claire had not abated. The lack of her was still a raw wound.

Prince Jon-Landon came to visit again, and this visit was intolerable for he brought with him Sir James Wigant. Sir James is all smiles and witty banter, but he's truly an eel, and I despise him. I was much shocked to see him again, let alone in the company of the prince, as if they were suddenly boon companions. Duke Wigant responded to the call to arms and brought an army down from Dundrennan. I don't know whether James slipped away while his father was absent. I don't trust him and think he has less brains than a badger if he's trying to get in the good graces of Jon-Landon.

His smirks and knowing looks were made even more insufferable because of the news he brought concerning Ransom. News that Ransom didn't share himself, although I understand why he didn't think I'd wish to know that he has been asked to marry another woman. Honestly. Some badgers are more brainless than others. I think it delighted Sir James to tell me that the Elder King has promised the newly conquered duchy of Bayree to Ransom if he accepts the duke's niece as his wife. Sir James also said that he hopes Jon-Landon will not be named the Duke of Glosstyr after all. He gave me a knowing smile. I tried to reveal nothing, but I think Sir James knows he bothered me. Let him feel like the victor. At least I got news from someone.

—Claire de Murrow
(trapped amidst commotions and intrigues)

CHAPTER NINE

The Lilies of Bayree

Ransom sat in the solar with Dearley, enjoying a companionable silence. It was a new feeling, being the master of a castle, and he found he rather liked it. Dearley was reading a book, and Ransom stood overlooking the lazy river and the village road, watching as the men walked by. They'd all eaten, but most had decided to visit the town to spend a portion of their pay.

Dearley broke the silence. "When do you anticipate riding to Bayree, if you don't mind my asking?"

Ransom turned away from the window. "Tomorrow, I think. The horses will be rested and ready for another journey. Duke Ashel will grow vexed if we wait too long."

"What do you make of Lord Ashel? He seems a brooding sort of man."

"He's been loyal to the king for many years. He served Devon Argentine during the wars with King Gervase." Ransom looked back outside again. "He's seen many troubles in that time. No doubt they press on him."

"I hope the troubles are nearly over," Dearley said, his tone thoughtful. "The battle seems like a strange dream now, but so many died. So many knights fell, never to rise again. And here we are now, far away from that field." He shook his head. "Well, I'm talking too much. Have you been to Bayree before?"

"No," he answered. "I don't know much about Bayree, just that it is renowned for its fishing, and there's a famous dye they export. I imagine they will be nervous about meeting us, so we will need to put our best foot forward."

He heard the noise of the door latch and looked toward it as it opened, revealing Elodie.

"You want me to come?" Dearley asked with anticipation.

"You are my first knight," Ransom answered. "Of course. Hello, Elodie. Welcome."

Dearley turned and then rose and bowed quickly to the young lady. The warmth in his smile seemed to confirm Ransom's suspicions.

"I was hoping . . . if I might have a word with you?" she said to Ransom.

"I should go," Dearley said, setting down his book on the table. He promptly left the two of them alone.

Ransom remembered his conversation with Maeg. He'd been so busy afterward that the matter had entirely slipped from his mind. He gestured for her to take Dearley's chair, but she only approached and stood behind it, her hands fidgeting before she pressed her palms on the top of the padded chair.

"I'm glad you called on my sister to come," Ransom said.

"I enjoy her, I truly do," said Elodie. She looked uncomfortable, hesitant. "I'm grateful for your suggestion."

Ransom waited, wondering what she was going to say or if he should just let her know his thoughts quickly and end the suspense. "Elodie—"

"If I may," she interrupted. She took a deep breath, then bit her bottom lip. "When the king took me under wardship, the master of the rolls explained that my guardian would have the right to choose my husband." She gave him a worried look.

"I know," Ransom said gently.

She flushed and glanced away, then took another breath. "I confided in Dearley, while we were waiting for you to arrive, how nervous I was. But then I met you, and you were nothing like I dreaded you might be. You both left quickly, and Dearley's note arrived soon afterward. I think he was trying to be helpful, but he may have given you the wrong impression." She looked down. "I am . . . willing . . . you see . . . I know my duty . . . that I have no right to choose. If you want it . . . me . . . I'm . . . I'm making a fool of myself right now." Her cheeks had flushed scarlet, and she turned to leave.

"Wait," Ransom said, surprised by her words, her confession. This was not at all the conversation he'd expected them to have. "Please, Elodie. Don't go."

She hurriedly wiped her eyes but did not turn back to face him.

"I should have been more up-front with you," he said, taking a few steps closer. "The master of the rolls told me the same thing. He encouraged me to marry you as the king wished. Now the king has changed his mind again. He would prefer for me to marry the heiress of Bayree. But I tell you this, truly, there is but one woman whom I love. She has been my friend since we were children. I wait on her and no one else."

Elodie turned her head slowly, a look of relief on her face. "Do you mean Lady Claire de Murrow?"

"She is the one," Ransom said. "I gave Dearley permission to write to you, to let you know that I will not force you to marry anyone, let alone *me*. You are my ward, it is true, and I want you to be happy. In fact, I think Dearley cares for you."

Elodie's smile brightened the room. "Do you think so?"

"I'll let you decide that for yourself. As far as my intentions are concerned, I should have been up-front. I don't intend to marry any woman but Claire."

"But what about the king? Won't he be angry?"

Ransom sighed. "Perhaps. I can only hope I'll earn his approval. In the end, Lady Claire is the one who chooses her fate. She cannot be forced to marry, as per the custom of her people."

Elodie looked at him seriously. "I've heard Lady Claire serves Queen Emiloh now. I feel sorrow for both of them. That tower must be a lonely place."

"It is," he agreed. "Do you like staying at Josselin?"

"I do," she said brightly. "It's a beautiful castle. I will make it a place that you will want to bring Lady Claire to someday. I could look for some tapestries from Legault, perhaps?"

"That would be splendid. Thank you."

Elodie smiled at him. "I'm grateful you shared what you did. I wasn't opposed to the match. I didn't expect you to be so . . . kind."

Her praise embarrassed him, so he said nothing. She left, and he walked across the room to the other window, the one overlooking the castle gardens. A few moments later, he spotted Elodie and Dearley walking side by side down the gravel path, talking animatedly to each other.

The sight made him smile, but there was a heaviness in his heart as he imagined doing the same with Claire. Would it ever happen?

✕

Within three days, Ransom reached Lord Ashel's camp on the border between the Vexin and Bayree. The men had been provided for, and there were provisions to spare for Ransom's men when they arrived. He walked with Dearley to Lord Ashel's pavilion, which was soot-stained and dirty. The men had not been given any respite since the battle, and they looked tired and ill humored.

Lord Ashel was eating a bit of roasted chicken when Ransom entered, his fingers wet with grease. His gray-streaked beard had specks of food in it.

"Took you long enough to get here, Barton," growled Lord Ashel after licking his dirty fingers and rising.

"We came as quickly as we could," Ransom answered.

"Pardon my grousing, but I'd like to get back to my own duchy. Let me tell you where things stand."

"I'm eager to hear it."

"Good, although I'm not a man of many words. I delivered the news to her ladyship, Lady Alix, at Kerjean. The duchy had six hundred knights who fought with the duke in the battle, and they've lost over half. They are ill prepared to resist. The injured have returned and are being cared for at the manor. She hardly had time to speak to me, and I didn't want to linger because the whole place stinks of blood. Enjoy your new duchy, Barton. You're welcome to it."

Although Ransom had assumed Lady Alix wouldn't be happy to meet the man who'd slain her uncle, he hadn't considered how the casualties of war might impact the duchy. He was coming as a conqueror.

"Thank you, Lord Ashel. I'll see you again at Kingfountain, I'm sure."

"Indeed. We'll meet again when the king gets the urge to grab something else. Hopefully he'll want to rest his old bones as I do. If I were you, I'd leave most of your men here in camp. Kerjean is full at the moment."

"It is good advice. Thank you."

Ashel started eating the chicken again. "Oh," he said around a mouthful. "Duke Bennett came by on his way back to Auxaunce. He said he wanted to see you when you arrived. You are neighbors with him now." A caustic smile came to Lord Ashel's face. "Good luck with that."

Ransom left the tent, and Dearley looked at him with raised eyebrows. "A pleasant enough fellow."

"He's weary. I don't blame him. I hadn't thought enough about the wounded of Bayree. Send a knight back to Josselin. Perhaps candles may be of use while they tend to the wounded. Tell the knight to gather several cartloads and bring them to Kerjean. And to send word for barbers. I will pay them well if they hurry."

Dearley looked pleased by the order. "I will see to it. Perhaps some food as well?"

"Yes. Some sheep from Josselin, and we can arrange for supplies to be brought from my other castles. They cannot turn to Pree for help right now. We'll do what we can."

"I will see it done. Are we riding to Kerjean, then?"

"Immediately," said Ransom.

As Dearley went to fulfill the command, Ransom walked through the camp, surveying the weary men and their filthy armor. There was a feeling of malice in the camp, of tempered anger that showed these men were at their limit. It was good that they'd be leaving. Their dissatisfaction could easily turn violent. He ordered twenty of his knights to ride on to Kerjean while the rest stayed behind and reclaimed the camp from those who were moving on.

He made sure Dappled was fed and had water to drink before mounting him again and preparing to ride the rest of the way. A messenger was sent ahead to warn Lady Alix that Ransom was coming with a group of knights. The road to Kerjean was narrow and flanked with trees. The trees reminded him of the terrain in the Vexin, and they passed a hill that sparked memories of his wearying voyage with Lord DeVaux and his men after he was captured. The recollection brought with it a dull ache in his leg and the feeling of being permanently cold after sleeping in the wilderness for months.

"You look pensive," said Dearley, coming alongside him. "I imagine you'll be received with coldness."

"That's not it. It feels like I've been here before," Ransom said. He felt solemn, and his concern began to increase.

Another piece of scenery sparked recognition, and then another. He *had* been here, or very near it. His Fountain magic began to thrum inside him. Was it responding to his mood, his memories, or revealing danger ahead? As the sunlight began to fade, he wondered if they'd be caught in the dark before reaching the castle.

The woods finally opened up, revealing a quaint little town, windows glowing with light and smoke drifting lazily from stubby chimneys. There were lilies growing everywhere. Ransom saw them in planter boxes beneath the windows of the houses, growing in rows in open fields, clustered around trees, and being bundled and loaded onto carts to sell. The townsfolk were out and about, and as Ransom and his men rode down the main street, still following the road, they were met with spiteful looks.

The road eventually led to a gate, at which point it turned into a long paved path leading to Kerjean castle, a small building of Occitanian design. Only a few of the windows were illuminated against the growing dusk, giving the darkened ones a feeling of gloom.

As soon as he saw the castle, Ransom felt sure his instincts had not betrayed him. He *had* been there before. The slope of the roof, the steep pitch of it, reminded him of a fever dream he'd had during his injury and imprisonment. Of the place where he'd nearly died.

The gate was open. He felt sweat begin to trickle down his back as he rode Dappled down the paved path, hearing the echo of the hooves as they struck stone. There were two great fields of sod on each side of the road and distant hedges lined them, creating a border before the tree line, which now looked ominous and dark.

About halfway down the path, Ransom began to sense her presence in the castle ahead. It struck him like a bell, a sound that only he could hear. The toll of another Fountain-blessed. Yes, this was the poisoner who had killed the Younger King. The one who had also shot Ransom in the leg with a crossbow in the dungeon of Beestone castle. The one who appeared to be Queen Emiloh's natural daughter.

He had never known her name, but he knew it now.

Alix was also the lady who had snuck him bandages when DeVaux had forbidden anyone to heal him, and this was the castle where it had happened. His hands gripped the reins, and he felt Dappled's mood alter along with his. The horse snorted distrustfully.

The poisoner was the lady of the castle now, and the Elder King wanted Ransom to marry her.

Was this why Estian the Black had laughed?

Still no word from Ransom.

The king has returned, and the whole palace is con-sumed with tales of the fighting. Many knights were lost on the battlefield. A knight cannot be replaced easily. It takes years of training for one to be ready, which is why war is of such consequence. The wounded are being cared for, but some bear wounds that will mark them for a lifetime.

Prayers have been said and coins plopped into foun-tains. What a waste of good money. Tomorrow has been established as a day of solemnity, but the Elder King is any-thing but solemn. He brought with him the first payment of the truce terms, which he's added to his hoarded treasure.

Sir Dalian said that Prince Jon-Landon made a com-motion in front of the king's council. He demands his own lands, his own rights, more than just a single castle. He was angry to have been left behind, to have been "robbed" (his word) of his share of the honor. In all likelihood, the barmy codsockle would have ended up dead had he gone there.

He didn't ask for Glosstyr. He's asking for the Vexin. No, he's demanding it. And from what Sir Dalian implied,

the king may consider giving it to him if Ransom takes
Bayree.
   Who will I get, then?

—*Claire de Murrow, Rightful Queen of Legault*

CHAPTER TEN

The Fisher Kings

Kerjean castle was a structure with four walls joined in a square around a stone courtyard. The front gate was stone, decorated with sculpted effigies of knights and ladies, with flourishes of waves and fish carved into the design. The courtyard beyond it was thronged with horses and empty wagons, and the smell of manure hung thick in the air. At the far end of the space, a grand entrance stood between two shelves of steps, revealing a stone manor built into the far end of the castle, with enough windows to show that it was four stories tall, including the dormers in the slanted rooftop at the pinnacle. The walls on the eastern and western sides of the courtyard boasted guest quarters with doors leading into them. It was a noisy yard, and Ransom continued to tense as they rode toward the doors, feeling the presence of his nemesis grow stronger.

"What a foul stench," Dearley said, grimacing. "The duke wasn't jesting."

But it wasn't the smell that made Ransom so uneasy. As they reached the bottom of the platform at the edge of the stairs, he dismounted, then looked at the knights he had chosen to come. Many were gazing up at the decorative manor. As a castle, it was not formidable. Ransom had seen no one guarding the ramparts leading into it.

"Be ready for trouble," he said to the knights. "Do not let your guard down. We are enemies in this land. Never wander off alone. Keep your heads up and your eyes open. We are not here to cause offense."

He looked from man to man, letting them see that he was serious about his order. Then he marched ahead and mounted the steps as Dearley fell in beside him.

"Are you very uneasy?" his ward asked him.

"More than you know," he replied. "I do not trust this place. Keep the knights together as much as possible."

"What concerns you?"

"I'll tell you later," Ransom replied. When they reached the top of the steps, they were greeted by a young man in a servant's livery. The tunic was blue with the emblem of a fish on the front.

"Greetings, my lord," said the boy. "Lady Alix is in the hall."

"Thank you," Ransom answered. "Take us there, please."

As they entered, they needed to walk around the men sleeping on the floor of the corridor. The marble floor was filthy with mud. Broken pieces of armor were strewn about. Some of the injured warriors glanced up as Ransom passed. He sensed their pain, their fevers, their sickness. Coughing echoed down the length of the corridor, and the stench of stale vomit hung in the air.

As they walked toward the set of doors at the end of the corridor, he could sense the presence of the poisoner. The boy tugged the handle of one of the doors, but he struggled with its weight, so Ransom grabbed the edge and opened it effortlessly.

The hall was a mirror of the corridor. The furniture had all been shoved to the side, and men slept on pallets throughout the room. Some had bandages wrapped around their heads. Some were missing limbs. Other writhed and groaned in pain. The scene was awful, but Ransom's senses cut through the injuries to the woman he sought.

Lady Alix knelt by one of the couches, blood up to her elbows as she tended to a dying soldier who moaned with pain at her ministrations.

It shocked him to see her like that—out in the open, working to save a life rather than destroy it. The cloak that had concealed her identity was gone. Her golden hair, so much like Queen Emiloh's, was disheveled. She wore a black-and-gold brocade gown that seemed especially out of place in the gory scene around her.

"This way," said the boy, and he started walking toward the lady.

As they came closer, Ransom realized she was in the process of sewing the man's side wound closed. As he approached, she finished and then put a slab of moldy bread on the wound before bandaging it. Seeing the splotches on the bread brought back memories that roiled his emotions. Memories of this woman saving *him*.

She turned, noticed him, and shook her head. There were bloodstains on the gold of her gown. A smear of it on her breastbone.

"I don't have time for you right now," she said wearily. "If I don't tend to some of these men, they'll die before dawn."

"How can we help?" Ransom asked, stepping forward, feeling his concern grow despite his wariness.

"Unless you can gut a fish, you'll only be in the way," she said. "We have barrels of rotting fish and no time to prepare and cook them. Some of these men haven't eaten in days."

"Dearley," Ransom said. "Take the men to the kitchens. See that they help."

Lady Alix's eyebrows lifted in surprise. "Thank you. There are servants digging graves beyond the walls. They could use some help as well."

"I'll see to it, my lady," Dearley said. He turned and began dividing up the men.

Ransom noticed Lady Alix had a long strand of pearls wrapped around her left wrist. The pearls were covered in blood, and it seemed odd that she should wear such a thing while treating the men. Was it something she had won from the Fountain on her own quest to the oasis? He knew she'd gone on one, for the deconeus of St. Penryn had told him so.

"What can I do?" Ransom asked, coming closer to her.

"That one is already gone," she said, pointing to a man who'd collapsed on the floor. "Carry his body to the doors over there. They'll bring a wheelbarrow and take him to the pit."

Ransom did as she asked, bending down and hoisting the corpse up over his shoulder. As he looked around the room at the other men suffering, dying, he couldn't help but think of his own gift from the oasis. With the Raven scabbard, he could help heal these wounded men, one at a time. But if his relic were discovered, it might be stolen from him. Someone might kill him for it. *She* might kill him for it. It would be prudent to keep it secret, but he could at least help these men with his hands and his strength.

He worked side by side with Lady Alix, helping where he could—pressing bandages to wounds, moving men, and doing whatever else was asked of him. The manor became darker and darker, and he noticed the candles were indeed sparse and more would be welcomed. Food came in later on, carried on trays by the knights he'd brought with him. They went from person to person, offering pieces of roast fish to the wounded, the dying. Other knights brought tureens of water and helped the injured drink.

It was long after midnight when they were finished tending and feeding the injured. Lady Alix bathed her hands in a water dish, turning it pink as she scrubbed her fingers clean. She dried them on a towel.

"My uncle's room is yours," she said, looking at him with sad eyes. "I haven't had the heart to go in there since I learned he was gone. There's a chamber for your knights next to it. Get some rest, Ransom. We will talk on the morrow."

She looked utterly exhausted. He wasn't sure what he'd expected, but it wasn't this. Her compassion for the injured had awoken his gratitude. Whatever else she'd done, there was no denying she'd saved his life. Perhaps she'd even told Queen Emiloh about him. For all he knew, that was why the queen had paid his ransom. Looking at her face, he saw plainly the resemblance. His curiosity about her origins tantalized him . . . and yet, she'd murdered his friend and king, and she'd almost certainly killed Claire's father too. All of which made him feel supremely conflicted.

"Tomorrow, then," he said. He was weary but still too anxious to want to sleep.

The duke's private chamber was on the upper floor of the castle. Ransom and his men had to climb the steps with only one candle to light the way. The anteroom for the knights had enough pallets for the men to sleep on, and they gratefully hunkered down for the night. Ransom and Dearley explored the duke's dwelling place, which was nicely appointed and decorated with the motif of fish.

"Our horses were brought behind the manor," Dearley said. "They've been cared for and fed provender." He touched one of the curtains, admiring the velvet. "This duke was a wealthy man. That bed could hold three people." He stifled a yawn. "I'll be in the next room if you need anything."

"No, I'd like you to stay. I don't trust Lady Alix. One of us needs to stand guard. We'll take turns sleeping."

Dearley laughed. "Are you thinking she might try to murder you in your sleep?"

Ransom didn't smile. "Get some rest, Dearley. I'll wake you when it's your turn to keep watch."

"You're serious?"

"Very," Ransom said. "Get some rest."

It wasn't long before Dearley was snoring softly on the couch. Ransom continued to inspect the room, to stop his own eyes from drooping. In the back of his mind, he was thinking of another time, of the small dungeon in the basement of this castle. Would it look the same now as it had then? Years had dulled the sharpness of his memories, already hazy from his illness.

He wasn't sure how much time had passed before he sensed her presence coming up the stairs. A prickle of apprehension shot through him as he stared at the door, waiting. She came down the corridor, unable to hide her presence from him. It was still deep into the night.

Dearley slept right through the knock that sounded at the door. Ransom walked to the door and twisted the handle, positioning the tip of his boot to catch the door when he opened it. The lit candle from his room had nearly burned out, so he barely saw her in the gap in the door. She had not brought a candle.

"If neither of us is going to sleep, then we should talk," she said.

His lips curled into a wary frown.

She sighed. "I'm not going to attack you, Ransom." She held up her hands, showing that she carried no weapon.

"I wish I could be sure of that."

"A truce, then? Just until dawn?" She gave him a tired smile. He did not feel a threat coming from her, and her exhaustion was obvious in the slump of her shoulders.

"Truce," Ransom agreed.

"There is a little nook down the hall with a window seat. Shall we?"

He was grateful she didn't demand to enter the room. Glancing at the couch and the slumbering Dearley, he nodded in agreement and then left the door open so it would be obvious he had left. She led the way to a nook at the bend in the hall, equipped with a window seat where the moon shone brightly. She sat down first.

Her gown was no longer the soiled one she'd worn earlier. Her hands rested on her lap, and he saw the coil of pearls around her wrist. The blood had been cleaned off. She wore no other jewelry, but he noticed a birthmark dotted her breast above the edge of her bodice.

Ransom sat down on the other side of the bench, his emotions still conflicted. "I didn't expect to find you here," he said, offering a bemused smile.

"Do you even remember coming here when you were injured?"

"The castle was vaguely familiar, but I was delirious at the time."

"You were indeed." She offered a pretty smile that snagged at his chest. "DeVaux came in through the rear of the castle. It looks very different on that side. The villagers didn't know he'd come until after he was gone. My uncle was at the tournament in Chessy at the time."

"Who are you?" he asked intently.

She glanced down at her hands before she looked up at him. "Who was I then, or who am I now?"

"There is a difference, then?" He leaned toward her.

"Yes." Her eyes peered into his. "We are both Fountain-blessed, Ransom. We are not like other people. When you were wounded, the Fountain told me to heal you, even though I risked my own safety by doing so."

His feelings churned with uncertainty. He'd always felt a great curiosity about the woman who'd saved him. He'd fallen a little in love with the idea of her, before discovering she was the cloaked lady. The mystery of it had been alluring, although his feelings for Claire were much stronger. Now his savior, Devon's killer, sat with him, and he struggled to reconcile her with the things she'd done.

"Are we the only ones?" he asked.

"The only ones I know of," she answered. "I was just beginning to learn about my powers when they brought you here. I sensed something different about you. Afterward, I heard about how you'd stood alone against DeVaux's knights. They couldn't defeat you. It reminded me of stories I've read."

"What stories?" he asked with interest.

"The legends of King Andrew. This castle plays a role in that history. Before it was named Kerjean, they called it the Castle of the Fisher

Kings. It draws those who are Fountain-blessed. It drew me here. And now it's brought you."

She looked into his eyes, her expression full of wonder and confusion. "You are part of something greater than yourself, Ransom. Can't you feel that? We both are. It is so strange meeting you like this. I didn't think there was any chance you would ever come here voluntarily. Yet . . . here you are. It's a miracle to me."

"What is significant about this castle?" Ransom asked. "I've never heard of the Fisher Kings before."

"I'm sure you haven't," she said. "This castle has been here for as long as written history. This place used to be its own kingdom. There has always been a deep connection between this place and the Fountain because the people are so dependent on the streams and the ocean, and the bounty they provide, for their livelihood. The folk who lived here were called Fisher Kings. Now it is just a duchy. But in days of old, the Duke of Bayree would have been a king. The people here treated him as one."

Ransom felt a twinge of sorrow for having killed the man. "He was your uncle, then?"

She shook her head. "But that was what I called him. That was what everyone believed. As you may have guessed, I am the natural daughter of the Duchess of Vexin. Your queen." She seemed to wrestle inwardly with some dark emotion, then shook it off and continued. "The Duke of Bayree thought to woo her after her father died. He sent his first knight to win her trust, to see if she would be amenable to such an alliance, but another offer had come in from the Duke of Westmarch. That duchy was more significant, more powerful than Bayree. In his zeal to persuade my mother to love his master, the knight . . ." Her voice trailed off. Her lips pressed tightly together. "Let's just say they failed to suppress their affection for each other. I was born of their union. I was their shame. Queen Emiloh got rid of me as soon as I was born. She ordered her lover, the knight, to take me away. And I was brought here.

My uncle, the man I call my uncle, took me in. And now he is dead, and he has named me his heir."

She breathed out slowly. "King Lewis had other plans for me. He sent me to be trained by an order of women in the kingdom of Pisan. To be used as a tool to ensure that his son, the Black Prince, would one day rule over all the kingdoms. I have been their tool for most of my life, Ransom. But what has happened now . . . it changes everything. The game of Wizr is almost over, and Devon will likely win it."

"Game?" Ransom asked with confusion. He felt his pulse in his ears as she told her story. She knew things that he did not. She could help him understand his place in the world, and he was hungry for it.

"A magical Wizr board has been handed down for generations among the kings of Occitania. Lewis, and now Estian, knew what would happen in our conflicts because of that board and what it reveals to him. I've seen it, Ransom. I know where Estian hides it. If your king had it, he could defeat Occitania. You and I have been enemies playing each other across that board, both of us pawns of our kings. This is the chance to change that. If you become the Duke of Bayree, if you take *this* land, then it will change my allegiance. It will break the curse that I'm bound to." She shook her head. "There's too much to tell you. Too much you don't know." She put her hand on his, and he felt the pearls of her bracelet graze his skin as her eyes bored into his. "You have a decision to make."

*Another outburst erupted in court today. The prince contin-
ues to make demands. I cannot help but see the influence of
James Wigant in all of this. He has spent so much time with
the prince of late. What is in it for Sir James, I wonder?
What does this turmoil give him? I cannot see it unless his
aim is something totally foolish like wanting me for himself. Surely he's not that simple. Or maybe he just thrives on
creating discord. One cannot be too careful in choosing one's
friends . . . or enemies.*

—Claire de Murrow
(missing Legault . . . longing for a walk among
the barrow mounds)

CHAPTER ELEVEN

A New Future

Ransom stared down at the hand covering his. The warmth and softness caused unfamiliar feelings to stir inside him. Dangerous feelings. He pulled his hand away and then stood. Her eyes lowered in embarrassment.

"What decision?" he demanded.

"About *us*, Ransom," she said, her gaze still downcast. "This is the first glimpse of freedom I've ever had. A chance to change sides. I can only do that if you accept me. If you become the Duke of Bayree." She looked up at him. "I'm not your enemy, Ransom. I am loyal to Estian because I *have* to be. If your king discovers who I really am, he will forbid us to marry. You've seen what he's done to the queen. To my mother." She swallowed and then stood and approached him. She gently touched his face. "You're exhausted, and I've added to your burdens. Get some rest. I promise I will not harm you or any of your knights. I wanted you to see that it is in my best interest to accept you. To accept this twist of fate." She lowered her hand. "I have feelings which . . . they are difficult to express. I've seen you from the shadows for so long. As a danger to my missions, yes. But I've also seen you as a man. An honorable one." She shook her head sadly. "There is no honor in Pree. The tournaments, the fanfare. It's all a show. Think about what I've told you. We can talk on the morrow." She started to walk away but then paused. Without looking back, she said, "I know your heart has been committed elsewhere. I only ask that you consider what may be."

His heart churned with warring feelings as he watched her leave. He thought of Claire, picturing in his mind her hair, her smile, her laugh. It pained him to think of giving up hope. Of relinquishing what his heart had wanted for so long. But the king had made it clear he never intended to yield. And now this . . .

Should he confide in King Devon the truth about Alix of Bayree? His sense of loyalty trembled at the thought of concealing it, but she'd seemed so sincere, so eager for his help.

He felt her presence fading as she went down the stairs. Weary to his bones, he walked back to his room and found Dearley still sound asleep on the couch. Ransom went to the chair by the window and sat down, mulling over the strange things she had said about magic Wizr boards and curses of allegiance. And he fell asleep soon afterward.

The following days were much like the first. Ransom and his knights helped in the kitchens, buried those who had died during the night, and cared for the horses that cluttered the inner yard. Alix spent the day treating wounds, using her skills to heal and comfort. He watched the care she showed to the injured, and his confusion about her only deepened.

One late afternoon, weariness overcame him, and he wandered through the square castle a little until he found a reading room stacked with books, most of which were written in Occitanian. He took a book of stories of the Fountain-blessed to a couch and stretched out on it, starting to read. The script was difficult to translate, which taxed his mind, and he fell asleep.

He dreamed and knew it was a dream. In it, he was walking in the gardens at Josselin castle, hand in hand with Alix. The bright sunlight flashed off her golden tresses as they made their way through the gardens, and he felt a powerful sense of peace and contentment. In the dream, he saw Maeg walking with Sir Kace, the two of them smiling at each other shyly, and his heart swelled with gratitude. He brought Alix's hand to his mouth and kissed her knuckles. There was a smell to them. A perfumed smell. When had he ever experienced a dream so real, so intense?

It was a dream. It had to be a dream.

And he awoke to the feeling of a kiss on his brow.

Ransom's eyes fluttered open, and the chains of sleep began to loosen, although the exhaustion did not lift. He felt weighed down by a suit of armor, even though he only wore his hauberk and a tunic. Lady Alix knelt at the edge of the sofa, pulling away from the kiss she'd just given his forehead.

"I should have let you sleep," she said, smiling as if she'd just received the greatest news in the world. "But I couldn't. I had to wake you." Her smile brightened even more. The light was beginning to fade outside the window. It was nearly sunset.

Ransom grunted as he sat up, and the book tumbled from his lap, thudding on the floor. She reached out and smoothed his hair. "They just arrived, Ransom. Carts full of candles from Josselin castle. Food. And barbers. At least a dozen. They came because of you." She sighed in wonderment. "Thank you. I don't know how to thank you, but . . . thank you still." She pressed a kiss to his cheek. "You are a lovely man. Now I feel I can finally get some rest."

He was gratified by her words and her appreciation. The scene from his dream was still overpoweringly real in his mind. Had it been a vision from the Fountain? It felt like it.

"I wanted to help," he said, swinging his legs down. The fog in his mind lifted slowly. "I know the costs of war."

With him sitting up, she was slightly lower than him, looking up at his face. "You do." She leaned against the couch, resting her head on her arms. "When DeVaux's men came all those years ago, they said you'd murdered so many of his knights. It can hardly be called murder since they were trying to capture . . . the queen." Her pause was deliberate, her eyes touched with pain. "I've heard other stories about you too. They say that you cannot be defeated. Your gift from the Fountain is a brutal one . . . but valuable in our world. My gift is similar." Her eyelashes lowered. "I know how to hurt people, or prevent them from being hurt. I sense the potential for death in everyone. Except for you. I shouldn't tell you this, but something has changed, and I know I can't kill you. When we met in the dungeon at Beestone castle, I could have killed you easily, but I didn't wish to. I'm sorry I shot you, though." She touched his injured leg, patting it gently. "I wish I could have done more when DeVaux brought you here. I would have."

The pressure of her hand on his leg caused warmth to radiate throughout his body. "You saved my life, Alix."

"Even then, I saw what was needed to save you," she said, removing her hand. "Are you hungry? You must be. I don't think you've eaten since you came."

"I've had a little," he said, amazed by how much his feelings had changed. Although he would have thought it impossible a few days ago, he was beginning to trust her. It felt good to talk to another who wielded Fountain magic. It was something they shared that he would never share with Claire. And yet, he could not be comfortable with the situation, knowing that King Devon knew nothing about it. His sense of loyalty to Claire, to the king, nagged at him.

"I will have a tray brought here. Perhaps we could share it together? The barbers have started working on the injured. I just need to change out of this dress . . . it will take days for my maids to clean all the blood off it."

He could see some stains on her sleeves, but it didn't bother him. If anything, her hard work, her fortitude, was something to respect.

"I would like that," he said, nodding. He reached down and picked up the fallen book.

Her hand touched his. "That's not the best story. One of the others talks about a Fountain-blessed knight whose horse was cut in half riding beneath a shutting portcullis. A brutal tale, but I think you'd like it."

"It sounds intriguing," Ransom said.

She smiled and took the book from him, returned it to the shelf, and searched for another. Moments later, she slipped the slim volume into his hand.

"This one. The story of Sir Owain."

Ransom took it and then watched as she left. She paused by the door, looking back at him with such an expression of gratitude that his heart melted in his chest. As soon as she was gone, he set the book down, rose, and began pacing. It was a quandary. The vivid dream, her manners and kindness, the gentleness of her violent hands . . . Feelings came and left of their own accord, his mind a jumbled mess. Was this why the Fountain had taken the bracelet from him at the oasis? To prepare his heart for a change? Or was he looking for meaning where there was none?

Dearley knocked on the door before entering. He had a knowing look and a wry smile. "I'm assuming Lady Alix told you that the supplies arrived? Ah, good. The knights have cleaned up the courtyard, although a little grudgingly. I wouldn't hear any excuses, though."

"Thank you, Dearley."

"This castle isn't as grand as Josselin, but it is an opportunity. Are you considering it?"

"I have to say that I am," Ransom said, running his hand on the top of the sofa. "It's not what I was expecting."

"I've barely seen Lady Alix, but she seems pleasant enough. Wouldn't you agree?"

"I've had my heart set on one person for so long," Ransom said, wrinkling his brow. "But what if it was never meant to be?"

"I have to say," said Dearley with a look of concern, "you've changed your thinking rather quickly. You just met Lady Alix under dolorous circumstances."

"No," Ransom said in disagreement. "We first met years ago."

"Truly? I thought you said the duke's heir was a stranger to you."

"Remember the story I told you about serving Lord Rakestraw? How I was captured by DeVaux and held hostage for months?"

"Yes. What's the connection?"

"After I was injured, they brought me to this castle. To the dungeon, actually. Not that I could have escaped with my injured leg. The Duke of Bayree was at the tournament I had just left. A lady brought me moldy bread and linen bandages. The moldy bread to help treat the wound and the clean bandages because I'd been tearing strips from my dirty tunic. That was her." He sighed heavily. "That was *her*, Dearley."

The look on Dearley's face showed a change of feeling. "I owe her a great deal, then. She saved your life. You saved mine. Now I'm even gladder that you sent for the candles and food and such." He looked around the room. "It's a smaller castle, but it has a pleasing sense of antiquity. I could get used to it, I think." He smiled at Ransom. "But I hope we'd still visit Josselin on occasion." He cheeks flushed, and an embarrassed smile tipped up his lips. "I'll leave you to your thoughts."

He was likely thinking about Elodie. Ransom nodded to him and turned to the book. Holding it in his hands, he walked to the window and looked outside, staring down at the vast lawns stretching into the distance. There were no trees within the outer walls of the grounds, only the lawn. No gardens either, which was disappointing. Ransom enjoyed Josselin for that reason. The stone wall surrounding the grounds was thin and had a ditch on the other side, beyond which trees grew in abundance.

The room became so dark that Ransom couldn't read, so he left and started down the corridor, only to see a servant coming toward him with a tray. Alix followed holding two fat tallow candles. He retreated to the room he'd just left and held the door open for the servant.

"Set it in the middle of the floor, please," Alix said, and the man obeyed.

When he left, Alix went and set down the candles near the tray and then seated herself on the floor, knees tucked under her. Ransom joined her, finding the candlelight especially flattering to her green brocade dress.

She clasped her hands before her and bowed her head. "To our Lady, we give thanks for the abundance provided."

They ate together, talked together, and shared the evening in a pleasant way, telling stories from their childhoods. She especially wanted to hear the tale of how King Gervase had almost hung him from a trebuchet for his father's disobedience. As he told it, her eyes filled with emotion.

"That story moves me," Alix confessed, hand on her breast. "I wish . . . I wish there were something I could have done to help that little boy."

An uncanny feeling passed between them, like the ripples of a pond after a stone was cast in. They exchanged a look, and Ransom knew they'd both experienced it.

"I feel strange," she whispered.

"So do I," he answered.

They ate in silence for a while after that, and Ransom only knew that his heart was changing. It was uncomfortable, painful even, like a potter squeezing clay.

"When must you go?" she asked quietly.

As he struggled for an answer, Ransom realized he didn't *want* to leave. There was a pull, a strong urge to declare that he'd stay at Kerjean for the rest of his life. Would it hurt Claire if he chose Alix? He'd made no vow, yet it wouldn't feel right to move on without first discussing the situation with her, seeking her pardon and her blessing. Would he be able to do that when he returned to Kingfountain? Would the Elder King let him?

"Soon, I think," Ransom said. He looked down at the bones and scraps on the plate.

Her shoulders drooped, and her countenance fell.

"But I should like to come back. Duke Benedict wished to see me. And I owe my king an answer about Bayree."

She leaned forward, looking at him intently, worry and hope in her eyes. "What will you tell him?"

Ransom didn't know. He still didn't know.

"There are places I wish I could take you," she said. "Bayree is beautiful. It's every bit as pleasant as Brythonica, although there is more fog. The cliffs of Shialle are so lovely. And the trees. There are trees here that are older than the world, I think, with trunks so wide it would take a dozen knights to encircle one. And the fishing boats in the waters . . . there are so many varieties of fish to catch, some that are only found here. But you must make up your own mind. My need cannot outweigh your loyalty." She offered a sad smile and looked away. "It'll be you or another noble. An old man like Lord Kinghorn whose wife died long ago? Duke Wigant's son? To me, there isn't much of a choice. I have a strong preference, but I know it's not the same for you."

Ransom didn't want to disappoint her. Conflict roiled inside him again. He'd enjoyed being with her, talking with her. The master of the rolls had advised him to find a wife quickly. *Posterity is power.* Of course, the man had also suggested he'd be a good match for Claire.

"It's late," Ransom said, feeling lethargic. His chest ached with the pressure.

"It is," she said. And she rose and took the candle that hadn't burned out yet. Only a small stub of it was left.

He offered her his arm and escorted her to the stairs. They climbed together, the castle dark and quiet. He could smell the tallow smoke wafting in the air. On the second floor, she released his arm and offered him the candle.

"I can find my way in the dark," he said, refusing it with a little wave.

She nodded and started down the corridor to her own chamber. His heart burned within him as he watched the light dim. She opened the door and disappeared inside, quenching the small flame. There was enough moonlight coming through the windows that he could make out his path. He groped the banister and began to climb to the higher level.

There was no warning before the attack. He smelled the stink of sweat and blood, and then felt the heat of another body before it collided with his. A dagger stabbed his thigh, plunging deep into the muscle before hitting bone.

Ransom grappled with the man, his leg afire with pain, and then they were both tumbling down the stairs.

I received a secret note from Sir James this morning, delivered with our morning meal. It immediately disturbed my appetite. He wants to meet with me today when the queen and I visit the cistern garden. The reason—he's heard that Sir Ransom will marry the heiress of Bayree. They say the king will give the duchy of Vexin to Jon-Landon and name Benedict heir to the throne. He may even give him the Hollow Crown.

Sir James knows I do not care for him, but he wishes to make an alliance with me regardless. Flattery I'm immune to. He's learned as much. So he has taken a more practical approach: If we marry, I can rule Legault, and he will live apart from me in Glosstyr. If Benedict rebels, James plans to support him . . . so long as the prince agrees to this design.

I have agreed to speak to James in person if he can arrange it. Things do not always turn out the way we wish. I'd be foolish not to consider any option that will take me from this tower.

What would Jon-Landon do if he knew of his friend's double-dealing?

—Claire de Murrow
Queen's Tower
(hoping for freedom)

CHAPTER TWELVE

The Threat of Revenge

hen their bodies struck the bottom of the stairs, Ransom felt the dagger strike his ribs, but the chain mail of the hauberk saved him from a death wound. Stunned, surprised, Ransom rolled over on the fellow and grabbed his wrist to hold the weapon at bay. A boot struck Ransom in the stomach, knocking him back.

"You will die . . . ," the man wheezed in Occitanian, "for what you did! I served the duke. I will *never* serve you!"

He lunged at Ransom again. Twisting to the side, Ransom pivoted on his feet, and the fellow crashed into the stone wall at the edge of the stairs. The door to Alix's chamber yanked open, spilling candlelight onto the scene. The man Ransom faced looked to be a knight, his face bruised, and he, too, wore a hauberk and bloodied tunic. Ransom saw the bloodstain on his side, saw the way his elbow pressed against it, the grimace of pain on his mouth.

His stores of Fountain magic had not yet been replenished, but he reached out with it and sensed his opponent was nursing injuries that were days old. He'd been at the battle.

Alix rushed down the hall. The rogue knight looked toward the light, and Ransom recognized his opportunity to charge him. He drove the other man back, bringing his forearm into the man's throat. The knight jabbed him twice with the dagger before Ransom managed to deflect the blows with his arm.

"Die, you murderer!" the knight snarled.

Alix reached them and shoved the candle at the knight's face, splashing him with the hot wax. The knight screamed in pain, and Ransom used his temporary distraction to knee him in the stomach. When the man collapsed, Ransom felt the visceral urge to bash his head onto the stone floor, but he tamed himself before the rash thought became realized.

"What happened?" Alix demanded with concern.

The knight groaned on the floor, covering his scalded face with his hands.

"He attacked me on the stairwell," Ransom said, breathing fast. Pain lanced down his leg from the first stab wound.

"Are you hurt?"

"Not badly. His wounds are worse."

"I'll get another candle," Alix said. She picked up the fallen knife and then handed it to Ransom. "I'm so sorry."

"It's not your fault," he said, grunting. He leaned back against the wall, his leg on fire.

"I will be right back." Alix hurried to her room and returned with a torch. A knight came with her, one of her guards. She held the torch over the fallen man. "Who is it?"

Her knight pulled the man's hands from his face. Some of the wax had hardened, and his nose was bleeding freely.

"It's Sir Etienne," said the knight, frowning in disgust.

"Take him to the dungeon," she said with a look of anger.

"Yes, my lady." Her guard hoisted the man up beneath his arms and began dragging him away.

Alix held the torch closer to Ransom, looking at him worriedly. "You're in pain. Come, let me treat you."

He knew the scabbard would render her efforts unnecessary. "I will be fine."

"Please, Ransom. Let me tend to you. Let me heal you."

He looked in her eyes, saw the compassion there, and he felt inclined to let her do as she asked. The need to do so pulsed through him. But he didn't want her to trouble herself, not when he knew it wasn't required.

"I would accept your help, only it's not necessary. I will be fine."

Her brow wrinkled in concern. "Are you sure?"

"We tumbled down the stairs is all," he said. The pain from the dagger was fierce, but he shoved it down. No blood came from the wound.

She reached out and pressed her hand to his cheek. Her thumb grazed his cheekbone. "I'll check on you in the morning with some breakfast. Shall we share it together as we did tonight?"

He smiled through the pain.

Her look was tender. "I'm worried about you. I feel very protective right now."

"This is far from the worst injury I've ever had," he said. "Go get some rest yourself."

She nodded and carried the torch back to her room. He leaned against the wall and began slowly moving up the stairs, one step at a time. Why hadn't the Fountain magic warned him as it had in the past? He could still sense her, as bright as the flame she carried, but he hadn't felt any danger on the stairwell. In her presence, he'd thought of nothing but her.

As he walked, he saw a blue light glowing from the Raven scabbard belted to his waist. It was dimmer than it had been before, the buzzing noise more muted. The sudden change alarmed him. Was it simply because his injuries were less serious, or had something muted its power?

He staggered up the rest of the steps and finally made it to his room, where he found Dearley asleep on the couch again. He slid the latch into place, securing the door, then hobbled over and flopped onto the bed. As he lay there, he tried to sense Lady Alix down below. A giddy feeling inside his heart made it impossible to fall asleep. She was no delicate demoiselle. As soon as danger had presented itself, she'd leaped into action. It was a quality he admired—in fact, it was one of the things he loved about Lady Claire.

Claire.

Thinking of her sent a ripple of guilt through him. He had feelings for both of them, although his emotions were bubbling like the contents of a kettle on a raging fire.

King Devon wanted him to marry Alix, and he'd indicated he'd never agree to a match to Claire. If he wished to wed Alix—and he did, didn't he?—all he needed to do was keep silent about her true identity. At least until after they were wed. The thought of having her as his wife caused the burning sensation in his heart to flare even more. He lay on the bed, feeling the mixture of pain and attraction until sleep finally swept him away into another dream.

It was a dream he didn't want to be awakened from. In it, Alix was sitting on his lap, and they were kissing each other with a ferocious need, her hands touching his face. A firm shove against his shoulder interrupted the delicious sensations, and his eyes opened at the same moment he heard Dearley's voice.

"You normally don't sleep this late," his ward said in a jovial way. "But Lady Alix is at the door with a tray of food. I thought it would be rude not to wake you."

Ransom lifted his head, seeing the sunlight spilling in through the sheer curtains. His skull throbbed with a headache, but the pain in his leg had gone. He quickly sat up, feeling himself restored to health, yet the sluggishness of sleep clung to him like heavy chains.

"Of course. Send her in. We were going to breakfast together."

"Are you all right?" Dearley asked with a tone of concern.

"I was attacked on the stairwell last night," he said. "One of the duke's knights wanted vengeance."

Dearley gaped at him. "I'm sorry, Ransom. We should have been guarding you."

"I'm capable of defending myself, but I should have foreseen it. It will take time to win the trust of these people."

Dearley nodded. "I'll let her in. I imagine you would like to talk privately with her."

"Thank you," Ransom said. As Dearley was about to leave, he caught his arm. "We'll be riding back to Kingfountain. Prepare the horses."

"Will we stop by Josselin first?"

"No. We've been invited to Auxaunce, however, and we'll stop there and at the castle of the Heath on our way back."

"Very well." Dearley went to the door while Ransom scratched his head and tried to shake off the torpor. He saw the hole in his pants from the dagger wound, but there was not even a scar on his skin. The pain of his injuries was gone, except for the strange ache in his mind.

He rose from the bed and walked without a limp as Alix brought in the tray. She set it on the floor as she had done the previous evening. Her smile was bright, but she studied him carefully, as if still concerned about his condition. Dearley hid a smile before leaving.

"You look healthy. I don't see any bruises."

"There are none," he answered. The tray featured a variety of dishes, from cooked eggs with flecks of green spinach to sliced fruit and an array of cooked fish.

"This is river trout," she said, pointing to one of the plates. "This other one is a deep sea fish called tuna. They're quite large and have to be speared. A wagon came with them during the night. Our food supplies have been restored thanks to our hardworking fishermen."

Ransom tried all the dishes and found them cooked to perfection. The tuna had an interesting taste, the flesh harder than that of other fish. Most of all, he enjoyed being in Alix's company. He felt at peace with her, and he listened with interest as she described the life of the fisherfolk in Bayree.

When the meal was done, she gave him an intent look.

"What is it?" he asked.

"I don't want to say it," she said. "I don't want to break the spell."

He gazed at her in confusion. "What spell? Are you a Wizr?"

She smiled at the statement and shook her head no. "There are none. Not since Myrddin vanished. Do you believe in the old legends, Ransom?"

He looked toward the window, considering her question. "The ones about King Andrew and Leoneyis, the kingdom that was drowned in the sea?"

"Yes. That's what I meant."

He looked back at her. "Do you?"

Her eyes showed her sincerity, but she only held his gaze for a few moments before looking down at the tray and the remaining scraps of food. "They aren't just stories, Ransom. They're real. I know they are."

"How do you know for certain?"

"I can't tell you. Nor can I show you. Not until you become the lord of this castle." Her eyes met his again, her look pleading. "I cannot speak freely until the curse is broken. There is so much I *want* to tell you." She looked away again. "I'm sorry. I'd nearly given up hope that I'd find a partner who could understand me. Someone I could be my true self with."

He gazed at her and nodded, feeling a deep sense of connection. He did understand her, in a deep way he suspected only another Fountain-blessed person could. "I must go today."

Her shoulders slumped. "I knew you might need to leave. I shouldn't try to hold you here."

"I want to stay," he said seriously. It had crept up on him, the desire to stay, but there was no denying it was strong.

Her smile was full of hope. "Do you? Since you came, I've had dreams about us every night. Isn't that strange?"

He felt his eyes widen in surprise. "So have I."

"Truly?" she asked with a smile of pleasure.

"I have. I think it's the Fountain's way of telling us we are supposed to be together."

"I feel the same way," she said with conviction. "I didn't want to frighten you."

"I'm not afraid of you," he said.

She reached over and pushed the tray aside. "I think you are," she said, giving him a welcoming smile. An invitation.

Ransom had never kissed a woman before. He'd never practiced on the lasses at Averanche like Sir James had. He felt wholly ignorant and shy but knew what he wanted to do, even as he knew what it would mean. If he kissed her, it was akin to deciding this was the life he wanted, that he was leaving his old ambition, his old love, behind. Edging closer, he felt the heat coming from her. She swallowed, and he saw the motion in her throat. He was the world's biggest fool, but the feeling swelling inside of him couldn't be denied. So he leaned forward and kissed her mouth. It was a gentle kiss, not like the one in his dream.

She tasted of the honeyed melon that she'd had with breakfast.

He leaned back, looking at her pleased expression, and she laid her hand atop his.

"That was nice. I look forward to more." The warm look in her eyes shifted to something worried, even desperate, and she said, "Please don't tell the king about me. About my mother. I don't want to lose you."

She kissed him again before he left, this time in front of all his knights. It made his cheeks burn with self-consciousness, but she didn't seem embarrassed. As he rode across the inner courtyard on Dappled, he caught Dearley smirking and gave him a look of rebuke.

"I'm sorry," Dearley said. "I'm happy for you, truly."

Ransom noticed there wasn't a single weed throughout the grounds. Not a single one. They passed the well-sculpted lawn, the horses' hooves crunching on the gravel drive, and then cut through the village of Kerjean, where they were met with more warmth than when they'd arrived. Ransom thought about making Alix his wife, almost dizzy with gladness. He wanted to kick Dappled into a gallop and whoop out his feelings. He glanced back at the castle, taking note again of the ancient carvings on the gate. It likely had some connection to the legends of the Fisher Kings. He craved to learn more about them, about all the Fountain-blessed.

When they reached the knights still encamped at the border, he described the assistance they'd already given and ordered the men to enter the duchy and do as the lady of the castle commanded them.

Ransom's small group camped off the road at the border between Bayree and the Vexin. He'd hoped to dream of Alix again, but his sleep was dreamless, and he awoke disappointed. Had it been the castle itself that had infiltrated their dreams?

By the end of the second day, they reached the castle in Auxaunce. The steward brought Ransom to the training yard, where he found Benedict in full armor with a battle axe, fighting against two knights at once. The bout did not end until both knights had been knocked senseless. Benedict removed his helmet, his face flushed, his beard a tangled mess. He set down the axe and took a water skin and gulped down his drink. When he finished, he slapped it on the table and turned to face Ransom.

"Could I persuade you to fight me, Sir Ransom?" he asked, his blue eyes flashing with a challenge.

"Is that why you asked to see me?" Ransom asked, looking at the king's son with indifference. He'd never been close to Benedict, although he bore no ill will toward the man. Of all the Argentine children, he was the most like the father—quick to anger, relentless, and a true warrior. He lacked the manners and grace of Devon the Younger, and he'd always fixated on defeating Ransom.

"No, by the Lady! I think I can beat you. But it's possible my pride will destroy me if I fail. Maybe it is better if we never know. But thank you for coming out of your way."

"It was not far off course," Ransom said with a shrug. "What do you want?"

"What? No friendly chat between neighbors? I don't like the castle at Kerjean. It's too small. What did you make of it?"

"It suits me well enough," Ransom said evenly.

"The lady suits you too, does she?" asked Benedict, then grinned. "I've tried to meet Lady Alix, but I could never get her uncle to permit it. She was always off visiting Pree for this reason or that. It made sense, to me anyway, that Bayree and the Vexin should be on good terms, but I don't think the duke wanted me to marry his niece. Maybe he knew our personalities would clash. What do you think?"

Ransom didn't want to offend Benedict, but he wasn't about to disagree either, especially given what he knew about Alix's parentage. "Yes."

Benedict snorted. "I should punch you for being so honest. I didn't push for it hard, anyway, because I suspected Father wouldn't permit me to marry her. It wouldn't have suited his ambition. Or mine. I am grateful we will be neighbors, though, if you've decided to accept your fate?"

"There are worse things than becoming a duke," Ransom said.

"Indeed there are. Like getting gout. I hope I die young." He pulled off his gauntlets and tossed them onto the table where he'd placed his helmet. "Father trusts you. And you served my brother well, except for all that nonsense at the end. I don't care about any of it. What I want is your honest opinion. Do you believe my father will give me his throne?"

Ransom wasn't surprised by the question. Nor did he find it difficult to provide an answer. "I do. He may not have officially named you his heir, but he acts as if you are. I suspect it will happen soon."

"Of course I'm his heir," Benedict said peevishly. "But that wasn't my question. Do you think that he will *give* me his throne, or must I *take* it? I know Devon, my brother, came to realize that Father never gives away anything. He clings to Westmarch with white-knuckled fingers when anyone can see it should be Lord Kinghorn's. Do you understand what I'm saying, Sir Ransom? He may name me his heir, but he will not give up one scrap of power until he's dead or he's compelled to. If I allow him, he'll put me in the same position he did my brother."

Ransom felt queasiness in his stomach. He saw the ambition in Benedict's eyes. The determination.

"Don't fight against your father," Ransom said in a low tone. "Bide your time, and it will *all* be yours."

"That's the problem, you see," said Benedict. "What you're asking requires patience. It requires me to see my father not as he is, but as he wants to be seen."

Ransom cocked his head, silently inviting him to continue, even as he dreaded what would come next.

"I never knew King Gervase. I was very young when all that nonsense happened. But even as a boy, I began to see the truth about my father. How he thrived on taking the glory for everything anyone did. He cannot share power, Ransom, because he is incapable of believing anyone else is worthy of it. Because he enjoys the adulation too much. I've spent years seeking to win his approval, but I'm done with that. My brother had it right. Father will not accept anything less than total surrender to his will, his fame." Benedict waved his hand. "He is the sun, and everyone else must remain in his shadow. I know he's putting you in Bayree to keep your sword poised at my back. I see through the ploy. But remember this, *neighbor*. What happens next is between my father and me. I won't countenance any meddling from you. I fear you not, Ransom. And if you're wise, you will come to fear and respect me. Now go and tell these things to my father. I am not to be trifled with. I've heard whispers that he intends to strip the Vexin from me. Let me be clear: That will not be allowed. Tell him to beware lest he provoke my rebellion."

The cold look in the blue eyes promised revenge and retribution. Ransom knew exactly how the king would respond to such a threat. Because, in a sense, Benedict was correct—anyone who challenged the king's authority would face his wrath. Even his own sons.

Oh, Sir James is a sly one.

I must give him credit for his boldness. He takes such small liberties they seem like trifles, only they add up to something more. Smoothing a hair from my brow. Jostling my elbow. Grazing my fingers. And his words are designed to appeal to me. His offer, for example. Should we be married, I would reign in Legault, and he would rule Glosstyr. He's paid some nefarious badgers, no doubt, for the news he brings from Atha Kleah. They are trying to forbid my house from returning, he says, words intended to cause distress. To give me the impression that time is running out—that if I remain here, trapped in the palace of Kingfountain with a disgraced queen, I will never see my homeland again, nor will they want me.

Oh, he's a cunning one. There was no proclamation of love or sentiment. Yet still he kept touching me, as if I didn't already know the power such simple gestures can invoke. A cunning one. But I am not taken in.

How I wish I would hear from Ransom.

—Claire de Murrow, the True Queen of Legault
(frustrated)

CHAPTER THIRTEEN

Honor or Truth

I am grateful you came, Marshall, truly," said Marcus, gripping Ransom's shoulder as he prepared to mount Dappled. "I'm proud of all you've accomplished."

"I'm glad we spent the night," Ransom said, smiling back at his elder brother. "It was good to see you all again."

"You do justice to our family name." His brow furrowed. "I should like Maeg to return, though. There is a young man I would like her to meet. I hope you will not need her for much longer?"

It was a subtle prod, a reminder that Ransom was not the one responsible for overseeing Maeg's fortunes and future.

"It is your right to do as you wish," Ransom said, looking his brother in the eye. "But I hope you consider her feelings in the matter."

"What do feelings have to do with such things?" Marcus quipped. But his grin faded when he realized Ransom was serious.

"They matter a great deal," Ransom said, feeling anxious for his sister—and for himself. His feelings, which had been so clear in Bayree, had become more confusing since his departure. The closer he came to Kingfountain, the more it felt like his heart was returning to its former affections. The more he found himself thinking of Claire. It unsettled him and made him want to delay his return to that place. Yet he knew he shouldn't. He'd kissed Alix in front of his men. His sense of honor compelled him to follow such a display with marriage.

He hadn't written to Claire since he'd agreed to visit Bayree. At first, he'd held back because he didn't want to worry her . . . and then because he'd felt it would be better to tell her about Alix in person. Now, he was no longer sure of anything.

Marcus gave him a look, shifting Ransom's attention back to their conversation, and he said, "If the dowry is a problem, it need not stand in the way. You know I fully intend to help."

"It is your right to choose for your wards, Ransom. It's not your place to dictate what happens with mine."

"I'm not trying to," Ransom said, trying to stifle his frustration. "I just ask you to give more thought before making her so very unhappy."

"She's told you about Sir Kace, then, has she?" Marcus said, his eyes flashing. He snorted in contempt.

"Maeg didn't ask me to speak for her. I do it because I care about her. Father cared more about stones than he did about our hearts. Just . . . consider things carefully, Brother. That's all I'm asking."

"I'm twenty-six and unmarried," Marcus said. "The king hasn't seen fit to direct his favor my way. I'm not jealous. It just feels I can never get ahead. I need her to make a good match, one that will promote our fortunes, and I need to do the same."

Ransom gave his brother a sympathetic look. Pushing the point further would only cause ill will between them. It would not change Marcus's mind. "I can see that. It's your choice, as is proper. It was good to see you. I hope Mother gets over her cough soon."

"She'll be right as rain in no time," said Marcus. They hugged each other one last time, and then Ransom mounted Dappled.

Dearley was already mounted, along with the other knights who'd accompanied them. After they rode past the village of Heath, Dearley edged his mount closer.

"And Sir Kace is part of your brother's mesnie, is he not?"

"Yes, he is."

Dearley had a dour look on his face. "I don't see why he isn't given preference, then."

Ransom understood Dearley's interest in the matter. He had feelings for Elodie—but his fate, and hers, was up to Ransom to decide.

"It is the duty of a lord to provide for those who serve him," Ransom said.

"It is indeed," Dearley said with a longing sigh.

"Then it should please you to know that I will not force anyone to marry against their will. That's the custom in Legault. It should be here as well. If she wants you . . . I won't object."

Dearley's eyebrows lifted, and a smile brightened his face, bringing a flush to his cheeks. "I think she does—well, I *hope* so at least. I wouldn't want you to compel her. That is, I would be honored if . . . I-I'm flummoxed. Thank you, Ransom. I'm relieved to hear you say it."

"You are both still very young," Ransom said. "There is no rush. But don't play with her affections. Treat her honorably." He found himself thinking of Alix again, of the scene they'd put on outside the castle. Such behavior was totally unlike him. All these years of wanting Claire, of yearning to marry her, and he'd never once kissed her.

His heart grew more troubled.

"Of course!" Dearley said. He couldn't stop grinning, and Ransom had an idea of how he might be feeling.

Only he didn't quite feel that way about his intended anymore.

They rode into Kingfountain in the evening, the noise of the falls thundering in Ransom's ears. He felt at odds with himself, a feeling that had grown starker since leaving Bayree. He was nervous about seeing the Elder King for multiple reasons. Part of him wanted to disclose the information about Lady Alix and her position as King Estian's poisoner. Yet she had pleaded with him to remain silent on that point, for fear the king would forbid their marriage. And after everything that had happened between them, he felt beholden to marry her. Part of him still *wanted* to marry her. But his gaze shot to the queen's tower, aglow above them, and he had to acknowledge his feelings for Claire.

Then, of course, he had to communicate Benedict's threat to rebel if forced to yield the Vexin. It was entirely possible war would erupt again between father and son, even after they'd joined forces to fight Occitania.

"I'll see the horses are cared for and that your room is ready," Dearley said after they dismounted in the courtyard.

"Thank you," Ransom said, dropping his hand to his sword hilt and starting toward the palace doors. He hadn't gone far when he encountered Sir Simon, who approached him eagerly.

"Welcome back, Ransom!" he said in a breathless way. "Might you have a moment to talk before seeing the king?"

"The hour grows late," Ransom said. "I wasn't sure he would want to see me."

"Of course he does!" Simon said with a laugh. "He's been restless lately, anxious for news from Bayree after Duke Ashel returned. You met the duchess, then?"

"She's not the duchess yet. At the moment she's still a ward," Ransom said, feeling the conflict seething inside him. "The title and the duchy must be sealed through marriage." They walked together down the corridor.

"You don't seem pleased. Is she pox-ridden or deformed in some way? No one I know has met or described her."

No one knew that Lady Alix was the queen's illegitimate daughter. It would be obvious to anyone in court who saw her. That added to the tension of the situation.

Simon's brow furrowed with concern. "You won't refuse to marry her? That would be . . . how shall I put this tactfully? Imprudent? Ungrateful? He's offered you a duchy!"

"You mistake me, Simon." Ransom clapped him on the back. "No, she's . . . she's quite pleasing to look at." His heart panged strongly, tugging him as if he were a bone fought over by two dogs. He felt he would lose his mind.

"So you *will* marry her?"

"I think so."

"That's a relief," Simon said. The adamancy of his reply surprised Ransom.

"Why do you say that?"

"It's the reason I wanted to see you before you met with the king. We're walking too fast. Can we slow down?"

Ransom slowed his pace. He glanced at Simon with concern.

"I suspect Sir James has been trying to win Lady Claire's favor."

The news struck Ransom like a fist to the stomach. He stopped abruptly and stared at his friend in astonishment.

"I'm telling you this as your friend, but I have little evidence," Simon said after halting. He looked at Ransom earnestly. "They've met in private on occasion. Sir Dalian, Lord Kinghorn's son, told me so himself. He is supposedly wooing her for the king's son, but Sir Dalian fears he has his own interests in mind. So do I."

"It sounds exactly like the sort of underhanded thing he'd do," Ransom agreed, his sense of restlessness growing.

"If there is any interest on her side, I don't know. She's held off on choosing a husband, which has provoked the king to no end, I'll add." He shook his head. "She's got fire, that lass. And not just in the coloring of her hair. If you marry the Duchess of Bayree, then don't be surprised if she . . . well, that would just be conjecture on my part. It's possible he really is trying to ingratiate himself with the prince, but you and I both know Sir James cares most about Sir James. And . . . beware of what you say in response, for there they are."

Ransom turned his head and saw Sir James and the prince walking toward them. For a moment, the surge of anger and resentment overwhelmed all his other confused feelings. Immediately, those visceral emotions began to war within him.

Jon-Landon wore an expensive blue tunic gleaming with metal studs. He had the surly look of a young man thwarted. His hair was dark and wavy atop his head, but he didn't wear it long in the fashion of his brothers. He seemed to have grown a hand's width since the last time Ransom had seen him.

James had clearly noticed them, but he didn't seem frightened of Ransom. He continued to approach them, a crafty look in his eyes and a bit of a strut in his walk.

"Back so soon?" he said to Ransom, stopping well out of reach. It was obvious he hadn't forgotten what Ransom's fist felt like. The prince looked at Ransom with neither malice nor pleasure.

"I just arrived," Ransom said coldly.

"Well," said the other. He looked between Ransom and Simon, and the corner of his mouth ticked up. "I hope you are well enough. Does Bayree suit you?"

He was seeking to get Ransom to reveal his plans. He wouldn't.

"Good evening," Ransom said with a slight nod of his head and then continued walking, Simon hastening to catch up.

"It's a small duchy," James said from behind. "But I think it will suit your ambition."

Ransom ignored the jibe, but he frowned in annoyance. From behind him, he heard Jon-Landon mutter in a mocking tone, "Don't provoke him, James. He's savage."

"Positively," agreed James, and Ransom could hear the smile in his voice.

As soon as they rounded the corner, Simon sighed heavily. "Those two are plotting something," he said in an undertone. "I've heard the prince demand his father reward James with some new castle or lands. He's always pleading his cause. It doesn't speak well of the prince's judgment, particularly since James is trying to charm Claire behind his back."

"Has the king agreed?" Ransom asked, trying to temper his rage.

"Not yet. He's too greedy. He doesn't want to give anything away. Well. I've told you the worst. I don't know what Lady Claire will do. But given your history with Sir James, I thought it best to warn you."

"And I am grateful, truly."

Yet, it wasn't gratitude that Ransom felt churning inside him. He wanted to punch the stone wall with his fist. Yes, Claire could choose whomever she wished. But the thought of her marrying Sir James made him bristle with jealousy.

"I'll leave you to your interview, then," Simon said. "He's in the solar at the moment. Is there anything you need reimbursement for from the king? Lord Ashel said you had wagons sent from Josselin with supplies for Bayree. Is that true?"

"It is, but I seek no compensation for doing the right thing," Ransom said.

Simon smiled and chuckled. "Everyone is always begging for something from the king's coffers. You might as well join them."

"It's not necessary," Ransom said. He nodded to Simon and continued on his way to the stairs leading to the solar, leaving his friend behind.

After climbing up several steps, he stopped and put his hand on the wall, lowering his head to steady his emotions before he saw the king. His fingers coiled into a fist, and he shut his eyes, trying to let the anger leach away. How long he waited, he didn't know. But he stayed like that until he heard footsteps coming, and then he started up the stairwell again, feeling the heat of the torches hanging from sconces in the wall as he passed them. His emotions were still churning, but not at the same fevered pitch.

When he reached the top, he went to the solar and tapped on the door.

"What is it?" barked the king's voice.

Ransom pushed on the handle, and the door opened, revealing the scene within. A fire sizzled in the hearth, and the windows had been left open, letting in a cool night breeze and the sound of the distant falls, but the pleasant atmosphere was soured by the look of ill will between the king and Lord Kinghorn, who'd clearly been in the midst of a fraught conversation.

"I'm disturbing you." Ransom apologized and started to close the door.

"No, come in," said the king. "You are late, Ransom. I expected you yesterday."

Ransom had not agreed to return at a certain time, nor had he been asked to. He eyed Lord Kinghorn worriedly, seeing the anger in the other man's eyes.

"You may go, Bryon. We'll address your concern in the king's council tomorrow."

"If that is what you wish," said Lord Kinghorn. Ransom opened the door wider. He'd never seen the king quarrel with Lord Kinghorn before. It increased the unease in Ransom's stomach, particularly since he valued his kinsman's judgment. Lord Kinghorn nodded to him, but his brooding expression held no warmth. He shut the door behind him.

Ransom looked at the king, who seemed no less agitated than he had in the midst of the argument. "So. Have you come to gripe at me as well?"

"No, my lord," Ransom said, his confidence beginning to waver.

"I gave you Lady Elodie and her lands. You sniffed and turned your head." The king folded his arms, pacing a few strides before turning back. "Now I give you a duchy in enemy territory, which will increase the size of our kingdom and protect our borders. But you don't care for the girl. Is that it? Your desire is still fixed on that Gaultic . . ." He seemed on the verge of using a slur, but he held it back. "Is that it, Sir Ransom? You came to tell me no?"

Ransom felt the conflict writhing inside him. He should reveal what he had learned. Didn't the vows he'd taken command it? But the king was in an especially dark mood, and he couldn't bring himself to share the news. Not yet. And his feelings were still a confusing knot of emotions, his loyalties confused.

"No," he said to the king.

"I knew it," snarled Devon angrily.

"You mistake me, my lord. I was disagreeing with you. My feelings are different from what you suppose."

His words caused a look of surprise to radiate across the king's face. "Indeed, lad? You will do as I command? For the good of the kingdom?"

"It was not what I expected," Ransom said. "Lady Alix and I had met before."

The king gaped at him. "How can that be?"

"When I was a hostage to Lord DeVaux," he answered. "I didn't realize it at the time, but Lord DeVaux fled to Bayree to hide from your wrath. I was delirious. I'd lost a lot of blood. Lady Alix brought me bread and bandages. She saved my life that day."

The king's look transformed to one of exquisite joy and wonder. "That is an astonishing coincidence. She helped heal you? I'm agog. It's rare for me to be at a loss for words." He strode forward and hooked his hand around Ransom's neck, as if he were one of his own sons. It made him feel disloyal for withholding part of the truth. "Good for you, Ransom. If she pleases you, that is even better. I propose a winter wedding, when there will be peace, not because of a treaty but because of deep snow."

"Thank you, my lord," Ransom said, feeling simultaneously grateful and guilty. The urge to speak filled his chest, but the words refused to rise.

"I couldn't be more pleased with you. This is news of the rarest kind . . . good news! I have some errands for you to perform for me in the interim. We must make good use of the season before it changes. There isn't much time."

"Much time for what?" Ransom asked.

"I intend to send you to Brugia to deliver a threat and arrange a peace. A marriage proposal, if you will, for Benedict. We've had too many Occitanian entanglements of late. And you have a reputation in Brugia, because of the way you fought the last time they attempted an invasion." He grinned like a wolf. "A bride for Benedict—one who comes with extensive lands, of course—and one for yourself. I intend to make him my heir and crown him as I did his brother, but he needs a queen. All he has to do is give up the Vexin to Jon-Landon." He rubbed his hands together. "Everything will be settled at last."

"I don't think Benedict will be agreeable to that," Ransom said in a wary tone.

The king snorted. "Nonsense. He's no fool. I fully intend to give him the power he thinks is his due. Within five years, he will be ruling most of the kingdom. I'll transfer control gradually so that he can prove his capability. Plus I'll give him some livres to sweeten his sorrow at losing the duchy. He'll accept it. Trust me. This is what he wants."

Ransom didn't want to spoil the moment with the truth, but he dared it. "I think you're wrong. He told me that nothing would persuade him to peacefully part with the Vexin."

The king sniffed at Ransom's answer. "I'll send a courier. I trust my judgment more than yours."

So the rumors are true. Ransom has returned to Kingfountain, and he is promised to the future duchess of Bayree. He could have told me himself, the brute.

I didn't believe Sir James, not at first. One shouldn't make a habit of trusting serpents or eejits. But Sir Dalian confirmed it, having the news from his father. Why am I so surprised? I shouldn't be. There was no promise between us, no talk of a shared future. And I haven't received a letter from him for some time. Yet it still hurts. The queen says she understands the pain I feel—the shards of a broken heart dig deeper than any sword. How maudlin I've become.

The world is not fair. Why should I have expected it to be fair to me? Sir James's offer hangs over my head like a sword of doom. Yet the thought of him touching me fills me with revulsion. I don't think I could bear it.

—Claire de Murrow
(forlorn isn't the right word . . . some words do not
do justice to pain)

CHAPTER FOURTEEN

The Ghost King

Sleep would not come to Ransom's eyes. The churning feelings of anguish, guilt, and concern battled inside his mind and heart, offering no relief, no solace. He thought on Claire, imprisoned in that tower, and it made him want to weep. He thought about the look of pleasure on King Devon's face, and it made his heart shrivel with guilt. He considered what Lord Kinghorn would think of him if he learned the truth, and it made him more than miserable. He was positively wretched.

It was after midnight, and Ransom lay on his bed, hands behind his head, staring at the beams supporting the ceiling. Moonlight streamed through the window in silvery beams. He tried to summon memories of Alix to quiet the torment, but the thought of her kisses only made him feel guiltier because he hadn't told the king what he knew about her. Because he hadn't spoken to Claire about any of it.

Because he was no longer sure how he felt about the heiress of Bayree.

What would happen after the truth came to light? He had witnessed firsthand how the king had reacted to his sons' betrayal. The memory of that cry of pain from the pavilion had haunted him for years. And the king still had not visited his wife, Queen Emiloh, in her tower. Ransom did not want to disappoint the king that way. He did not want to be yet one more person to disappoint him.

Frustrated, he rose from the bed and dug his fingers into his hair. He felt like crying. No, he felt like going down to the training yard, bastard sword in hand, and taking his feelings out on an opponent or two.

He'd been back in Kingfountain for two days, and each moment he felt more conflicted, less certain of his path. Ransom had written a letter to Alix letting her know of the king's intention of a winter marriage, but he wished he could call back the courier. Part of him still felt he should marry her—a strong part of him wanted to—and yet doubt had welled through him. Did he only wish to wed her because he owed her a debt for saving his life? She had killed the Younger King, his former master, but she'd been ordered to do so by Estian's father, who should rightly bear the brunt of the blame. And what of the curse she'd mentioned?

Ransom went to the window, parting the curtain. He could see the courtyard below, dark with swirling shadows. Sentries bearing torches patrolled the grounds as their duty required.

That idea mocked him. What duty required. Duty required him to tell the king what he knew. There was no way around it.

Ransom.

He heard the whisper and started. It had been felt more than heard, although he sensed this wasn't the voice of the Fountain. He turned around abruptly, noticing a strange blue light emanating from the corner of the room. The raven-head sigil on his scabbard, which was slung on a nearby chair, was shining. He blinked in surprise, his concerns shoved aside by a growing sense of dread and fear.

It usually didn't glow on its own, only when its magic was healing him.

Ransom.

He heard the whisper again, although this time it sounded farther away. There was a pleading quality to it. A beckoning.

Was his mind playing tricks on him?

Perhaps, but Ransom felt compelled to leave his room. Cautiously, he went to the chair and pulled his tunic on over his undershirt. Then he wrapped the scabbard belt around his waist. As he cinched it, he felt comforted by having his weapon with him. He finished by tugging on his boots and went to the door and pulled the latch.

He gazed out into the darkened corridor and saw nothing but shadow. He didn't know which way to go, so he started toward the stairs leading to the main floor of the castle. Having spent many years here as a child, he knew the palace better than most. Memories of those sunlit afternoons made his heart pang with loss. He gritted his teeth and slowly made his way down the steps.

He wandered the halls, empty now of servants, looking for something he couldn't explain. He could barely see, the glowing raven sigil his only source of light, but his other senses guided his steps. The hush of night over the castle brought a feeling of stillness that went as deep as his bones. He walked steadily, peering through the darkness. And then, he saw another source of blue light glowing up ahead.

He slowed his walk, his heart tugging with unease.

Ransom.

The voice was coming from the blue light. It sounded . . . familiar. A man's voice. His heart hammering with emotions he didn't understand, Ransom walked faster, approaching the light. As he approached, he could see it emanated from one of the decorative fountains in the palace. The lapping of its waters filled his ears as he entered the anteroom containing the fountain. Bizarre light suffused the space, emanating from the very waters of the fountain. A spray of mist rose from the depths, creating a sheath of vapor that rose to the ceiling, and standing within that swirling pillar of mist was King Gervase, a ghostlike apparition.

Ransom stared at him in shock as the old king looked on him with a smile of welcome and kindness. As soon as he registered what he saw, he dropped to his knee, bowing his head, his emotions unraveling into a chaotic mess.

My boy. It is I.

Again, he heard the voice in his mind rather than with his ears. The words penetrated his heart like a lance tip. Tears began to streak down his cheeks.

"M-my lord," Ransom gasped, feeling like a child again. He felt too overwhelmed to look up, too fearful of seeing judgment in the old king's eyes.

Look at me.

Ransom dreaded it, but he obeyed. The ghost king's eyes were wells of compassion, and there was a kindly smile on his bearded face. He missed seeing that face. King Gervase had made him feel safe and appreciated. At home. When had he felt that way since? It had all been ripped away upon his mentor's death. He gasped again, trying to compose himself, but failed.

I've missed you, my boy. But I'm at peace now in the Deep Fathoms. I've come to warn you.

Ransom blinked away tears, but they wouldn't dissipate, so he swiped them with his wrist. "Warn me?"

Confined in the mortal coil, you are blind to so much around you. I was the same way. I spent my life half blind. Will you heed my warning, my boy?

Ransom swallowed and nodded emphatically. "I will. I will do whatever the Fountain bids me to do."

Even if it causes you pain? Even if you must die?

The thought filled him with dread, but he was resolved. "I will do it."

The ghost king smiled again. *I see much better now the role I played during my reign. Much of what I thought was important is not. I needed someone like you, Ransom, an advisor I could trust implicitly. One who would tell me the truth. The Fountain chose you to help the Argentines because of your feelings of duty. You were chosen before you were born.*

Ransom looked at him in astonishment. "How is that possible?"

I did not understand it myself at first. How can I expect you to? When I was king, I felt as if every choice I made had been predetermined. The actions that led to my rise. My fall. It was all decided in advance, and I was dancing to a tune plucked by a minstrel I could not see. My actions were often prompted by the obligations I felt at the core of my being, ones I'd carried from a previous existence.

In wonderment, Ransom shook his head. "That feels unjust. How can our choices matter, then?"

The ghost of Gervase smiled knowingly. *Like the abhorrence of murdering an innocent child? Circumstances may suggest such an action is prudent, especially when power is to be gained or kept, but we cringe involuntarily from such horrors. Yet the choices we make are always our own. The obligations we feel belong to a different world, founded on kindness, scruples, sacrifices—a world entirely different from the one you're still in. The Deep Fathoms is the place from which we emerge to be born, before returning thither, to live under the empire of those unknown laws we have strived to obey because we bore their teaching within us without knowing who had taught us. Yet still we choose which world influences us most in our earthly existence.*

He looked at Ransom with utter sincerity and conviction. *We mortals instinctively trust people to tell the truth because we are, in our hearts, truthful beings. That is the law we no longer remember. But in the mortal coil, we are susceptible to deception.*

Ransom found himself trembling, his entire body quivering as if he bore the weight of the entire castle on his back. The phantasm before him spoke words of truth that echoed within the deepest reaches of his being.

You were chosen, but you can still be deceived. I cannot make your decisions for you. It is up to you. But I came back to warn you. I still love you, my boy.

The look in the king's eyes turned fiercer, more determined.

You already know what you must do. You've known for some time. You merely have to muster the courage to do it. I wish I had had someone like you to serve me when I was king.

The ghost king reached out his wraithlike hand, and streams of mist curled from it. The touch, when it came, felt like the morning fog.

"Thank you," Ransom choked out, trying not to sob.

The ghost king looked around at the anteroom, a smile of contentment on his mouth, and then he dissolved into vapor, and the churning of the fountain ceased.

Ransom collapsed onto the floor.

A hand touched his shoulder and shook him. "Are you unwell? Why are you sleeping on the floor?"

Ransom blinked awake, blinded by the sunlight streaming in through the window. He raised his hand to block the light and felt stiff and uncomfortable.

He lifted his head and found a serving girl crouched next to him, looking at him with confusion. She was probably twelve years old, and her expression indicated she thought he was either very drunk or very foolish, or maybe both.

"Is it sunrise?" he asked, sitting up and stifling a groan. His strength was sapped and weak, as if he'd run against the surf for days.

"Can't you see the sunlight? You're lucky I found you first, or you might have gotten a scolding from your lord."

He sat up, and it was then he remembered the vision of King Gervase. His mentor's words still burned in his heart. They had awakened him to the truth. He rose to his feet, and the serving girl did the same.

"Thank you for waking me," he said. "Go about your business."

"The same with you," said the girl with accusing eyes. She tossed her head as she walked off.

Ransom rubbed his arms, his mind in a fog. He knew it had been no dream. His sword was still strapped to his waist, although the raven's head wasn't glowing anymore. All the conflict and angst he'd felt over the past days had been crushed beneath the certainty of what he needed to do. It wouldn't be easy. King Devon would likely be furious with him.

None of that mattered anymore. The Fountain had sent King Gervase to him, and he intended to take his advice with the utmost seriousness. He needed to be honest. If Alix had indeed deceived him, it explained why his feelings had altered so much after leaving Bayree and why she'd been so eager for him to return quickly. Being away from her had lessened her hold on him.

He left the alcove and walked to the king's private chamber. When he got there, he saw two of the king's guards, Sir Axien and Sir Thatcher, on duty.

"The king didn't summon you, Sir Ransom," said Sir Thatcher.

"I know, but I must speak with him urgently."

Both knights looked confused, but Sir Axien opened the door and slipped inside. He returned a moment later and gestured for Ransom to enter.

The king was holding out his arms as his manservant put a royal robe on his shoulders. A discarded meal was on the table, along with many scrolls and papers.

"This is unusual," the king said with a grin. "Are you so eager to set sail for Brugia that you've come for your orders?"

"No, my lord," Ransom answered, bowing his head in greeting. "I need to speak with you."

"Obviously, or you wouldn't have interrupted my ablutions so rudely. Well, speak up, man! There is much to do today, and I must get to it!"

"Could we speak privately, my lord? What I have to say is of a sensitive nature."

King Devon rolled his eyes and swatted at the manservant, who was holding up a pair of shoes he'd selected for the king. "Be gone! I can put on my own shoes today." The servant departed through a side door and shut it behind him, leaving the two of them alone.

The king walked to the breakfast platter and picked up a cube of cheese. "Have you eaten yet? I'm about finished. They always give me much more food than I need."

"I'm not hungry," Ransom said, and it was true. His stomach squirmed with the knowledge of what he had to do.

"Speak, then. You are not going to refuse to marry the girl, are you? You can't go back on it now, my boy."

The endearment, so recently heard from Gervase, made Ransom flinch. The two kings couldn't be more different in temperament. With Devon the Elder, there was always an edge of sarcasm, prepared to become sharp and cutting if the situation changed in a way that was not to his liking.

"I will if you still command me to. But in my desire to please you, I left out news that I should have shared. It may . . . change your mind."

The king had been biting through another cube of cheese. His expression became wary, then angry, and he set the half-eaten morsel back down on the platter. "What are you saying, Ransom? You lied to me?"

"I withheld the full truth from you, my lord. And I am sorry. I've had two . . . restless nights now because of it. Let me be frank with you, my lord. I wanted to please you. I wanted to marry her, at least I thought I did."

"You're not making any sense," the king growled. "Out with it!"

"I told you I knew Lady Alix. That she's the one who healed me. But she is also a trained poisoner who served King Lewis and now answers to King Estian. She wants to serve you . . . or so she has claimed."

The king's face became pale with the news. He blinked quickly, absorbing the information. His cheek muscle twitched. "A poisoner?"

"Yes, my lord. There is more."

"Did she . . . was she the one who killed my son?" he asked, his voice suddenly raspy.

"It was her," Ransom said. "She was there at Beestone castle."

The king glanced away. "There is . . . more, you say? You've already ruined my entire day. How much worse can this get?"

Ransom licked his lips. "Lady Alix . . . if that is her true name . . . this poisoner is also the daughter of . . ." Words failed him, but the king's eyes widened with shock and understanding.

"Emiloh?" the king whispered in horror.

Ransom nodded. "I should have told you before."

"By the blazes, yes, you should have!" the king thundered.

Ransom's stomach shriveled. "I apologize, my lord. I discovered, two years ago, that she was the queen's daughter. I also knew she was the one who had healed me. I had no notion that she was the Duke of Bayree's niece. Except she isn't, I think. I believe he took her in and claimed her as his own." Ransom was talking too fast, so he shut his mouth.

The king stared down at the ground in disbelief, his face a mask of unspeakable pain. He shook his head, blinking rapidly.

"There is more," Ransom said.

The king stared at him in disbelief. Shocked into silence.

"My lord. You should also know that she is Fountain-blessed. And so am I. I do not know what her powers are, but they are formidable. She has made me believe things that were not true."

The king glanced around until he saw a chair. He went to it and sank down on the cushion, his shoulders slumped under the load of surprises unburdened on him. He stared at nothing, rubbing his lips with his finger, silent and thoughtful.

"I see now why you didn't tell me," he said finally. "You feared my reaction, *and* you were under her spell." The king's haunted eyes looked up at Ransom. "There are many deceits tangled into this mess. Is what she told you the truth . . . or just an elaborate ploy? Did she attempt to use her magic to turn you against me? Or will she truly help us crush Estian if I pardon her for these *serious* crimes against my sovereignty?" The king shook his head. "I don't know. But I do know this. You have proven yourself to be worthy of sitting on my council. I must include Lady Deborah in this secret. She, of anyone, can help me unravel this tangled knot of allegiances."

"That sounds wise," Ransom said, but he knew another person who could also help. "What about the queen?"

The king flinched, but then he nodded. "Painful as it is to consider, you're right. I swore I would never look at her again. It wounds me to even think of seeing her. But no, this thorn must be pulled at last."

There is something about the queen's past she never speaks about. We've become as close as sisters, sharing stories and learning from each other. I know her heart is still tightly bound to her family lands, the Vexin, but something happened to her there long ago. Something that still causes her pain. I've heard that a knight serving a neighboring duchy seduced her. Is that true, or is the story more tangled?

—Claire de Murrow
Kingfountain
(prisoner still)

CHAPTER FIFTEEN

Bitter Memories

Not wanting to alert anyone to what was happening, Devon carried on with his scheduled meetings while Ransom sought out Lady Deborah at the king's request and explained the situation. She agreed that there would be much to gain from talking to Emiloh. Yes, it would be painful, but they would have a better notion of how to manipulate the situation if they fully understood it. Although Ransom would have preferred not to take part in so personal a conversation, the king had insisted that both he and Lady Deborah should be there.

And so Ransom found himself pacing inside the solar that afternoon while he awaited the arrival of the queen. His mind lingered on Claire. Would she come with Emiloh? What would it be like to see her again?

The king stood by the veranda door, looking down at the palace gardens, his manner and expression subdued. The weather had been bright and sunny the last couple of days, but when Ransom glanced out the window, he saw thick clouds had gathered in the sky. A rumble of thunder presaged a storm.

Voices could be heard coming down the corridor, and Ransom forced himself to stop pacing and clasped his hands behind his back.

Lady Deborah opened the door, and his eyes immediately shot beyond the queen to the woman who entered the room with her. Claire.

The sight of her hair, neither brown nor red, caused a tightness in his chest that nearly stole his breath. She looked startled to see him, her eyes widening with the surprise, her lips parting to reveal her teeth and even a glimpse of her pink tongue. She wore a fetching gown of green and gold that added to her natural beauty. He stared at her, unable to look away, and the years they'd spent apart seemed to disappear. Seeing her now, there was no doubt in his mind that Alix's magic had manipulated him. His feelings for Claire were real, and any force capable of muffling them was frighteningly strong.

Claire studied him with equal intensity, but a look of brooding anger quickly replaced the surprise. Her lips pressed closed, and he saw her hands clench into fists. She tried to look indifferent as she stepped to one side, giving him another sidelong look.

Once she had passed, he glanced at the queen. She looked paler than she had in the past. She'd aged in her confinement, with more wrinkles about her eyes and a frailer form. Ransom remembered her riding skill and imagined she missed the freedom of it. The king was staring at her with an almost frightening intensity.

"Here you are," the king said, his voice tinged with resentment. "Lady Deborah, if you'd escort Claire to another room to wait . . . ?"

"Yes, my lord," said Lady Deborah. She was a small woman compared to the queen, but she held herself with poise and self-command. "Come, Claire. We shall visit while they talk."

Claire looked at Ransom with an accusing gaze, wondering perhaps why he was permitted to stay.

He gave her an apologetic look, a slight shrug, and felt the squeezing of his heart increase after she was gone.

Emiloh stood by the entrance, taking in the scene and the audience. "What is this about, Devon? I was under the impression that you never wanted to see me again."

"That would be my preference," Devon said. "But alas, it cannot be helped." The hostility between them made Ransom squirm inside. He felt loyalty to them both—although he'd made his vow to the king, it was the queen who'd ransomed him back when he was a prisoner.

"You'll forgive me if I'm ignorant as to how I may help you," Emiloh said. "Some news does mount the steps now and then, but I don't know much about the current situation."

"It is not for the present that I seek you out. It's for the past."

The queen's brow furrowed. "Have we not hurt each other enough with that topic?"

Devon pursed his lips. "Maybe. But there's something more I need to know."

Emiloh's gaze remained fixed on the king. "And why must Ransom be here? Does it concern him?"

"It does indeed, my dear. You may have heard we defeated Estian and were given the duchy of Bayree?"

"I have. What of it?"

"Tell me what you know of the duke's niece. You were neighbors with the man, after all."

Ransom watched as the queen's eyes narrowed with suspicion. "What do you wish to know?"

"Do you know her *name*?"

"Alix, I recall," said the queen stiffly. Her wariness increased. "What of it?"

The king turned toward the window again, his cheek muscles twitching. "Is she your daughter, Emi?"

Ransom watched the queen, waiting for a reaction. He wasn't sure what to expect, but he wasn't prepared for the pain and guilt in her eyes. That look betrayed her. She must have known it, for she stared down at the floor.

"Yes," she said huskily. "I believe so."

The king sniffed, still looking away. He seemed to be wrestling with his own emotions. "You had an affair with the Duke of Bayree, then? Before we were married?"

"No," said the queen.

The king winced. "*After* we were married?"

"You know that's not true," said the queen, her voice throbbing with anger at the accusation.

The king turned, staring at his wife with torment. "Do I?"

"Alix isn't his daughter. She's Lewis's."

Ransom stared at her in surprise. The daughter of the King of Occitania? The king's reaction was even more stunned. He gaped at his wife.

"I thought . . . it was a knight," Devon said, perplexed.

"Of course you believed that. It sounds far more romantic that way," said the queen, her voice betraying bitterness. "I was very young, Devon. I didn't understand the nature of some men back then. He came to visit me, to offer his . . . protection. But his actions belied his motives. I was frightened. My father was dead. I had no one to protect me."

Devon stared at his wife, a gamut of feelings playing across his face. This was news.

"I tried to keep the pregnancy a secret," she said. "Lewis knew and offered to take the child. This was before Estian and Noemie were born, and he and his wife had no children. He was . . . greedy about it. He wanted her. I think he feared for his kingdom's future if he died without having a child. I did not give myself to him, Devon. I was too frightened to refuse."

The king looked down and nodded. "You deceived me," he said.

"I did," she answered. "On our wedding night. I confess it. But I never intended to hurt you."

A frown twisted Devon's mouth.

Ransom stared at the queen in pity. This was not the story Alix had told him. Perhaps she didn't know the truth herself but had been fed the lie since her youth. Lewis was dead now, beyond the reach of retribution.

Something in the queen's words triggered a memory in his mind. A memory of Lewis's daughter, Noemie, and something she had said to Ransom when she had tried to manipulate him. He hadn't thought on that encounter in a long time, and he vaguely remembered her words, her urgency. Had it all been a trick? Or was there indeed a magical game of Wizr at work that controlled the fates of kingdoms? How could he know what was a lie and what was truth?

"I might have forgiven you if you'd told me," he said. "I very much wanted the Vexin, and I very much wanted *you* at the time. Now, things are different. You twisted my sons against me. You poisoned them."

"I did not," said the queen, shaking her head. "You still cannot see it, Devon? You have done the poisoning yourself. Pride is a poison. And you've drunk your fill of it."

The king flinched, her words landing a blow. "And what of your pride? What of your conceit? You drove my sons to rebellion!"

"You blame me for their insurrection still. But it was you yourself who caused it. Your determination to persecute Occitania gave Lewis the opportunity to draw them in. I never told my sons that they were making friends of my enemies. I kept that pain to myself."

The king held up his hand, visibly frustrated. "There is no point discussing this further. Instead of being grateful I delivered you from bondage to that wily king, you have castigated and condemned me. I'll hear no more on that score. Tell me, then, truthfully. If Alix is your daughter and Lewis's spawn, then she is no true heir of Bayree. Nor is she an heir of the house of Vertus. She's illegitimate and thus cannot inherit anything. Do I understand well the laws of Occitania?"

"If you accuse her, yes," said the queen. "But in doing so, you challenge the honor of Pree, and thus void the treaty of peace you've just established. To what end, Husband?"

He flinched at the word. "Do not call me that!"

"But I am your wife in the eyes of the Lady and our people. Think, Devon! If you deny her, will it not cast in doubt the legitimacy of your own sons, who also came from my womb?"

The king's cheeks were flushed, his breathing growing sharper and sharper.

"I swear on the Lady that the sons I bore you are your offspring. I have been faithful to you, even though you've cast me aside. But if even one person sows doubts . . . That is why I've never spoken of this. To protect you and our sons. Leave the girl alone. None of this is her fault."

Devon slumped into a chair, pressing his face into his hands. He coughed and then lowered his hands and glared at her. "She killed our eldest child, madam. And others. And if I send Ransom to her, she'll likely kill him too. Or anyone else I allow to marry her."

The queen stared at him in confusion.

"Lewis made her a poisoner! He must have sent her to that accursed place in Pisan when she was old enough. You never knew this?"

By the look of shock and horror on the queen's face, it was obvious she had not.

"No, Husband. I did not know that."

"So you've never seen her? You don't know your daughter?"

The queen's face crumpled in anguish. "Not since her birth. I placed one kiss on her bloodied scalp, and then she was rushed away from me and taken to Pree. I didn't even give her that name. But I've heard of her resemblance to me . . . that it has caused rumors and idle stories."

"Perhaps I should capture her and send her to the tower to be your companion!" said the king harshly.

The queen, who had been standing by the door the entire time, rushed forward and knelt by the king's chair. "I beg you, Husband, do not be so cruel. Have I not suffered long enough? Release me."

Ransom's throat tightened as he listened to her plea. The entire situation was horrible, none of the possible outcomes desirable. Would the king force him to take Bayree and send Alix away in humiliation? He did not want that to happen either. Even if she had knowingly deceived him, he still believed there was good in her. He'd seen her tend to the wounded for days, tireless and unflinching.

"I'll not hear of it!" thundered Devon. He clambered out of the chair and left her on her knees, her eyes wet. "You think I am fool enough to be convinced by tears to do something that would only hurt me?"

"Have you not had enough revenge?" the queen pleaded. "Send me to Auxaunce. Banish me there that you may never see me again."

The king choked down a cruel laugh. "Oh? And what about when I give the Vexin to Jon-Landon? Will you be so keen to live there then? He's not so fond of you as the others."

The queen gazed at him, her mouth turning down in a look of dread. "Surely you are not that foolish."

"The kingdom is mine to do with as I please. Benedict will be heir to Kingfountain, and the Vexin will go to Jon-Landon. Surely Bennett wouldn't want it the other way around?"

The queen hung her head, her golden tresses hiding her face. She looked so like Alix at that moment, and Ransom's heart burned with grief for both of them.

"You do not know your sons as well as you think," the queen whispered.

"Do I not, madam? I know Bennett is jealous and vengeful. He's strong and cunning, but his resentment is a flaw that is easily exploited. Goff is content where he is. He's busy seeking trading partners and increasing his wealth. He lacks the spine to rule a kingdom. Jon-Landon has suffered with want of a mother's kindness. Of all our children, he loves me best. He's cunning and quick-minded. He'd make a good king, although he cannot defeat Bennett. Not yet. But with me as his mentor and guardian, he wouldn't need to. I am willing to give the throne to Benedict if he has enough sense to claim the opportunity. But if he defies me again, I will give it to the youngest, who deserves it more."

The queen lifted her head, her eyes burning with controlled anger. "Unless Bennett takes it from you."

"He's tried. Or have you forgotten?" said Devon. His look darkened. "Go back to your tower, madam. Before I change it to the dungeon."

Queen Emiloh rose to her feet and brushed off her hands. She nodded to her husband, then gave Ransom a pained smile.

"She still cares for you," the queen said softly.

"Out!" shouted the king.

The queen turned back to her husband, giving him a final look before she let herself out of the room. Ransom's heart bled with agony as he watched the king pace the room, muttering to himself. He was desperate to leave, both to escape the king's emotional torment and so that he might see Claire one more time before she went back to the tower, but he knew it was impossible.

Finally, the king stopped pacing. "How she vexes me," he said angrily. "But now the thorn is pulled out."

Ransom didn't know what to say, so he said nothing. He just looked at the king expectantly.

The Elder King's eyes flashed with cunning. "You cannot marry that girl," he said. "The duchy of Bayree has no heir. That means it belongs to the crown. It is for Estian to decide who gets it, and he has given it to me on the condition that one of my people marries the heiress." He frowned and shook his head. "Unacceptable. That is why he laughed, Ransom. That is why he laughed! Well . . . I will be the one who laughs now. I'm not sending you to Brugia. I'm sending you back to Pree."

I saw him today. I wish we could have spoken, but I was dismissed to Lady Deborah's watchful care while the king and queen argued loudly. Ransom remained behind, although why I do not know. When he saw me, there was a curious look in his eyes. I wish I had the power of second sight the Aos Sí possess. I couldn't interpret my own feelings, let alone his. All I know is that my heart hurts, I'm confused, and I cannot stand this palace prison any longer. My heart screams for freedom.

When Emi was dismissed, we were escorted back to the tower. Sir James was waiting at the door, a sly smile on his face. He said nothing as we passed, but he took my hand and pressed a kiss to it, giving me an impertinent look that made me feel like flinging myself out the tower window so I could be done with all this madness. No, better yet—I would fling him out the window. After he did it, I looked him in the eye, and with all the sincerity I could muster, I told him that if he ever did that again, I would claw out his eyes with my fingernails.

—Claire de Murrow
Tower
(washing her hands)

CHAPTER SIXTEEN

The King's Errand

Ransom hurried down the corridor toward the queen's tower, hoping to catch Claire before she returned to her prison. He'd overheard a couple of passing servants talking about the queen, saying she'd just come by with her companion. If he caught up with them, he wasn't sure what he'd say to her, but that didn't stop him. He felt a powerful need to speak to her.

When he turned the corner, he saw Emiloh enter the doorway leading to the stairs. Guards were posted there, as always, and it required special permission from the king in order to visit the tower room—permission that Ransom didn't have. Someone else was loitering by the door, someone whose presence was an unwelcome surprise: Sir James. Ransom stopped in his tracks, staring in shock as his childhood enemy took Claire's hand in a familiar and clandestine act and pressed it to his lips. The sight of it struck him like a blow to the ribs. The fiery autumn of her hair filled his eyes as she turned her head slightly and said something to Sir James that Ransom couldn't hear. And then she followed the queen through the doorway.

Ransom stood frozen in the corridor, powerless against the rush of jealousy and hatred that swirled through him. He wanted to destroy Sir James. As he wrestled with dark emotion, his old companion looked down the corridor and caught sight of him, giving him a gloating look. Blood pounded in Ransom's skull as he watched the other man walk toward him.

When James reached him, he said nothing, but he gave Ransom a knowing look. It was a look that said, *See? I prevailed in the end. She chose me instead of you. And there isn't anything you can do about it.*

Sweat itched on Ransom's brow. The violence inside him could not be tamed. He glared at Sir James, but he did not strike him. Instead, Ransom went straight to the training yard. It was hailing outside when he got there, the tiny pebbles of ice rattling and rolling against the stone. The wind whistled, and thunder rumbled overhead. Ransom didn't care. He went out in the midst of it, feeling the little stings as the hail lashed at his flesh. The raven's head on his scabbard began to glow. Ransom unsheathed his sword and began to practice, yielding his body to the rage surging through him. He swung his blade until his arms ached with the effort. He swung it until he was soaked to the skin. There was no one there to fight, and that was for the best.

In his dark mood, he may have killed someone.

When he returned to his room, dripping wet, he found Dearley inside pacing. His ward's eyes widened with concern.

"You were out in that strange storm?" Dearley asked.

Ransom nodded, feeling his misery keenly. He unstrapped his sword belt, slung it over the chair, and started stripping off his soaked tunic. Dearley went to the clothing chest and knelt by it to retrieve fresh clothes and a towel, the latter of which Ransom used to mop his face before he changed. Because of the storm clouds, he had no idea the time of day. Everything seemed darker, both within the castle and without.

"The king sent for you," Dearley said. "Are you all right? You look . . . terrible."

Ransom grabbed the sword belt and wrapped it around his waist, leaving the wet clothes in a heap on the floor by the hearth. His hair felt heavy, and he rubbed his chin, feeling the thick stubble there and on his cheeks. The violence of his emotions had passed, but he still felt sickened by the thought of Sir James marrying Claire.

It was not like him to avoid answering a question, but he didn't want to let any of his dark thoughts out.

"What happened?" Dearley asked in a kindly way. "You weren't here this morning when I came for you. A servant said you'd been found asleep next to a fountain. Have you been drinking, Sir Ransom?"

He shook his head no, finally able to speak. "I told the king the truth," he said. "I haven't even told you yet." Breathing out slowly, he turned and looked at Dearley's compassionate expression. "Lady Alix, it turns out, isn't the true heir of the duchy of Bayree."

Dearley's eyes widened. "By the Fountain," he whispered.

"It's worse than that. She is the King of Occitania's poisoner, and it turns out she's also his illegitimate sister. And if that weren't bad enough, I saw my old enemy, Sir James, kissing Claire's hand." The words sounded ridiculous as he said them, coming after the weighty revelation about Alix, but he realized he cared more about the latter disappointment than the former. If he'd wished for a way to know his own mind, his own heart, it seemed he'd found it. "Sir Simon warned me that he might be courting her. But seeing the evidence with my own eyes made me sick." He gave Dearley a wan smile. "It's been a difficult day."

Dearley was flummoxed by the news. "That's awful."

"I'm conflicted, to say the least. It's possible that Lady Alix doesn't know the full truth about her parentage, but she may have been feigning her interest in me." He sighed, again feeling the weight of the sorrow on his heart. "I wanted to believe her. I suspect she has an uncanny power that *forces* people to believe her. Still, she saved my life . . ."

"I don't even know what to say," Dearley said in amazement. "Her affection for you did seem real, as far as I could tell. And yet, if you're right about her, none of us can trust what we experienced around her. You told me she was Fountain-blessed too, but I never would have suspected that."

"Well, the matter is moot. The king has forbidden me to marry her." He paused, considering the situation, and added, "Being in Bayree turned my head around in a way I don't fully understand. I realize my feelings for Claire haven't changed."

Dearley nodded slowly. "And Sir James is courting her. From what you've told me, I doubt he intends to seek the king's approval. That . . . that is unpleasant."

A knock sounded on the door. Dearley crossed the room and opened it, revealing Lady Deborah in the entryway.

"My apologies!" Dearley said when he saw her. "Sir Ransom just returned, and he was—"

"I know," she said with a quirk of a smile. "Half the servant girls in the palace were crowded around the windows, fawning over the sight of him in the training yard."

Ransom thought she was jesting, but the look on her face indicated she was sincere.

"You were quite a specimen, I've been told. They're all aflutter now. Shall we?"

Embarrassment twisted in his stomach. It hadn't occurred to him that others might be watching. It had been storming fiercely, unnaturally, and he'd probably looked like a fool eejit out there, as Claire would say, swinging at nothing. But he didn't have time to dwell—the king expected him, and Ransom doubted he was in any mood to wait. He nodded and started toward the door. Dearley touched his arm on his way out, giving him a look of support.

As Ransom and Lady Deborah walked into the hall, she gave him a surreptitious glance.

"Heartsickness is a malady with no easy cure," she said. "I was young once, although you may not imagine that possible. I was given to the lord of Thorngate castle when I was sixteen and he thirty. It was quite a shock in the beginning. Not a marriage of the heart, you might say. Not at first. Political marriages rarely are."

Her words seemed intended to ease his pain. He appreciated it.

"I imagine it was that way for my parents as well," Ransom said. His parents had never seemed affectionate toward each other. He thought about his sister, Maeg, and Marcus's objection to letting her marry as she wished. If Dearley and Elodie still wanted to marry in a few years, he'd make sure it happened. Happiness should not be impossible to achieve.

"What matters is making the best you can of any given situation. Would you hear my counsel, Sir Ransom?" she asked.

"I will if you have any to give," he replied. They'd reached the stairs and started down them side by side.

"It is my belief that Lady Alix did intend to deceive you. Someone like her—a woman trained as a poisoner—could not have been kept in the dark forever. She would have found out her true parentage. Would she have betrayed Estian, her brother? Possibly, but I doubt it. She may have killed her other brother, but she was raised with this one. She was raised Occitanian. Her insistence on keeping her identity a secret only strengthens my view. It has long been a practice in Occitania to prefer political intrigues to war on the battlefield. Her efforts to entrap you fit into that tradition. So I've advised the king not to allow the marriage."

"Yes, well . . . I can't say I disagree with you. I'm not surprised by your counsel."

"I haven't given it yet."

His brow furrowed in confusion.

"I've advised the king that you would be a better match for Lady Claire de Murrow."

Ransom halted and turned to stare at her in disbelief.

"The duchy of Glosstyr has been vacant for far too long. The king needs a strong man in that position more than he needs the additional income. Also, we would regain loyalty from the Legaultans, which would be to our benefit should war break out with Occitania or with one, or more, of the king's sons. You've proven your loyalty, Ransom. I think it would not only be a pragmatic decision, but it would tie your interests to the king's. My counsel to you, young man, is to ask for it yourself."

Her words lifted some of the darkness that had descended on him—they gave him something he'd been lacking all day: hope. "I have, but he's denied me before. And I may be too late. Another man is seeking her favor."

"She despises Jon-Landon. That's plain to see."

"I was talking about Sir James."

She frowned. "The king wouldn't trust him to guard a cow, let alone a duchy," she said. "No, that won't do, and I'd advise against it. Is this palace gossip? Ignore it. To rule Legault, you'll need sufficient coin and bravery to tame their nobles. It wasn't easy for Lord Archer, nor would it likely be easy for you because of your youth. But I think you're the far better man for such a duty."

He thought again of James kissing Claire's hand. The memory still made him queasy. Did she have feelings for him, or was the attachment one-sided?

"The king told me he'd never allow it," he reminded her.

"I know. He's stubborn. But I think he'll come around. Ask for it, Ransom. Demand it. He respects persistence."

He looked at Lady Deborah with admiration. "Thank you for your counsel. I've always been . . . fond of her."

Lady Deborah smiled. "I know. The cook told me about the two of you." Then she winked at him and continued down the steps.

When they entered the king's private chambers, allowed in by his guards, he was pacing restlessly. Hail tapped at the windows outside.

"Accursed storm!" railed the king, glaring at the water-stained windows. "The day started so pleasant. Where have you been, Sir Ransom? I don't like to be kept waiting."

"I'm sorry, my lord," Ransom apologized, but he offered no explanation or excuse.

Lady Deborah approached the king. "I've shared with him my views on Lady Alix and her intentions."

The king gave her a knowing look and then pointed to Ransom. "You seem a little glum, but if Deborah says the poisoner has tricked you, believe it. They're a cunning lot. She nearly tricked us all."

"I understand, my lord. What do you want me to do?"

"What do I want? I want you to lead an army and blast through the walls of Pree! But I need to get out of the treaty first. I'm finished playing games with Lewis's brat. It will not be said of me that Devon the Ursus doesn't keep his oaths. Go to Pree with a sizable host and tell him that Bayree is mine by rights and that he shouldn't have made it conditional on marrying the girl. If he balks, tell him you know the truth. If he wants the rumors to get out, then that will be his decision, not mine."

Ransom had an uneasy feeling about the whole thing. Estian had proven he was perfectly capable of tricking and manipulating them. Any concessions he made would come with barbs.

"What if he gives you Bayree outright?" Lady Deborah asked. "He just might do it to prevent the scandal."

The king nodded sagely. "I'll give it to Sir Ransom, and he can take her as his ward. But I want her confined." He looked at Ransom with great conviction. "I don't want that poisoner running around. But honestly, I don't think Estian will grant our request. And he won't let her be taken hostage either. She knows too much. You must capture her, although it won't be easy. If you can get to Bayree first, you might be able to bring her into our territory before Estian finds out."

Ransom remembered something she had told him, something he hadn't revealed yet in the furor of all his other revelations. "My lord, she would know I'm coming."

"Why? Because of that Fountain-blessed nonsense?"

Lady Deborah looked at Ransom in confusion.

"It isn't nonsense, my lord. It's the truth. Ask Lord Kinghorn if you don't believe me. But that's not what I meant. Alix told me that Lewis, and now his son, has a Wizr board, one that has been handed down for generations."

The king looked skeptical. "It's a popular game. What of it?"

"This board has been gifted with power from the Fountain. The game is real. The pieces represent real people, I believe. Through it, she told me that Estian knows all of your moves as you make them. He knows when you are working against him. Based on what she told me, that, my lord, is how he knew we would attack Occitania and not the Vexin."

"What madness is this?" the king murmured.

Lady Deborah just cocked her head, waiting for him to continue, but she had a skeptical look on her face.

"I'm just repeating what she told me. The Wizr board is hidden in Pree. She said she knows where to find it, and if you manage to claim it, she can change sides. Some curse binds her to play for him. If it's true, we'd do best to find it. It could change everything in our conflict with that country."

The king folded his arms across his chest, and a sour expression twisted his mouth. "I'm doubtful of her story, Ransom. She may actually believe it's true, but that doesn't make it so. Yes . . . I have often wondered how the Occitanians knew of our movements. But I've attributed it to men they've hired to spy on us. This is a large castle, and I cannot vouch for the loyalty of every man, woman, and child who lives and serves here." He paused, as if thinking on it. "But let us pretend this is true. The board is in Pree? Very well, go and fetch it. Send word to Lady Alix that you've been sent on a mission there. Have her steal it for you. Inspect it yourself. If it is true, then I will reconsider keeping her in a dungeon. Be careful, though. If she learns what you've told me, then your life will be in danger."

"I will go," Ransom said, nodding with conviction.

The king wrinkled his nose. "I don't know if you have the talent for deception, however. This mission requires some guile. I suppose you will do the best you can."

"A bold plan, my lord," said Lady Deborah.

"Confound it, I've told you both I detest such formalities! Go to Pree, Ransom. When you return, I will summon the lords of the realm to meet with me. I wish to name Benedict my heir and to see him crowned. The question is whether he will acquiesce to my demand that he give the Vexin to Jon-Landon. We shall see. Do you believe he will?" He looked at Ransom and then at Lady Deborah.

"I know he won't," Ransom said. "He's told me as much."

The king snorted. "Deborah?"

"I don't think so. He's too much like you."

King Devon chuckled. "Then my son will earn another lesson in humility."

I watched this morning as Ransom departed on his ugly dappled horse with a cohort of a hundred knights to enforce the king's will on some matter or other. I asked Emi what she thought would happen next. She knows her husband better than any other person. She said he would try to force Benedict's obedience once again through promises of wealth and land but without ceding true power to him. And she predicts that her son will do something rash in response. I asked her what he might do. She looked at me, her eyes gleaming with mischief. She knows, but she won't tell me.

I hate this tower. I hate this entire palace.

—Claire de Murrow
(mired in the troubles between kings and queens)

CHAPTER SEVENTEEN

Enemies Forever

t took them three days to ride to the borders of Occitania, and another to reach Pree itself. Ransom had sent a courier ahead to Alix, asking her to meet him in Pree to discuss their marriage, and to bring the Wizr board with her. Although he knew it was unlikely, he still hoped she might switch sides. As an enemy, she was dangerous; as an ally, she'd still be dangerous, but hopefully more dangerous to the other side.

The wind had become cool on the journey, and the leaves on the elm trees began to turn yellow, some purple. It would be winter in short order, and there would be no armies, no long rides, and no more contention between the king and his son.

If only it were winter already.

The Occitanian palace rose above the city of Pree, with ribbons of smoke coming from the hundreds of chimneys beyond the fortress walls. It was a splendid structure, but one that contained too many dark memories for Ransom to view it with anything but trepidation and mistrust. He had wondered whether they would encounter Occitanian knights along the journey, especially since he rode with so many warriors, but the road had only been full of carts and wagons, tradesmen and merchants roaming the realm to provide their goods.

Jeff Wheeler

When they reached the gates of Pree, Ransom announced himself
and asked for a writ of safe conduct to see King Estian. Was Alix already
there? He couldn't sense her yet. It was granted in short order, along
with permission to bring twenty of the knights as an escort. Ransom
asked Dearley to remain behind with the other eighty, and to be on the
lookout for any trouble.

"Do you think the king would attack us now?" Dearley asked with
a frown of concern.

He would if he realized it was Ransom's intention to steal the Wizr
board and his poisoner.

"I don't. But neither do I trust him," Ransom answered. Then he
parted ways with Dearley, taking his smaller group into the city. The resi-
dents of Pree glared with open hostility at the knights wearing the badge
of the Silver Rose.

As much as he worried about the confrontation with King Estian,
Ransom felt more anxious about seeing Lady Alix. If she came. Would
she affect him the way she had in Bayree? Was her power so strong it
would sway his will even now?

Was it even possible to manipulate a person who could magically
influence others? He aimed to try. He hoped he could persuade her to
take the Wizr board out of the city. It would require more deceptions
on his part, but lying to her was a little easier because he suspected she'd
already deceived him.

When they reached the palace courtyard, he sensed Alix's presence. His heart began to pound faster, but he hid his reaction as he
dismounted and then followed the royal steward through the gates of
the palace.

"The king is meeting with his council at the moment," the steward
said to him as they walked. "You will be permitted to speak to him
when they are finished. There is, however, someone who wishes to speak
with you beforehand. The heiress of Bayree is here."

"I was hoping for a chance to talk to her. And I would prefer to address the king in private," said Ransom, knowing the demand he was about to make would be offensive to their nobility.

"That is for the king to decide," said the steward brusquely. They were brought to a set of huge oak doors, the wood divided into many squares decorated with intricate carvings of knights, fleurs-de-lis, and banners. The walls around them were bedecked with tapestries made of fine cloth and stitching. Ransom's gaze took it all in, but his other senses were focused on Alix, and when she came down the corridor toward him, he turned to look.

She was alone, dressed in a hooded cloak that hid her hair and features. When she got his attention, she turned into an alcove midway down the corridor and disappeared.

"Ah, there she is," said the steward. "You may speak privately in that alcove."

Turning to one of the knights, he said, "I'll be back in a moment."

The knight gave a shrug and continued milling about with the others while Ransom walked down the corridor. As he approached the alcove, he heard the splashing of fountain waters coming from ahead. The interior was full of shadows, but he spied Alix standing on the other side of the water.

He entered the space cautiously, his eyes adjusting to the dark, and she hurried around the fountain to embrace him, pressing her cheek against his chest. His first response was to flinch, but he recovered quickly and wrapped his arms around her.

"When I heard you were coming, I couldn't come fast enough," she whispered. "I've missed you."

"Did you bring it?" he asked.

She looked up at his face, a smile parting her lips, and nodded. Relief surged inside him. He didn't see any sort of bag or carrying case nearby, but it was dark still.

"Where is—?" he started to say, but she wove her fingers through his hair and brought his mouth down to hers for a fierce kiss.

Surprised by this, his mind quickly went blank except for the press of her mouth against his, her fingers digging into his hair, and his whole body reacted to her closeness, to the smell of lilac on her skin. The kiss was powerful, intoxicating, and his resolve began to waver.

Suddenly she stopped, pulling back, her eyes narrowing. He was breathing fast, trying to control his rampaging emotions. Despite his better judgment, he wanted more. But it felt dangerous.

"A kiss never lies," she said, shaking her head, backing away from him.

"What?" he asked in confusion.

"A kiss *never* lies." The look of rapture on her face transformed to wariness and then hurt. "That is one of the lessons we were taught in the poisoner school. When a man's heart has changed toward you, then you will tell it from his kiss. You told him, didn't you? You told your king about me."

It wasn't so much a question as an accusation. He swallowed as his Fountain magic prickled, warning him of the danger she presented. Reminding him that, whatever else this woman was, she was also a murderer. The sound of the splashing waters filled his ears.

"I did," he answered truthfully.

Her face crumpled with disappointment. "Oh, Ransom," she said bitterly.

"I am loyal to my king," he said firmly. "And you are not who I assumed you were. I know who your father is. And the story you told me is not true."

Gone were the loving looks she'd given him in Kerjean. She stared at him with eyes full of distrust, hurt, and even malice. Had her behavior in Bayree been entirely an act?

"You *think* you know the truth, but you know nothing, Ransom. You have no idea what this game is or what it's about. Yes, I'm King

Lewis's daughter. I was going to tell you that. I was going to tell you everything. But I cannot now. Now we must be enemies." The hurt look on her face intensified.

"I don't want that," Ransom said.

"But you chose it," she answered. "I was willing to betray my brother for you. All I asked was for you to do the same for me." She closed her hands into fists and then pressed them against her eyes. "I don't want to hate you. But I must."

"Come with me," Ransom said, taking a step toward her. "Bring the Wizr set and come back with us. I will protect you from Estian."

She lowered her fists and shook her head no. "I can't break the curse myself. And neither can you. I had it all figured out, but now there's no escape for me. I almost gave you the set first. I'm so glad I didn't."

"Alix," he said, confused and troubled. "We can still be allies."

"No, Ransom. Estian was right about you. He said you're a man who will never betray his principles. And now I must hurt you for it. Your king must die. Good-bye."

He moved to block the opening. "I won't let you," he said.

But she didn't move toward the opening. She stepped into the fountain itself and said a word he didn't understand. And she was gone in a plume of mist. He sensed a surge of power, one that grated through his bones. He stared at the fountain in disbelief. No longer could he sense her presence. She had literally vanished into the waters through some magical means he didn't understand.

The king was in mortal danger. And there was no way Ransom could warn him.

Ransom stormed away from the alcove, his heart on fire with worry and bitterness. He had to get back to Kingfountain, but he could not leave without fulfilling his mission. He stormed up to the heavy oak doors.

The steward still stood there, along with four guards. It was obvious no one intended to let them in anytime soon.

"I'll see him *now*," said Ransom angrily.

"It is not your place to demand anything here," said the steward dismissively.

Ransom marched past him and grabbed one of the heavy decorative handles. Two of the knights standing guard tried to restrain him. Ransom shoved one of them back into the door hard and then kneed the other in the stomach before shoving him down too. He yanked the door open violently before the other two knights had a chance to react to their fallen comrades.

The door creaked open, revealing the throne room beyond it. Estian sat on the throne on a raised dais, wearing a black velvet tunic stitched with silver fleurs-de-lis. Six decorative chairs formed a row on each side of the dais, twelve in all, and the nobles of the realm sat on them. One was empty. It was a gloomy chamber, the curtains drawn shut, and the only light came from circular fire pits spread throughout the council chamber.

As Ransom marched down the center aisle, he saw Benedict sitting in the chair closest to the king. His stomach dropped at the sight of the Prince of Ceredigion next to the man who should have been his enemy, drinking from a jeweled goblet. Benedict didn't look uneasy. When Ransom reached the end of the line, the prince met his gaze and gave him a nod of recognition.

"Of all the formidable qualities our neighbors from Ceredigion possess," said King Estian with a cunning smile, "perhaps the most pronounced is rudeness."

Ransom heard a scuffle break out behind him, but he didn't turn around.

"What's the meaning of this?" Ransom demanded, glaring at Estian, but he nodded toward Benedict.

"Is it not fitting and proper that the lords of Occitania should assemble to advise their king and do his bidding?" said Estian. "Sit, Sir Ransom. There's a chair here for you as well."

"I am not your vassal," said Ransom.

"He's too pompous to do what's best for him," said Benedict boldly. "He will not serve you."

"Will he serve you when you are king, I wonder?" asked Estian, leaning forward. "I know you came bearing a threat, Sir Ransom. I'm weary of Devon's intrigues, so I thought I might try some of my own. The duchy of Vexin is now part of the kingdom of Occitania. Benedict has knelt and sworn fealty to me. That puts him under the protection of the treaty that you so recently forced me to sign. A two years' truce, if you remember. Bayree belongs to Devon if he still wants it. I care not. But you must cross *my* lands to get to it or otherwise take a ship. I don't really care." He scratched the wooden armrest of the throne with his fingernail.

A sense of betrayal roiled inside Ransom's chest. He glared at the nobles of Occitania, feeling their rancor in return. His gaze fixed on Benedict. Had Alix known all along that Estian intended to pursue an alliance with Prince Benedict?

She'd never intended to switch sides. Her sole purpose had been to get him to do so . . . or to distract him from what was unfolding.

"What did he promise you?"

"More than I ever got from my father," said Benedict. "Including his latest offer, which a courier brought to me just yesterday. It's time to alter the game. Instead of taking Father's bribe, I've agreed to give the King of Occitania the duchy of La Marche. In return, I'll get to keep the Vexin, Bayree, Brythonica, and the rest once I become king. I never liked Westmarch anyway. When you go back to Kingfountain, be a good man, and tell Father I'm coming." He looked confident and aloof. "And when I do, I'll take it all away from him."

It was a blow to Ransom's heart. "Don't do this," he said.

Benedict took another sip. "He's done it to himself. He may say he'll share his power, but I know better. He'll never give it up unless forced. The money he offered is an insult. Did he truly think I'd accept so little so late?"

"The last time you rebelled against him, you failed. Do not expect his forgiveness this time."

"I'll take your words to heart, Sir Ransom. It's not too late for you, you know. Join my side. Swear fealty to me as the rightful king of Ceredigion, and it will end with less pain and suffering."

Ransom hung his head. "You'll break his heart."

"I intend to break more than that," said Benedict coldly.

Alix had left the palace. She was going to Kingfountain to murder King Devon. The certainty of that blazed in his mind. He turned to leave and saw guards had come and disarmed the knights who'd accompanied him. One stood out from the rest: Sir Robert Tregoss in the black tunic of the king's knights. The recognition of the man who had helped destroy Devon the Younger jolted him. The danger he was in was immense.

"You broke the peace when you stormed your way in here," said Estian in a mocking tone. "I'll have these twenty as punishment for your discourtesy."

The rush of the falls filled Ransom's ears, as loud as he was angry. Benedict's betrayal would injure the realm. Alone, he could not face his father and win. But with help from Estian and his mysterious Wizr set, he would likely prevail. Assuming the king survived long enough for there to *be* a war.

He reached for the hilt of his bastard sword and drew it from the sheath in a single fluid movement. He lunged forward and held the tip at Estian's throat, pushing him back into the throne with his other hand.

Shocked cries of outrage came from the throne room.

"Stay seated or he dies," Ransom threatened.

Estian's eyes widened with surprise. He swallowed once, and the bulge made his throat brush against the tip of the blade.

"That would be murder," Estian said.

"Which is no less than what you are planning. Release my knights."

Estian squeezed the armrests of his throne. Ransom felt the king's vulnerability. One thrust was all it would take to destroy him. How he wanted to, even if it ended in his own slaughter!

"Don't be a fool, Ransom," growled Benedict. "You cannot defeat us all."

"I don't need to," he answered, glowering at Estian. "Just him. That leaves your sister, Noemie, does it not?"

Sweat had formed on Estian's brow and began to trickle down his cheek. "Sir Robert, be so kind as to let our guests leave the palace."

"Aye, my lord," said Sir Robert in a disgruntled tone. Ransom hated the man even more now. It was obvious he'd wanted to slaughter his own countrymen.

He turned his head and saw Sir Robert returning the knights' weapons. A sense of danger to his left shifted his gaze to Benedict, who was tensing as if prepared to spring from his chair and tackle Ransom.

"I wouldn't if I were you," Ransom said to the prince in a menacing way.

"Benedict, I forbid it," said the king. "Your men are leaving, Sir Ransom. Lower your sword. You may go free as well."

"I intend to," Ransom said. More sweat trickled down Estian's face. "Call her off, my lord."

"Who?"

"You know who I speak of. Your poisoner. If Devon is dead when I return, I swear on the Fountain that I will be back to take off your head."

Estian licked his lips. "Very well."

"You have a way to stop her?" Ransom asked, pressing his hand harder against the king's chest. His sword arm burned from holding the same position for so long, but he ignored the sensation.

"I will recall her," he said. "It's that simple."

"It better be," Ransom said. "Your life depends on it."

"I understand you. Lower your sword."

Ransom did so, although it was now aimed at Estian's stomach. The urge to drive it through him was so powerful he almost shook with it. He wanted to rampage throughout the throne room, to slay all of them in his fury, even though he knew he would die doing so. Or would the scabbard miraculously keep him alive?

No, he didn't believe it was that powerful. It made him difficult to kill, not immortal.

"We are enemies now," Estian said softly. "You realize that. I will never permit you to step foot in Pree again on pain of death. I banish you. Your lands are forfeit. But go in peace. I swear before my nobles you will not be harmed."

Ransom wasn't surprised. "I don't intend to come back," he said curtly.

He lowered his hand from the king's chest until his sword pointed at the floor. He turned, basking in the enmity focused on him. Then he marched past the nobles, watching as some of them shrank from him. When he reached the door, he exchanged hostile glares with Sir Robert Tregoss.

"Until next time," Sir Robert said with the promise of vengeance.

"I look forward to it," Ransom shot back.

It has been over a year since I last scribbled on these pages. I think my loathing of this confinement made me loathe this little book as well. At least I've had letters aplenty from Ransom. Quite a few of them talked about his past conflicts with Sir James, which leads me to believe someone told him about that fool eejit's interest in me. I like that he wants to protect me, and I truly wish I could have been there in his youth to see him take on James and his moody henchlings when they were at Averanche together. So many stories. I cherish each one. He also told me about Lady Alix and her role in the Occitanian court. I've spent the afternoon reading through those letters as well as these pages again, sometimes with a smile, sometimes with tears. Sir Dalian says the dungeon is full of prisoners now, and many of them are sick and dying. I don't know how those poor souls can live with their chains. My captivity isn't nearly as onerous as theirs, but a caged bird is still caged, no matter how expensive the bars.

Well, if Benedict wins, we will shortly earn our release. But at what cost?

As I understand things—you must pardon me, future reader, if any of my facts are in error—the Elder King intended to press his son to relinquish the Vexin lands to his youngest brother, Jon-Landon, in return for being named heir presumptive and crowned King of Ceredigion. Of course, he would be king in name but not in power. Both father and son are stubborn men, which needs no further elaboration on my part. Rather than heed his father's wishes, Benedict went to Pree and swore fealty to the King of Occitania, returning the Vexin lands back to their previous loyalty. I assure you that the queen was not in favor of this outcome. She offered to go to the Vexin herself to persuade Benedict to make peace, but her husband refused, believing she would once again betray him. So he lost his greatest ally, the one person who has influence in those lands, because he could not trust or forgive her.

Ransom discovered Benedict's treason during his mission to Pree. He told me that he held a sword to Estian's throat and threatened to dispatch him then and there. You can imagine the Elder King's rage when he learned of Benedict's defection. He promptly sent a force to the Vexin to secure the duchy for himself, and at the same time, Benedict invaded Westmarch. The son's move proved crippling for the father, for the king kept a good deal of his treasury secreted at Tatton Grange, which the young duke quickly claimed for himself. The money has enabled him to hire his own mercenaries to further his cause. Estian claimed that the Elder King violated the terms of the truce and has refused to pay as previously agreed upon, even though Devon argued that he was attacking his own land and not Occitania's.

The fighting stopped during the winter season, although both sides positioned men and supplies to begin a spring offensive. When the Elder King tried to drive Occitanian forces out of Westmarch, Benedict attacked Glosstyr. You can imagine how sick with anger it made me to hear that my father's lands were being ravaged, and there was naught anyone could do about it. This forced the Elder King to strike at his son, who feinted around the army and went farther north, *threatening Duke Wigant's lands. Meanwhile, Occitania captured Southport and defeated Duke Rainor in a consequential battle there. The duke himself is now being held for ransom back in Pree.*

Father and son fought through the year and even into winter before each side retreated to strongholds. The Elder King is staying at Beestone castle. Lord Kinghorn has been defending Kingfountain. And Ransom has been seeking allies on behalf of the king. His own fortunes have fallen along with his master's. His castle in Occitania was forfeit, which leaves him a small manor in Ploemeur and only one castle—Josselin, and that has been threatened multiple times by Benedict's men. At one time he was supposed to marry the heir of Bayree, but that has all been upended by this conflict. I wonder how he feels about it. He comes and goes so frequently. We haven't seen each other since that day the king called Emi in to talk. I don't know whether to hope or give up hope. I still have that little bit of braided leather that reminds me of the one I gave him. Sometimes I hold it to my nose and smell it.

If the Elder King had any sense at all, he would have made Ransom the Duke of Glosstyr by now. But I think the queen understands that he cannot bear to give up power after he has it in his hands.

—Claire de Murrow
The days of war
(like olden times)

CHAPTER EIGHTEEN

The Winds of Change

Snow crunched beneath Dappled's hooves as Ransom and his knights traveled the northern road. The air was crisp with cold and smelled of pine. Birds were charging about, some black-and-white breed trimming bits of bark from the shrubs, and the sky was mottled with clouds. The landscape had a bleak look to it that made him think with longing of the wildlife of Legault. Claire had described it so vividly in her letters he felt like he'd visited the green, lush land himself.

"How far is Dundrennan?" asked Sir Dawson. He'd joined Ransom's mesnie as a knight in training six months earlier and had already earned the rank. Dawson was seventeen, tall and athletic, and had the look of a soldier who'd already seen many conflicts. And indeed he had. They all had.

"If it were spring, we'd be hearing the falls already," answered Ransom, watching the plume of fog come from his lips as he answered. "They slow during the winter and aren't as loud, but we're close."

He turned his neck to glance at the other twenty riders following behind him in tight ranks. Dearley wasn't with them. He'd stayed back at Josselin to protect the castle in case Benedict tried another go at it. Ransom's two wards had gotten even closer during the winter's confinement, while he had traveled under less than pleasant circumstances on errands for his king.

Each of the men had two lances, and while Ransom wasn't expecting a brush with Benedict's knights this far north, it didn't hurt to be cautious. The snow had already melted farther south, but the climate of the North required heavy cloaks and thicker padding beneath their armor.

"How many times have you been there?" Dawson asked.

Ransom shrugged, swiveling back and fixing his gaze on the road. "Once. Duke Wigant couldn't spare any men to help the crown last season—he was too busy pushing back the Atabyrions. But we've lost Lord Rainor, so we need Wigant now. Dundrennan can hold out for a long time if it's attacked."

Once they cleared the rise, the view opened up, and they could see Dundrennan amidst the snowy mountains. The falls next to it seemed like a white tongue of ice, although the sound of falling water could still be heard.

"Now that's a sight," Dawson said in awe.

It was. Smoke from the many hearth fires in the castle added to the layering of clouds, some of which were low enough to smother the highest peaks of the mountains. Birds chirped and fluttered from tree to tree with giddy excitement, as if promising the riders that spring was on its way.

As they rode down the slope on the other side, coming to the town at the base of the mountains, a group of six men rode forward to intercept them. Ransom appreciated that the duke had posted guards to keep watch for incoming troops. It was what he would have done.

The lead horseman had the badge of an eagle, the symbol of Wigant's house. Ransom didn't recognize him, but he slowed and raised a knightly salute.

"You wear the Silver Rose," said the knight to Ransom. "Who are you?"

"I'm Sir Ransom," he replied, gazing at the men, each one in turn. He felt a sudden prickle of unease shoot down his shoulders. His Fountain magic was warning him of something, of some danger that lay ahead.

The knight looked startled. "You've come on a long journey, Sir Ransom. Did you come to see the duke?"

"Yes, with orders from the king," Ransom said. He had the sealed writ in his saddlebag.

"We'll escort you," said the knight, and he turned. The other riders did as well, and they started toward the town.

"How's the food here?" Dawson asked in a low voice, a grin on his mouth.

Although Ransom had been thinking about that himself a few minutes ago, dreaming of roast turkey and bronzed yams, he didn't respond. The strange prickling sensation troubled him still, giving him a sensation of unease. He called ahead to the knights leading them. "How were things in the North this winter?"

"Cold," one of the other knights grunted.

The feeling that something wasn't right increased. The knights ahead exchanged a look. They didn't strike up conversation amongst themselves, nor did they ask how things were at the palace or with the war. A feeling of doom came over Ransom as he stared at the fortress built into the mountainside.

"How is Duke Wigant doing?" he asked.

"Oh . . . the duke is quite well," said the lead knight.

Looking ahead, Ransom saw that the road opened up as it approached the spiked timbers of the wall surrounding the town. The pine trees crowded the road on each side, creating a dense mass where it would be easy to hide troops or cavalry. His stomach twisted into a knot of worry, and his eyes lifted from the town to the castle. He had the distinct feeling of being a child again, standing on a barrel in front of the castle of the Heath with a hangman standing next to him holding a rope.

Ransom held up a hand to alert his men to stop and then eased Dappled to a halt. He glanced at the trees on both sides of the road. Although he couldn't see past them, he felt sure there were soldiers hidden beyond, waiting to flank them.

"What's wrong, Sir Ransom?" Dawson asked in a wary voice, his hand seizing one of his lances. He'd learned to respond to Ransom's instincts.

The other riders kept going before one of them noticed they weren't being followed. He said something in an undertone, and the others stopped. The leader turned his rouncy to the side.

"Oy!" he called. "What's the matter?"

"Who do you serve?" Ransom asked in challenge.

"The Duke of North Cumbria," said the man.

A ripple of distrust went through Ransom's bones. "And who is that?"

The man stared at him in confusion, or perhaps he was feigning it. "You're a nervous one. Come to the castle."

Ransom didn't trust it. "I want a writ of safe conduct first."

He heard some of his own knights inhale sharply at the request. One asked for safe conduct from an enemy, not an ally. The implication was that Ransom didn't trust the king's liegeman in the North.

The lead knight from Dundrennan snorted. "You are daft, man. You want to linger in the cold while I fetch one? So be it."

"Thank you. We'll come no farther without one."

The riders continued on to town, and as Ransom watched them go, he wondered if he was being overcautious.

Dawson looked both ways through the woods. "Do you think Duke Benedict is waiting for us?" he asked worriedly.

"I don't know," Ransom said, "but I sense something's wrong. Dismount. Give the horses a rest and some provender. It could be nothing."

"I don't believe that," Dawson said, shaking his head. "But we will do as you ask, my lord."

They all dismounted and began to care for their horses. Ransom kept looking back at the town and peering into the woods. The distrustful feeling began to fade, and he worried he had misunderstood the Fountain's promptings.

"They're coming back," Dawson said urgently.

Ransom mounted again. The cold had settled in his hands and feet after the brief wait, but he moved fast in spite of it. He gazed at the town, and his stomach dropped when he saw the numbers coming through the wooden gate. Five turned to ten, and then twenty, and then fifty or more. One carried a battle flag with the Eagle standard on it.

"They don't look friendly," said one of the other knights.

"Ride," Ransom ordered, turning his destrier around. He looked at Dawson. "Get to Blackpool as fast as you can and send word to the king that there is treason here. You go ahead of us."

"I want to fight," Dawson said, his eyes fierce.

The young man reminded Ransom of himself, but if they fought here, now, they'd lose. They at least needed to bring the fight somewhere they'd have an advantage. "Obey me, Dawson, or you have no place in my mesnie."

Dawson gritted his teeth in frustration, but he nodded and spurred his horse ahead of the others. Ransom and the knights followed him, charging back up the slope the way they'd come. He was grateful they'd stopped, even more so they'd given their steeds a needed rest and some food. Dappled grunted with the mounting tension as the noise of the advancing knights grew louder.

They made it to the top of the hill without being overrun. Ransom saw Dawson charging down the other side at breakneck speed, but

Ransom reined in and turned. The other knights followed suit. They wouldn't all make it to Blackpool.

"What shall we do, Sir Ransom?" asked one of the others with worry in his eyes.

"We're outnumbered," Ransom said. "Their horses are fresher. But right now, we have the high ground. That will help. Let's break some lances, lads."

Ransom took down five knights before both of his lances were destroyed. He charged into the thick of their attackers, swinging his bastard sword overhead as he rushed into the press of men. The power of the Fountain gushed into him, filling him with strength. Shouts of battle surrounded him. He felt blows striking him, but he turned and countered, driving his attackers away. His knights were surrounded, and one by one they started to fall. Each loss filled him with battle rage, which made him relentless in his attack.

His screaming horse bit down on a knight's arm and dragged him off the saddle, where he was promptly crushed beneath a hail of hooves. Two knights charged Ransom at once, and he roared in defiance, spurring his destrier between them and swinging at them both. He used the hilt to pound the helmet of one while the other hacked at his armor viciously, trying to take off his arm holding the reins. The knight he'd bashed in the helmet toppled off his horse, and Ransom swung back, jamming his blade into the other knight's visor.

"*Dex aie!*" Ransom shrieked, reviving the war cry of the Younger King. It was joined by the calls of others in his band. He saw a knight attacking one of his fellows from behind and rode up to the man and stabbed his horse in the rump, which caused the beast to groan and flail, spilling the knight backward off the saddle.

A flash of familiar armor caught Ransom's eyes. Sir James. Ransom couldn't see his face or the white-blond hair, but he recognized the man's posture. A spurt of anger rushed through him as James struck at one of Ransom's knights and killed him. He charged at his old nemesis, but three other knights intervened, blocking him. Ransom fought all three, one of whom held a studded mace he used to hammer relentlessly on Ransom's arm until a counterstroke proved fatal and ended the assault. Ransom saw James turn and face him, saw the look of fear in his eyes beneath the visor.

And then Sir James cried out the order to retreat and started riding back to town. The attack broke, and suddenly knights were fleeing the scene, charging back down the road. Ransom saw writhing, groaning men in snow speckled with mud and blood. He saw eight of his own still on their horses, weapons in hand. Broken lances were strewn everywhere.

Ransom wanted to ride after James and take off his head. The rage of battle pounding in his ears, his chest, he spurred Dappled to charge after him.

Someone else cried *"Dex aie!"* and soon the surviving knights were riding behind him, rushing back down the hill and chasing the larger force as it abandoned the field. Ransom saw James turn his neck and gaze backward and then spur his horse faster. Ransom's thirst for vengeance overpowered him. Dappled responded to his prodding, and they began to gain ground, even though the other horses were fresher.

It was a race to the wooden palisade, and Ransom was determined to win. Even though there were only eight, he felt enough wrath that he could have defeated the entire garrison. But Sir James and his men had fresh horses, and they rode through the gate before Ransom and the others could engage them. He pulled up short, snarling. He wanted to shout insults at James, to demand he come out and face him in single combat. But he knew James wouldn't, not even with his men gaping at him.

"My lord! Crossbows!"

Ransom felt the danger before he saw it. Men were climbing up the ladders to the railing wall behind the palisade.

"Retreat!" Ransom ordered, and they rode away as the bolts launched at them from the walls.

A few bolts landed in the snow ahead of him. One struck his armor from behind, which felt like a blow from a hammer, but it didn't pierce the armor. Soon, he and his knights were out of range of the crossbows, and they worked their way back up the road to the scene of the fight. Some of the wounded knights still lay groaning in pain.

"See if any of ours still live," he said, panting, when they reached the scene.

His knights dismounted and began searching. One of their men had hit his head after falling off his horse, but he was able to ride again, and they helped him back onto his mount.

Another man wearing the badge of the Eagle cowered as Ransom rode up to him.

"Are you a knight?" Ransom demanded. His anger had cooled, but he was still glowering.

"I'm Sir Honald," said the young man.

"Do you yield?" Ransom asked, staring at him.

"Yes," stammered the young knight. "I yield to you, Sir Ransom."

"Who do you serve?"

"Duke James of North Cumbria."

Ransom blinked in surprise. "What happened to his father?"

"He died a fortnight ago," said the young man. "A fever and cough went through the palace. Many died, Sir Ransom."

"Why wasn't word sent at once to Kingfountain?" Ransom demanded. He gazed at the crumpled men littering the road. The vacant eyes staring through the slits in the helmets. They'd been out-numbered, but Ransom's smaller force had won the day. His arm throbbed with pain, but he saw the raven symbol on the scabbard already glowing.

The young man looked fearful. "Because . . . because it was sent to the Vexin instead."

Sir Dalian told us this afternoon that North Cumbria is now supporting Benedict. I could hardly believe it at first, but he said the news came from Ransom, who had gone to Dundrennan on a mission for the king to seek aid from Duke Wigant, only to discover the old duke perished during the winter and Sir James is now lord of the North. Through some intervention of the Aos Sí, Ransom suspected a trap and escaped, bringing a hostage with him to verify the news. I could kiss him, I'm so relieved.

The king has ordered a council of war to be held at the palace in two days. I wish I could attend it. I'm jealous of Lady Deborah in that regard. All the nobles loyal to the Elder King are commanded to attend on pain of forfeiting their land and titles. It is a meeting where he will ask the council to prove their loyalty. If he asks for hostages to ensure that loyalty, then I fear we are about to tumble back into the abyss.

—Claire de Murrow
Kingfountain Palace
Winter's end

CHAPTER NINETEEN

The Call of Loyalty

Ransom looked over at his battered suit of armor hanging from the rack in his room. The palace blacksmith had work to do on it, and quickly, for Ransom knew he would be sent on another mission soon. The remains of some poached eggs, bread, and a half-eaten trout were all that remained of his morning meal.

Dawson entered the room, holding a sealed scroll.

Ransom took a quick swallow from his chalice and nodded to the letter. "What is that?"

"A message from Dearley. It just arrived from Josselin."

Unopened messages were a cause of anxiety for Ransom these days. Wherever he was in the realm, trouble had a way of finding him through pen and parchment. He waved Dawson to hand it to him and quickly broke the seal. The knight lingered, his brow furrowing with worry.

> My Lord,
> Some of the local shepherds said they noticed knights riding through a grain field at Ashton. I sent scouts to investigate, and they, too, saw the riders. They may have only been foraging, but I'm concerned Duke Benedict has his eyes on Josselin again, as we last

spotted his knights over a fortnight ago. I've increased the watch, and the townsfolk are under orders to flee to the castle quickly. We have enough stores, but I'm worried the duke may be coming in person this time. That he's trying to draw you here so you will leave the king unprotected. We will hold out as long as needed, Sir Ransom. Elodie is concerned, but I think this old castle can withstand the attack. I will send further messages as required. Your presence here is greatly missed.

Your servant,
John Dearley

"Were they attacked?" Dawson asked worriedly.

"No, but some knights were spotted in a farmer's field."

"Scouts for Duke Benedict?"

"Likely. Dearley will let us know if more are seen. That castle is strong and protected by a river. It wouldn't be an easy target."

Dawson began pacing, his worry evident on his face. "What can I do while you are at the king's council? I wish I could go with you."

"Go to the training yard. I know you're upset you missed the fighting outside Dundrennan, but you will get your turn again very soon."

"I will do that, my lord. Thank you."

Ransom donned his sword belt, pausing to rub the raven sigil on the scabbard, and left the room.

When he arrived at the council room in the great hall, it was noticeably quiet. A few chairs were empty. Duke Wigant's chair was the newest vacancy. Duke Rainor's had been empty since his capture. Benedict's seat was empty, as it had been since his rebellion, and Goff's sat vacant beside it. That caused a sickening feeling of dread in Ransom's stomach. While Goff's lands bordered the conflicted grounds, he could have easily taken a ship from Ploemeur and been the first to arrive. Had he joined his brother in rebellion? Were they now fighting two of the king's sons?

Duke Ashel sat next to one of the empty spaces, scowling, stroking his peppered beard as he gazed at the floor. Lady Deborah was also present, her expression tight with concern, and Sir Iain sat fidgeting in his chair. Lord Kinghorn raised his eyes as Ransom approached the gathering and took the seat next to him. Simon's brow was furrowed as he read a piece of correspondence. The king had not yet arrived.

Lord Kinghorn leaned over to him. "How is my cousin, Lady Sibyl? Have you heard from your mother recently?"

"I have," Ransom answered. "My brother is joining the knights of Heath to support the king's forces at Beestone castle."

"How many have remained behind to guard the Heath?"

"I don't know, but Mother isn't a fool. She'll defend the castle."

Lord Kinghorn smiled knowingly. "You're right about that." The smile slipped as he surveyed the room. "Too many empty chairs," he murmured.

They waited a long time for the king, who was normally very punctual. When he finally arrived, he came with Jon-Landon, his arm draped around his youngest son's shoulder. Jon-Landon wore a dark green tunic that was nearly black, and his dark hair looked tousled, as if he'd just been in bed. The young man roved his gaze around the assembly as he entered, giving off a feeling of discomfort.

"Where do I sit, Father?" Jon-Landon asked when they reached the other members of the council.

"Sit there," the Elder King said, gesturing.

"That's Benedict's seat," said Jon-Landon with a frown.

"And that is why you will sit there," the king said.

The prince went and slumped into the chair. Duke Ashel shook his head subtly, his nostrils flaring. The youngest Argentine son had a reputation for being surly and more interested in acquiring power and wealth than in learning how to use either.

Dressed in his sable cloak with wolfskin trim, the king strode to the center of the council. Ransom saw the agitation in his eyes, in his clenched fists. He paraded in front of them all, going from person to person as if passing judgment on an unspoken crime.

"Another one of my sons is missing," said the king after his circuit around the chairs was complete. He stepped up onto the dais and lowered himself onto his throne, leaning forward and projecting his anger.

"Is he delayed?" asked Lady Deborah.

The king shook his head no. "The herald I sent to Ploemeur just returned. Goff wasn't at Ploemeur. He never got the summons."

Ransom looked down at the floor. He could hear the pain in Devon's voice.

"So I brought another son. My *only* loyal son. He will be part of the king's council from now on."

Ransom glanced at the prince, who looked thoroughly ill at ease. Jon-Landon was nearly the same age as Dawson, but he suspected Dawson would have been a better choice to sit in the chair.

The king raised his hands and shrugged. "I must assume that Goff has also betrayed me. We've lost Bayree, the Vexin, and now Brythonica. Wigant's brat has also turned on us. Thanks to Sir Ransom," he added, gesturing to him with a pleased look, "he was chased back into the castle like a whipped pup in front of his men. But my scouts have already confirmed that Sir James is not lingering in the frozen North. His army has left the gates."

"Any word on the Duke of Vexin's movements?" Lord Kinghorn asked. "Where did he spend the winter?"

"My spies say he was in Pree," answered the king. "But since half of my treasury was stolen, it's possible they've found someone who'll offer them more coin. Maybe Bennett wants me to *think* he's in Pree. Regardless, we must choose a target and strike. Who here can best think like my son? What will Bennett do next? I have an idea, but I don't want to limit your thinking. Give me your counsel. What must we do to regain all we've lost?"

Sir Iain scratched his chin. "The boy wants to be king. That means he has to come here. Draw your force together and wait for him. Let him stretch his lines. He cannot exert dominion over so much land."

The king nodded in a noncommittal way and looked around the room, seeking other advice.

Lord Kinghorn spoke next. "The duke knows you are unpredictable and has sought to be the same way. He wants to keep us guessing. But his heart is loyal to the Vexin. Make his people suffer, and he'll abandon his pursuits to come to you."

"Interesting," the king said, but showed no emotion.

Lord Ashel snorted. "He won't come. He'll not let emotion rule him. If we attack the Vexin, we leave our lands open for the same treatment. I'm not worried about Sir James. He's a stripling and knows a farthing about war. Did the knight who Ransom captured reveal anything more? Does he know where they were to meet?"

The king glanced at Ransom. "No. He wasn't given that knowledge."

"Perhaps a little pain will help him remember?" Lord Ashel said viciously.

Ransom shook his head no. "My lord," he said, looking at the king. "I received word today from Sir Dearley at Josselin. Some farmers saw knights passing through. He suspects Benedict may attempt to take the castle again."

The king's brow furrowed. "That is good to know. What else? What would you do, Sir Ransom?"

"The herald you sent to Ploemeur. Did he tell you anything else? They truly didn't know where Goff had gone?"

The king gritted his teeth. "What they said and what they knew are two different things. He said they seemed overly nervous, agitated about the summons, as if fearing that their lord was in a place where he ought not to be. I can only assume it was Pree. So what do you say, Ransom? Forget about Goff. What will *Bennett* do?"

Ransom wanted more time to think on it, but the answer that came to his mind was simple. "He will go wherever *you* are, my lord. He wants to beat you in subtlety and beat you in battle."

The king stared at him intently, leaning forward in his throne. "You think he wants to kill me? If that were his aim, surely the poisoner would have carried through Estian's threat long ago."

Ransom shook his head no. "My lord, he'll put you in the tower. He will give the Vexin lands back to his mother. He will strip away members of your council, one by one. Choose your ground. He will come."

The others were all looking at him. He could feel their scrutiny and see it from the corners of his eyes. But he kept his gaze fixed on the king's.

"Lady Deborah?" the king asked, still looking at Ransom.

"There is only one course that has not been suggested. Nor do I recommend it. I think Ransom's counsel is the most prudent. Pick your location. Westmarch, perhaps. You were the duke there, and many of the people are still loyal to you. If you lose to Benedict, demand that you remain as duke. Your son has not made any mistakes so far. Give him time, and he will, and you can step in and exploit them."

As always, she delivered good advice.

The king inclined his head toward Lady Deborah. "What course has not been suggested? Say it."

"I would rather not, my lord."

"Say it, Deborah," the king said icily.

"Abdication. If you fight him and destroy each other, we all perish. We've already lost so many knights. If we keep fighting, we'll be too weak to defeat King Estian when he rides in to claim what's left. Abdicate and give Benedict your strength. Give him what you didn't give the Younger King."

A look of rage and anger trembled on Devon the Elder's face. Ransom could see that the strategy made sense. It would keep Ceredigion whole and turn Estian into a rival. But like Lady Deborah, he knew Devon was incapable of doing what Gervase had done. Even Gervase had only decided on that course after losing everything.

"No," said Lord Ashel angrily. "I'll not hear of it."

Ransom glanced at Jon-Landon, whose gaze had sharpened. Lady Deborah had mentioned a maneuver that would overlook him as the possible heir, and the acid in his gaze was unmistakable.

"Be silent, Ashel," said the king, waving his hand. "That is why I value her input so much. She says what no *man* among you is brave enough to say. You'll notice she didn't suggest this course, merely mentioned it. I can assure you I won't do it, but I need to see all of the choices before I make a move." The only sign that he was overwrought was his red, splotchy cheeks. "Like in Wizr, when you make a move, you cannot undo it."

The door to the audience hall opened, and the king's steward rushed in, his face pale. He hurried up, bent over, and whispered in the king's ear.

Devon straightened, his eyes widening with shock. "Bring him in," he commanded.

Lord Kinghorn steepled his fingers over his mouth and leaned back in his chair. Ransom wondered what had happened, but his suspense was soon lifted as a man entered wearing the livery of Occitania. He was not a knight, just a messenger. His black tunic bore the silver symbols of the fleurs-de-lis. He had doffed his velvet cap, and he came before them and bowed. The gray in his hair showed his age, as did the creases on his cheekbones.

"Well met, herald," said the king. "I used to know your name. You served King Lewis."

"My name is Moquet," said the man in a strong Occitanian accent. "I was chosen because I did, indeed, serve our old king. My lord, I bring evil tidings."

"I know," said Devon. "Or you would not have come. Do you have a message for me?" He opened his palm.

The herald shook his head no. "These words are from King Estian himself, from his lips to my ears to yours. It grieves me, truly, to bear such evil tidings. Your son Duke Goff of Brythonica died in Chessy two days ago in an accident. He fell from his horse while hunting a white elk and was . . . he was trampled, my lord."

A sickening feeling shot through Ransom's heart. The man looked utterly convinced he was speaking the truth. There was no lie in his eyes, and the grief with which he delivered the news seemed genuine. But Ransom couldn't accept it was an accident.

"My king was so overcome with grief," said the herald, "that he wept openly before the people. I have never seen him so sorrowful, my lord. Truly. It was an accident. I swear it on the Lady of the Fountain."

Ransom still didn't believe it. He shifted his eyes to the king, who looked dumbstruck. Devon the Elder's hands gripped the armrests of the chair, his knuckles white as bone.

The king found his voice at last. "What . . . pray tell me . . . was he doing in *Chessy* in the first place?"

"The p-prince . . . my king," stammered Moquet, "had called for a tournament to welcome the spring. Your son Benedict invited his brother to the tournament. And so he came."

Ransom glanced at Lady Deborah. Her expression suggested they were thinking along the same lines. Had Benedict caused his own brother's death, to remove another obstacle to him taking the throne?

Or was this Estian's ploy?

This bondage presses on me like an ache that will never heal. Emi and I had a long talk this morning. She sees my souring mood, the tears I try to hide. I abhor everything about this tower except my friendship with her. When I think of Atha Kleah, I cannot help but grieve that I may never see it again. Or Connaught or the barrow mounds. What if I never hear the lilting tongue of my true people from any mouth but my own? What if I am cursed to stay here until the end of time? Emi says I should not stay out of loyalty to her. I hold the key to my own prison. All I need do is agree to marry. I told her that my heart belongs to one man, and until he drowns in the Deep Fathoms, it is where it will belong.

I cannot tell Ransom this, for we agreed at the beginning that we would only write as friends and share nothing of our feelings. Feelings that, for me, grow stronger with every letter. He reveals only what he can about the war and a little about himself. I tell him about Legault and the Aos Sí, and what little stories I can of my long, tedious days. And I wait. And wait. And wait.

—Claire de Murrow
Cursed Tower, Kingfountain

CHAPTER TWENTY

The Test of the Heart

The news struck the king like a lance. He slumped down on his throne, head in his hands, and that was enough to dismiss the members of the council. Ransom wandered the palace aimlessly, feeling wretched at the news, convinced that Goff's death was no accident. Had Alix played a role in the deaths of two of Devon's sons? He was grateful he'd told the king about her when he did, but that did not lessen the feeling that he had failed to protect the king's sons. Three heirs to the throne remained: Benedict, Jon-Landon, and now Goff and Constance's son, who was still just a small child. They'd named him Andrew after the legendary king.

He found himself near the part of the palace with the cistern. The place was pleasant, full of memories that were more so, and no guards blocked his path. He went out there and found the little square empty. The solitude was just what he needed. He paced around the hole leading down into the cistern, wondering what the future would hold. The Elder King was now outnumbered in the coming conflict. James was coming with an army from Dundrennan. Benedict had Estian on his side and enough funds to summon an army of mercenaries to boost his forces from the Vexin. No help was expected from Brythonica; Lady Constance would not want to leave herself vulnerable in Brythonica after her husband's death. Duke Rainor had been captured, and Westmarch was mostly overrun. In truth, Benedict had done a much better job of inciting a revolt than his older brother had. He'd learned from his mistakes and turned himself into a formidable enemy.

Ransom clenched his fist and grimaced. It was the king's own fault things had come to this point. His arrogance and pride had led to this rebellion. And certainly Estian had done his part to curdle the milk.

Go to the king.

He recoiled upon hearing the whisper from the Fountain. He did not want to see the grief of Devon at that moment, nor did he imagine he would be of any comfort. What he *wanted* to say would be salt, not a balm. Yet the command had unmistakably come from the Fountain. It had not sprung from his own thoughts.

He'd promised to obey the voice.

Raking his fingers through his hair, he breathed out in a grunt. His stomach twisted with agitation. The very last thing he wished to do was confront the king, but he *would* do it. Even though he had no idea what to say.

Ransom left the courtyard and started walking toward the king's personal chamber. Before reaching it, he encountered Lord Kinghorn, who looked grave as well.

"Are you looking for the king?" he asked.

"Yes. I was just on my way."

Ransom was afraid his kinsman would counsel him to leave the king in peace, but the older man surprised him. "He's out at the dock to be alone. I've wrestled with this feeling that he needs someone right now, and I am not the one. Will you go to him, Marshall?"

He nodded, feeling it was no accident he'd met Lord Kinghorn in the corridor. Ransom turned and hurried away, walking in long strides to the doorway leading to the dock along the river. Sir Harrold and Sir Axien guarded it, which did not come as a surprise, but they both knew Ransom and let him pass without a word.

He found Devon standing on the planks, gazing at the mighty river as it swept toward the falls. Memories poured over him of lifting the funeral boat, of hoisting Devon the Younger into the river. No doubt that was what had drawn the king there, although this time his grief was all inside. The palace of Kingfountain rose behind Ransom as he walked away from its shadow. He gazed over his shoulder at the beautiful stone walls, the intricate towers. When he turned back, he saw the Elder King had also turned, and he stood facing him, arms folded.

The rush of the falls in the distance grew louder as Ransom approached, mingling with the Fountain magic burbling inside of him. The king looked much older than his years, his emotional torment manifesting in physical pain. Thick clouds loomed in the sky, threatening rain. A distant rumble of thunder boomed far away.

"How did you know that you are the one I wanted to see?" the king asked, his voice raw with grief.

Ransom felt sorrow for him. Although he did not always agree with Devon's judgment, the king was a man of deep feeling. "The Fountain told me to come," he answered.

"Did it now?" the king said, eyebrows lifting in surprise. "That is very interesting. I've been thinking about you, Ransom. Isn't that curious?"

A prickle of unease tugged at the knots of dread already in his stomach. "Why did you want to see me?"

"You are loyal to me, are you not? You will not abandon me during my hour of need?"

"I am your sworn man, my lord."

"We are alone, Ransom. I hate such formal little speeches. Are you faithful to me or not?"

He felt his dread increase. "I am."

The king nodded, his brows furrowing. "I will tell you what I was thinking." He turned his head and looked back at the river. "I was never close to Goff. I did not hate him. I just found his manners . . .

tedious. But he was my son, and I did not wish him any ill will. Now his son has been left without a father." He turned and looked at Ransom again, his eyes fierce and determined. "He needs a protector, my boy. I want you to marry Constance and be that boy's guardian until he is old enough to rule the duchy himself. He's an Argentine. I must look after his interests."

It felt wrong from the first utterance of the king's words, and the feeling of wrongness only intensified.

"I cannot," Ransom choked out.

The king's lips went tight with anger. "Are you loyal to me or not, Marshall Barton? I cannot trust Jon-Landon with this task, for I know he will see the boy as a threat. I need someone with Gervase's sentiment, someone who would have compassion on a little boy and spare him! Can I not rely on you, of all people, to do this?"

His reasoning was sound, and yet it still felt wrong. Utterly and completely.

"Of course you may rely on me to protect the boy," Ransom said. "To see him become a noble duke. I will grant you that. But she is not the lady I am supposed to marry. I think the Fountain brought me here to prevent you from making another mistake."

The king recoiled. "Are you so wise in all your vast years?" he said, disappointment and grief warring on his face.

"I don't pretend to be," Ransom said. "None of us can know everything. Do you know who you remind me of right now?"

The king shut his eyes. "Don't say it. Don't you dare compare me to him!"

Ransom didn't have to. The Elder King had already recognized the truth for himself. Devon the Younger had been just as convinced he would come out victorious in the beginning—and in the end he'd been equally unwilling to acknowledge the role he'd played in his own doom.

"I stayed with him to the end," Ransom said. "And I will do the same with you, come what may. But surely you must see that you've made enemies of your sons. It is the duty of a knight to serve his lord. To be faithful to the master of the mesnie. But it is the master's duty to reward obedience. To be generous and praiseworthy."

The king lowered his gaze, as if reluctant to look at him. "Are you not being selfish, my boy? You say this because you want the girl. You want that proud shrew from Legault. Glosstyr has prospered under my control. Its revenues are worth three times now what they were under Lord Archer. And Legault is ripe for the plucking! Isn't it your own ambition that drives you to speak thusly to your king?"

Ransom hadn't known about that, although it didn't surprise him to hear the duchy of Glosstyr had prospered under the king's royal favor. It certainly had nothing to do with his interest in Claire.

"Please do not call her a shrew," Ransom said softly. "She is the lady I love and always will."

The king whirled away from him, and Ransom saw the man's shoulders shaking with emotion. Ransom stood there, fixed to his post, listening as the river rushed by, giving Devon the Elder his privacy. His declaration had brought a feeling of peace in his heart. It was a deep truth, and there was something especially valuable about such truths in a time so rife with deceit.

After a long pause, one with gasps of pain and tears from the king, Devon turned around again, his face haggard.

"You are sincere," the king said. "I once loved as you do now. I cannot help but feel a little jealous as well as worried for you. Marriage isn't easy. The greatest source of pain I experienced in my life, as a child, was witnessing my parents bicker. They hated one another, although they were shrewd allies. I swore . . . it would not happen to me when I wed. And now look at me. I grieve with no source of comfort. My lady love is locked up in that tower. And despite all the pain she's caused me, I cannot bring myself to let her go."

Ransom nodded, listening carefully. Hoping. Waiting.

The Elder King sighed, his shoulders drooping. "She is yours, my boy. And I'll not speak ill of her again. I apologize. Her tenacity is admirable. And so is yours." He sniffed. "You realize this will make you the most powerful lord in Ceredigion? And that your seed will rule Legault as kings or queens in their own right?"

Ransom's shock quickly gave way to a rush of heady joy. He smiled and said, "It's best not to count the harvest before the first rows are even furrowed."

The king chuckled. "Well, you've got what you've wanted. Deborah has been vexing me about this as well. I shall tell Master Hawkes to prepare the rolls, the pedigree, and Sir Simon to give you an accounting of your domains and funds. The investiture cannot happen until the two of you are wed, and that cannot happen until the lass gives her consent. As well I know! And I daresay the people of Glosstyr will revolt if you aren't married at the sanctuary there if she does accept. But we must turn the tide of this situation and bring my son to heel. Peacefully, if possible."

"I agree with all my heart," Ransom said, unable to suppress a grin of delight.

The king nodded slowly. "You've spoken the truth, Ransom. And Lady Deborah has as well. Hard as it is to admit, I have not been innocent in this situation. I do not intend to abdicate my throne, but I think I can offer terms that would be more to Bennett's liking. Let me ponder it more. You, on the other hand, have tidings to bring to the tower."

Ransom's heart thumped with eagerness. "Have you told the queen about Goff's death?"

The Elder King shook his head. "I will send Bryon to impart the news. His son, Sir Dalian, will escort the lady and meet you . . . where?"

Ransom thought a moment and then remembered the part of the garden where he and Claire had gotten stuck in a tree as children. He'd been a little in love with her even then. "The garden with the magnolia trees."

The king gave him a sly look. "Whatever for?"

"There are memories there," Ransom answered, "from long ago."

The sly look faded, replaced by a confident nod. "I keep forgetting that you were both children here. Hostages."

"It wasn't really like that," Ransom said. "The king was a father to me. The hollow crown was a burden to him, as it is to you."

The king gave him a sad smile, but the clouds that had been there earlier were parting now, spilling sunshine down on them. The warmth felt good on Ransom's cheeks.

"Your words are more appreciated than you know," said Devon. "I was too busy basking in my own triumph to see the weight in that old man's heart. You were always a comfort to him. Just as you are a comfort to me in my hour of need. Now go and claim your prize. If she'll have you."

Ransom turned and started to walk away, but he paused midstep and turned around. "Thank you, Devon. Words fail me. *Thank you.*"

And he saw that his simple words meant more to the king than anything else he could have said. Tears filled the Elder King's eyes, a flush of emotion rising on his cheeks. Was this what the old king had craved all along? Some gratitude and appreciation from his family for what he had done for them, provided for them? The truth struck Ransom solidly in the chest. What a strange and curious thing to expect from others without showing or giving it himself. The king clenched a fist, trying to compose himself once again.

Ransom went to him and embraced him. And held him while the king wept the tears of a grieving father.

A bird flew into the open window this afternoon. Poor creature, it was startled and frantic to get out, but it kept crashing into the closed window on the other side of the room, thinking it was the way to escape. Emi and I tried to guide it out, but it wasn't having it. It was a little comical to watch the wee thing, but it wore itself out until it suddenly went the other way and found freedom. It felt good to laugh again.

—Claire de Murrow, the Bird Keeper
(I wish I had wings also)

CHAPTER
TWENTY-ONE

A Promise Kept

A knot of nerves had wound itself up inside Ransom's chest as he paced the garden lawn, waiting for Claire to arrive. The scene in front of him was lovely—the onset of spring had brought the birds back to Kingfountain, and the trees were covered in green buds—but the feeling in his stomach made it impossible to hold still. He kept clearing his throat, wishing he'd brought a flask of water. Every moment that passed was a painful torture.

What if she says no?

Confusion and eagerness raged inside of him. It was a long walk to the top of the tower and a long walk back down. Should he have met her inside the palace instead?

At the sound of approaching voices, he tensed like a bow string and looked in the direction they came from. Letting out a fierce sigh, he loosened his shoulders and stopped his vicious pacing. Claire's face was turned toward her companion, Sir Dalian, and the sunlight splashed prettily on her hair and her green brocade gown. Her smile was easy, untroubled. And then, as if sensing Ransom's presence, she turned her head and saw him standing by the tree they'd climbed as children.

She stopped instantly, her smile vanishing as the surprise of the moment caught up with her.

"My duty is fulfilled," said Sir Dalian, bowing to her. There was a wistful look in his eyes, one that Ransom didn't fail to see. The familiarity between them showed some degree of intimacy and friendship. The worry in his heart swelled.

"Thank you," Claire said, touching Sir Dalian's arm, but her gaze was fixed on Ransom. As she came toward him, he noticed the sadness in her eyes, the look of gloom that had come over her.

"What are you doing here, Ransom?" she asked him, her voice still rich with a Gaultic accent, although it had faded since their youth.

"I got permission from the king to see you," he answered.

"Of course you did, or I wouldn't be standing here. Why didn't you come to the tower?"

He looked down at the grass and then back at her face. Was that fear in her eyes? His courage began to melt. "Lord Kinghorn was sent to tell Emiloh the news. Her son Goff died in Pree."

Claire's eyes widened in surprise. "That is terrible news!"

Ransom nodded.

"Was he murdered?"

"They say it was not," Ransom said, shrugging. "He fell off his horse and was trampled. I don't know the truth of the matter."

She looked him in the eye. "Was it her? The poisoner you warned us of?"

"Again, I don't know," he said, feeling miserable and inept. At some point he would have to admit to her that he'd almost wed that very woman, something he wasn't proud of, even if she had used her power to sway him. "We only have the information that the herald brought. It's all a mess right now. Sir James . . . I mean, *Lord* James is now ruling Dundrennan. His father died during the winter."

"I heard the news," she said. "I'm grateful that you were uninjured."

If it had upset her to learn her admirer had been implicated in treason, it didn't show. Her kind sentiment helped steady him a little.

Before he could decide what to say next, she closed her eyes and squeezed her hands into fists. "Just tell me the news, Ransom. Your storytelling is driving me barmy with suspense." She opened her eyes again, her lips quivering. "Let me guess. The king wants you to marry Goff's widow. To safeguard his son and heir, the little child."

"He did ask me to do that."

He saw her flinch, the color drain from her face. She stared down at the grass, as if she couldn't bear to look at him. "I see. The duchy of Brythonica. It's . . . it's an important duchy. More significant than Bayree."

"I told him no," Ransom said.

She fell silent, but she still wrung her hands in agitation. Then she slipped one hand into the pocket of her gown. "No?" She looked up at him, her lashes fluttering.

"Well, I said I would defend Brythonica if he wanted me to. But I refused to marry the duchess. There is only one duchess that I *want* to marry."

She blinked quickly. Then an angry look stole across her face, and she stamped her foot. "Stop toying with me, you fool eejit! Tell me now, or I swear I'll . . . I'll strangle you!"

From her pocket, she withdrew a small braided bit of leather with tarnished silver ends. She squeezed it hard, as if she intended to use it to fulfill her threat. He blinked in surprise when he saw it.

"Where did you get that?" he asked, gazing at it fiercely.

"Why?" she demanded. "Tell me what you came to tell me, Ransom."

"I lost the one you gave me," he said, stepping forward, gazing at the very bracelet he had worn. The one she'd given him at Chessy. It had even worn out in the same way.

"I found this one by the cistern well," she said. "Two years ago? It reminded me of the one I gave you. But you were gone . . . in the East Kingdoms . . ." She looked at him in confusion.

He'd lost it going into the well at the oasis. *A gift for a gift.* His knees began to tremble. It was the same one. It had to be. The Fountain had brought it to her. It had intended for them to be together all along, from the very start.

"Are you going to stand there gawping like a fish? Please tell me!" Her voice was desperate with worry.

He was still shocked to see the bracelet in her hand, the one he'd lost, but he forced himself to shake it off. She deserved an answer.

"I asked the king for your hand," he said in a rush, looking into her eyes. "He finally said yes. The king said yes. If you're willing. It is your choice. It's always been your choice. If you've given your heart to someone else, I'll—"

"Please! Be silent before you ruin this," she said, reaching out and touching his chest. She bowed her head and shut her eyes, the sunlight playing on her hair in a way that made his heart ache to touch it.

Then Claire sank to her knees in front of him, shaking her head back and forth. He dropped down to one knee, putting a hand on her shoulder. "I love you, Claire, but am I too late?" he whispered, unable to read her reaction. Was she saying no?

But she lifted her head, and the exquisite joy of her smile reassured his feelings at last. She flung her arms around his neck and kissed him on the mouth. Her lips were so soft, yet so ardent, he felt a thrill down to his feet. And it was a completely different feeling from what he'd experienced with Alix. A deeper pleasure from a deeper connection. This, this was bliss. Wrapping his arms around her, he pulled her even closer. She began sobbing and laughing during the kiss and broke away, her feelings such a tangled mixture they bewildered him.

"Will you have me?" he pleaded.

"Brainless as a badger, but I love you anyway," she said, laughing in disbelief. Her laughter prevailed over the tears, and her smile was the most brilliant thing he'd ever seen. "Of course I'm yours! I've only always been yours." She stroked the edge of his mouth with her forefinger. "Do you think I would have stayed in that tower this long for anyone else? But *you*," she added, giving him a playful shove, "you nearly married the Duchess of Bayree. Nearly broke my heart. No, I'm sure you did break it. I'm addled. That's my problem. I should make you beg." Her smile was a teasing one.

Ransom had never felt so happy as he did in that moment, kneeling in the grass, with her so close he could feel her breath on his face. He tried to take her hands, but she was still holding the bracelet.

"You lost the one I gave you, did you?" she asked suspiciously. Then she started to fasten it to his wrist.

"This is the same one," he said.

"Only the Aos Sí could have arranged that," she said with a smirk. She pressed a kiss to the bracelet, and then she kissed the knuckles of his scarred hands. "Do you know what you have given me, Ransom?" The look of gratitude on her face made his throat thicken with tears. "It means I can go home at last. I can be with my people again. With you! There is so much I want to show you, to share with you. I think my heart is about to burst. Is it possible to die of happiness?"

She interlaced their fingers, and he lifted their joined hands to kiss hers. "It may not be for a while yet," he said. "But I desire to see Legault. I want to reclaim your birthright for you."

She released him, but only so she could dig her fingers into his tunic. "You'll let me *help*, surely? You cannot have all the war to yourself."

Her emphatic words made him smile. Oh, how he adored this fierce Gaultic woman. "I don't think I could stop you. I wouldn't dare try."

And he kissed her again, warmth and contentment filling him to the brim. He couldn't believe they were together, that they would be allowed to stay together. He would do anything for her.

She broke the kiss and leaned her head at an angle, smiling content-edly. "Have you had much practice with kissing, Sir Ransom? I fear I may swoon."

Guilt trickled into him at the thought of Alix. "I'm not like Sir James," he said.

Claire wrinkled her nose. "You are not. You are *my* Ransom. I'm the one who gave you that name, and then everyone stole it from me." She hugged him and pressed her cheek against his chest. "I want it back. I knew you before anyone else did."

He lifted his hand and began stroking her hair. The feeling of it made his chest burn. He could get lost in her hair. He kissed some of the locks.

"You fancy my hair, do you?" she said with a teasing voice. "Everyone else thinks it's a cursed color. I'm afraid you won't think it so special anymore once we're in Connaught."

"It will always be special to me," he said.

"Are you certain you haven't been studying how to flatter me, Ransom? You're doing it very well."

"I'm not trying to flatter you, Claire. I'm too much of an eejit to try."

She pulled away from his chest and gave him a sly look. "How long am I free from the prison? Do I have to go back to the tower soon?"

He ran his finger down her nose. "I don't think you have to go back at all."

He felt her body shudder, and she closed her eyes as if he'd just cast a spell on her. When she opened them again, her smile was so pleased it pained him. "Good," she said. "I'm not done kissing you yet."

Ransom looked at Simon in astonishment. "How much is Glosstyr worth?"

His friend laughed and gripped his shoulder. "Are you deaf? This is why the king hasn't been quick to find another duke; he's been enjoying the benefits himself." He turned to Claire, who sat next to Ransom at a table in the palace kitchens. "My lady, you are the wealthiest heiress in the land. Why you would settle for him is beyond me."

Ransom gave Simon a wounded look, but he knew his friend was jesting.

Claire propped her chin on her palms, her elbows on the table. "I didn't feel very wealthy confined in that tower, Sir Simon." She took one of her arms and hooked it around Ransom's. "And I have a feeling we'll need it in order to bring Legault to obedience. I don't want to ask the king for help as my father did. I think the two of us can do it."

Simon smiled and gave her an approving nod. "I'm glad to hear it, as the king's coffers are decidedly barren. Master Hawkes is writing up the records as we speak. A courier will be sent to Glosstyr to inform the castellan with a writ. Spring is an excellent time for a marriage. Although I'm not sure Duke Benedict will wait for your nuptials before he attacks."

"Has Benedict ever defeated you, my love?" Claire asked Ransom with a bright smile.

The endearment made him giddy inside. "No, and I don't intend to let him win now. I hope the king will be able to broker a peace that will end this conflict."

"As do I," Simon said. He slapped his palms on the table. "I'm glad I found you here. I must get back to the king."

Simon started to rise, but Ransom caught his arm. "Have a room prepared for Claire if you would. She is no longer confined to the tower."

Simon glanced between them and nodded. "I will inform the king of Lady Claire's consent and your wishes. I don't think he will begrudge you anything right now."

After he left, Claire entangled her fingers with Ransom's, and they sat at the table talking until a strange but pleasant smell wafted over.

"What did you ask the undercook to make?"

"It's a surprise. Do you remember Siena, the cook who used to work here when we were children?" She scooted even closer on the bench until their hips touched.

Ransom thought a moment, and the memories began to return. "She was Gaultic. I do remember her."

"This palace has so many dark memories for me now." She glanced up at the rafters, then at the cooks who were cleaning after the evening meal. "I want to cherish as many good ones as I can before we leave this place forever. Remember when we met in Chessy and you gave me that little morsel of penuche?"

"Of course."

"Well, this is something I wanted you to try. Ah, here she comes."

The undercook was carrying a large bread paddle with four slices of bread on it. It looked almost burnt, and the sight of it made Ransom wrinkle his nose, but the smell was intriguing and sweet.

"What is this?" he asked as the cook set the paddle down on the table before him.

"Just try it," Claire said. She took one of the four pieces. When she bit into it, there was a nice crunch, and she smiled in enjoyment.

Ransom took one of the pieces and smelled it first. The spice was slightly familiar, although he'd never tasted it before. He thought it might be something he'd encountered in the oasis. The morsel was still steaming, but he took a cautious bite and then smiled as the sugar melted on his tongue, leaving him with the flavor of the spice.

"It tastes a little like penuche," he said with a grin.

Claire grinned and nodded. "I thought so too, which is why I wanted you to try it. It's a delicacy in the Vexin, one that Emi is fond of. They call it *qinnamon torrere*."

"I've never heard of it," Ransom said, taking another delicious bite. The bread was soft, but the topping was thin, crispy, and sweet.

"Qinnamon is a rare bark from a tree in the East Kingdoms. Genevese merchants transport it, and it's very expensive to buy. The sugar is also from the East Kingdoms. Not from beets but from a different plant that only grows over there. The cook puts some butter on the bread to help it stick, and it bubbles and hardens in the oven."

"If my lady loves it, then my lady shall have it whenever she desires," said Ransom with a smile. "A duchess can afford such a delicacy."

She flashed a smile. "I didn't want to tell you first that you were eating *bark*. Well, bark that is ground in a pestle until it's powder."

He looked at her face, and it pleased him to think that he'd be looking at it for the rest of his life. Her smile was warm, but then she looked over her shoulder, and her eyes crinkled with worry.

Lord Kinghorn had entered the kitchen and was walking up to them.

"I think the queen could use some comfort this evening," he said to Claire.

She nodded. "I imagine so. I'll go to her."

Lord Kinghorn shifted his attention to Ransom. "The king would speak to you. Another messenger just arrived." He pitched his voice lower. "Benedict just arrived at Beestone castle. It surrendered to him without a fight."

The sweet taste in Ransom's mouth turned sour. He glanced at Claire and saw her countenance had changed with the news.

Without speaking, they understood each other. If Benedict won the hollow crown and defeated his father, what would become of their future together?

◊

My hand trembles as I write this. I don't think my heart can hold so much happiness without bursting. Sir Dalian brought me from the tower on the king's orders and took me to one of the palace gardens. Ransom was waiting for me. I didn't know how to interpret his mood. He was flustered and uneasy, and I dreaded the worst. By some miracle of the Aos Sí, he has freed me from this prison. He is to be mine, and I am to be his. The news about Goff is dark indeed, but I can't help but feel joyous about the future.

Sir Simon gave us a reckoning of my father's estates and lands. Legault is an unruly mess, but when word reaches Atha Kleah about the change of events, I am convinced many of the nobles will flock to me and my future husband. If only this disorder with Duke Benedict can be resolved quickly. I do not want this war to continue forever. I do not want anything to ruin our future together.

I love thee, Ransom Barton. I say it freely and want to shout it from the window. This tower will be my prison no longer, although my joy cannot be complete because I know it will remain Emi's cage.

—*Claire de Murrow, Queen Again at Last*

◊

CHAPTER
TWENTY-TWO

High Commission

Beestone castle had its share of ghosts, but Ransom was determined to face them. He had received a high commission from the king to broker peace with his wayward son. Now that Ransom had been named the future duke of Glosstyr, he had plenty of motivation to see the assignment accomplished successfully. But he knew it would not be easy, particularly since Benedict was on the verge of winning the war.

He rode with an entourage of fifty knights, each man wearing full armor and carrying lances at the ready. His brother, Marcus, accompanied him on the journey, having obeyed the king's summons to bring ten knights to Kingfountain for duty. It was the first time the two brothers had served together, although Ransom had the command. Scouts had been sent ahead to preview the ground and warn of possible ambushes on the road.

Ransom was anxious to get back to Claire. Her good-bye kiss still lingered on his lips. At the pace they set, there wasn't much opportunity to talk to his brother, but it had interested him to see that Sir Kace was one of the knights in his brother's retinue.

When they arrived at the outskirts of the village at dusk, the scouts they'd sent ahead were waiting for them. Dawson led the group, and he approached Ransom on horseback as they came closer. Torches shone from the walls of the castle, showing it was prepared for an assault.

"What have you learned?" Ransom asked Dawson.

"Duke Benedict's men wear the badge of the Lion, and they're roaming about the village," said Dawson. "The first one I met asked if we'd come to swear fealty to him as the rightful king of Ceredigion." Dawson grinned. "I asked if Benedict was up at the castle, and the man said yes. I didn't feel it was my duty to speak on your behalf. Nor did I tell him whom I served. We're clearly not the first to have come."

Marcus turned in his saddle to face Ransom. "It seems Benedict is confident there will be more defectors from his father."

"I agree," Ransom said. He gazed at the castle atop the small rocky hill. Few people knew, but there was a secret way into the keep. He'd discovered it himself after the Younger King had perished by poison, for Alix and Sir Robert had used that passageway to escape. Did Benedict know of it? Ransom was tempted to find out, but it would be dangerous to enter the palace that way without having an exit planned.

He turned to his brother. "I want you to ride ahead and seek a meeting with the prince. Tell him that I've come to negotiate with authority from the king. He can meet us here, or I will come to him if he provides a writ of safe conduct."

He had stopped in a strategic spot outside town—there was an open meadow on each side of the road, which would make it difficult for anyone to sneak up on them.

Marcus nodded. "Would you like me to bring you some supper as well?" he asked with a joking smile.

"We'll fend for ourselves in the village. I hope he will meet with me tonight."

"So do I," said Marcus. "I'd rather sleep on the floor in the castle than in that meadow yonder." He clicked his tongue and gave his horse a nudge with the spurs.

Ransom watched him depart. The shadows thickened, and the night crickets began their song. "Dawson . . . Kace. See if you can get us some food."

They obeyed, and Ransom stayed atop Dappled, who snorted for some fodder. He stroked the beast's neck and offered a soothing murmur while the other knights shifted restlessly. Stars began to appear in the sky, one by one, and the castle continued to shine like a beacon on its hill. Occasional bursts of noisy laughter came from the village.

In due time, Dawson and Kace returned with some sausages, bread, and a tankard of ale for them all to share. Not long after the meal was done, Marcus rode back to them bearing a scroll.

"Benedict is glad you came," he announced as he rode closer, tapping the scroll to his forehead. "He's anxious to speak with you and bids you come up to the castle. He offered the safe conduct without being asked for it." A curious smile came on his face. "I think he's going to try and woo you, Brother."

"Maybe he'll offer me the duchy of Glosstyr," Ransom said with a grin.

Some of the knights chuckled around him.

"I serve the king," Ransom said forcefully. The words, the sentiment behind them, sent a surge of Fountain magic through him.

"Shall we go with you?" his brother asked.

Ransom imagined that the castle was already full of Benedict's men and possibly some Occitanian troops. "Wait until I call for you," he said. "I'll go on alone."

"I should come as your guard, Master," said Dawson with a bit of impetuousness.

A prickle of unease went through Ransom's heart. He shook his head no. "I'll send for you if all is well. The watchword is . . ." He thought for a moment. "Gemmell."

"That was your horse, wasn't it?" Marcus said, his brow furrowing.

"Aye, he was a gift from King Gervase," Ransom said. "If all is clear, I'll send someone down to bring you up. I don't know how long it will take, so be ready and keep watch. Don't let your guard down, Marcus."

"I won't, Brother. These are our fellow knights, not our enemies. I don't think Benedict would dishonor himself."

"I hope not," Ransom said, but he'd learned to listen to his instincts, and he couldn't shake the uneasy feeling he'd had moments before.

With a nudge from his thighs, he directed Dappled to canter down the road toward the village. As he approached the town, he saw there were knights in abundance, but none wore full armor, only hauberks and tunics with the Lion badge. If Ransom had brought an army, he would have caught them by surprise. His cloak bore the badge of the Silver Rose, and many of the men looked at him with open curiosity, but none seemed resentful. No one confronted or barred the way. A few even called to him by name.

As he started up the road to the top of the rocky bluff, he sensed Lady Alix's presence in the distance, just like when he'd come here to sit at Devon the Younger's deathbed. He gritted his teeth. He hadn't expected her to be there. Did this mean that Benedict's life was in danger? Or his own?

The warning feeling in his heart didn't compel any action. He didn't feel he should turn around and leave, nor did he feel it was safe to go on. It was an unpleasant sensation, one that filled him with dread. He had no wish to face Alix, but he had a mission to fulfill . . . and he supposed she did as well. Had she known of his travel through the Wizr board and come to intercept him? Or had she already been here with Benedict?

There was no way of knowing.

The castle gates stood open, guarded by ten knights with spears.

"Welcome, Sir Ransom," greeted the captain. "The duke is waiting for you in the solar."

Ransom nodded to the fellow and rode into the courtyard. He passed the well that was connected to the secret passageway, but he did not sense Lady Alix in it. No, the feeling of her came from within the castle.

When he reached the main door, he dismounted, and a squire came to attend to his horse. He took in the celebratory atmosphere within the courtyard. There were bedrolls strewn about, and men were laughing and toasting one another with cups. With one hand gripping the pommel of his sword, pressing the scabbard against his metal-shod hip, Ransom marched to the door, which was opened as he reached it. He knew the way but was met by a servant.

"This way, please," said the man.

As Ransom followed him, he sensed he was getting closer to Alix as well. He licked his lips, his heart shuddering with dread at the upcoming meeting. When he reached the solar, the servant who'd guided him there opened the doors. Benedict was moving in a restless manner that reminded Ransom of his father, and he had a tangle of grapes in his hand. He wore a hauberk beneath a dirty tunic stained with faded blood. His long hair was a bit wild, and his beard showed his defiance of the Occitanian preference for clean-shaven men.

Lady Alix stood off to one side, no cloak or hood. He recognized her golden dress and felt a strange surge of protectiveness. She still wore the bracelet of pearls around her wrist. Her expression was hard and distrustful.

"Ah, welcome to Beestone, Ransom!" Benedict said, setting down the grapes. He approached and gave a knightly salute. "I'm glad you are here."

"It's good to see you again," Ransom answered, still suspicious. Lady Alix offered no greeting. Her beauty made the back of his neck itch. Memories of kissing her began to roil inside his mind.

"You've met Lady Alix already," said Benedict. "She is my body-guard on this expedition. A good conversationalist, expert at stratagems and the like. You were foolish not to wed her yourself."

Ransom stared at Benedict in disbelief.

"What? You think I did? No, she's my half sister—don't be absurd. I'm just saying you were foolish not to. I shall be a king and must make a strategic alliance suitable for such a rank. Lady Alix has been advising me on the possibilities."

"Come back with me to Kingfountain," Ransom said, wanting to shift the discussion to the business of his mission. "End this senseless conflict. You will rule half the realm in your own right. And I believe that we can, if you return with me, persuade your father to release your mother. Show him you're willing to discuss terms. He's ready to hear you."

Benedict snorted and smiled pleasantly, but the look in his eyes indicated he took offense. Nor did he seem at all interested in the proposal. "I do intend to go to the palace," he said. "*After* I've won."

A feeling of inevitability struck Ransom in his chest. He saw Benedict's confidence, his swagger, and the determination in his eyes. But there was something more. It was the look of a man who'd had too much to drink. A man under Alix's influence.

"Bennett," Ransom said, coming closer. "This conflict with your father is unnecessary. Name your terms. I think you will find him agreeable to them."

Benedict chuckled. "I know him far better than you. He doesn't want to lose. Yet he is going to." His eyes became deadly serious. "I *want* to defeat him."

"It will cost lives. There will be bloodshed. It will weaken us against our true enemy."

"Our true enemy? There you go, spluttering the same words that Father uses. Estian's father had Devon killed, but the son shouldn't be made to suffer for his crime. We have provoked this conflict, and I seek to end it! And since when are you squeamish about bloodshed? If I recall, you severed the arm of the duchess's champion in Brythonica."

Ransom bowed his head, trying to master his feelings, trying to understand the confusion rattling inside his skull. There was some power at work. Something related to Lady Alix's mysterious abilities.

"I'm not afraid to fight you," Ransom said. "And neither is your father. But he is prepared to give you a crown to wear. Half of the kingdom, Bennett—now. You don't have to take the whole."

"I don't believe in his promises," Benedict shot back. "Not anymore. He's losing, and he knows it. Nothing will entice me to back down. I have a superior force, a better strategy, and every likelihood of winning. I am not my brother Devon."

Ransom sensed the situation was hopeless. "Your brother had many advantages too, yet he failed twice. No battle is ever certain. Much can happen on the field."

"I know," said Benedict. "I've been training all my life to defeat you, Sir Ransom. I'm ready to prove it. By now you know of my alliance with Sir James, the new duke of the North. Earlier today, I sent out two hundred letters rallying the people of Ceredigion to my side. Two hundred letters, Ransom. I wrote each of them myself. I made promises to some and threats to others. Men are motivated by their hearts. By ambition and by fear. My father has taught me well, and it shouldn't surprise him that I've learned from him." Benedict shook his head. "But I have none of his bitterness against Occitania. If he does not want this war, then have him come to Beestone on his knees and beg my pardon. I'm sure he'll find the tower to be suitably comfortable."

Ransom tried not to let his anguish show. "There is no need to humiliate him. It is beneath you."

The jab at Benedict's honor stung, and it showed. He turned around, his face muscles twitching with raw emotion. He walked back to the table against the wall and took a cup and drank from it. He swallowed and then steadied himself. Gone was the rage and bluster. The man's mastery of himself impressed Ransom. Alix did not interfere at all. But that did not mean her presence wasn't influencing the scene.

"Father always criticized us if we were too emotional," Benedict said. "Yet he's always had the biggest outbursts of any of us. I've made up my mind, Ransom. He will yield and face imprisonment, or he will fall in battle. War is the ultimate test of manhood. Such was his example to me. And by his example shall he fall. The letters are sent, Ransom. I cannot unsend them."

"You will break his heart," Ransom said.

The duke shrugged and took another sip. "Just as he broke Mother's? I do this for her as much as for myself. He promises to release her, but when? He'd haggle and delay, all the while preparing to double-cross me. She deserves better than that. She deserves her freedom now. I've learned much about her in her homeland." He looked at Lady Alix and smiled. "And of what she has been through in her life."

"You trust Estian at your peril."

"I have more reason to trust him than I do my father," Benedict said with a frown. "I would welcome you to my side, Ransom. If you forsook him, it would end. Everyone, even Lord Kinghorn, would follow your example. But you won't. Alix told me you won't, and she is never wrong."

Ransom looked at her, saw the cold defiance on her face.

"I'm sorry," he said to her.

She didn't respond with words, but her disdain was evident.

He turned his gaze back to Benedict. "And I'm sorry for your brother's death. What a terrible . . . accident." He let doubt thicken his voice.

Benedict scowled but didn't rise to take the bait. "You are welcome to spend the night in Beestone, but I have a feeling you're anxious to return to my father. Like a faithful hound."

It smarted, but Ransom ignored it. "She does not serve you," he said, pointing to Alix. "She may be your sister, but she killed your brother."

"I know this already," Benedict said with exasperation. "She only did it at Lewis's command. He's responsible for what happened. He's dead, and Devon too, and that cannot be cured. I could have asked Estian to have Father poisoned. But I don't want to win the throne that way. I don't *need* her skills to defeat him." His brows contracted. "You've chosen your side. I've chosen mine. We shall see who prevails and who can fulfill the promises they've made."

Those words haunted Ransom. He took the prince to mean that he would not fulfill the Elder King's promises.

"I've delivered my message," Ransom said.

"You have. Your duty is fulfilled. Farewell, Ransom. Until we meet again with steel and helm. This time it will not be on the tournament grounds or the training yard."

Ransom eyed the prince and pushed his Fountain magic out against him, trying to tell if he had weaknesses. Benedict looked at him, unaware of what was happening, and Ransom pried into his soul. He was strong and fit, an able warrior, but he lacked Ransom's ability, his prowess. And he didn't have a scabbard that would prevent him from bleeding to death. In a contest, it was only a matter of time. Ransom would win, and he knew it.

"I'll be sorry on that day, Bennett," he answered. "But I will fight for the king."

"I know," Benedict said. Then he gave him a nod of dismissal.

Ransom turned and left the solar, his heart discouraged at his failure to reconcile father and son. Partway down the passage, he sensed Alix coming up behind him. He turned to face her, in part to let her know that he was aware of her presence.

She didn't attempt to hide her approach. Her eyes burned with anger, and she didn't stop until she was close enough to touch him.

"I gave you a chance to stop this madness," she said softly, "but you refused me. Remember that. What happens next is your fault."

He looked at her and felt an overwhelming sense of confusion. His love of Claire shrank in Alix's presence, but his convictions did not.

"What is your power truly?" he asked her. "You said it was one thing, but I don't believe you. I sense you using it even now."

A smirk twisted her mouth. "We all have our secrets, Ransom. Even you."

He heard the sound of boots behind him in the corridor and felt a throb of danger. She looked over his shoulder, which made him copy her.

Sir Robert Tregoss was the one approaching.

Ransom's hand dropped to his sword.

He didn't realize his mistake until Alix grabbed his elbow. He felt a little sting. A needle.

He turned back to look at her in disbelief.

"It's too late," she said with a cunning smile. "I've already won."

In moments, he felt his legs turn to jelly. A fog engulfed his mind. Sir Robert caught him beneath the arms. Lady Alix still had not released her grip.

"Take him to Kerjean," she said to Sir Robert. "To the dungeon." She squeezed his arm harder, driving the needle in deeper. "I'll come after this is done."

I cannot sleep tonight. The moon is bright with a tinge of pink. I should be happy. I've felt little else of late, but tonight my fears mix with the shadows. I'm worried about Ransom. His mission should be a simple one. Why should it distress me so? I know Benedict is an eejit, but he would do nothing more than reject an overture of peace. He wouldn't imprison Ransom. Perhaps what leads me to grab my quill and write in the darkest part of the night is that while I've always worried about Ransom, now he is my *Ransom. That makes his danger mine too. I know he would have asked for a writ of safe conduct to see Benedict. Yet still, this nagging feeling in my heart warns me that all is not well. What can I do from so far away?*

—Claire de Murrow
Still of the night
(and a pleading heart)

CHAPTER
TWENTY-THREE

Hostage Again

The poison wore off, bringing him back to his senses slowly. Ransom felt the swaying of a horse beneath him, the dizzying sensation of riding. His head lolled with the motion, and his body would have slid off if his legs hadn't been bound. Darkness blinded him until he looked up and saw the teeming stars swirling overhead.

Panic thrummed inside his body. He tried to move his hands, but they were bound at the wrists, the rope so tight his fingers stung with pricks of pain. He was riding among other men. Although he could barely see them in the dark, he could hear their horses.

And then the moon rose on the horizon, dispelling the gloom and making the stars bow in reverence to its superior light. He twisted his neck, looking from left to right. There were about a dozen riders, all wearing armor and carrying lances. He was mounted on a dark rouncy, and the knight in front of him held the guide rope in one hand. A horse would always follow the promptings of the man who held his guide rope rather than the one on his back—a trick Ransom had learned during his tournament days. He thought about jumping off, but the knots securing him to the saddle would prevent it. He was a prisoner again.

Memories of those dark months he'd spent with DeVaux and his men came rushing back, filling him with doubt and dread. They were bringing him to Kerjean. He remembered Alix saying so before she'd rendered him helpless with her poison. He had no notion of how far they'd traveled, but they were not on a road. Grass whisked against the horses' withers, and the muted thud of hooves on earth was different from the sound on a well-trodden road.

As the moon rose, he stared at it, feeling desperate to escape. Thoughts of Claire warred with worries about the king. What would Dawson and Marcus and the other knights waiting for him think when he didn't come back? Would they assume, as he would, that he was being held prisoner in Beestone? If so, there was nothing they could do but ride back to Kingfountain and warn the Elder King.

Ransom tried to break the knots at his wrists, but the ropes groaned with his effort. They loosened slightly, but the pain in his hands only grew worse. He tried again and again, wrestling with the knots.

"He's awake!" one of the knights shouted in Occitanian.

Ransom turned and saw one of his escorts staring at him. The moonlight showed a clean-shaven face. A knight of Occitania, although he wore no badge or symbol to declare himself as such.

"We're not stopping until dawn," called back one of the other riders. It was Sir Robert Tregoss's voice, and Ransom's hatred for that man made his heart rage.

Judging by the direction in which the moon had risen, Ransom knew they were riding north, or slightly to the northwest. They were heading toward the Vexin lands, and he knew that Bayree lay beyond them. It was a long journey, and the farther they went from Ceredigion, the less hope he had of being rescued or of freeing himself.

Sir Robert was as good as his word. They'd ridden into the dawn, changing course to due west as the sun came up behind them, casting long shadows of them and their horses. The smell of meadow grass began to mix with trees and brush. Ransom recognized the landscape, for they were close to Averanche, which lay directly north of them at the coast. He had trained there with Lord Kinghorn and his knights. It had been taken by Benedict already, so it wasn't the safe haven it had once been.

Sir Robert led them to a wooded area in the rolling hills, and the men finally stopped to rest. Some knights relieved themselves in the woods, while others prepared to feed their horses. Hooves were examined. Ransom sat on his mount, waiting for someone to attend to him, furious at the situation.

Sir Robert uncorked a flask and gulped down something that looked like water. Then he walked up and handed it to Ransom. "Thirsty?"

Ransom took it, even though it was awkward with his bound hands, and tilted his head back to drink. The water tasted leathery and stale, but it soothed his aching throat. He wanted to kick Robert in the face, but his bonds prevented it.

After he'd drunk, he handed the flask back.

"Whatever you are being paid," Ransom said, meeting his eyes, "I can pay you more."

Sir Robert snorted, and a wicked smile stretched his lips. "I know you are rich, Barton. Simon always compared us to you and your skin-flint ways. I don't do this just for the money. There will be a change of power now, and I will rise, while you fall."

"You've been promised much by your king? I'm speaking of Estian, of course, not Benedict."

"I have. And what I've been promised suits me very well. You will rot in Kerjean. No one will even know you are there, wasting away in a poisoner's dungeon."

Ransom felt a surge of blackness in his heart. He wanted to rage at the man, to accuse him of all sorts of infamy, but he recognized that was what Robert wanted. He closed his eyes, thinking of Claire, worrying about her and what would happen if Devon fell. Promises made by dead men—or forgotten men—were useless.

When Ransom opened his eyes, he noticed a bracelet encircling Sir Robert's wrist. It was the leather bracelet that Claire had given him. The urge to kill that man was overpowering. He tried to summon his Fountain magic, to break free of his bonds and exact retribution. But no feeling of trickling water came. The knots were steadfast.

Then Ransom also noticed that his sword and scabbard were gone. His elbow ached with pain from where Alix had pricked him. The wound had not healed because they'd taken away his source of healing.

"Where's my sword?" Ransom demanded.

"I thought it best to keep it out of your reach," Robert answered snidely. "I would have stripped away your armor as well, but we were in a hurry. I'm done talking to you. I want food." Robert turned away with a smug look, but Ransom wasn't finished with him yet.

"I challenge you to single combat," Ransom said. "I may be a prisoner, but I did not yield. Let me fight for my freedom."

Robert turned his head partway and chuckled. "I'm not a fool."

"Three against one, then," Ransom said angrily. "If you do not accept my challenge, you will be branded a knave and shamed for it. Fight me, or let me go."

Sir Robert barked out a laugh. Then he turned all the way around and looked at Ransom incredulously. "I slept with Devon's wife," he said with swagger. "The code of *honor* you speak of means nothing to me. No one truly abides by it . . . only the few . . . the *fools*. What happens at court in Pree is the same as what happens in other courts. Virtus is a lie . . . a trick designed to deceive the childish. Men like you." He spat on the ground and looked at Ransom with eyes that held no remorse. "If I wanted to fight you, I'd do it with you bound, on the ground and helpless. And I'd kill you with your own sword. Those are my terms." He jutted out his chin. "Only she wants you alive. Maybe she wants to make a sort of *pet* out of you. If it were up to me, I would have spilled your blood in that dungeon at Beestone three years ago."

"You're a knave and a coward," Ransom said to him coldly.

Sir Robert shrugged. "I care not what you think of me. Befoul yourself when you need to. I won't trust you without ropes or shackles. And I won't be feeding you until we reach Kerjean. Let your hunger be your penance for worshipping the false goddess of Lady Pride. For claiming to be Fountain-blessed when you are but a mortal man. If you are more than that, prove it. Break free of those bonds, and I'll believe in you."

Please free me, Ransom prayed silently. *I swore I would serve you. Do not let this happen. Give me deliverance from my enemy.*

He strained at the bonds, but he felt as weak as a man. His stomach growled, and his bowels yearned for release.

Sir Robert stared at him mockingly. "I thought so," he said and walked back to his horse.

Ransom couldn't sleep during the day. He sat with his back to a tree, another rope wrapped around his chest. One of the knights scraped a whetstone against his dagger. Two others gambled with small wooden dice. Some slept but most just waited out the day.

Birdsong sounded overhead, and Ransom found himself envying them their freedom. He'd held his water so long everything inside him ached. It was wise just to relieve himself and deal with the stink. But the thought made him so angry he rebelled, determined to hold out.

Despair brooded in his heart. He thought about the cold look Lady Alix had given him while he spoke to Benedict. Surely Claire would pay for his freedom, but the offer would never be accepted. Alix wanted to break him, to seduce his mind and his heart, to crush his spirit until he yielded to her dominion.

What confused him was that the Fountain had not warned him away from the mission. He'd felt nothing but a small prickle of unease. Well, he'd done his duty and ended up in bonds. He doubted Benedict knew, or that he would have taken part in such trickery. That it had happened after Ransom was dismissed indicated this was Estian's plot.

Why had the Fountain forsaken him? Why had it allowed him to stumble into bondage when he should be trying to save his king?

He found himself recalling what he'd been told after the scabbard healed his battle injuries. *The scion of King Andrew will be reborn through an heir of the Argentines. They will try to kill the heir. You are all that stands in the way.*

What did that mean, exactly? Did Estian intend to kill all the Argentines? He was allied with Benedict at the moment, but he could just as easily turn on him. That would leave just Jon-Landon and Goff's son, Andrew.

A prickle of unease shot through Ransom's heart. He'd promised the king that he would look after Goff's son. If he were in bondage, he could not do so. In fact, Alix would be able to mingle among the Argentines without anyone discerning her presence. His heart began to quiver with dread.

He pressed against the ropes that bound his chest, straining with all his might. The knight scouring his blade stopped and looked at Ransom as if he were daft. Then he shook his head and resumed what he was doing. No power flooded into Ransom. No rushing water filled his ears. And still he continued trying. After several more failed attempts, he sagged back against the tree, exhausted and sore. His effort had created a little slack in the rope, and it settled farther down his chest. The knots were all behind the tree, so he had no way of working them loose.

Please help me, he thought in desperation. He didn't want to go back to Kerjean, to be at Alix's mercy. To listen to her honeyed words as she tried to persuade him to change sides. His recollections of his time there made him even more certain Alix's power was not as she had said. There was something about her that twisted a man's heart, and he didn't want to feel his love for Claire wrenched away from him.

Please, he thought in the silent halls of his mind. He yearned to hear an answer, to receive assurance that the fate he dreaded would not be forced on him.

But he heard nothing but his own troubled thoughts. And so he summoned up memories of Claire. The sound of her voice, the color of her hair, her strength and wit. Everything he had been given had been stripped away suddenly. Again. But he had her love and admiration, and that was what mattered most.

◊

It wasn't a groundless worry. Word arrived at the palace that Ransom is being held prisoner at Beestone castle. A writ of safe conduct was granted, only to be violated by that treacherous son of Devon. Word has also come that Duke Ashel has fallen ill. He's sent his eldest son to lead the knights of his duchy, but the father's experience is sorely needed. Other nobles who were ordered to bring forces to Kingfountain have made excuses as to why they cannot come. These are desperate hours. Benedict is coming and brings with him a host of mercenaries as well as Occitanian forces. The king is readying his men and will march westward to meet him. This time, he brings his youngest son with him. If Devon wins, I presume he will name Jon-Landon his heir. After such treason, I do not think he can ever trust Benedict again. I surely never will.

—Claire de Murrow
The end is near
(broken peace)

◊

CHAPTER
TWENTY-FOUR

The Raven Sigil

Ransom's insides throbbed with pain and growled with hunger. He was given water to drink but no sustenance, and he felt himself growing weaker by the hour. They'd rested half a day before Sir Robert had led them out again, and they kept a punishing pace to fulfill the task given them by Lady Alix. Every sunset had heightened his dread. He wasn't tied to the horse any longer, but his wrists were still bound in front of him so he could grip the saddle pommel and not fall off. Each league that went by thickened the anguish in Ransom's soul. They were well past the borders of Westmarch, and he recognized the terrain as they approached the Vexin lands.

He had continued working on his bonds, but he'd only succeeded in bloodying his wrists and adding to his discomfort. His elbow throbbed from the needle that Alix had used to poison him. He stank of sweat and his own filth, but his innards were still twisted into knots that made him miserable. The sun began to sink, which blinded their eyes as they rode into its glare. To the north lay the vast woods that signified the border of Brythonica, but Ploemeur was fifteen leagues away, and they'd passed the road leading to it long ago. He thought of the manor there, which he owned but hadn't visited, a gift from a tournament victory before his journey to the oasis. It felt like part of another life.

His fate now was to go to Kerjean castle in the duchy of Bayree. When he thought of it, he imagined the castle walls were made of bleached bones and not stone. It was like some giant skull waiting to receive him until his own flesh turned to dust.

His horse suddenly slowed, breaking him from his dreamlike reverie. The sun had nearly set, its golden rays knifing through the tree-lined hilltop to the west. He felt a sluggish ripple from his Fountain magic.

"Whoa there," said Sir Robert in a wary voice. He held up his hand to signal a warning and then grabbed one of his lances.

Squinting into the sunset, Ransom saw a row of horses lined up to confront them. Sir Robert's retinue slowed further. The other knights copied their master, and each took up a lance, except for the one holding Ransom's lead rope.

Ransom craned his neck, trying to see through the glare of the setting sun. The knights blocking their way had a single banner with the raven sigil, the symbol of Brythonica. What were these knights doing so far south? Ransom saw that the numbers were even or nearly so. A spark of hope began to quicken in his chest. When he heard the lapping sound of water in his ears, that hope began to flame.

Sir Robert ordered a halt. He twisted in his saddle, giving Ransom a brooding look, and then turned back to those blocking the way. A single rider came forward. Not the one carrying the banner, but a solitary rider enclosed in a shell of iron.

Sir Robert edged his horse forward to meet the man. As they drew near, Ransom saw that the knight in front of them was missing an arm. His right arm ended at the elbow. It was Ransom's sword that had taken his arm, for this could only be Sir Terencourt, the champion of Brythonica.

"What's the meaning of this?" Sir Robert said angrily. "Stand aside."

"You bring armed knights through Brythonica," said Sir Terencourt, his voice familiar. "Are we not entitled to investigate?"

Did Terencourt hold a grudge against Ransom for injuring him in the tournament? He'd said all was forgiven, but was that true? The Fountain magic swirling inside Ransom made him believe that these knights were his allies. "Hoy there, Sir Terencourt!" he shouted.

Sir Robert's horse began to fidget. "Let us pass."

"You may pass," said Sir Terencourt. "But you'll leave your prisoner with us."

Robert let out a curse. "I will not, by the Lady's blood."

Sir Terencourt drew his sword with his left hand and brandished it. "Your prisoner, sir."

Ransom knew this was his only chance to escape. Now that the horse had stopped, he could dismount without breaking his neck. So he did.

One of the knights positioned behind him came up with his lance, aiming the tip at Ransom's chest.

"Don't move!" he barked in command.

Ransom grabbed the lance with one hand and twisted his body, trying to pull the knight off his horse.

"Ready to lose your other arm?" Sir Robert snarled to Sir Terencourt and then jammed his spurs into his horse's flanks.

Chaos exploded in the clearing. The lance was ripped out of Ransom's grip, but he sidestepped as the man's horse went by him, hooking his bonds in the rider's spurs. He was dragged off his feet, and the knight was yanked off his horse. The man dropped his lance as he landed on the ground, groaning in pain. Ransom descended immediately, kneeling on the man's leg and using the spur to saw at the ropes. When the knight tried to rise, he kicked his helmet.

The sounds of battle became louder as the two sides engaged, horses charging at each other, and Ransom paused from his sawing to look up. Sir Terencourt swung his blade at Sir Robert, who had drawn his already.

The ropes frayed and finally spilled away from Ransom's wrists. The knight on the ground swung an arm backward, his elbow coming at Ransom's face. With both hands free, he blocked the elbow and then yanked the man around on his back. He found a dagger sheathed at the knight's waist, and the two wrestled for it for a moment. But Ransom's determination to free himself gave him a surge of strength that ended with the dagger plunging into the knight's neck.

He felt no remorse for killing the man. No, his heart pulsed with the need to do battle, to defeat these men. Some riders were unhorsed in the first round. A Brythonican knight came right at Ransom, but the man swerved his lance to the side as he prepared to turn around for another run at the enemy.

Ransom threw the dagger aside and drew the sword from the dead knight's scabbard. With a new weapon in hand, he felt his energy surge, and the Fountain magic roared inside him. A feeling of danger came from the side as he saw one of Robert's knights charge toward him with a lance aimed at him. Ransom stood his ground, staring at the oncoming warrior, and then flung himself to the side at the last moment, slashing at the man's beast as he went by. The horse screamed in pain, and its forelegs tucked, driving both animal and rider to the ground. Ransom found the weak spot in the knight's armor and stabbed through it, killing the man before he landed.

Another throb of danger. He whirled around, finding another knight bearing down on him, not with a lance but with a sword. He blocked the attack, knowing he was at a disadvantage since he was on foot and lacked a helmet. He feinted to the left and then came around the other side of the horse. He whacked its rump with the flat of his blade, making it buck, which sent its rider backward. The knight held on to the reins, trying to prevent his fall, but Ransom grabbed his arm and pulled while the horse charged forward. The knight collapsed in a heap of metal, choking to breathe through the sudden loss of air, and Ransom finished him off.

He turned, hungry for vengeance, and saw Sir Robert stab Sir Terencourt through the ribs, at the seam of his armor. His missing arm made it all too easy. Ransom saw the Raven scabbard and his own sword fastened to Sir Robert's destrier. He ran forward, jumping over a fallen knight to get closer.

Sir Terencourt tilted in his saddle, and he dropped his sword to grab the saddle horn to keep upright. He stayed in his seat, but Sir Robert slammed his beast into him, and Ransom heard the man's leg get crushed. Robert hacked at Terencourt again, his blows deflected by the armor, but the other man lacked a weapon, and it looked like he would prevail.

Ransom reached them. Dropping the sword he'd claimed, he grabbed the scabbard and hilt and tried to wrench them free. Sir Robert turned suddenly, his eyes glimmering with fear when he saw Ransom at his flank, and he glanced his spurs against his horse. The beast leaped into action, and Ransom was dragged a ways before he had to let go of the scabbard. Sir Robert's horse began to flee.

Breathing in quick bursts, Ransom turned and saw Sir Terencourt's horse lacked a rider. The Brythonican knight lay on the ground in a heap. Ransom hurried to the beast and mounted it. He charged after Sir Robert, and the animal rode like a lightning bolt. It was a magnificent chestnut, a heavily muscled warhorse bred for stamina. The knights were still embroiled in a bitter fight, but he ignored them and went after Robert.

The two raced each other, but Robert's horse was already fatigued from the strenuous ride of the day. Terencourt's was fresh, and it followed Ransom's lead as if it had served him all his life. He gained ground with every stride. Robert glanced back, seeing who was bearing down on him, and used the flat of his blade to swat his horse again. But it wasn't enough. There was no pain in Ransom now, even though his wrists were worn raw and he'd been weakened by the journey. He had to kill Sir Robert. The need for retribution burned so hot inside him, it blinded him to all else.

When he overtook Robert's horse, he leaned from the saddle to grab the man. Robert attacked with his sword. Sir Terencourt's horse bit Robert's beast, and the other capitulated and stopped running. It hung its head, swooning with exhaustion, and no matter what Robert did, the beast wouldn't move. Ransom swung about and watched as Robert dismounted, holding his sword out in front of him, his eyes wide with fear.

Ransom had no weapon himself, but he didn't care. The man's obvious fear indicated he knew it wouldn't save him.

Swinging off the horse, Ransom stalked toward his enemy, holding his arms out in a gesture of defenselessness.

"You've always wanted to beat me," he said angrily to Robert. "Now is your chance."

Robert was panting. "I don't . . . want to fight . . ."

"I don't care what you want!" Ransom shouted at him. "Do your best, and I will do mine."

Robert stared at him, his face chalky with dread. Ransom sensed he was planning an attack. He was preparing to fling himself at Ransom. He would come from the left.

"They say you don't even bleed," Robert said. "It's all stories and fables."

"Do your best," Ransom taunted.

Robert lunged at him from the left before twisting around and swinging his sword, trying to decapitate Ransom.

But Ransom sensed all his actions before they unfolded. He paused, ducking so that the blade sailed over his head, and then tackled Robert onto the meadow grass. The two wrestled for a few moments, but Ransom was stronger and easily pried the weapon from his hand.

Robert tried to knee Ransom in the groin, but he sensed that too and twisted his hips in time to avoid it. He hefted up the sword and rose with it. Robert lay on the grass, panting heavily, and gazed up at him.

"You won . . ." he panted. "I yield."

Ransom stared at him with contempt. He took a step closer, feeling his strength grow.

"I said I yield!"

Ransom shook his head. "For *shame*. I was there when Devon died," he said. "You betrayed your king. You cannot beg for mercy now."

Robert Tregoss squeezed his eyes shut, lying on the meadow grass and waiting for death.

It came swiftly.

The army of the North is coming. Instead of venturing south to connect with Benedict, James has swung east and marches on the palace. Lord Kinghorn is set to defend it. The Elder King has taken his army to confront his son, who has left Beestone and marches east. There are a number of castles along the way, the question is which one the king will choose to defend his crown. He must choose one of them because he is so outnumbered. He will force Benedict to besiege the castles one by one as he retreats back to Kingfountain. That is what Sir Dalian said the strategy was as he heard it from his father. The best way to stop a sword from cutting off a limb is blunting it. Will this buy us enough time? I offered to go to Glosstyr and summon those willing to fight to aid the king. Lord Kinghorn was grateful. There just wasn't enough time to get there and back to make a difference.

—*Claire de Murrow, Duchess of Glosstyr*
(the painful silence before the storm)

CHAPTER
TWENTY-FIVE

The Guardian's Ring

After Ransom finished strapping the scabbard to his waist, he saw the raven sigil begin to glow and felt the first stirrings of relief. He took Terencourt's horse by the reins and then walked back to the remains of the battle. Of the two dozen knights who'd clashed in the meadow, only six remained upright, five standing and one kneeling. Each had a shield with the Raven on it, so he knew which side had won and decisively so.

The knight kneeling was doing so by Sir Terencourt, who lay in the trampled grass, his breathing shallow and ragged. Blood trickled from his chapped lips. They were moving slightly, as if he was whispering something, and Ransom hurried toward them as the knight uttered his plea: "Bring my body . . . to Ploemeur."

If he used the Raven scabbard to heal the knight, he risked revealing its nature, but this man had saved him, and Ransom was willing to take that risk. But as he started to unbuckle the sword belt, he felt a gentle push to stay his hand.

Kneel, Sir Ransom. His time is at an end.

Ransom obeyed and knelt by the fallen warrior. One of the knights standing nearby sniffled. This was his mesnie. Ransom understood the grief and pain they felt at the loss of their master and their brothers-in-arms. In his mind, he heard the rushing of the waters.

Sir Terencourt's eyes found his, and the bloodied lips twitched with a smile. "I am dying," he whispered.

Ransom grasped the fallen knight's gauntlet in his hand, adding gentle pressure to it. "You rescued me, Sir Terencourt. I am grateful. I am sorry you had to trade your life for mine."

Terencourt pressed his lips together and shuddered. "The Fountain . . . bid me come. Take off my gauntlet. Quickly."

Ransom did so, tugging off the metal glove. Terencourt's hand was pale from lack of blood, his knuckles scarred from a warrior's life.

"The ring," said Terencourt, seizing Ransom's hand.

Ransom's brows wrinkled in confusion. He saw no ring.

"You will feel it, Sir Ransom. It cannot be seen when worn." His blue eyes looked at Ransom fiercely, his voice straining as it became weaker. "It is yours. You are the champion of Brythonica now. Protector of the family. Master of the wood and keeper of the Gradalis." His breath began to fail.

Ransom stared at him in concern. "What does this mean?"

"The duchess . . . will explain. Good-bye, Sir Ransom. Until we meet in the Deep Fathoms."

The knight squeezed Ransom's hand, but his energy soon failed him, and his grip went slack. Ransom squeezed it in return, trying to lend the man some strength. But the knight had finally yielded his life. The sound of the waters faded to a trickle, and then it faded away.

With curiosity, Ransom touched the base of the man's fingers, feeling for the ring, and found a metal band around his forefinger. It did not take effort to pry it away and when it slipped off, the ring could be seen. It was a simple band of white-and-yellow gold. Around the band were overlapping circles. He stared at it in his palm, feeling the weight of the ring and the sense of responsibility it imposed. Then he rose and stuffed the ring in his pocket.

"His last wish was to return to Ploemeur," he said to the others. "It is on the way back."

"Are you coming with us, Sir Ransom?" asked the young knight who had knelt by the body. His face was grief-stricken, but he had a look of hope.

"I am," he said. "But I cannot stay long. Our king is in danger."

They reached Ploemeur at dawn, having ridden all night. He sent one of the knights ahead to inform the duchess of what had happened and that they were coming. He was utterly spent by the time they reached the city, but the scabbard had healed his infirmities. He rode Sir Terencourt's horse, and they'd strapped the old champion to another mount for the journey back to his home.

When they reached Ploemeur, the streets were full of soldiers and knights. They were informed that the duchess was at the Hall of Justice in the town proper and not up at the palace, which would have taken them longer to reach. Ransom dismounted and followed the knight to meet with her. He was ashamed to encounter her, filthy as he was, but there was no time left.

When they entered the audience hall, the Duchess of Brythonica, Lady Constance, descended the throne to greet them. The other chair, the one previously reserved for Goff, sat empty. She wore a black velvet gown and a black veil. Clinging to her hand was a small child who looked up at Ransom hopefully at first, perhaps expecting his father, then looked away in disappointment. Ransom had met the duchess before, but they'd only exchanged a few pleasantries. He could see the kohl marking her eyes beneath the veil.

"Sir Ransom," she said as he gave her a bow.

"I am sorry for all that has befallen your family. My words are inadequate compensation for your grief."

"These are dark times," said Lady Constance. "I did not want my husband to go to Pree. I don't trust Estian. I never have."

Ransom nodded in agreement. "I brought Sir Terencourt's body with me—"

"Did you bring the ring?" she interrupted.

Ransom dug into his pocket and retrieved it. "He gave this to me as he lay dying."

She looked at him, her frown serious and concerned, not angry. "You are to wear it."

Ransom sighed. "He told me as much, but I don't understand what it means. He said you would explain."

Lady Constance turned away from him and told her son to sit on the throne. He toddled over and climbed up onto the footrest before clambering onto the seat. She watched him, her shoulders shaking with suppressed emotion.

"He's all I have left," she whispered. When she turned to face Ransom again, he took a step closer. "The ring is an artifact of the Deep Fathoms, Sir Ransom. And so is the scabbard you wear. When you were last here, you were not wearing it. But I recognize it as an heirloom of this ancient land."

"My loyalty is to the King of Ceredigion," Ransom said, "but I promised him that I would guard your son. His grandson. Are you . . . do you hear the voice, my lady?"

"I do, Sir Ransom. The voice bid me send my knights to rescue you. You are Fountain-blessed. I've known it for some time, and not because of the rumors." She looked down, gathering her thoughts. "When you first defeated Sir Terencourt in the tournament, he told me that you would replace him. I didn't want to believe it at first." She looked at him again. "He told me that Sir Robert Tregoss would be the man who killed him and, in doing so, become the protector of Brythonica by right. But he also said that you, Sir Ransom, would kill Sir Robert and win that right yourself. You have been chosen by the Fountain to defend the Argentine line, from which will come the rebirth of King Andrew. It is my hope that it comes through my son, which is why I named him Andrew. He cannot defend himself, nor can I defend him from the threat of the King of Occitania, who will surely seek the boy's life. With this ring, you will be able to protect him."

It shocked him to hear her say it, but there was no denying her story matched what the voice had told him—that the scion would come from the Argentine family. "How?"

She stepped closer, dropping her voice to a whisper. "There is magic in this world, Sir Ransom, that you do not understand. When the Wizr Myrddin was banished to another world, he was sent away with an artifact more powerful even than that ring or your scabbard. It is a silver bowl called the Gradalis. It was once kept at Kerjean castle in Bayree by the Fisher Kings, but it was taken from that place by a champion of King Andrew. A champion much like yourself. The Gradalis is here in Brythonica in a secret place. If you put on that ring and accept the role of master of the wood, I can use it to summon you. If someone tries to steal the Gradalis, it will summon you as well. That is the power of the ring. And the responsibility." She grasped his arm. "I need you, Sir Ransom. My son needs you. Do you accept your role as protector?"

He swallowed his nervousness. Much of what she said confused and baffled him, starting with the fact that Sir Terencourt had apparently presaged his own death, but he felt reassurance from the Fountain. Its soothing burbling filled his ears.

"The Fountain bids me accept," he answered her.

"Put on the ring," she told him. "It is yours until you give it to another when your time is fulfilled or you are defeated in single combat. I bless you by the Fountain, Sir Ransom. You are needed more than you know."

He gazed at her face through the veil. "I will do my best."

"It is enough. Now, put on the ring."

Ransom stared down at it in his hand. Sir Terencourt had worn it on the forefinger of his left hand, so he would do the same. As Ransom lifted the ring to put it there, the duchess whispered a word he didn't understand. The ring slid on effortlessly. As soon as it was on his finger, it vanished, although he still felt its presence.

The duchess smiled and lifted the veil. He saw a tear streak down her face. "Thank you, Sir Ransom. You are a good man. And now that you are Brythonica's protector, I give you the right to command her knights. I've been preparing ships all night long to send aid to King Devon. The tide is going out soon. Go with them, and defend our king!"

His heart surged with hope. This was why the Fountain magic had not come to him before they reached the borders of Brythonica. He was meant to be here, in this place. There was still a chance they could win the war and stand strong against Occitania.

A chance was all they needed.

"My lady, I'm not as familiar with the coasts. Where were you planning to send them?"

"Averanche is under Benedict's control. I was going to send them due east to Glosstyr. What do you think of that?"

Ransom smiled. "My lady . . . I am to be the new duke of Glosstyr."

"Is that so? I rarely know all the reasons behind the whispers that come to me, but I know the Fountain is with us. It is with *you*, Sir Ransom." She squeezed his hand and gave him a warm smile. "We depend on you."

Sleep had eluded Ransom for days. But in the stateroom on board the Brythonican ship, he was finally able to rest. The weariness and exhaustion of his captivity was washed away by cleansing sleep. The room was dark, and the swaying of the ship didn't trouble his stomach as it had in the past. In fact, he felt more comfortable, more at peace, in the sea's embrace.

His slumber was disturbed by one of Terencourt's knights.

"My lord. We're nearing Glosstyr."

Ransom sat up on the cramped bed. The refreshment he felt was enormous. He looked at the knight standing in the doorway, recognizing him as the young one who had knelt by Terencourt in his last moments.

"What's your name, lad?" Ransom asked.

"My name is Guivret," said the young man. He looked down. "I was Sir Terencourt's squire."

Ransom swung his legs over the bedside. "I don't have a squire. Would you be willing to serve me? I have a small mesnie."

The young man's face brightened. "I would welcome the opportunity, my lord. Truly. Is there anything I can do for you?"

Ransom rose and stretched. "How about some food? What time of day is it? I can't tell since there isn't much light in here."

"The sun is waning. We'll be at Glosstyr before nightfall."

"Good. Fetch me paper and ink as well. I need to write my lady a letter and tell her what's happened."

"Gladly, Sir Ransom! Thank you! I cannot thank you enough!"

Ransom watched him depart with haste and exuberance. He rubbed his thumb across the ring on his finger, feeling the little circles engraved in the band. What was the significance? He'd heard stories about the Ring Table and King Andrew, tales of the Fountain-blessed, but he'd paid little attention to them at the time. He wished he knew more. Alix had said she had many books with the old stories. Did she know about the Gradalis, or had he perhaps learned something she had not?

His thoughts shifted to Claire and the letter he was to write. He'd always imagined visiting Glosstyr with her first. Rather than wait in his chamber for Guivret to return, he strapped on his sword and bounded up the stairs until he was abovedeck. There were twelve ships in all, each full of knights and soldiers hastening to defend the king. He grabbed a rope to steady himself as the deck pitched. The fortress of Glosstyr lay before him, the town set within the bay. It rivaled Ploemeur in size and grandeur, but the city and bay were not as large, and there were fewer ships at port.

Waves crashed against the rocks beneath the massive castle built into the coast south of town. The sight of it gave him a thrill of wonder.

It would be his if they won this war.

It would be *theirs*.

A letter arrived today that brought such joy and relief. Ransom escaped from the murderous villains who had abducted him, thanks be to the Duchess of Brythonica. He wrote to me from one of her ships, and the message was sent from Glosstyr. He has men-at-arms now and is hastening to meet the king at Dunmanis castle, where the king assembled his forces to withstand the attack from King Estian and Duke Benedict.

Duke James's scouts have reached the edge of the city of Kingfountain. I don't think he will attack us. I believe his goal is to prevent the king from returning. However, his presence will make it difficult for us to hear any news that doesn't arrive by sea.

This is such a reprieve. I'd feared Ransom would be held hostage again, just as he was before. He didn't mention any injuries, but he's just the sort of fool eejit who wouldn't talk about something like that. I'm pleased he went to Glosstyr to bring aid to the king. There are still some puffs of smoke coming from the ashes of this fire. Perhaps some fresh wood will cause it to blaze again. I hope so. Oh, how I hope so!

—Claire de Murrow, Duchess of Glosstyr
(the tempest is coming)

CHAPTER
TWENTY-SIX

Dunmanis Castle

Ransom and the knights from Brythonica and Glosstyr arrived at Dunmanis at midday, riding in from Glosstyr. There were puddles and mud everywhere, showing a rainstorm had swept through the area. Dunmanis was a sizeable fortress, although not as powerful as Beestone. It wasn't situated on a hill, which would have added to its defensive position, but it did have a river on the south side of town, creating a natural moat to help defend the town.

His arrival at the north gate with additional forces was greeted with cheers from King Devon's bedraggled troops. Knights and soldiers thronged the rain-soaked cobblestone streets, their grinning faces and salutes indicating the reinforcements could not have arrived at a better moment. The boisterous welcome made Ransom smile as he rode through the throng on Sir Terencourt's destrier.

A group of knights approached them from the castle, and Ransom was delighted to see John Dearley at the head of the group. Dawson was with him, along with other knights from Josselin.

Dearley's face was bright and joyful. "I didn't let myself believe the news until I saw you with my own eyes. But it is you!"

Another cheer went up from the soldiers who'd accompanied Ransom and the knights down the road.

"It's a story I'll share later," Ransom said. He nodded at Dawson, whose grin was almost as wide as Dearley's. "Where is the king?"

"He's at the castle waiting for you," Dawson said. "Your brother is also there."

"Good," Ransom said. "How are things at Josselin?"

"I left ten knights to defend her," Dearley said. Then he flushed. "The castle . . . I mean. I meant the castle."

"How many men does the king have on his side?"

"There are about two thousand gathered here." His eyes turned worried. "We need more."

"It's easier to defend a castle than to take one," Ransom said. "We have enough to hold them off."

"I hope you're right," Dearley said.

"We'll fight to the last man," Dawson said with a dark look. He was always hungry for combat, and Ransom didn't doubt he'd get his fill.

"I hope it doesn't come to that," Ransom said. "But we defend the king, no matter what." He saw Guivret out of the corner of his eye, watching them, and he gestured for him to join them. "This is my new squire, Guivret of Brythonica. He's joined the mesnie."

Dearley looked surprised but pleased, but Dawson looked at the younger man with the eyes of a rival. Leading a mesnie presented its own set of challenges, something he would have to maneuver more with each person he added. Each young knight or squire had a different temperament and personality. It made him understand and appreciate Lord Kinghorn all the more. He had always made it look easy.

"Let's go to the castle," Ransom said.

They rode to Dunmanis and dismounted in the bailey. Guivret began to tend to the horses while Ransom and Dawson followed Dearley, who knew the way. The king was atop the battlement walls, wearing not even a hauberk, although his sword was nonetheless strapped to his waist, and he had on his black cloak with wolf trim. Immediately, Ransom sensed the pain in the king. The grimace on his face showed that he was suffering, that his insides were on fire, but Ransom could tell that it was not an injury. His heart sank. Now, he knew why Alix had not traveled with them. She'd had another assignment.

"Ransom!" the king said, forcing a smile. He embraced him in a bear hug and then clapped him on the back. "It was storming every day until your news arrived, and now the clouds have lifted."

Ransom saw his brother, Marcus, grinning at him nearby, along with the other lesser nobles. He was surprised to see Prince Jon-Landon atop the battlements too, standing in the king's shadow. When Ransom met the prince's eyes, he saw a look of contempt and anger gazing hotly back at him. Was it because of the king's warm greeting, or was some other resentment festering inside the young man? Had he planned on taking Glosstyr for himself?

"I came as soon as I could," Ransom apologized.

"I shouldn't have been surprised by such treachery," the king said. "I'm only too grateful that you made it out alive. This is a desperate hour, my boy. But this old wolf isn't dead yet."

"You're in pain," Ransom said in a low voice.

Jon-Landon was close enough to hear it and scowled.

The king draped an arm around Ransom's shoulder in a warm, easy gesture that reminded him of the Younger King's affability. "I *am* suffering," he said in a quiet way. "It started after you left for Beestone. It's not gotten worse, but it feels like I've swallowed hot nails. This is not the time to be indisposed." He grunted with pain and then shook his head.

Ransom gazed at him with concern. "I think it's poison, my lord."

The king nodded curtly. "I've thought the same. How she got into the palace is a mystery, but you once saw her disappear into a fountain—we know she has uncanny abilities." He sniffed. "They want to end this conflict. A missive arrived from Estian this morning, asking to broker a peace between me and Benedict. What cheek he has. Is not that why I sent you to Beestone? My strength is failing. Soldiers are deserting in droves. But your arrival . . . it's truly a gift from the Fountain. Bless you, my boy. Thank you for your loyalty."

Ransom felt his stomach clench with dread. He'd never seen the king's health so compromised. Usually, he was so strong and hearty.

"We should go back down, Father," said the prince. "You need to rest."

"I'll rest when I'm good and ready!" snapped the king. The discomfort was making him irritable. "You need lessons in war, boy. That's why we are here." He thumped Ransom on the back again and then turned to his youngest son. "Look down from the walls. Tell me what you see with a soldier's eye."

The prince blinked with surprise, but he sidled up next to his father, arms folded. "The bridge is made of wood. It'll burn."

"Exactly. But flames can be doused and wood takes time to burn. I have men with axes at the ready, waiting for my order to demolish the bridge. Look at the river. What are those men doing?"

"Catching fish?"

"No! We have plenty of stores already. We can survive a siege for quite some time. They are putting sharp wooden stakes in the river. Why?"

The prince's brow wrinkled. "I don't know."

"To block the fords," said the king patiently. "We don't want to make it easy for them to cross, you see. Every trap we set delays them. They'll get across the river. I have no doubt of it. But we must ensure each step costs them in pain and frustration. Once they do wade across, if they do, then we burn the town. That adds smoke, you see? Makes it difficult for them to breathe and fight."

"Difficult for us too," said Jon-Landon.

"True. But we hold the ramparts. The fires will burn for days, making it costly and dangerous to attack the walls. The river is the best protection we have. That alone will hold them off."

"What if they try crossing a bridge to the east or west of us?"

"I know this river, lad. It is called the Pervenshere, and it runs nigh Tatton Grange. It'll cost them many days to go either way. And we'd follow them, forbid them to cross." His eyes had a far-off look. "I know this area better than anyone. I used to hunt the woods north of this castle when I was your age."

Those reminiscences seemed to fill him with sadness, with regret.

"You never took me hunting," said the prince.

The words were like a blow to an exposed wound. Ransom wanted to chide the young man, but it wasn't his place.

The king simply nodded. "Let's go back down. Have the cook bring some milk. It's the only thing that soothes my stomach."

"Very well, Father," said the prince, and he started off. His fashionable clothes and the dagger dangling from his belt looked out of place when war loomed so close.

The king shook his head and turned to gaze at Ransom. "How is Constance?"

"She's grieving," said Ransom. "Sir Terencourt died rescuing me. I promised her that I would protect her son's life."

"My only grandson, and I haven't seen him yet," said the king wistfully. His expression hardened with wrath. "Estian demanded I relinquish Brythonica. He wishes to take Constance in as his ward, and I'm to believe Goff's death was an accident." His nostrils flared. "I feel like a wounded elk with the birds pecking at me before I've become a carcass. Everything I wanted to give my sons is being torn away, bit by bit. Benedict will regret this alliance he's made. No matter the results of this war, he'll lose more than he ever would have by giving up the Vexin."

"What would you have me do?"

The king stared over the battlement walls. "Tomorrow morning, I want you to take some scouts and cross the bridge. I need to know how much time we have."

"Isn't it possible they'll strike at Kingfountain first?"

The king pursed his lips. "He wants the crown. And that's why he'll come here. I'm sure of it."

Long after nightfall, Ransom went to check on the king. When he tapped on the door, Sir Iain answered it. He was the only other member of the king's council present, but he was aged and would be of limited help should a fight break out.

"Can I speak with the king?" Ransom asked.

"He's asleep, finally," said Sir Iain. He opened the door wider. "See for yourself."

Ransom peered into the darkened chamber. A fire crackled in the hearth, providing light and too much warmth. The king lay on the bed without any covers, still wearing his clothes from the day, although his cloak had been tossed on a chair. Ransom ventured in, hearing the faint whistle of breath coming from the sleeping king.

No one else was there. "Where is the prince?" Ransom asked.

Sir Iain sighed. "He'll be back before dawn."

Ransom looked at him in concern.

The aging knight sighed again. "He sneaks off after the king falls asleep."

"Where does he go?"

"A lass in the village has caught his fancy. I haven't told the king yet. He has enough worries."

Sir James had been a companion to the prince. No doubt he'd educated the young man on the ignoble arts of carousing. It pained Ransom that the prince was off pleasing himself at such a moment. "Tell me he has a bodyguard?"

"Sir Kyle is very discreet."

Ransom breathed out through his nose. Then he approached the bedside of the king and gazed down at him. He could feel the man's indisposition through the Fountain magic.

He unbuckled his sword belt.

Sir Iain gave him a questioning look but said nothing as Ransom laid the scabbard atop the king as gently as he could, trying not to wake him. He didn't know if the scabbard would heal the king, but he had to try.

When he let go, he stared at the symbol of the raven, wishing it would brighten the way it did when it was healing someone. But nothing happened. Perhaps the only wounds it healed were injuries of war. For all he knew, it might only work for him. Disappointment coursed through him. After waiting several moments, he retrieved the weapon and buckled it back on.

When he returned to his own room, he found the others asleep on pallets on the floor, except for Dearley, who sat with a small oil lamp, a piece of paper, and an inkwell at the humble table near the window. He was tugging on his bottom lip, so lost in thought that he didn't notice Ransom's return until he heard the door shut.

Ransom sidestepped a sleeping body and slumped into the chair next to him, glancing at the half-written letter. He wanted to write to Claire again, but he knew it would be difficult, if not impossible, to get a message to Kingfountain before this battle was done.

"Your brother came by looking for you," said Dearley. "He'd like to join the scouting expedition in the morning."

Ransom nodded in agreement. "I would like that."

"The world is upside down," said Dearley with a small chuckle. "The elder brother now seeks permission from the younger."

"It is upside down," agreed Ransom. "The second son seeks to wear the crown. Your letter is only half finished. Have you run out of words to Elodie already?"

Dearley's smile was sad. "I'm afraid to write what I want to write."

Ransom gave him a questioning look.

Staring down at the paper, Dearley sighed. "I fear the future, Ransom. I don't want to give up hope, but even with the forces you brought, we are still mightily outnumbered. They have Genevese mercenaries, the Occitanian army, and Prince Benedict and all his men. We are so few. The king is ailing. If he dies . . . then all of my dreams may be shattered."

"How so?" Ransom asked.

Dearley wouldn't meet his gaze. "I'm your ward. If Benedict becomes king, then you won't be on the king's council anymore. And he could strip your rank away with the snap of his fingers."

One of the knights on the floor mumbled in his sleep, causing them both to look that way. The quarters were cramped at the castle. They both smiled when the chamber fell silent again.

Dearley spoke in a whisper. "I can't imagine what you must be feeling," he said. "I'm in anguish. I love Elodie, but I'm afraid to express it for fear of what will happen should we lose. Why raise her hopes only for them to be dashed?" He hung his head. "I don't know how you can look so calm. I'm a wreck."

Ransom did feel calm. Yes, the future was uncertain, but he'd become accustomed to that feeling. He'd suffered so many setbacks and losses the fear of it had drained away. But he remembered how crushing those first reversals of fortune had been, and he felt compassion for Dearley.

"Well, if you have nothing else to say in the letter, may I finish it?" Ransom asked.

Dearley gave him a perplexed look. "Of course."

"Hand me the quill."

Dearley did. "What are you going to tell her?"

"Some news I think she'll be grateful to hear. I'm going to tell her that you both have my permission to marry. Whatever happens here, it doesn't mean the two of you can't be together. If we prevail, the deed is done. If we fail, it will still take Benedict time to reach the palace and take over. He may become king, but he cannot override the sacrament of marriage."

Dearley stared at Ransom in disbelief. "But what about you and Lady Claire?"

The words tugged at Ransom's heart. He'd never so keenly felt the distance between them, even when she had been locked in that tower, but he simply dipped the quill in the ink. "I'm giving you what can be given. Hope for the future."

The army from Dundrennan has begun arriving, which has prevented communication from the Elder King from reaching us. The pompous duke of the North requested a meeting with Lord Kinghorn, but he was refused. The guards around the palace have been increased out of fear that someone within might betray the king and let the duke's forces in. The dock warden of Kingfountain has ordered people to remain inside. We still control the ports, and so there are ships sailing in and out. Everyone is tense, worried that every plume of smoke might be a sign of a siege beginning.

And so we wait. And hope.

—*Claire de Murrow, Duchess of Glosstyr*
(waiting for the end)

CHAPTER
TWENTY-SEVEN

Banners Unfurled

The previous day had been beautiful and clear, but a thick fog rolled in during the night, adding wetness that dripped down their armor and brought out the smells of dirt and grass. It was the kind that appeared in the early morning hours and tended to dissipate in the morning sun. The arrival of dawn was imminent, and Ransom hoped it would relieve them of the burden so they could see. He and his scouts had just ridden over the wooden bridge straddling Pervenshere River, venturing into the vast haze. The small group included his brother, two knights from the Heath, Sir Dawson, and Guivret. Ransom had asked Dearley to remain behind to defend the bridge with a host of men.

Those who had been on patrol during the night had reported nothing amiss. A few deer had been seen nipping at the meadow shrubs. That was all. But Ransom needed to discern the truth for himself.

"Can't see a thing in all this gloom," muttered Sir Dawson. Trees ghosted in and out of view.

"How far will we ride this morning?" Marcus asked Ransom.

"Farther than the patrols went," Ransom replied. "If Benedict has turned toward Kingfountain, we'll want to know."

"Do you think he will? Or is he coming this way?"

Ransom sniffed. "He'll batter down the walls of Dunmanis if the king stays."

"Do you think he'll be the next king?" Marcus asked in a low voice.

"I know he wants it." He glanced at his brother. "How are Mother and Maeg holding up? Are they frightened?"

"They're safe at the Heath. I think the castle can hold out for a long time," Marcus answered, which was no answer at all. "These are dangerous times. We've been loyal to the Elder King for many years. I'm hoping that loyalty isn't misplaced."

Ransom frowned. "Keep your voice down."

Marcus nodded, but the worry didn't leave his eyes. If Benedict won, those who had faithfully supported his father would pay. Literally. Power would change hands. Lives would be transformed. Ransom's gaze dropped to the leather bracelet he once more wore on his left wrist. A familiar ache throbbed in his heart.

If he could marry her now, this very minute, he would, but an untold number of troops stood between him and Kingfountain.

As the sun rose, it began to scatter the fog as predicted. They'd ridden perhaps a league away from Dunmanis, keeping an easy pace, when Ransom felt a prickle of warning go down his back.

"Hold," he ordered, lifting a fist into the air. Their mounts came to rest, some nickering and stamping on the dirt road.

"Do you see something?" Marcus asked in disbelief. The fog had thinned, but it still hung in the air like a shroud.

Ransom gazed ahead, unable to discern the source of the warning. He sniffed the air for a clue but smelled nothing unexpected.

"Just wait," he said softly, easing his shoulder muscles. The noise of the birds grew into a steady chatter, drowning out all other sounds. His steed stamped again with impatience.

"Scouts," Dawson whispered.

Ransom looked up and saw three knights coming up the road at a leisurely pace. There were eight in Ransom's group, which gave them an easy advantage.

"Shall we take them?" Marcus asked softly. "See what we can learn?"

A dark premonition filled Ransom's mind. "Not yet. Wait."

Still they lingered as the knights drew closer, seemingly oblivious to the danger they were blundering toward. The fog continued to abate, bringing in fresh streamers of sunlight.

And then, as if a wind had blown out a candle, the fog lifted, revealing an army stretched like a python down the road. Two banners hung side by side, held by heralds. The Lion of Benedict and the Fleur-de-Lis of Estian. Row after row of knights rode toward the castle, the sunlight now winking on the metal curvature of their armor.

Ransom could feel the vibrations of the hooves now, the implacable enemy approaching.

"They are coming, just as you said," Marcus acknowledged. "We'd better ride back and warn the king."

"How many do you think they have?" Dawson asked in wonder.

"Too many," Ransom answered.

The scouts noticed them at last. A cry of alarm sounded.

"Ride," Ransom ordered.

When they reached the bridge, Ransom gave the order to begin demolishing it. The men with axes began their work immediately, but he lingered, intent on defending the bridge should any of their foes arrive before it fell. Wooden pegs and supports were chopped furiously as he waited with bated breath, watching the road. Sure enough, knights were bearing down on them, hoping to stop them before they informed the king of the onslaught.

Ransom ordered his knights to prepare for a charge and lowered his lance. But the first shattered planks of the bridge began dropping into the river as the enemies drew up to it. He felt the Fountain magic stirring within him, preparing him for combat, but the invading knights were cautious and outnumbered. They gazed sullenly as they watched the bridge collapse section by section.

"Back away, my lord," said one of the warriors with an axe. "It won't be up much longer."

Ransom and his knights retreated, and he waited until he was satisfied the bridge was truly impassable. He rode hard into Dunmanis and was told the king was up on the battlements again, so he dismounted and joined him there.

The prince was with his father once more. He didn't look at Ransom with hatred or scorn. He seemed afraid. King Devon eyed the advancing army with a shrewd eye.

"I told you he'd come," said the king when Ransom arrived.

"Are you going to burn the town now?" the prince asked his father. There was a worried tone in his voice, a concern that might be related to a certain lass in town.

"No! Don't be daft. Your brother has to get across the river first. This will test him, to be sure. He will lose many men before he crosses the river." He sounded almost fond as he said it. Then he turned to look at Ransom. "Did you get a view of his army?"

"There are two armies coming this way," Ransom said. "Estian the Black is riding with him."

Devon the Elder scowled. Ransom could still sense the pain attacking his innards, the bite of whatever poison he'd been given. "You should have taken his head off in Pree. No matter. That river will drown many of their knights before this is over. Mark my words. All we need to do is stand firm." He gazed back at the scene unfolding across the river. "Come and get me, boy. You chose this fight. Not I."

Jon-Landon shot a wary glance at his father. "What do we do in the meantime, Father?"

"We wait. It will take today and probably tomorrow for the rest of the host to arrive. They'll set up camp. They won't even start attacking for two days. Maybe three. We have time."

"But what will we *do*?"

"If you were wise, you'd spend time in the training yard with Sir Ransom," said the king impatiently. He glowered at his son. "Your brother has."

A sudden fury flashed in Jon-Landon's eyes, and he turned and stormed off toward the stairs leading off the wall.

"Boy! Don't be petulant!" The king's teeth showed, and he cursed under his breath. After Jon-Landon was gone, Devon glanced at Ransom. "He's too young. In another three years, he would have been ready for this."

"He didn't have the same opportunities as his brothers," said Ransom solemnly.

The king chuckled. "Thank you for that, but he did. He wasted them. Always pining for some bit of land to rule. I tried giving him Glosstyr." He flashed Ransom a chagrined smile. "But we'll say no more on that score. He's always wanted Kingfountain. Maybe I should have given it to him and let Benedict rot in the Vexin."

Ransom approached the edge of the battlements and set his gauntleted hand down on the wall. Knights were streaming in from the road. Some were riding on the meadow grass bordering it. He felt a throb in his chest and gazed into the press of men.

"I think that's him," he said to the king, pointing.

Devon looked in the direction he was indicating and then breathed out slowly. "Yes. That's my son." He grunted in pain and doubled over, grasping the edge of the wall to steady himself.

"You need to rest," Ransom said.

The king grimaced again. "You think it is easy to sleep feeling like I do? No, I must be up and moving. I will not give up my kingdom so easily. Not after all the years I've spent building it up." His gaze was still fixed on his son across the river. A look of self-loathing crossed his face. "How did I lose so much so quickly?"

Ransom pitied him. The seeds of this moment had been planted years before, even before the Younger King first rebelled. It was a bitter harvest.

"Let's go down," he suggested to the king.

"I agree," said Devon. "I must speak to the men. They need speeches in times like this." He began to pant with weariness. Then he turned and looked Ransom in the eye. "Don't you betray me, Ransom. I don't think my heart could bear it."

"I won't," he promised and felt the power of the Fountain surge within him. The king put his hand on Ransom's shoulder and smiled weakly, and the two walked side by side down the steps.

Many knights had assembled in the courtyard. Most had smudges under their eyes from sleeplessness. As he beheld them, the king straightened and removed his hand from Ransom's shoulder.

"Why the glum faces?" the king said brightly, touching the wall with his other hand to steady himself as he continued down the steps. "This is not a siege to be dreaded. My friends, we have ample provisions and game in the forest to feast on for months. You may have heard that the duke's men have arrived. Ha! They are just beyond the river. And yes, the King of Occitania has ridden against us too. It is no matter. My son is proud. That is his weakness, and it will be his downfall."

He'd reached the bottom of the steps and started walking among them, touching shoulders and clapping backs. "We've been through worse storms than this one. Every man they steal from us will cost them ten. Now is not the time to be fainthearted. We are on the eve of victory. And when victory comes, and it *will*, I will chasten my son, and he will be ashamed he rode against us here. Courage, lads. Drop a coin in the fountains throughout Dunmanis. Make the waters quiver with them. The Lady is on our side and ever shall be. Spend this day in prayer, and tomorrow you shall witness the fate of those who dare to attack a city so defended by the Lady's own power!"

A weak cheer rose from the knights. Such a speech deserved a stronger response, and the king seemed shaken by the lackluster reception to his words. Were they so lacking in faith? Had they lost the battle already?

Ransom stepped down the rest of the way. "My lord," he said, his voice pulsing with anger. "Give me command of the gate. Let me hold it in the name of the king."

Devon turned and looked at him, his dismay turning to hope. "Yes, Sir Ransom! Duke of Glosstyr in spirit if not in right. I put you in charge of the defense of Dunmanis!"

A cheer rose from the crowd of knights, one much more enthusiastic.

Sir Ransom glared at them, angered by their failure to show proper respect for their king. This was the time he needed them most, and they'd distanced themselves, reconciling themselves to possible failure. "Prepare for battle!" he shouted. *"Dex aie!"*

In a thunderous response, they shouted the battle cry back at him.

Duke James said a knight was captured trying to sneak through his army bearing tidings that a battle had been fought at a castle south of Glosstyr. The king is dead, he said, and Duke Benedict is now king.

I thought it more nonsense from that brainless badger, but Lord Kinghorn came to visit Emiloh with the report and asked for her counsel. Emiloh said that it was a deception, a trick to get us to open the gates and allow James in to conquer the city. When Lord Kinghorn asked why she thought that, she said if Benedict had won, he would have come in person.

—Claire de Murrow, Duchess of Glosstyr
(insufferable eejits)

CHAPTER TWENTY-EIGHT

Hidden Ford

The morning birds were beginning to sing. Ransom paced at the gate, watching as the men slumbered. He could find no rest himself, having a brooding sense that danger was near. He'd sent out three patrols of men in the night to roam the streets beyond the wall, and there were guards posted at the river's edge to keep watch on the army, which had assembled the previous day. And yet, he could not bring himself to leave the gate in case Alix ventured near. So far, he hadn't felt any inkling of her presence. That surprised him, for he had thought she might be with Estian's army. Each report back revealed that nothing had happened or was happening. All was quiet.

And yet he felt that itching sense of anger from the Fountain, and it had never once been wrong.

"You should sleep, Ransom," said Dearley, who had remained by his side throughout the long dark night. "I promise I'll send word if there is so much as a stray arrow shot our way."

The suggestion made Ransom's stomach shrivel with queasiness. He frowned and shook his head. "Something is coming. I don't know what it is."

"How are they going to get across the river?"

"I don't know," Ransom answered. "I just feel uneasy."

The gate that he guarded was the main entrance to the inner part of the city, but there were smaller buildings and homes outside the walls. Most of the citizens had moved to safer ground the previous day, having been informed of the king's intention to torch the city to make it harder for Benedict to seize Dunmanis. Many had dared to remain behind.

"Someone's coming," Dearley said, gazing into the gloom of the town. The eastern horizon was just starting to brighten, but daylight was still a ways off.

It was true. The bootfalls of two men could be heard heading up the road toward them. The next watch wouldn't report until sunrise, so it was unusual to hear someone approach at this hour.

Soon the travelers became visible as they reached the edge of the light emanating from the torches mounted on the exterior walls of the gate.

Ransom recognized the prince, Jon-Landon, who walked toward the gate confidently. He was wearing a chain hauberk over his tunic, and his cloak was open to reveal it. A gorget covered his neck, and he had bracers on his arms. Walking about ten paces behind him was a cloaked knight who looked to be the prince's protector.

Ransom hadn't seen him leave, which meant he had probably used one of the other three gates, which were all locked now. He had given orders to keep each one secure, rendering the main gate the only way to enter or leave the fortressed town.

As the prince approached, Ransom felt disappointment curdling inside him. The prince saw him—although he still wore his armor, he'd left his helmet near the gatehouse—and his cocky smile faded.

Ransom remained where he stood, letting the prince come to him. He folded his arms.

"You've caught me in my misdeeds, Sir Ransom," said Jon-Landon. "Are you going to tell my father?"

"You shouldn't have been out last night," Ransom said, trying not to scold but unable to keep his voice as neutral as he wanted.

"I wore armor. I'm not the fool you take me for."

"I'm not accusing you of anything. You're a target for anyone seeking favor with your brother."

Jon-Landon stiffened. "You think Bennett would hurt me?"

"I don't. But there are others in Occitania who would. Get back to the castle before your father knows you're missing . . . again."

The prince frowned at him, the chagrin of being caught turning to fierce anger.

"I don't live by your standards, Sir Ransom," he said in a low voice.

Ransom took a step toward him, and the prince immediately backed away. "What harm have I ever done to you, Jon-Landon? Have I given offense?"

The young man's lip twitched. "She was supposed to be mine."

Ransom understood now. Jon-Landon had convinced himself that Claire would accept him eventually. That his father would eventually win out. He understood things better now. Disappointment was a bitter taste. Some found it impossible to endure.

"I know what it's like to be a younger brother," Ransom said. "I'm not your enemy, lad."

The prince looked down, either ashamed of himself or unsure of what to say. "Don't tell my father."

"Then get back to the castle before I *have* to tell him," said Ransom.

The prince nodded, still sulking, and then marched past Ransom through the gate. He took one of the castle horses tethered there for running messages and mounted it to ride the rest of the way back to the castle. The knight who'd followed him gave Ransom a nod of thanks as he jogged past him to get his own mount.

Ransom returned to where Dearley still stood. He'd witnessed the whole encounter, although Ransom wasn't sure how much he'd heard.

"What was that all about?" Dearley said. "Why was Jon-Landon wandering the town at night?"

"We'll not talk about it now," said Ransom, staring at the eastern sky, which continued to brighten.

Dearley looked confused for a moment, but then his eyes widened, and he nodded.

When the sun finally peeked over the eastern hills, the last watch arrived back at the gate, led by Dawson, who was accompanied by Guivret and six others.

"Any signs of trouble?" Ransom asked.

Dawson shrugged. "They're rousing already. A few have started campfires. But we couldn't see anything except for the scaling ladders they were building yesterday. Oh, they also have sentries at the river's edge, watching us. One called over and asked if the Elder King was still here, but we didn't answer him."

"Good," Ransom said, relieved. Of course, Estian likely had the magic Wizr board with him, in which case he knew Devon was there. And that Ransom was too. "What of the other gates?"

"They're still shut. But to be honest, Ransom, it wouldn't take much to break one of them open. If three of us grabbed a bench and used it as a battering ram, we'd be through in a trice. Not this gate, though. It's the strongest one. But what good will it do us if they manage to cross the river? They'll go for one of the others instead."

It was a good point. The main gate of Dunmanis was the obvious target, because of its size and proximity to the broken bridge and the street leading up to the castle, but Dawson was right—other breaches could be made more easily.

"Get some rest," Ransom said. "You've done well."

His men smiled with relief and walked past him through the gate. Others had begun to rouse, and a few men ran up to ask questions about the report from the watch. Then Ransom heard the noise of horsemen riding from the castle, and he and Dearley turned to see who was coming. The colorful dawn showed the arrival of the king, his son, and some of his household guards.

Ransom walked back through the gate to meet the king on the other side. The king wore no armor, only the hollow crown and his tunic and black cloak, although he did have his weapon. Jon-Landon and the rest were wearing armor.

"What's the matter?" Ransom asked with concern as the king reined in. He still sensed the pain the king was feeling, but it had lessened somewhat from the day before.

"Nothing's the matter. We're going to inspect the riverfront. I want them to see that I'm here waiting for them. We'll pay our respects at the shrine of Our Lady and then come back. Take off your armor and come with us."

A throb of warning went through Ransom again.

"I'll come with you, but I'd advise you all to return to the castle and prepare your arms. No doubt they have crossbows on the other side. You'd be vulnerable, my lord."

The king arched his eyebrows, eyes narrowing with offense at Ransom's gentle rebuke. "Are they preparing to attack now?"

"No. It's been quiet all night, but I'm troubled. I fear they will attack today."

The king chuffed. "I'm counting on it. I'd like to bloody Bennett's nose a bit on the first day. I see Jon-Landon has your paranoia. He said he rode down this morning to examine the defenses." His voice throbbed with pride in his son. It was a lie, but Ransom thought it prudent to remain silent about it. He glanced at Jon-Landon and saw a guilty look on the young man's face.

"No, I don't want to show fear in front of those Occitanian dogs," the king insisted. He turned back to his knights. "Remove your armor. We ride to the river as if we haven't a care in the world. Come join us, Ransom. You do the same."

The other knights looked at the king and then began removing their bracers.

Ransom shook his head. "My lord, I will go with you, but I'm going as I am. Whatever we face today, I want to be prepared. Riding to the river is a needless risk. I have a foreboding feeling about the day."

The king scowled. "Then keep your foreboding to yourself and stay here, by the Fountain! I'll not allow you to ruin my plan. Come on, Jon—take off the hauberk! We'll show them our mettle. Our defiance. Small acts of bravery will inspire the hearts of the men."

Ransom bristled from the scolding, but he remained in his armor because he felt the king was being unnecessarily foolish. The king's household knights removed their armor, including their hauberks. The men who'd been sleeping at the gate had risen, and they helped take the pieces of armor from the knights. Jon-Landon gave Ransom a grateful smile for not revealing him, but he said nothing as he handed over his armor. The king whistled, and they rode their horses down the street.

"That was strange," Dearley said to Ransom under his breath.

"The king is a proud man," Ransom replied. "It blinds him sometimes."

"Do you think he's in danger?"

"It wouldn't be an easy shot, even with a crossbow. And I don't see how the knights can cross the river. Perhaps I'm being too cautious. But I remember what it was like to be caught unprepared. Still, I don't think they'll be down by the edge very long."

From his vantage point at the gate, he saw the king and his fellow riders reach the edge of the river where the ruins of the bridge, whatever had not been tossed into the river, had been stacked into piles. The king inspected the bridge and then rode to the edge of the river.

"Look," Dearley said, pointing.

A group of knights wearing Occitanian-style armor approached the other side of the river on horseback. Had they responded to the king's approach? Another row of knights began to assemble behind them, followed by footmen with pikes.

"What are they doing?" Dearley asked in bewilderment.

"That's the vanguard of the army," Ransom said, his insides squeezing with concern. "They're preparing to attack." His guards, the ones who'd been sleeping, stared in confusion. "Put your armor on!" he barked at them.

One of the enemy knights rode his horse into the shallow bank of the river.

"There isn't a ford there," Dearley said. "The river is deeper than his horse's neck."

Ransom felt a thrum of power coming from the knight in the river. Fountain magic, and it wasn't attached to the poisoner. For a moment he just stared, immobilized, and watched the rider continue into the river. The other knights began to follow him. The king sat on his horse, staring at the scene without moving. Then the lead Occitanian knight raised a fist, as if making a command.

Ransom gaped in shock as the waters seemed to cease flowing, opening a gap that stretched from one border to the other, creating a path right before the gathered men.

The knight kept his fist raised, and Ransom sensed, preternaturally, that it was Estian himself using some artifact of the Fountain. He and his knights began to ride through the gap, advancing to the other side.

Ransom nearly screamed at the king to ride away, but the king realized the peril. He turned his horse and took off at a gallop toward the gate. The soldiers patrolling the edge of the river came rushing toward the opening en masse to try to prevent the knights from reaching the other side.

"Get my helmet," he told Dearley with rising passion.

His ward hurried to obey.

The king and his son rode furiously toward the gatehouse. One of the king's knights turned around, grabbed his lance and shield, and went back to attack the invaders. Ransom watched as he galloped toward the lead knight, who had just reached the other bank. Was it Estian? Now he wasn't so sure. Although the Occitanian king was unpredictable, he suspected he wouldn't risk himself by crossing first. The lance shattered as it struck the Occitanian's shield, but it didn't unhorse him. His horse clambered up the bank, and suddenly it was on the same side as the castle.

Another one of the king's knights turned to face their attackers, trying to buy time for the king to escape. He, too, shattered a lance on an enemy and managed to knock him off his horse, but three knights rode forward to challenge him. He tried riding away but was struck from behind by a lance.

"Here!" Dearley said, holding up the helmet.

Ransom put it on, understanding now the source of the prickles of warning he'd been experiencing throughout the night. His senses sharpened as he felt the rush of the waters inside him. Once his helmet was in place, he turned to Dearley.

"Torch the town. Get every building you can blazing. Have the townsfolk flee through the other gates."

"What about this one?" he asked in concern.

"I'll hold them off myself," he said. "I need my horse."

"You can't hold it alone!"

Ransom turned back, watching the king approach and seeing a look of horror on his face. Jon-Landon was pale with fear. Behind them came a rush of enemy knights, all determined to catch the king before he made it through the gate.

Every day that passes, every moment spent in suspense, is more terrible than the last. Lord Kinghorn will not relinquish the city unless he is ordered to do so by the Elder King or the king is killed. The latest word we have from Dunmanis is that they are preparing for a siege. Estian's army has arrived with Benedict's. I don't know much about the town, other than that it is south of Glosstyr and a river protects it on the southern side. A siege could last for weeks.

Ransom could be trapped inside the city for a long time. I feel better that he is with the king. How long can they hold until the tide turns or defeat is unavoidable? It's possible that James will abandon Kingfountain and try to cut off their supplies.

In such times, wisdom is the dearest companion. I wish I could be there amidst the smoke and carnage instead of here. I would have taken a bow and done my best to shoot down enemies.

I see the sun cresting the hills. What will this new dawn bring? Fight hard, beloved. Don't let them through.

—Claire de Murrow, Duchess of Glosstyr
(restless still)

CHAPTER
TWENTY-NINE

The Fires of Dunmanis

Ransom only had time to mount his destrier and grab a lance. He would have to face the onslaught alone at first, the other soldiers having ridden off to start fires or put on their armor.

He gazed down the street at the king and his small cohort charging for the gate, followed by at least eight knights bearing down on them with lances. There was no way to shut the gate on the enemy now. Ransom saw the look of terror on Jon-Landon's face as he kept glancing backward, seeing the knights closing in. King Devon had mastered his fear, so he didn't show it, but he looked determined to escape death.

Ransom cradled his lance and urged his destrier to ride forward to meet them, quickly building speed. A frontal attack would allow the king's cohort to go around him through the gate, while he tried to hold the Occitanian knights from passing through it. If the invaders won the gate this early, before the fire started raging, all was lost.

Feeling the Fountain magic ripple through him, Ransom lowered his lance. The king looked at him with a satisfied grin before charging past. Jon-Landon's eyes were fixed on the gate. A moment later, Ransom's lance exploded against a shield, sending fragments spraying everywhere and rocking him back. He unhorsed the other knight directly into the path of the other riders.

Yanking hard on the reins, he swerved his steed around to block the advance of the enemy knights. He moved so quickly the sights and sounds beyond his helmet were a blur, but he sensed the other knights' positions and quickly backed up his steed to block another man from getting past as he yanked his bastard sword out of the scabbard. It was seven against one, although not all of them could strike at him simultaneously. He blocked and countered, hearing the shriek of beasts as they responded to their masters' haphazard jerks.

But the numbers were so squarely against him, he found himself being driven backward as he defended himself against the attackers. More knights were crossing the river as the enemy vanguard continued to press through the magical ford their king had summoned. He managed to grab one of the knights by the collar and yank him off his horse. But still they pressed him backward, toward the shadow of the gate, their weapons smashing against his armor.

"Over here! The Fountain! The Fountain is with Sir Ransom!"

The shout came from guards atop the wall behind him. Emboldened by the cheer, Ransom fought back and stopped giving ground, holding the knights at bay until he heard the sound of hooves coming from behind him. Three knights of Ceredigion charged in on their horses, their presence evening the odds somewhat. More reinforcements were still pouring through the river.

They had to get the gate shut before the enemy arrived in force. Before the acrid smoke that was even now filling the air engulfed them.

A sword slicked through Ransom's armor, and he felt the sting of it, but immediately the scabbard began to glow and no blood flowed from the wound. He countered and smashed the Occitanian in the helmet with his hilt, stunning the man. Another knight was already bearing down on them, wearing black armor emblazed with the Fleur-de-Lis. Ransom recognized the armor, for he'd seen it during tournaments at

Chessy. This was Sir Chauvigny, the first knight in King Estian's mesnie. He was followed by other knights in black tabards.

Ransom dropped the horse's reins and cried out a warning to the others. Turning back, he saw more knights of Ceredigion coming from the gate, rushing to join the fray. He tried to fight his way to Sir Chauvigny, but several enemies blocked his path. His mind went numb to everything but the surge of battle, the determination to defeat his foes at any cost. Once more he was on the road to Auxaunce. But this time, he had armor and a strong destrier. Roaring with fury, he hacked a path to Sir Chauvigny, who saw him approach and didn't hesitate to engage him. Sir Chauvigny also wielded a bastard sword, and he fought with strength and skill. The two battered into each other, their horses joining the fight.

The rush of incoming Occitanian knights was driving the Ceredigion forces back, Ransom with them, and he once again found himself trying to stop a flood. He felt the arch of the gate looming up behind him, but he wouldn't back down, even though they were outnumbered again.

"Dex aie!" Ransom roared, the battle cry of the first king he had served, the cry of his father and of the knights of Westmarch.

Sir Chauvigny swung at him constantly to beat him down, but Ransom held his own, deflecting what blows he could with his sword and the rest with his armor. He fought back, matching stroke for stroke and sensing the other man was wearied by the ordeal. Realizing this, Ransom drove harder, and Estian's first knight began to give way. Smoke drifted through the scene, but Ransom could still see Sir Chauvigny's eyes through the opening in his helmet. They were wide with fear as he realized his skills and stamina could not match his opponent's. There was no way to retreat, the two blocked in on every side.

The battle cry was shouted all around him as the knights of Ceredigion began to drive the Occitanians back. The heat from the fire was stifling, and the smoke stung Ransom's eyes. It felt as if the whole world were burning, but it was nothing compared to the flames raging inside him. The Occitanians gave ground again, shoved back by the sheer might of will coming from the knights who had rallied to Ransom's side.

Smoke obscured the road and the oncoming soldiers, but Ransom saw some of the Occitanians turn and flee. Perhaps they feared they'd be burned alive in the blazing town. Sir Chauvigny turned in his saddle, looking to see what had become of his knights, and Ransom lunged forward and grabbed the other man's horse by the bridle strap. He clenched it in his hand and then turned his own steed and dragged the other toward the gate. Sir Chauvigny nearly fell off the horse at the sudden lunge but managed to keep his seat. Ransom hauled both horse and knight toward the gatehouse, where he saw and heard cheering men atop the walls.

Sir Chauvigny tried to wrest control of his horse again, but the beast followed Ransom docilely despite its rider's objections. Stones were hurled down from the walls, several of them striking Sir Chauvigny on the helmet and breastplate. Ransom gritted his teeth and kept pulling, hearing the cheers grow louder.

As he reached the gate, he saw Dearley and other knights had assembled to guard it. A huge stone was flung down, hitting Sir Chauvigny on the arm he'd lifted to defend himself from the blow. The knight let out a bark of pain, and Ransom saw that the stone had broken his arm.

Ransom tugged the man through the gate and handed the bridle to Dearley. "Disarm him," he ordered. "He'll make a good prize."

"Aye, my lord," said Dearley, beaming with pride at Ransom's feat. The smoke from the burning town rushed in through the gate, but Ransom turned back to join his comrades who were still battling the Occitanians. A small group of knights from Ceredigion was holding off the vanguard, thanks to the narrow street, the smoke, and the determination to prevail. Indeed, neither side was prepared to relent.

Ransom brought two more hostages back to Dearley, and each time he arrived with another victim, cheers went up from the men.

One of his fellows turned to Ransom. "Shall we stand our ground longer, my lord? I think we can defeat the whole army!"

Ransom chuckled at the man's bravado. "We've held it long enough. Back to the gate before we cook inside our armor."

The heat from the flames grew more oppressive as the fire spread. The homes outside the walls of the town were blazing, but at least Estian wouldn't be able to use them for firewood or shelter.

He motioned for the others to follow, and they rode back to the gate, where Dearley and the other guards awaited them. Ransom tried moving his left arm, but the armor was so dented and battered around his shoulder that his range of motion was severely limited. He imagined his helmet had also been mangled during the fight. But he was proud to have stopped the advance.

As soon as Ransom and the others reached Dearley, the men on guard shoved the doors of the gate closed and settled the crossbar into place.

"Your horse is wounded," Dearley said to him.

Ransom raised his crooked visor so he could see better. He looked down and then back, and saw that the horse's rear flank had been scraped by a lance he hadn't even seen. The beast was bleeding profusely, but it had not wavered during the battle.

Ransom quickly dismounted and patted the horse along the neck. Memories of Gemmell, the horse that Ransom had lost after his first battle, brought a throb of sadness. "You served Sir Terencourt and me well." He turned to Dearley. "Get this beast back to the castle and have him tended to. I hope the wound isn't fatal."

"I will," Dearley said. Then he pointed to another horse, the one that Sir Chauvigny had been riding. "This one can serve in its place."

King Devon strode up, still not wearing any armor. Ransom was surprised to see him. He'd expected the king would ride up to the castle.

"My lord," Ransom said in concern.

The king gripped Ransom by the shoulders, his big hands grasping the dented armor. "You fought like ten men out there," he said, beaming with pride. "I'm agog at what I saw. You *are* Fountain-blessed. I've no doubt on that any longer."

"I did my best," Ransom said. "The smoke will hold them back for a while, but we need to guard all the gates."

The king shook his head. "This is the strongest one. The others will fall, and we can't defend them all at the same time."

Ransom's stomach shriveled. "What do we do?"

The king shook his head. "I didn't think they'd get past the river so quickly. You saw what happened. We must abandon Dunmanis. There might be a way into the castle we don't know about. I don't trust that it's safe." The king grunted, his face blanching with pain. "My guts are flaming again. If they lay siege, I will die in this place." His eyes burned fiercely. "And I do not want to die here. I'm taking my son and riding out of here. You're coming too."

Ransom lowered his head. He wanted to argue, but there was logic in the king's strategy. If they went to the castle, they'd be trapped inside. At that point, it would only be a matter of time and suffering.

"You were right," the king said, hooking his hand around Ransom's neck. "You were right about the armor. I should have listened to you. This pain has made my mind a fog. I don't have the strength to flee all the way to Kingfountain."

"Let's go to Glosstyr," Ransom said. "We can take a ship from there."

The king's expression turned dark, brooding. "I hate this," he said. "Everything I've built is crumbling. It's slipping through my fingers."

Ransom suppressed a coughing fit, his throat sore and rough from all the smoke. "I understand what that feels like, my lord."

The king pursed his lips, eyeing Ransom with a look of wisdom. "Defeat is worse than poison. I'd forgotten its bitter taste. Let's round up those who are still loyal outside the castle. We must go while we still can."

The king mounted his horse, and Ransom lifted himself into Chauvigny's saddle. His mesnie gathered around him, even Dawson, who had returned after hearing about the fight raging in town. Guivret looked particularly worried.

"We ride with the king," he told his men.

"What about the gate?" Dearley asked.

Ransom shook his head. "Leave it."

As they rode up the street, Ransom took in the disorder and chaos. People were dragging things from their homes and shops, frantic to save their possessions. Smoke filled the air.

The king gazed at the wretched conditions, his expression bleak. "The fire spread within the gates," he said to no one in particular. "There will be nothing left here by morning. Everything I touch bursts into flames."

Truth is rarely pure and never simple. There was a commotion at one of the city gates last night. A group of merchants who were feeling the pinch of confinement, which spoiled the cabbages in their carts, thought to break through the gate and flee Kingfountain. There were enough to make a mob, but it was quickly quelled by the night watch. They care not who rules them. Their only wish is for the gates to be open. Nothing will drive a man madder than uncertainty.

—Claire de Murrow, Duchess of Glosstyr
(on the consequence of spoiling cabbages)

CHAPTER THIRTY

The Fate of Choice

here was so much smoke in the air that the sun looked like a shield of pale bone in the haze. Flames scoured the city relentlessly, and the townsfolk were drawing buckets from the wells to douse the houses and shops that had not been burned yet, to prevent them from being lost to the fire. Dunmanis would be left desolate.

Ransom sat astride his new destrier, the one taken from Chauvigny, holding a fresh lance in one hand and the horse's reins in the other. The Elder King coughed into his fist, his lungs plagued by the smoke. His son Jon-Landon sat astride his own horse, his expression that of a greensick lad. A few other nobles had gathered with them at the rear gates of the city.

Dearley suddenly appeared through the gloom, his face blackened with smudges from where he'd rubbed his face. When he reached them, he shook his head.

"The town is lost," he said. "The Occitanians have withdrawn back over the river again, but they wait there, watching the city burn. The men abandoned the outer walls because of the flames. There are no defenses now."

Devon looked at Ransom with a bleak expression. Pain still writhed inside the king—he could sense it—and this foul news made it worse.

The stand, which should have lasted several fortnights, had ended on the first day. It was a miserable defeat.

"We ride north, then," said the king. "Abandon the town."

"What of the soldiers fighting the fires?" asked one of his knights.

"I don't think Benedict will murder them," he said. "Only those with horses can escape." He looked at one of his knights. "Axien . . . ride back to Kingfountain. Tell them we've abandoned Dunmanis and are heading to Glosstyr."

The knight balked. "My lord, your life is more important than this news. Do not send me away. It's my duty to protect you."

"It is your duty to do as I command!" barked the king. His eyes flashed, but then the intensity guttered out. "Somehow you need to get past Wigant's army. Do your best. Fulfill my command."

Sir Axien looked stricken, but he nodded in capitulation.

Devon turned to Ransom. "You are my bodyguard. We fight from Glosstyr next with what little strength is there. The knights are scattered and bewildered. Leave a man to send word for all who are left to rally at Glosstyr Keep. Avoid Benedict's army if they can. But we must ride *now*. Every moment we wait increases the chance we'll be captured."

"As you wish, my lord," Ransom said. He turned to look at his small mesnie. "Dearley, you and Guivret ride with me. Dawson, fulfill the king's orders. Gather as many knights as you can and meet us in Glosstyr."

Dawson nodded and turned back to ride into the burning town. Those who would be riding to Glosstyr had already removed their armor, Dearley and Guivret included. If they were to flee the distance required to escape, they would need to travel as light as possible. The horses were already weary enough from the fighting of the day, and there were no fresh mounts. Every beast had been taken, some stolen, in the commotion.

With lances poised, they rode out of Dunmanis into the midmorning, reeking of smoke and determined to reach their destination swiftly.

The king had six knights left from his guard and a half-dozen lesser nobles traveled with them, including Ransom's brother, Marcus. It felt wonderful breathing clean air again, hearing the noise of birds and the thump of the hooves against dirt instead of cobblestones. Pervenshere River snaked on their left, but they rode away from it, leaving the Occitanians behind.

"My lord!" called one of the lesser nobles from behind.

Ransom turned in the saddle, and his stomach dropped when he saw men giving chase on horseback, their tunics that of the Lion.

The king looked back as well, recognition dawning in his eyes. "It's him," he declared over the wind rushing past them.

Ransom saw Benedict at the head of the pursuers, his beard noticeable, and his wild hair fanning out behind him. There was a reason they hadn't fought any of the duke's men during the fight. They'd come around from behind to cut off escape, and now their quarry was running for it. The trap had been sprung.

One of the king's knights, Sir Thatcher, turned around and went to face their pursuers. He did this without being commanded to. His action was misinterpreted by a few of the others, who suddenly broke ranks and fled, abandoning the king. Ransom stayed alongside Devon, but he looked back. One of Benedict's knights rode ahead and met the charge. He took the lance on the shield, and it shattered but didn't dislodge him from the saddle. Sir Thatcher was quickly captured while Benedict continued his pursuit. He was farther ahead than his other men, coming at them with purpose and determination to halt the conflict quickly.

Ransom's heart rushed in his chest. If Devon were captured, it would be the end of his reign and the end of Ransom's hopes. He would never be allowed to marry Claire, and the Occitanians would have free range on Ceredigion. The heir the Fountain had spoken of might never be born. They were in the meadows now, rushing through the tall grass, trying to get a lead. But Benedict's horse was fresher, and he was gaining on them. However, he'd separated himself from the rest of his men, leaving himself vulnerable.

The king gazed back at his son, a mixture of admiration and pain on his face. Ransom knew what he had to do. He barked Dearley's name, causing him to turn his head.

"Protect the king and the prince!" he shouted. "Get them to Glosstyr!"

"What are you going to do?" Dearley demanded, eyes wide with surprise.

"I'm going to stop Bennett," Ransom declared.

They were going at full gallop, and so Ransom had to convince the beast to slow before it could be turned. He wrestled with it a bit before turning around and plunging back the way they'd come. He met Marcus's questioning gaze with a nod as he passed, then spurred his horse to ride hard at Benedict. Ransom positioned the lance, cradling it, preparing to take aim.

Benedict rushed headlong at him. He wore no helmet. In fact, Benedict didn't even have armor, although his tunic was drenched from crossing the river. No doubt he and his men had doffed their armor before crossing in case any of them fell in. The man also had no lance, only a sword, and was thus utterly defenseless against his charge.

Fountain magic bubbled up inside Ransom again, sharpening his senses and lending him strength. The two were on a collision course, but this wasn't Chessy. One of them could die. Ransom sensed the duke's weakness. There was no armor protecting him from a lance. He'd ridden ahead foolishly, determined to capture his father. He'd jeopardized his own life in the process.

Ransom lowered the lance into position as his destrier picked up speed.

Memories battered at him in the crucial moment. Once again, he felt the strange cyclical nature of time. Years before, he'd ridden toward Auxaunce with Queen Emiloh, and they'd been chased by DeVaux's men. The constable, Lord Rakestraw, hadn't been wearing armor that day, and Ransom had watched as he'd been impaled on a lance.

Ransom knew that the queen would not want her son to be killed in the same way. And truthfully, the young man's father wouldn't want that either. Ransom had witnessed the king's grief when the Younger King and Goff had died. No matter how strained their relationship was, Benedict was still his son. One of only two left.

"Are you going to kill me, Ransom?" Benedict shouted worriedly, seeing Ransom's lance aimed right at him. "By the Lady's legs, I've no lance!"

No one could have stopped Ransom from doing so. It was just the two of them facing each other, coming together like a clash of worlds.

Ransom felt the thrum of the Fountain in his heart. He *couldn't* kill the prince. He knew it would be a wicked act. But he wouldn't let the lad capture his father either.

"I won't," Ransom said as the two horses rushed at each other. "Let the Deep Fathoms take you where it will!"

He shifted his aim from Benedict's chest to his horse at the last moment. The horse died on the spot, pierced by the lance in the breast. Ransom released the lance, which hadn't shattered, and veered away. Looking over his shoulder, he watched as Benedict fell over the horse's head to the ground with a jolt. The beast collapsed, but the duke rolled a few times before coming up again to his feet. Although clearly stunned and dizzy, he managed to find his sword in case Ransom came at him again.

Their eyes met, and Ransom tapped his own breast in the salute that knights gave one another. Benedict stood in the meadow, powerless to give chase as Ransom rode away. There could be no doubt between them who had won.

He wondered what Benedict's feelings were in that moment, his eyes blazing as he stared at Ransom riding away from him. Was he grateful his life had been spared? Humiliated at his defeat? Benedict's recklessness and impulsiveness had nearly cost him everything. Ransom could have tried to capture him—something that would have ended the conflict—but he knew the duke would have resisted, which would have given his men time to arrive and capture Ransom.

When Benedict did become king—for surely it would be a matter of when and not if—Ransom would be punished, which would once again leave him without someone to serve. He could be banished from the realm forever, or even killed. Yet he felt a calm assurance he'd done the right thing, that he had performed a final act of loyalty to his king.

With sadness chafing in his heart, he left the meadow behind as the other knights of the Vexin approached. He rode hard to try to catch up with the king, who was still fleeing for his life.

When he caught up with them at a distant hilltop, they were waiting for him. Ransom reached them, out of breath, and saw the king gazing back at the black smudge in the distance, the smoldering wreck of Dunmanis. His eyes seemed haunted.

Ransom looked back and saw that they weren't being chased anymore.

Dearley edged closer on his horse. "They stopped hunting us. They went back and are helping put out the blaze."

It was the right thing to do, and Ransom respected Benedict for the choice he'd made.

The king turned to Ransom. "You killed the horse instead?"

"Yes, my lord. I wouldn't have killed your son." As he said this, he saw a look of anger kindle on Jon-Landon's face. The prince's future was ruined—Benedict would win the throne. So be it. That was what the fates had written.

The king stiffened and then groaned, clutching his belly with one arm. Jon-Landon looked at his father worriedly.

"We need to get you to a healer," Ransom said. "We should ride on."

"You ride on to Glosstyr," said the king, grunting in agony. "I don't think I can make it that far."

"Father?" Jon-Landon asked fearfully.

"I'm dying, boy," said the king. "Ride on to Glosstyr with Sir Ransom. Seek shelter there."

Dread twisted the prince's features, but after a moment he nodded.

"I'm not leaving you," said Ransom earnestly.

The king looked down, breathing in quick gulps. He clenched his jaw and shuddered with the torture. Then he gazed up at Ransom. "I want to die at Tatton Grange."

Ransom frowned at him. "My lord, it's in enemy hands now."

"I know that. My end is near. My body is at war . . . with itself and losing the fight. Take me to the grange. Have Bennett . . . and Estian . . . meet us there. This conflict must end. Too many have paid the price. I . . . I yield." He groaned again, nearly toppling from the saddle.

Ransom edged closer and grabbed the king by the arm to keep him from falling. He hated seeing the king in such pain. Poison was a coward's way, and he thought of Alix and of Estian with malice.

The king looked up at Ransom. "Will you . . . take me there, boy?" There was blood on his lips. "It was always the place that I loved best in all the world."

Grief overwhelmed Ransom. Although Devon and his family were more difficult than King Gervase, more mercurial, he had come to care about them as his own family. The pain of losing this king hurt just as badly as the loss of the old one. A feeling of failure weighed on him.

"I will, my lord," he answered.

"I'm not going into Westmarch," Jon-Landon said sullenly.

Ransom looked at Dearley. "Take the prince to Glosstyr. Then go to Josselin."

The message was clear—if Dearley was to marry his love, it would need to happen now. The young man's eyes shone with gratitude, and he nodded to Ransom. Then he turned to the prince. "Come with us."

As they rode away, the king hung his head and gazed at the distant smoke of Dunmanis. "Curse the Fountain for this ruin. And curse my feckless sons!"

✕

Disaster at Dunmanis. That is the only way to describe it. One of the Elder King's knights who was at the battle brought the tale through fire, smoke, and enemies prowling around Kingfountain. We were all astonished by the story of the parting river and the horror of Dunmanis's destruction. When last the knight had seen the king, he was fleeing to Glosstyr for refuge. It is my castle, and I cannot even be there to defend it or the king. No doubt Benedict and Estian will lay siege, and no doubt the king will flee by sea, but where? Where can he go? Everything is in ruin.

The knight also said that the king was very ill, that he could hardly keep atop his horse. I suspect treachery and poison.

Lord Kinghorn has ordered the queen to be released from her confinement. She is no longer bound to the tower. He said he would write to Benedict and pledge fealty to him if it is the Fountain's will that he should rule. Everyone will flock to the prince now. They are all sheep fearing the wolves that are coming. But not my Ransom. I can't imagine him changing sides until the very end, when the Elder King is bound on a boat and thrown into the waters. How long before that end? Only the Aos Sí knows.

—*Claire de Murrow, Duchess of Glosstyr*
The kingdom withering

✕

CHAPTER
THIRTY-ONE

The King's Curse

After clearing the final rise, they saw Tatton Grange in the valley below, looking just as it had when Ransom had last been there, except for the conspicuous flags showing the Fleur-de-Lis hanging from the turrets. The king's face was gray as chalk, and he swayed in the saddle, his strength having withered even more during the journey.

"It pains me to see Estian's flag hanging there," said the king to Ransom as they paused atop the hill. "It ruins the view."

Ransom stared down at the grange, the center of power in the duchy of Westmarch, now ceded to the Occitanians by Benedict. It was strange to think they were inside the borders of Occitania now, in land that had been ruled by the king who sat hunched in his saddle, his eyes watery, his lips flecked with blood.

They cantered down the hill with the few knights who remained with them. Ransom wondered where his own men were, the ones he'd brought from Brythonica and Glosstyr to Dunmanis. How many were still trying to reach Glosstyr? How many had been captured by their foes? The defeat they'd suffered was crushing.

During the journey, he had thought about the consequences about to befall him. There was no doubt in his mind that Devon was dying, that he had perhaps a few days left, if that. Ransom would surely lose everything he had gained, a reality that loomed over his head like the clouds that had gathered over them during the ride. He still bore the ring of the guardian of Brythonica. Would he end up in that duchy, in service to the duchess? How long would it be before Benedict drove him from that position too? Thicker clouds loomed on the horizon, a coming storm that was completely out of the ordinary.

As they advanced on Tatton Grange, Ransom felt a prickle of awareness go down his back. Alix was there, waiting for them. He sensed her clearly, her presence now unmistakable, and his heart seized up with dread. Had she come to claim him again as her prisoner? He glared at the walls with defiance. He would not become her captive. He would sooner die.

"She's here," Ransom said.

"Who?" the king asked wearily. "I don't understand you."

"The poisoner. She's here."

Was it possible she held the cure for the king's illness? Had she come to make some sort of bargain?

They reined in a good distance from the walls of Tatton Grange, although it was done from a habit of caution more than anything else. If riders came from within, there was no chance of escape. Their horses were weary, and the king couldn't endure much more.

"Well . . . see what she wants," said the king. "I'm spent, Ransom. I can't go another furlong."

Ransom turned and nodded to four knights, leaving one to safeguard the king. The five of them rode ahead toward the main doors of the castle. The doors were opened before they got there, and a man wearing Occitanian finery came striding out. He had a hooked nose and dark hair combed forward.

"Do you speak Occitanian?" he asked in a nasally voice.

"I do," Ransom answered.

"State your business. We were not expecting arrivals today. There are archers at the ready if you intend violence. You will find no shelter here."

"I would speak with Lady Alix of Kerjean," said Ransom. "Behind me is King Devon Argentine, the true duke of Westmarch. He has returned home to die."

The man looked startled by the news. "Is that truly him? By the Lady, so it is!"

"Tell Lady Alix I would speak with her."

The man sniffed. "Whether she will or not, I cannot say, but I will deliver your message."

"Thank you."

The man gave a little bow and retreated through the massive door, which was promptly shut behind him. Ransom thought he saw men through the arrow slits. He was exhausted by the ride and his use of Fountain magic, but its stores were still available to him should it be needed.

The sound of horses came from around the corner, and two riders charged away from the castle, riding fast and heading away from them. He did not sense danger from them, and neither of them was Alix.

The door creaked open again, and the man with the hooked nose returned. "The lady bids you welcome. If the king wishes to die here, it is so permitted. Riders have been sent to inform King Estian of your arrival. It will not take long before he comes."

"I should think not," Ransom answered. "May I speak to her?"

"If you wish. She promises you will not be harmed so long as *you* intend no evil here."

He nodded to the man. "Bring the king," he said to Sir Harrold and Sir Rawlin, gesturing at them. "Help him dismount. We'll go on ahead and find a place for him to rest." He then rode forward with the other two knights. They dismounted and followed the Occitanian into Tatton Grange. Ransom kept his hand on his sword hilt.

They were escorted to one of the waiting rooms at the grange. He eyed the furnishings, feeling a strange sense of familiarity despite the fact that he'd spent little time in the manor. It was a dizzying feeling, one that both alarmed and confused him. Shortly after their arrival, he sensed Alix's approach, and she entered from another door.

She stood there, wearing a cloak, and was escorted by three men of her own, each with brutish strength. From the looks they gave Ransom and his men, they wanted to attack them. Alix's expression was guarded, contemplative. He felt the stirrings of her beauty once again, but he was determined to resist whatever it was that made her so persuasive.

"You surprised me, Sir Ransom. That doesn't happen very often."

One of the knights standing by Ransom dropped his hand to his sword hilt. The two groups were now eyeing each other with open distrust and animosity. It was like two packs of wolves snarling at each other.

Lady Alix looked unperturbed.

"Can we speak privately?" he asked her.

"You mean before our men try to kill each other? If you wish. Have yours remain beyond that door," she said, indicating the one on his left. She waved to the door across the room. "Mine will stay behind this one. Agreed?"

"Agreed," Ransom said, giving the order to his men as she directed hers. Soon they were standing there, alone. The memory of her kissing him fluttered through his mind, and he clenched his hands into fists, willing it to leave.

"Are you happy with your choice, Ransom?" she asked him. "This is where it led. And it leads farther still."

"Can you heal the king?" he asked her.

She tilted her head slightly, giving him a pitying look. "The poison I gave him is doing what it was intended to do. Deliver a slow, agonizing death. He has, perhaps, two more days. He'll become delirious, fitful, and then his heart will literally burst. But you ask an interesting question. Can it be stopped?"

Her words made him struggle with his feelings. They made him want to wrap his hands around her throat and choke her until she told him there was a cure. His heart raced with anger, but he listened to her.

"Can it?"

"There is a special plant that could cure him," she said. "Even if you knew where it was, it would take you too long to get there, to return in time. He'd be dead before you tried. *I* could get there. *I* could fetch it. But I do not think you would accept my terms. What you must do in order to earn such a priceless gift."

He remembered the way she'd disappeared into that fountain in Pree and knew she could do what she said.

"And what would that be?" he asked tightly, still trying to master his anger.

"When Estian and Benedict arrive, kneel before them as if doing homage. Then plunge a dagger in Estian's heart."

A feeling of blackness came over Ransom. Not only did the thought sound intriguing, he wanted to do it. The darkness inside him reveled at the thought.

"I would have no compunction killing him on the battlefield," Ransom said. "But I'll not murder him."

Alix shrugged. "I know. But you could, Ransom. You're afraid of yourself. You always have been."

Her words rang true, and it rattled him. "I think we are done here," he said, turning toward the door.

Before he reached it, she called out to him, her words attempting to wind around him. "Don't you ever wonder what it might have been like? If you had only chosen differently? You betrayed me, Ransom. I warned you what would happen if you did."

His hand paused on the handle. He turned back to her. "You've made your own choices, Alix. You gave in to the darkness. I won't."

His words affected her. He saw her flinch, saw the blush rise to her cheeks. "If you find yourself without a place, with wounds that will not heal, you know where you will find me."

Ransom hoped he would never be so desperate.

Morning came, and Ransom awoke to the sound of the king's racking cough. The curtains had been pulled shut, but light leaked through in a couple of spots. Ransom had fallen asleep in a chair, hand on his sword hilt, and his back ached from the awful posture. His wounds had all healed, though, and he felt rested.

He turned and went back to the bed where the king lay in his sweaty clothes, his hand grasping the leather saddlebag that held the hollow crown. His eyes were feverish with pain, and he gave Ransom a helpless look, as if pleading for relief that could not come. An ache tortured Ransom's heart. It hurt to see his king suffer so.

"She came to me last night," the king wheezed.

Ransom blinked in surprise. He hadn't felt her presence, but then, he'd been exhausted and sleepless for several days.

"Alix?" he asked the king.

"Yes. The girl. The poisoner. She looked just like Emiloh. *Nngghh!* I thought . . . I thought it was a vision. So young . . . just as I remembered her."

Ransom stepped forward. "Did she give you anything?"

"No, my boy. Nothing. She touched my brow. That is all. Then she looked at you asleep in the chair. She cares for you. I think even a serpent can love. But she is . . . she is just as deadly as one." His voice dropped off as he panted, trying to endure the pain. "You chose . . . better . . . for yourself."

He had, but he suspected that door had forever closed when he'd lanced Benedict's horse out from under him.

Ransom approached the bed and gripped the king's hand, unable to offer any other comfort. The king looked toward the curtains. "Is it morning, then?"

"Yes," Ransom said. "Are you hungry?"

"I've eaten fire, and it burns me up on the inside," said the king. "Some water, though, might douse the worst of the flames."

After Ransom fetched a cup and gave it to the king, the door opened, and an Occitanian servant entered with a jovial look.

"Ah, he is awake!"

"I never slept," grumbled the king after slurping some water.

"My king has arrived. And so has your son, Duke Benedict of Vexin. They have come to negotiate a peace, an end to the war. Shall I bring them in, my lord?"

"You shall not!" wheezed the king. "I will meet them in the great hall. Ransom, help me up."

The man looked surprised by the claim. "Very well, Your Grace. I will inform them."

When the fellow had departed, Ransom helped the king rise. The only clothes he had were the ones he had brought with him, and despite the heat, he demanded to wear the wolf-pelt cloak. The king stood by the bedstead, his legs trembling to support his weight.

"The crown," he rasped.

Ransom opened the leather pouch and drew out the hollow crown. He felt its weight and heard the rippling of water in a distant stream. With a grieving heart, he helped put the crown on Devon's head. As it rested there, the king's eyes shut, his jaw muscles bulging. He reeked of sweat.

"Let me hold your arm," he asked, clutching Ransom like a staff.

They walked slowly to the door and found two of Devon's knights standing guard. One shuffling step at a time, they walked down the hall.

The king's eyes were fixed on the doorway leading to their destination. It took every measure of will and determination to make it, and his face shone with sweat by the time they arrived.

Within the great hall, there were tables spread for a feast. Estian stood there dressed in the finery of his rank. His armored knights were spread throughout the room, glaring at Ransom with vindictive fury. Benedict was there, looking weary but rested, his hair tamed, his beard long and imposing. When he saw his father's weakened state, a troubled look came in his eyes. But he did not come forward to assist him.

Ransom felt that he and the king were spectacles for derision as they approached down the center of the hall.

Estian seemed unnerved by the king's weakened state. "My lord, please . . . have a chair. I had no idea you were so ill." Was he being honest? Alix's offer nudged in the back of Ransom's mind. It unnerved him that he found it so compelling. If he had to go down, part of him wanted to take Estian with him.

"I shall stand," said the king defiantly. He glared at both men, but it lacked the power it had once possessed. His whole body trembled. After catching his breath, he looked at his son. "I know what you want, and it's yours. The throne. The entire kingdom. Your mother. The hollow crown. You've won. Take it. Take them all."

Ransom could almost taste the bitterness in the king's words.

Benedict didn't gloat. He stared at his father without love, but his expression lacked any antipathy. His heart was scarred as well.

"I wonder if this is how you felt after defeating Gervase," Benedict said. "I'd always assumed you had felt victorious. No matter. What's done is done. I am the King of Ceredigion."

"One thing more," said Estian, his mood altering slightly. "There is something else required to ensure the peace." He looked at Ransom, and his mouth twitched in a smile. "Seventy-five thousand livres to be paid annually over the span of three years beginning now and ending at the culmination of the truce." He smirked. "And the duchy of Bayree. I think those terms are more than fair."

Ransom winced at the reversal of fortunes. Of course, Estian had only paid a third of the agreed-upon sum before he'd found a way to slither out of the obligation.

The significance of the request was not lost on the king either. "Only seventy-five? So generous, Estian. So very generous of you. I shall leave the new king to pay my debt. He's already stolen my treasury."

"I will honor your agreement, Father," said Benedict in a subdued voice.

"It is settled, then," said Estian. "Peace instead of violence. It is the way of the Lady. May we conclude this truce with her kiss of peace. Between father and son at long last."

Benedict approached his father for an embrace. Had he expected to feel his father's pride? Perhaps he'd hoped to earn his respect by defeating him?

"I ask one more thing," said Devon, holding up his hand. Benedict stood there, his moment of triumph tottering, on the verge of collapse. Would his father refuse to concede defeat even now?

Ransom didn't know what the king was thinking. He remained stiff as a post, a source of strength for the king to lean on.

"What is it?" Estian asked, his words precise and clipped.

"Give me a list of those who defected," said Devon. "Let me know the names of the rats. James Wigant being chief among them. I want to know who else betrayed me."

"Very well," said Estian. "You shall have it by tomorrow morning."

The king bowed his head. "Thank you." Then he removed his hand from Ransom's arm and lifted the crown from his head. His arms trembled from its weight. Benedict stood in front of him, head slightly bowed, a look of remorse in his eyes. From his expression, it was apparent this moment had not lived up to his expectations, whatever those had been.

Devon put the crown on Benedict's head. "It is yours, my son." He pressed a gentle kiss on Benedict's brow and then grabbed his son's tunic in his fist, clenching it, his eyes wild with wrath. "May the Fountain grant I not die till I've had my revenge on you!"

I cannot shake this feeling that nothing will end well. I walk the corridors of Kingfountain, and all the servants are subdued and worried. Many whisper about what it will be like when Benedict is king. Everyone liked Devon the Younger. He always had a smile for people, even the lowliest. But Benedict has always been bold and impatient and relentless. The world exists to serve him and his interests. And then there's the talk about how relentless he was in taming the Vexin.

My stomach is in knots today. The duke has always been jealous of Ransom. I fear that he will brook no rivals. When a knight or a noble is of no use or no longer trusted by a king, they are sent into exile. That is the fate I fear for my Ransom. I would take him to Legault if I could. I would claim him as my own, and we would stay away from Ceredigion forever. But that would require me to abandon my father's home of Glosstyr. My fate is bound to both realms.

—Claire de Murrow, the Never Queen

CHAPTER
THIRTY-TWO

The Death of the First Argentine

The next morning waxed hot and oppressive. The previous evening had promised a storm, but the clouds had fallen apart, and a merciless sun beat down on Tatton Grange, unusually hot for spring. One of Benedict's knights, wearing the badge of the Lion, had brought Ransom the duke's parting message. *I will be at the sanctuary of Our Lady in Fountainvault. Tell me when he dies.*

Ransom thought it interesting that Benedict had chosen to wait out his father's death before returning to the palace to claim his kingdom. Was it distrust that motivated him? Or respect for his father and a desire to see that he received the appropriate funeral rites?

The smell of sickness in the king's chambers was overpowering. After surrendering his crown to his son and imparting his whispered curse, Devon had lost all his remaining strength. Ransom had carried him back to the room. He lay on the bed, thrashing in pain, asking again and again to see the list of those who had betrayed him.

"When my life is over," the king rasped, breathing heavily and with pain, "find my son Jon-Landon. See that he escapes."

Ransom, who had been pacing in the chamber, approached the bedside again. "If that is what you wish," he said without enthusiasm.

The king's eyes were bloodshot and fevered. "I gave the crown to Benedict on purpose, you know. If I'd denied him his victory . . . if I had refused to concede and named Jon as my heir instead, he would have k—" The king doubled over in a terrible cough, breaking up his words. It took several long moments and some desperate gasping before he was fit enough to speak again. "I know my sons. Despite what they might think. Jon-Landon is a good boy. But he's too young to be king. He's not ready for the burden. Ugh, but this hurts! He's in Glosstyr by now. When he's older and stronger, he can challenge Benedict for the throne. You see? I will get my revenge at last. But if I'd goaded Benedict, if I'd sworn that Jon-Landon was my heir, then he would have hunted down his brother. And p-put his head on a spike just to spite me. It's too soon. Too soon. *Gorm* . . . how it hurts!" He doubled over again.

"Do you want some wine?" Ransom asked softly.

"No . . . no thank you. I wish . . . I wish I could have seen Emiloh one last time. I . . . I miss her. She was meant to be a queen. Of Occitania . . . or Ceredigion. Without her support, I wouldn't have won it, you know. It took our combined strength to win." He gazed into Ransom's eyes, his words becoming more slurred and delirious. "I should have let her out of the tower. I should have . . . forgiven her." He panted through his words. "You don't understand, though, Ransom. You're so young still. I remember . . . it wasn't that long ago . . . I felt invincible. Like Benedict does. The fool." He stopped speaking, staring into the distance at his empty memories, seeing things that Ransom could not. "When a woman betrays you . . . it is the worst kind of pain." His teeth clicked together, rattling. "She cared more for her offspring than for me. Those little vultures that pierced me and tore me to pieces. I should . . . have . . . forgiven her. It sowed the seeds of my ruin. I see that now. How I see it!" He tried to clench a fist, but then his strength failed, and he slumped down on the pillows again, sweat streaming down his face. He passed out and slept. Ransom saw the jeweled rings on his fingers, a sign of his wealth and authority, but no amount of wealth could prolong his life or grant him another breath. The end was nigh.

Ransom backed away from the bed and went and sat in a chair, cradling his head in his hands. Gervase, then the Younger King, and now the father. Powerful men all, each had been humbled by death, which took a king as readily as it did a peasant. It made him feel the vagaries of life keenly.

He hadn't sensed Alix's presence since the previous evening, when Estian had left for Pree with his twenty-five thousand livres. Thinking on her made him want to do her violence. She'd caused so much death, so much pain. The cruel thoughts repulsed him, though, reminding him of what she'd said about his true nature.

Thinking of Claire didn't bestow the comfort it usually did. Their future lay in ashes.

In the silence of that miserable room, he begged the Fountain to reveal its will to him. To help him understand all that had happened. Was he truly intended to protect Jon-Landon, a boy who did not seem worthy of such loyalty? But there was only silence.

He didn't know how long he'd sat there in that state, mired in misery, but a swift knock on the door was followed by the sound of it clicking open. He saw his brother, Marcus, in the doorway. The king was still asleep. The knock had not roused him.

Ransom rose and met his brother at the door. "What are you doing here?"

"It's over, Ransom," said his brother with a sigh. "I've just come from Fountainvault. Don't condemn me, but I made peace with Benedict and swore fealty to him. He said I can keep the castle of the Heath. He's asked for the wardship of Maeg, for now, to ensure my good faith."

Ransom's stomach sank with the news. Maeg would be hostage to Benedict? That was a blow he hadn't expected.

"I don't condemn you," he said softly. "His rule is over."

"Is the king awake?" Marcus asked, trying to peer over Ransom's shoulder.

"No, he's—"

"Who's there? Who's talking?" Their brief communication had roused the king again. He sat up, his expression pained. "Ransom, who's there?"

He turned. "It's my brother."

Marcus paled and then handed Ransom a folded and sealed note. The wax was still warm. "This is the information he requested. About those who've made peace."

Ransom took the sealed paper.

The king grew impatient. "Quit whispering. What news? Is that a message? What's in your hand? Give it to me!"

Ransom met Marcus's gaze as his brother slowly shut the door, leaving them alone again. His heart panged for his sister, and he wished he could see her to offer words of comfort and support. But he pushed aside his own troubles and walked back to the king's bed, holding the list of those who had rebelled.

"Is that it?" asked Devon eagerly. A noise rattled in his throat, as if he would start coughing again. Ransom sensed the king's weakness, knew his time was measured in hours now.

"It just came from Fountainvault."

The king reached out a trembling hand. "Give it! This is important, Ransom. Jon-Landon's hopes hinge on this. Once I know who was faithful to me, I can tell you who you must rally to his cause. That's why I want to see it. It's the last thing I can do for my son, my faithful Jon-Landon. He deserves better than what he got. Ahhh!"

He took the proffered note and scraped at the seal with his fingernail until it peeled away. With shaking hands, he began to unfold it.

"Bring me light," he asked, and Ransom fetched one of the burning candles.

Devon's hands continued to tremble as he opened it. Ransom held the light closer so that the king could read the list. He got no farther than the first name.

"No," he gasped.

In the light, Ransom had seen it too. The first entry on the list was: *Jon-Landon Argentine, surrendered at Dunmanis at night.*

The king died at midnight.

He'd spoken no other intelligible words since that whispered *no.* But the grief-stricken wail he'd bellowed would haunt Ransom's memories until the day he, too, died. Ransom should have realized the truth about Jon-Landon's late-night visits to a lover. Reading Jon-Landon's name on that list had been an awful, devastating blow for the king—the crushing of a final, beloved hope.

Ransom had read the rest of the list, name after name of those who had betrayed the king. He even found Lord Kinghorn's name on the list, near the bottom, with an oath of fealty contingent on the death of the rightful king. It wasn't a betrayal, not like Jon-Landon's, and it didn't surprise Ransom to see it there.

When dawn finally came, Ransom left the king's corpse in the room and roused Dawson and Guivret, who'd been sleeping outside the door all night.

"Ready the horses," he said to them. "We're riding to Fountainvault."

"The king's dead?" Dawson asked with bleary eyes.

He nodded and watched as his knight and squire walked away. He had little left to reward them with. Soon Josselin castle would be taken by the crown. He still had wealth, but a king could strip him of that if he so willed. Benedict would need money, and quickly after having waged war, especially given the heavy cost of the peace treaty.

They rode out shortly thereafter, the rising sun already blistering hot. It would be another unusually sweltering day. But it felt good to be on a horse again. It helped improve his mood, if only a little.

The sanctuary in Westmarch was situated along a river that had been dammed to create a man-made waterfall along its length. Although pleasant to look at, it was not as grand or majestic as the ones in Kingfountain and Pree. When they reached it, they were met by one of Benedict's knights.

"I recognize you, Sir Ransom," said the man. "Do you bring tidings for the king?"

He nodded and dismounted. The knight escorted the three of them into the sanctuary. The new king stood by the one shallow pool. His expression was impassive, and he had a coin in hand.

"I was about to toss it in," he said as they approached. "But perhaps your news will suspend it from splashing." He turned to look at Ransom. His expression revealed nothing. "Is he recovered? A miracle?"

"No, my lord," Ransom answered. "He died in the night. The news about Jon-Landon broke him."

Benedict pursed his lips and rubbed his long beard. "I knew it would." He turned and tossed the coin into the waters. It sank immediately to the bottom, mixing with the tarnished coins already there. Then he folded his arms. "The prince sent a young lass from Dunmanis to plead his case. No one noticed the trick, not even the knight sent as his bodyguard. He knew Father's health was failing. And he made the right choice, joining me instead of dying." Was there the hint of a threat in those last words? A lesson intended for Ransom?

"I've fulfilled my pledge," Ransom said. "Shall I have the body prepared to bring back to the palace?"

"No," Benedict said, shaking his head. "He died as the Duke of Westmarch, and this is where he'll receive the rites. Bring his body here,

Ransom. We will do this properly. Then your duty to him is fulfilled. Besides, I wouldn't want you knocking down Sir James again like you did at my brother's funeral rites." He gave Ransom a wry smirk that made him bristle.

"Yes, my lord," Ransom answered stiffly. He bowed and left.

They rode back to Tatton Grange in silence, feeling the uncomfortable heat on their shoulders. The day seemed like any other, and the farmers and laborers continued their efforts without any awareness of the news. Or if they'd heard, they didn't care.

When they reached the bedchamber, Ransom was shocked to find it had been ransacked.

"By the Lady!" Dawson whispered.

The king had been stripped of his clothes, down to his undershirt and linens. His body was half off the bed, slumped over. Anything of value in the room had been taken, including the jeweled rings on the king's fingers. Ransom's fury roused, and he told his young men to find the servants. He went to the bed and lifted the king's frail body up, then wrapped it in a sheet. Seeing the vacant, soulless eyes nearly unmanned him. The king had always been such a force of nature.

When he'd finished, Guivret returned. "The servants are all gone."

The disrespect shown to the king made Ransom's anger intensify. He turned to Dawson. "Make a litter. We're going to drag the body to the sanctuary with the respect it deserves. I'm furious at what they did."

"He wasn't loved," Dawson said in disbelief. "Even among his own."

He almost rebuked the young man but stopped himself. He looked at each one of them in turn. "Let this be a lesson to all of us, then. To try and do better."

"Yes, my lord," said Guivret. "You treated Sir Terencourt with great respect."

"True. But it's easy to do the right thing when everyone is watching. Your true measure is taken when no one is."

Dawson sniffed and nodded. He glanced at Guivret and then back. "Whatever happens, Sir Ransom, we've both decided to serve you. We talked on it last night. We are with you, even as you tended the king before he died."

The look of entreaty on their faces made his throat catch. He put a hand on each of their shoulders. "Thank you. I won't hold you to it. It is likely the king will exile me."

"Lady Constance won't forsake you," Guivret vowed. "You wear the ring."

Ransom shrugged. "She may not have a choice."

"We'll follow you to the end," Dawson reiterated.

The young men arranged for a litter to be fastened to the horses, and Ransom carried the body, wrapped in a sheet, outside. As he rode to Fountainvault, he wondered if he'd ever see Kingfountain again . . . or Claire.

Benedict and his mesnie were waiting for them at the sanctuary, along with several lesser nobles who had gathered for the occasion. Marcus was among them. His friend Sir Simon had also come to pay his respects. He looked like he'd just arrived. His name had also been on the list.

Dawson and Guivret carried the litter with the king's body into the sanctuary of Our Lady, where a table had been prepared to receive it. Benedict uncovered his father's face and looked at it with tears in his eyes.

They performed the rites at midday. The deconeus of the sanctuary read the ceremonial words as they all waited along the shore of the river above the gentle shushing of the falls. Ransom felt bereft of his Fountain magic once again. His master lay dead. His future was as uncertain as a storm.

When the words were finished, Ransom looked at Benedict, who wore a rich velvet tunic despite the sweat glistening on his brow. It was a solemn occasion, and the new king showed a reserve and respect that was unusual. There was no gloating, no grin of victory. Indeed, Ransom could see Benedict was struggling with his emotions. He gave a curt nod to proceed.

The three on the right side of the boat were Ransom, Guivret, and Dawson. The three on the left were Sir Simon, Marcus, and Sir Thatcher, who had been captured by Benedict's men but allowed the privilege to see his master into the river. They walked to the edge of the river and then tilted the staves so that the canoe slid down them and landed with a splash. The sluggish current was quite different from the river before the falls at Kingfountain. They watched the boat gently bob as it went to the edge before landing with another splash on the other side. They stood there in solemnity, watching the boat until it turned a bend in the river and vanished from sight.

Ransom smiled at Simon, and he saw the look of disappointment in his friend's eyes. This wasn't how either of them had hoped things might turn out. Simon came closer to speak with him, but suddenly Benedict was there between them, arms folded imperiously.

"Sir Ransom. Come ride with me. We shall go immediately." He looked at Sir Simon. "You as well. There needs to be a witness."

It was not a request. It was a king's command.

Rumor wears a thousand masks. But what is the truth? Some say that King Estian will attack Kingfountain himself. Some say that Benedict beheaded his father at the end of the battle. There is no loyalty left to the Elder King. His reign has ended, whether or not he still lives. Some say he is in Glosstyr. Others say he went to Tatton Grange. All the while we wait for the new king to arrive and claim his dominion. The people of the city want the uncertainty to end. Sir James's army is still laying siege, although he hasn't done anything to try to breach the walls. So we wait, and wait, and wait until it is insufferable to breathe. Emiloh is hopeful this will be resolved soon, but there is still no word from her son. Time itself seems to hold its breath. And wait . . . wait . . . wait . . .

—Claire de Murrow
(in her new, larger prison)

CHAPTER
THIRTY-THREE

The King's Blindness

They rode in silence to a meadow north of Tatton Grange. Fat bumblebees droned as they flitted from plant to plant. A soothing wind came from the east, cooling the heat caused by the oppressive sun. Benedict led them to a copse of oak trees along a small stream, where they stopped so the animals could drink. Looking back, Ransom could see the grange in the distance. They'd left everyone behind them. It was just Ransom, Benedict, and Simon, pausing in the shade beneath the oaks.

Ransom's insides twisted with worry. Was Benedict going to challenge him to a duel? Was that why he had asked for a witness? And yet, he'd chosen one of the Elder King's servants rather than one of his own men from the Vexin. The situation was curious and strange, and Ransom leveled a look at Simon, who seemed equally perplexed. Unable to read Benedict's mind or judge his mood, Ransom waited, feeling his own destrier growing impatient beneath him. The brooding silence grew thick and uncomfortable.

Benedict stared into the distance, saying nothing. The new king was a little older than the age that Devon the Younger had been at his death.

The two brothers were so different. Whereas Devon had possessed an uncanny ability to put people at ease, Benedict had more brutal energy than he did charm. What kind of king would that make him?

At last, after an indeterminable length of silence, Benedict twitched the reins and brought his destrier around to face Ransom's. The image of impaling Benedict's horse out from under him rose to his mind. Was he about to pay for what had happened?

"The other day," he said, his voice flat and devoid of emotion, "you tried to kill me, Ransom. You would have pierced me through, unarmored as I was, if I hadn't deflected your lance with my arm."

Was this the reason Benedict hadn't left for Kingfountain yet? Was he trying to rewrite history to put him in a more favorable light? Only a few knew the truth of what had happened that day. Others may have caught a glimpse of their confrontation, but no one had been near enough to overhear the words spoken between them as their mounts charged toward each other. Sick dread coiled in Ransom's stomach. If he accepted the version that Benedict was proposing, then he would be admitting that he'd tried to kill him—which he deliberately hadn't— and that it was only Benedict's own reflexes that had forestalled a killing blow.

Or . . . was Benedict testing his honesty? Was he trying to determine whether Ransom would lie in order to help him save face?

Ransom felt Simon's eyes on him, but he didn't let himself look to his friend for encouragement or guidance. He kept his own eyes locked on Benedict's.

"I never wanted to kill you. I think you know that. If I'd wanted to, we wouldn't be having this conversation right now. I could have just as easily dispatched you as I did your horse, and we both know it."

He didn't regret saying the words, for they were true. But he knew that kings had brittle egos. And this one was still young, untested. He watched for Benedict's reaction, for a flare of his nostrils or a curled lip.

Benedict nodded to him with a humbled look. "Ransom, you are forgiven. I loved that horse, I'll not lie to you. And I know you've lost your own. In fact, there's an ugly dappled nightmare waiting for you at Beestone castle. All is forgiven. I mean that sincerely. I shall never be angry with you over that matter. Nor bring it up in any way to cast blame. Sir Simon is my witness. I swear it as a king and as a knight."

Relief flooded Ransom's heart. Benedict had indeed been testing him, only not as he'd thought.

"Thank you, my lord," Ransom said. "I'm relieved to hear it."

"And thank you for not skewering me that day outside Dunmanis. To be honest, I was a bit reckless. Haste has always been my way. I see now that it was a blunder. Not every knight would have been as forgiving. I didn't just bring you here to make peace on that score. I need you. I need your service, just as my brother did. Just as my father did."

Ransom swallowed in surprise and nearly choked. "Pardon me, my lord?"

"You heard me. My father was prone to harboring resentments. I cannot allow those to cloud my judgment. I need men around me that I can trust. Those who have shown fidelity and honesty throughout their years. I need the *best* men in the realm. So I want you on my council, Ransom. Let me be frank. I *need* you. Most of my father's supporters abandoned him at the end. And those same men and women would be quick to abandon me as well. You held out until the end. You stayed by his side until he died. That kind of loyalty is not only uncommon. It's remarkable."

The hope bursting through Ransom, raw and powerful, yet delicate, made him almost queasy. He couldn't believe what he was hearing. "I have only done my duty, my lord."

"Yes! Duty! That is what I need if I am to be successful. Too often my father convinced himself that he was right. His own success blinded him to his faults. I already know that I have a plentitude of them. I need men of good faith to advise me. Here is what I propose. Is it true that

377

my father promised you the duchy of Glosstyr and wardship of Lady Claire de Murrow? I do believe that I am well informed on that count."

"It is true," Ransom said. "Although the agreement was never consummated."

Benedict smiled. "Sir Simon? Can you vouch for this?"

"It is true, my lord," Simon said eagerly. "The papers were drawn up, but no ceremony has been performed."

"Then my first act as King of Ceredigion is to uphold my father's command. She's yours, Ransom. If she'll still have you." He smiled knowingly. "I jest. I've heard she has always kept you close to her heart. May the Fountain bless your marriage. All previous gifts from the crown are ratified as well. You will be, if I'm not mistaken, the wealthiest noble in Ceredigion when this is done. And you will add to our dominion when you tame those rascals in Legault. Some of them have vexed me in my own duchy because of how near they are. No more. What say you, Ransom? Will you serve me? I give you these gifts regardless of your answer."

Ransom blinked in wonderment, amazed at the king's offer, at the unexpected generosity. His mouth went dry, and he couldn't find words. Benedict beamed at him, looking eagerly for a yes. No conditions had been given, which surprised Ransom because of what he'd heard about Maeg. Surely Benedict had wanted to take her as a ward to control him as much as Marcus. Perhaps the conditions would come later.

"I must speak another truth, my lord," Ransom said, his mind buzzing with the opportunity. His steadfast heart insisted he take a risk that might yet cost him everything. "I don't think you'll want to hear it."

"All the more reason that I need to." Benedict said it without hesitation, though his joy had clearly been dimmed by the declaration.

"How can I serve you if you serve King Estian? He arranged for the death of your brother and now your father. It was poison that took both of their lives. Poison administered by Lady Alix. Through his machinations, I was abducted from Beestone castle despite the safe conduct you gave me. He is a dishonorable man and an enemy to Ceredigion. That is the truth of things."

As Ransom spoke, a dark look crossed Benedict's face. Was it anger? Dread? "Do you have evidence to support such an accusation, Ransom?"

Ransom breathed slowly, trying to maintain his calm. "Evidence? No, I suppose I don't, but I've experienced it firsthand. Lady Alix herself told me that Estian has used her to remove his enemies. She is Fountain-blessed, my lord. And so am I. We have a peculiar way of . . . of sensing each other. She has a gift, my lord, a power beyond the ken of mortals. I believe it is a power of persuasion. I've fallen victim to it myself. I've loved Claire my entire life, but I nearly abandoned my pursuit of her to marry Alix. You, too, have been under her sway. Have you not noticed that everything she says seems eminently reasonable? It's only after you put some distance between the both of you that the feelings start to fade."

A surprised look crossed Benedict's face. "What you say is true."

"My gift from the Fountain, my lord, comes with loyalty. For me to realize my own potential, I need to serve a cause greater than myself. If not, I would truly become a monster. I would become like him."

It was clear from the look on Benedict's face that he was absorbing the information, working through it in his mind. Silence prevailed for several long moments as the two men looked at each other.

"Did my father know of this?" Benedict finally asked.

"He did. Alix is dangerous. She can travel long distances in a manner I cannot understand, but it has something to do with the fountains within the palaces. I also know of a Wizr set that—"

"Yes!" Benedict said, interrupting him. "I've seen it. Estian showed it to me. It's an ancient thing."

So it did exist. He'd never truly doubted, but it felt different to know for certain. "It is indeed. It's connected to the Fountain. The hollow crown is as well. Alix told me they are relics from the past, from the days of King Andrew. A struggle has existed between our kingdoms. My lord, the Fountain told me that Estian intends to destroy the Argentine line. He is fixed on that purpose. He will use his poisoner to dispose of all of you. Even *you*. Your alliance was useful to him, nothing more."

As Ransom spoke these words, he felt and heard the rush of water in his ears. It seemed to flood from him to the king, and from the look on Benedict's face, it was obvious the power was affecting him. The two sat astride their destriers, face-to-face, connected by something invisible, yet stronger than metal.

When the rushing feeling subsided, Benedict panted in wonderment, his eyes fresh and alert. "I believe you, Ransom," he said. "It feels like I've awakened from a dream and see the world with fresh eyes."

Ransom smiled at him. "Welcome back, my lord."

"I think . . . part of me always suspected it. Something nagging at the back of my mind. Yet I justified my ignorance. I let myself believe my father was destroying Ceredigion. That his caprice and vengeful nature was only a manifestation of his ambition."

"He never trusted Estian or Estian's father," Ransom said. "He knew in his bones they were his enemies."

Benedict nodded. "This changes things, Ransom. It changes everything. I had hoped my alliance with Estian would usher in a period of peace between us. Instead, it's weakened our position. Estian has Westmarch now, and Bayree has been returned to him. I know his eyes have been fixed on Brythonica. He's spoken to me of a lord in Occitania that he would like to marry to the duchess."

Ransom frowned. "Your brother's son is one of three Argentines left," he said. "I've promised to protect him."

"And you shall," said the king forcefully. "The Fountain has washed the scales from my eyes. This is my intention. Advise me, if you will, and tell me if you agree. I intend to name my mother as the Duchess of Vexin, her ancient inheritance, hers by right and by blood. I need her to keep those nobles tamed once I claim the throne and rule from Kingfountain."

"I agree," said Ransom with a smile. "She will serve you well."

"I also propose sending you ahead to Kingfountain. Your first errand as my sworn man. I want Lord Kinghorn on my side fully. Promise him the duchy of Westmarch. We will wrest it back from Estian. With the two of you defending our western borders, we will prevail against any attack. Do you think Sir Bryon will serve me faithfully?"

"I do," Ransom answered. "He's an honorable man. What of Lord James? What of the North?"

"James is not someone I trust," said Benedict. "When his father died in the winter, he became an ally out of necessity. But I didn't want him anywhere near Dunmanis for fear he'd switch sides again if the opportunity presented itself. By right of inheritance, he is the duke of the North and must be part of my council. But you now have more power and influence than he ever will. And I look to you to keep him in check."

That was a relief. "I'm glad to hear you say it. I will serve you, my lord. You've given me all the assurance I need."

Benedict smirked. "I'd also be the world's greatest fool if I cast a man such as you aside. Mother always spoke highly of you. She encouraged me to adopt your ways. It did provoke . . . resentment. But she was never wrong in her encouragement."

"Your mother is patient and wise," Ransom said, his heart burning in his chest.

"I've always thought so," said Benedict. "Sir Simon, prepare the writs and bring them to me for my seal. Then the two of you will take some men and bring word of what's happened to Kingfountain. Have the good duke disband his army and remain at Kingfountain for the coronation. After that, we will go to Glosstyr and see that you and the lass are properly wedded. Fulfill my commands, Sir Ransom." He grinned. "If you please."

"With all my heart," Ransom answered, giving Benedict the knightly salute.

The king returned it with a satisfied nod.

Ransom rode Dappled over the mighty bridge suspended above the rushing falls. As he gazed up at the palace on the hill, his heart swelled with anticipation. He was about to see Claire again. Simon rode on one side of him and Lord Kinghorn on the other, having ridden out to meet them. A crowd had gathered on the streets, and the people of Kingfountain were cheering loudly that the war was over and the gates of the city had finally been opened.

James, astride a coal-black destrier, sulked as he rode behind them. Judging by his expression, he still had a sour taste in his mouth from the news that Ransom had brought. The sanctuary of Our Lady shone with splendor, and Ransom felt his heart quicken with gratitude as he beheld the spires. The deconeus and his underlings stood at the top of the steps, waving at the riders as they passed by the street.

For years Ransom had worn the badge of the Silver Rose. Now he wore the badge of the Lion, the emblem that Benedict had chosen and was determined to keep. He had on a chain hauberk under his tunic, but he felt no threat of danger.

"They should all go back to their homes," James said, loudly enough for everyone to hear. "What a nuisance."

After crossing the bridge, they rode up the hill, increasing to a trot as they ascended toward the castle. The anticipation was so keen it was almost painful, but he tried to remain calm outwardly. Guivret was part of his entourage, but Dawson had been sent to Josselin castle to alert Dearley of the change in their fortunes and to bring him—and hopefully his wife, Lady Elodie—to Kingfountain immediately to attend the coronation.

As they reached the gates of the palace, Lord Kinghorn signaled for the guards to open them. The winches were pulled, and the portcullis began to slowly lift.

"You must tell me the whole story sometime," Lord Kinghorn said to him. "If your new duties do not keep you too busy, my lord duke." He gave Ransom a knowing grin that took him back years, to the conversation he'd had with Lord Kinghorn after his fight with James.

"I'm sure he'll be eager to boast of it," said James.

Lord Kinghorn gave Ransom a quizzical look. "Did you hear something? I think that was a bird chirping. A bird called Envy."

Ransom shrugged. "Some birds just like hearing themselves squawk."

James gave him a venomous look, but Ransom met his gaze with indifference. After the portcullis was lifted, they rode into the courtyard, which was teeming with servants and knights, but his gaze didn't rest on anyone until he found her. She stood in the threshold with Queen Emiloh, the two of them arm in arm. Seeing her worried face made him want to grin to signal all was well, but he remained solemn. The occasion warranted it.

After they rode in, Ransom and the others dismounted. Silence fell over the courtyard as he knelt before the queen at the bottom of the steps.

"My lady—my queen—by my badge you see that I am now in the service of your son, King Benedict Argentine. He sent me ahead to make you aware of his approach. He is not far behind me and comes to Kingfountain to assume his right as monarch and ruler."

"Rise, Sir Ransom," said the queen, smiling at him with pleasure as the people in the courtyard began clapping.

He did and then took her hand, climbed two steps, and kissed her ring. "Your husband is dead," he said softly, just loud enough for her to hear it over the ruckus.

"I thought so," said Emiloh, her tone flat.

"You should know that he had regrets at the end," he said. "I'll share them when we have a quiet moment."

"Thank you, Ransom," she said, although he had no notion what she was feeling. "And Jon-Landon? Where is he?"

"He was waiting at Beestone for Benedict. They are coming together."

"I see," said the queen. Although she'd been freed from her tower, she didn't seem overjoyed. There was still too much grief mixed with her gladness. "Thank you for coming. And what of you, Sir Ransom? I will speak to my son and tell him of your loyal service to our family. I will plead for you and Claire."

Ransom released her hand and then turned to Claire, smiling at last. He savored the look of excitement, of realization winking in her eyes.

"It's already done, my lady," he said to the queen, although he was looking at Claire. "Everything the Elder King promised is to be fulfilled by his son. Our wedding follows the coronation."

Claire's eyes were so wide and relieved that she leaped from the top step. He caught her around her waist, hoisting her up above his head and grinning up at her like the biggest eejit in all the world. The relief he saw in her face, in her parted lips, told him her fears had matched his own. Slowly, he lowered her down and wrapped his arms around her, squeezing her with no intention of letting go.

Her face was just above his, her hair tickling his cheek. "You could have told me, you brute," she said, tears trickling down her cheeks. "A smile would have been enough. But you had to look so solemn, didn't you? You *wanted* me to worry. Admit it."

"There's so much I want to tell you," he said, listening to the cheers and clapping grow louder as they became a spectacle for everyone in the courtyard.

"Kiss me first," she said hungrily, and when their lips touched, the roar grew even louder. It didn't matter to him that everyone was there. Only she mattered.

When they parted, he set Claire down and noticed the queen wiping her eyes, smiling at them. He stared back at her, gratitude spilling from his heart. If not for her, he wouldn't be here. She'd paid his ransom and then called him into service for Devon the Younger. She'd given him the chance to prove himself, to be the man he was today.

He mouthed the words "thank you" to the queen as Claire nestled against his chest.

"We'll be married soon," he told his beloved. "And then you can take me to Legault. I long to see it. Where shall we go first? Connaught?"

Claire looked up at him and started weeping, unable to speak through her tears as she hugged him fast and sobbed.

We arrived on horseback at the fortress of Glosstyr last night. I cannot find words to describe how it felt to ride out of Kingfountain and gain my freedom. Ransom's horse is an ugly beast, but I love it for all its ugliness. I have met his mesnie, Sir Dearley, Sir Dawson, and the squire Guivret of Brythonica. The respect they have for my soon-husband is deep and so is their loyalty. This comes as no surprise, for I know my husband-to-be is deserving of such. I understand Dearley has married the heiress of Lord Kenford.

It has been so many years since my last visit to Glosstyr. Even though we arrived late, the town was waiting for us with torches, banners, and bright flower petals, which they tossed down on us from above. We thanked the knights from Brythonica, who had gathered to Glosstyr after Dunmanis fell. They'll return home to Ploemeur, but I've entreated the duchess to come for our wedding. It is not a distant journey. I hope she will. Ransom said that we can go to Legault after our marriage. He knows how I long to see it. How will the eejit nobles react when they learn we are coming? I don't know. But I know some of them are afraid, as they should be, and that gives me pleasure. We'll not let them run about and cause trouble any longer.

It is sad thinking of Da and all that he will miss. Of the grandchildren he will never know. But this is my life now, and it's time to get started living. It's about barmy time.

—Claire de Murrow, Duchess of Glosstyr, Heir of Legault
Eventide

EPILOGUE

A Storm by a Tranquil Sea

he sound of the surf crashing on the rocks could be heard through the open arches along the walkway. The smell of it was rich in the air, reminding Alix of the cliffs of Bayree. She walked down the corridor with Sir Chauvigny, feeling the coolness of the air from the open arches mingled with the pleasant warmth of sunlight. It was a beautiful day to be married.

That thought unleashed a ripple of jealousy in her breast. It was Ransom's wedding day and so most of the castle lay deserted. Everyone was gathered in town at the sanctuary of Our Lady of Glosstyr. King Benedict was there with Emiloh, the dowager queen. Alix wanted to see her mother, but if she got too close, she risked revealing herself.

She paused at one of the arches, looking out at the waves rippling to shore. There were plenty of ships docked at the city, bearing flags from many kingdoms. She recognized the Raven of Brythonica and felt another spurt of anger. Had the duchess brought her son? Were all of Alix's prey gathered together in one place? Benedict, of course. The boy heir, Andrew. And it was rumored that Jon-Landon had also come, showing he could play the role of dutiful brother.

Three Argentines left to murder. An opportunity like this might never present itself again. She could step into a fountain in the castle and magically appear in the sanctuary. She believed she could kill one, maybe two, if fortune favored her boldness. But she'd be caught. And that was not an outcome she would tolerate.

Sir Chauvigny had paused next to her, standing in the archway and looking down at the spray of foam on the rocks as the surf collided with them. He was a handsome knight, one of Estian's best men. His arm was still pressed between rods and bound in wrappings to help the break heal. Ransom had captured him at Dunmanis, expecting to receive a fee to earn release, but Alix had freed him from his confinement. She'd tended to his injury and placated him with words designed to win both his loyalty and his affection. He did not have all Ransom's skill, but he was a powerful warrior and one with great potential.

Chauvigny lacked one essential quality: he was not the man she wanted. As she thought about Ransom's rejection, the enmity burned hotter inside her. She felt . . . *jilted*. She could not remain aloof about it. The feeling twisted inside her like one of her deadly concoctions.

"Can he sense you from here?" asked Chauvigny. His tone revealed his feelings of rivalry against Ransom. He, too, wanted vengeance.

"It is too far," she said. "That's why we came through the fountain when we did. I had to be sure he'd be away."

"When my arm heals, I'd like to face him again."

So like a man.

"You'll have your chance. The king wishes him removed."

"Gladly," said Chauvigny.

The door at the end of the corridor opened, and a woman appeared, a servant by the looks of her, middle aged and doughy. She was startled to see a knight and lady standing there by the arch.

The woman looked at them warily and with concern. "What are you doing here? The wedding is underway at the sanctuary."

"I know," said Alix, shifting her speech to that of a fluent speaker of this realm. "Thank you, madam. But my husband fell ill last night."

She stroked Chauvigny's arm and gave a disappointed pout. "He's still recovering from the fight at Dunmanis. Poor thing."

As she spoke, she reached out with her Fountain magic and dispelled any mistrust or wariness the woman felt. Immediately the matron's expression shifted to one of regret.

"I'm sorry, my lord," she said, clucking her tongue. "How unfortunate for you to have come all this way only to miss it."

Chauvigny shrugged but didn't speak. His accent would have revealed him immediately. Little did he know, but it wouldn't have mattered. Alix's skill would have made the woman hear what she expected to hear.

"Do you know if the new duke and duchess of Glosstyr will be staying here awhile?" Alix asked sweetly, tilting her head to one side, giving the woman a feeling of trust in her. Alix's magic infiltrated the senses so subversively that it couldn't be noticed.

"They'll be going to Atha Kleah first," said the woman brightly. "Representatives from the nobles are here for the wedding. Rude sorts. But they came begging peace. Some of the lords have tucked their tails and run back to their castles. As well they should!"

"They've waited many years for the heir to return," Alix said. "Is she excited to be with her own people again?"

"As pleased as a cat in the cream," said the woman, sighing. "We'd just as soon keep her here. She may be the new queen of Legault, but she's Lord Archer's daughter first and foremost. And Lord Ransom . . . well, if he isn't a noble of the highest kind!"

"Yes, he is," said Alix with feeling, suffering another spasm of jealousy. "Did his sister come to the wedding?"

"Of course! And so did his brother and his lady mother. It is sweet seeing their family together. Good days are ahead of us, I think. Well, sorry to disturb you. I have duties to fulfill. Glad you came for the wedding."

"You are so kind," Alix said, withdrawing her magic as the woman turned and left the way she came.

Chauvigny grunted. "I wondered if you were going to kill her."

"There was no need. I do only what must be done."

Chauvigny gazed at her, his eyes full of speculative interest. "You announced me as your husband."

"Do you object?" she asked with a sly smile.

That only inflamed him more. "You are the heir of Bayree. Above my station."

She put her hand on his chest. "The same was true of Ransom. He's just an ordinary knight. A worthless second son." She looked down in a coquettish way. "If you ask the king, he may yet give you what you deserve." Glancing up again, she met his eyes in an entreating way.

As she lowered her hand, she saw him tremble. With Ransom, she had nearly expended her full stores of Fountain magic to disable his natural wariness, his deep devotion to his Gaultic obsession. It was exhausting maintaining such an effort. With Chauvigny, she didn't have to invoke anything. He had responded to every touch, every look with ardor.

"When we return to Pree, I shall demand it," he said, his voice thickening with passion.

"I should hope so," she answered, gazing out at the sea again.

She'd wanted Ransom to choose her. Yes, she'd been ordered to seduce him, but her brother, Estian, wasn't the only one with a taste for changing fate and upending the established leadership. Although her role was a valuable one, it chafed. She would be rid of her bondage someday. Just as the Gaultic girl had finally been freed from hers.

The image of Ransom kissing Claire made her blood heat with outrage. Her imagination might drive her to a frenzy. Make her risk all and throw away her life to murder everyone Ransom loved. Just to spite him. Just to punish him. In her raging thoughts, she imagined bursting from the fountain in the sanctuary, a poisoned crossbow in hand, all her knives and implements at the ready. She could do quite a bit of damage in so crowded a place. It brought her a little thrill to imagine him standing over her own dead body, her blood spreading across the floor and staining his boots. She stopped the thought before it tempted her too much. Patience. She had to be patient. To plan her moves carefully, secretly, deftly, the way any keen Wizr player would.

There was no cure for a broken heart. But there was revenge.

AUTHOR'S NOTE

One of my early readers of this book was on tenterhooks because she assumed that Owen and Evie's story would be repeated in this tale. I don't like telling the same story over and over, and thankfully history gave me an excuse not to. I have taken some authorial liberties from the written record, since the age gap between the two characters that Ransom and Claire are based on would be jarring to modern sensibilities, but the historical text that inspired this book ended up being a love story of the best kind. I'll share that source when the story is done.

Some of the situations in the book that might seem downright implausible, like the king mocking Ransom for keeping his armor on before going to the riverfront, are actually based on true events. It can be frustrating to read about people making decisions that feel so illogical, but we all make mistakes. Some of them just have a greater impact.

While history inspires me, fantasy gives me the freedom to twist the plot to tell a better story. I enjoyed weaving additional Arthurian legends into this story. The Gradalis for example (the silver bowl in the grove at Brythonica) is a stand-in for the Holy Grail. Many think of it as a special cup, but in the original legends, it was a dish. One of Arthur's knights, Sir Percival, found it protected by the Fisher King. There have been so many reinterpretations of the legend, and I found it fun to add my own.

I look forward to sharing the next book with you. The story continues with *Lady's Ransom*. If you think this is a reference to Claire, you may be surprised. As always, there will be many more twists and turns ahead before we reach the climax in book four. Thankfully, the next two books will not be long in coming.

ACKNOWLEDGMENTS

I'm always grateful to those who help get my books out into the world, to the many editors and professionals who use their talents to make this possible. I wouldn't be anywhere without you, and I appreciate the advice, care, and professionalism that goes into it.

Recently I got a note on social media from a fan who said my books have helped them get through the hardest time in their life. So many of us have experienced heartache and heartbreak of a thousand kinds. I'm not exempt. Some dear friends lost their baby grandson recently. A precious niece lost a child as well. And just this weekend, a wonderful friend passed away from ALS. He's the friend I dedicated this book to. After the news came, my youngest son held me and cried and said he didn't want to lose me. Life is fragile, and each day is a blessing. So I acknowledge you, especially the silent sufferers who carry pain other eyes don't see. One of my favorite hymns has the line: *In the quiet heart is hidden sorrow that the eye can't see.*

May you find a little comfort in your trials of the heart.

ABOUT THE AUTHOR

Photo © 2016 Mica Sloan

Jeff Wheeler is the *Wall Street Journal* bestselling author of *The Immortal Words*, *The Buried World*, and *The Killing Fog* in the Grave Kingdom series; the Harbinger, Kingfountain, and First Argentines series; and the Muirwood, Mirrowen, and Landmoor novels. He left his career at Intel in 2014 to write full-time. Jeff is a husband, father of five, and devout member of his church. He lives in the Rocky Mountains and is the founder of *Deep Magic: The E-Zine of Clean Fantasy and Science Fiction*. Find out more about *Deep Magic* at https://deepmagic.co, and visit Jeff's many worlds at https://jeff-wheeler.com.